THE MAID'S COURAGE

Devastated by the death of their mother, their two brothers and their sister, and with their father imprisoned for murder, Ginny and her little brother Charlie lose the only home they've ever known. Charlie is only eight and has a weak chest. He is taken to the workhouse before Ginny has a chance to save him. Lonely and desperate, Ginny finds work at a pie shop – until the unwanted advances of the baker leave her out on the streets. Then she remembers her father's final words – the housekeeper of Lamp Hill Hall will help her. After catching the eye of the house's mistress, she becomes a lady's maid.

THE MAID'S COURAGE

THE MAID'S COURAGE

by

Rosie Goodwin

Magna Large Print Books
Long Preston, North Yorkshire,
BD23 4ND, England.

British Library Cataloguing in Publication Data.

A catalogue record of this book is
available from the British Library

ISBN   978-0-7505-4561-7

First published in Great Britain in 2016 by Corsair

Published in Large Print 2018 by arrangement with
Little, Brown Book Group Limited

Magna Large Print is an imprint of Library Magna Books Ltd.

Printed and bound in Great Britain by
T.J. (International) Ltd., Cornwall, PL28 8RW

This book is in loving memory of;

Patrick Joseph Tracey (Paddy)
October 1933 – January 2016
Who began as one of my greatest fans
and became a dear friend.
R.I.P. Paddy, you were a true gentleman
and you are sadly missed.
God bless,
Rosie xxx

Chapter One

Nuneaton,
September 1860

'Shall I stay behind and help you to clear up, lass?' Blanche Jacobs asked kindly as she closed the cottage door on the last of the mourners.

It had been a long day and Ginny looked exhausted. And it's no wonder, Blanche thought grimly. This was the second family funeral in less than two weeks the poor little soul had had to live through. The terrible flu epidemic that had swept through the town had claimed four of the Thursday family now. Strangely it had been eight-year-old Charlie – who Ginny's mam had worried the most about, for he had always been the weakest of her brood – who was the first to come down with the infection. Yet against all the odds he survived, and it was Betty, Ginny's younger sister by three years, who caught it next and was dead within twenty-four hours. Poor Betty was closely followed by three-year-old George and, soon after, four-year-old Tim. A heartbreaking toll. It was from that moment on that Emily Thursday seemed to lose the will to live. Now, less than two weeks later, she too had been laid to rest with three of her five children in St Paul's churchyard.

Charlie, meanwhile, had begun to recover, but the family would never be the same again.

Blanche's eyes found him now, sitting stiffly on the hardbacked kitchen chair, his pale face looking completely bewildered. He was a scrawny little lad, small for his eight years and prone to attacks of coughing caused by his weak chest. Her gaze then moved to Seth, their father, who was a broken man. Seth had worked for Blanche and Wilf, her husband, since bringing his wife to the cottage as a bride, and over the past twenty years he'd become Wilf's right-hand man. Seth Thursday had always been a hardworking, gentle soul – but now he looked for all the world as if he had nothing left to live for.

'It's all right, missus. I can manage, thank you.'

Ginny's brave young voice made Blanche's heart swell with pity. Poor little lamb, at just sixteen years old she would have to become the woman of the house now and it seemed a huge responsibility to place on such slender shoulders. Thank God the epidemic had run its lethal course.

'Very well then, just give me a shout if you need owt … and Seth, the mister said you're not to trouble about turnin' in to work fer the next couple o' days. Yer need a little time to yourself. God knows we've another funeral to face tomorrow when they lay the Blights' two little 'uns from next door to rest.' She made the sign of the cross on her chest and a tear ran down her cheek. Two of the children in the neighbouring cottage had succumbed to the scourge of the influenza too, God rest their innocent little souls.

Seth was staring blankly off into space and was clearly locked away in a world of his own so when no answer was forthcoming, Blanche quietly slipped away.

'Right, I'd best get this lot tidied up.' Ginny rose from her seat and began to collect the dirty pots that were strewn about the place. It occurred to her then that she hadn't thanked Blanche for the lovely spread the woman had laid on for the mourners who'd wished to come back to the cottage following the service at St Paul's. Blanche and Rita Bradley, who lived in the adjoining cottage on the other side of them, had done a grand job – but then the girl supposed she could always thank them tomorrow.

Ginny was slim with long black hair that was unfashionably straight and hung down her back like a silken cloak. Her eyes were a curious dark blue-grey colour, exactly like her father's, whilst Charlie had curly blond hair and blue eyes like their mother's. She smiled at her brother reassuringly as he lifted Ginger, their cat, on to his lap and buried his face in his fur. Charlie was overwhelmed by all that had happened during the last two weeks and had clung to Ginny like a limpet ever since the day they had carried his mother from the cottage in a plain pine coffin. It was very hard for an eight year old to understand the finality of death and he was struggling to come to terms with the fact that he would never see his mother, or his sister and brothers, again. Ginny had gently explained to him that they had all gone to a place called heaven but he didn't want to accept it. He'd much rather they'd have stayed at home with him.

Ginny had almost finished clearing the mugs and the glasses from the table when Seth suddenly rose and, snatching up a half-empty bottle of whisky from the table, told her, 'I'm going up for a lie-down. Call me when the evening meal is ready, would you?'

Ginny bit her lip and nodded. She'd never known her dad to drink, apart from social occasions like Christmas or the harvest supper. But then she decided that if a drink would help him there could be no harm in it.

By the time she climbed the stairs to wake him later that day, the cottage was once again neat and tidy, as her mother would have wanted it to be, and a rabbit stew was bubbling away on the range. Ginny had made the fire up and closed the curtains against the chilly September night, and in the glow of the oil lamp that stood in the middle of the table everywhere looked warm and cosy but – empty. Normally at this time the younger Thursday children would have been playing with their toys, and Betty would have been telling Emily, her mam, about all she had done at school that day... Tonight, however, the cottage was deathly quiet.

Upstairs, Ginny shook her father's arm. 'Dad, your dinner is ready,' she whispered. Seth was lying across the bed still dressed in his Sunday best suit and she was alarmed to see that the bottle of whisky he had taken upstairs with him now lay empty on the eiderdown at the side of him.

'Wh ... what?' Seth started awake then groaned as his hand rose to clasp his forehead. He was going to have a terrible hangover the next day but at least the drink had dulled the pain in his heart for a short while.

'Your dinner,' Ginny repeated. 'It's almost

14

ready. Will you come down for it? And perhaps you'd like to get changed first?'

'Aye, aye I will,' he mumbled as he felt his way towards the edge of the bed. There was a hammer in his head battering away at the back of his eyes and as he stood up, his legs turned to jelly. Serves me right for drinking, he reproached himself as Ginny left the room.

None of them ate much of their evening meal and Ginny was relieved when she'd tucked Charlie into bed and her father had retired for an early night.

Only then did she allow the tears she'd held back all day to flow as she rocked to and fro in her mother's chair. Although she was only sixteen she knew that her life was never going to be the same again. Girlhood was over, and somehow she must become the woman of the house now and take care of her father and Charlie.

The next morning, Ginny was unable to rouse her father but she wasn't overly concerned. The Blights' children's funeral wasn't until later in the afternoon so she would have plenty of time to press his suit when he did decide to get up, and the master up at the farm had said he wouldn't be expected into work so there was no harm done. When he did get up shortly before lunchtime, however, he looked dreadful and to Ginny's horror he began drinking again.

'Dad...' she said tentatively. 'Perhaps you should get out of your suit so that I can iron it for you, and get yourself washed. The children from next door are being buried at three o'clock and it

15

would look disrespectful if you weren't ready.'

'I shan't be going to the funeral,' Seth growled in a completely uncharacteristic manner. 'I've had enough of funerals to last me a lifetime.'

'But Dad—'

'I'm not going! Didn't you hear what I said?'

Ginny looked stunned and Charlie's eyes welled with tears as Ginny placed an arm about his shoulders.

'Shall I go and tell them you're not well enough to attend then?' she suggested timidly.

'Tell them whatever you like,' he grunted as Ginny scuttled away. By teatime he barely seemed to know where he was as he alternately cursed and sobbed, and once again Ginny packed Charlie off to bed early and kept out of her father's way.

It was four days after the funeral when farmer Wilf came hammering on the door. Ginny answered it and he instantly noticed her red-rimmed eyes.

'Why hasn't your dad turned in to work, lass?' he asked. 'I know I told him to have a couple of days off but there's jobs as need doin' an'—'

'Me dad isn't well,' Ginny answered hastily, holding the door tight to her side so that the man couldn't see into the room beyond. She dreaded to think what he'd say if he saw the state her father was in. He hadn't been sober since the funeral.

'Aye well ... tell him I'll expect him tomorrow then,' Wilf said gruffly, and set off back the way he'd come, much to Ginny's relief.

Once she'd closed and bolted the door, Ginny went to her father's side and said, 'Dad ... can you hear me? The mister's just been and he says

16

you've to turn in to work tomorrow. Why don't we get you washed and shaved, eh? You'll start to feel better then.'

His head lolled senselessly to one side as Ginny hurried away to fill the tin bowl with water that was heating on the fire. He'd neither washed nor changed his clothes since the day of the funeral and now stubble was sprouting on his chin and the rank smell of him filled the room. Gently, she washed his face with a length of coarse hucka-back then shaved him carefully, and slowly he began to come to his senses as Charlie looked on from frightened eyes. He'd never seen his father like this before and Ginny prayed that he never would again. Thankfully there was no liquor left in the cottage now, so Seth would have no choice but to sober up. The night before, as he slept, she had poured any spirits she could lay her hands on down the deep stone sink.

'There,' she said eventually, as if she was speaking to a child, patting him dry. 'That must feel better. Now why don't you go up to your room and get changed. I've laid your clean clothes out on the bed.'

'Aye, lass, I will.' Seth staggered to his feet, swaying, and catching his arm Ginny led him over to the foot of the stairs.

'Now, I'll get us some breakfast, shall I?' Ginny turned with a bright smile plastered on her face for Charlie.

The boy nodded solemnly as she hurried across to stir the porridge that she'd had simmering on the stove. After ladling some into a dish she spooned in some honey, noting that it was almost gone, and carried it to the table for him.

'There,' she said encouragingly. She knew that she should have walked Charlie to school, but she hadn't wanted to leave her father in the state he was in. But I will get him there tomorrow, she silently promised herself. Once he's back into some sort of routine he might start to feel better.

Thankfully, as the day progressed her father managed to sober up and the next morning, much to Ginny's relief, he went to work at his usual time. She herself walked Charlie to the little school in Stockingford then hurried to the farm to begin her own chores, which would start with milking the cows.

'I see yer dad turned in today,' Blanche commented approvingly later that morning when she fetched her a mug of tea.

Ginny released the cow's udder and turning to look at Blanche from her three-legged stool, she nodded.

'Well, happen things will start to get back to some sort of normality now,' the woman said kindly before bustling back to the warmth of the farmhouse kitchen. Ginny sighed. She doubted if life would ever be normal again but for now she just had to try and get on with things.

Chapter Two

It was one evening in early November when things took a turn for the worse – although Ginny wouldn't have believed that they *could* get much worse!

It was a Friday night and although she had waited up till gone midnight there was still no sign of her father returning home. The last few weeks had been difficult. Since his first day back he'd missed many other days off work and staggered home late from the inn once he had been paid – but he'd never not come home before.

He's probably having a game of cards somewhere, the girl tried to convince herself, and after banking down the fire she made her way to bed where she lay shivering and fretting beneath the blankets until sleep finally claimed her.

The next morning she rose early, expecting to find her father sleeping in the chair, but there was no sign of him. It was a Saturday and as there was no school she let Charlie sleep in as she peered into the cupboard to find something she could make him for breakfast. Their food supplies were dangerously low and she needed Seth to give her some housekeeping money so that she could go and do some shopping. The little her mother had kept by for emergencies in the spare tin on the mantelshelf had gone some weeks before. As she thought of her mother, tears pricked at the back of

19

her eyes. Emily had been able to conjure up a tasty meal from almost anything – but Ginny wasn't finding it so easy, especially as most of her father's wages seemed to go over the bar of the Prince Inn, these days.

She had just carved the last of the loaf to toast it for Charlie when there was a loud banging on the door. It would no doubt be the farmer, come to find out why Seth hadn't turned in to work again.

'He ... he isn't here,' she told Wilf once she'd opened the door.

The large man frowned. 'Drunk again, is he?'

Ginny shook her head. 'N ... no, it's just he didn't come home last night and I've no idea where he is. But I'm sure he'll set off for work as soon as he does get home,' she ended desperately.

The man softened as he saw her distress. 'Aye, well, let's just hope as he does, lass. This state of affairs can't go on, can it? I need reliable workers to keep the farm runnin' smoothly.'

He turned and strode away as Ginny quickly closed the door and leaned against it with her heart hammering, only to find Charlie standing in the middle of the room looking apprehensive.

'So where *is* me dad then?' he asked.

'I don't know,' she answered truthfully, crossing to the table and stabbing the toasting fork into a slice of bread. 'But I'm sure he'll be home soon. Now you come and sit by the fire and hold this for me while I get the butter.'

Charlie obediently did as he was told as Ginny went back into the pantry, only to find that the butter was all gone. She knew that Blanche would give her some from the farm if she were to ask, but pride forbade her from doing so.

'We'll have to have dripping on our toast this morning,' she said cheerily, placing the earthenware dish on the table. 'It's good for you.'

Charlie grimaced. He hated dripping, as Ginny well knew, but it was better than nothing.

'Soon as Dad gets home with his wages I'll walk up to the farm and get us some more butter,' Ginny promised. *If there are any of his wages left,* she thought bleakly.

But Seth Thursday didn't come home that day, or the next – and Ginny began to panic. What if something had happened to him? What if he was hurt and lying somewhere with no one to help him? She went about her duties at the farm as usual and said nothing to anyone, although she knew that Blanche must be wondering what was going on. Blanche was well aware that Seth hadn't turned in to work but she didn't comment on it to Ginny. The way she saw it, the poor girl had enough on her plate with trying to look after her little brother.

By Wednesday, things were desperate and Ginny knew that she was going to have to take drastic action if she and Charlie were to eat.

'Wrap up warmly,' she told him late that afternoon. 'We're going into town to the market.' She'd seen women shopping late in the day when there were bargains to be had and she'd also seen them picking up the food that was discarded beneath the stalls. She had never thought that she would be reduced to such measures, but the fact was, she had no choice. It was either that or she and Charlie would have to go hungry until their father came home.

Charlie meekly did as he was told. It was a good step into town from Whittleford, where they lived, and Ginny talked to him all the time to try and take his mind off it.

At last the market was in sight and Ginny positioned him in a shop doorway, saying, 'Just stand there and be a good boy, Charlie, I shan't be a minute.'

The girl flashed a reassuring smile at her little brother as she darted forward to snatch up a bruised apple from beneath an empty stall. Many of the stalls had been emptied now, although the market was still busy as some stall-holders were packing their wares on to carts as the horses stood patiently in front of them munching on their nose bags.

Other women were also scrabbling about beneath the stalls and Ginny avoided their eyes as shame and despair pulsed through her. This was the first time she had ever been forced to do this and she hoped it would be the last. Then suddenly someone tapped her arm and, straightening, Ginny found herself staring into the spiteful eyes of Sally Moreton.

'Well, blow me down! I never thought I'd see *you* lower yerself to doin' this,' Sally crowed. 'But then I dare say you ain't got no choice now your dad's locked up in the clink.'

'My dad *isn't* in the clink,' Ginny retorted furiously as tears pricked at the back of her eyes.

'Well, he is accordin' to what folks are sayin'.' Sally was clearly enjoying herself and Ginny wished herself a million miles away. 'This is a far cry from the posh carryouts yer used to bring into school every day, ain't it?'

A little crowd was assembling to listen now and Ginny felt her cheeks flame with humiliation. She lifted her chin. 'Are you on about the carry-outs I used to share equally with you when you had nothing to eat?' she said steadily.

Sally looked suitably shamefaced as Ginny turned away and continued to hunt beneath the stalls.

Charlie stood patiently in the shop doorway watching his big sister dart from one stall to another looking for fruit and veg. The afternoon was darkening, and a bitter wind whipped through the marketplace. Charlie shivered and stifled a sob. He hoped that they would be able to go home soon, for he wasn't used to crowded places and after the long walk into town his legs were tired. He seemed to stand there for a very long time, his eyes following his big sister's every move, but at last she came towards him clutching her precious wicker basket full of treasures.

'We'll eat well tonight, Charlie,' she told him, forcing a note of cheerfulness into her voice as she took his hand. 'I found a couple of carrots, an onion and a whole cabbage as well as some odd bits of fruit. I'll make us a nice pan of vegetable broth just as soon as we get home. I've got a bit of dripping left so I can add that to it an' all so it'll be nice an' tasty, you'll see.'

Keen to get away, Ginny quickened her pace.

Charlie's eyes darted about as the noise assailed him from every side. Loud bangs as the stalls

23

were dismantled until next market day, men shouting and women haggling noisily over the last few items.

'What did that girl mean when she said our dad was in clink?' he asked breathlessly as he tried to keep up with her. 'What's a clink and who was she?'

'Oh, take no notice of her; she doesn't know what she's on about. She's just someone who used to be in my class at school.' Ginny didn't even try to explain what the clink was; hopefully he'd forget all about it. Sally had made it up, she must have. They'd probably get home to find their dad waiting for them, but then she'd been saying that for the last four days now and he hadn't shown up as yet.

As they neared the end of Queen's Road and began the steep climb up the Cock and Bear Hill the noise of the town abated and Ginny slowed her steps. Charlie was wheezing and she was fearful that if he became over-tired he would have one of his attacks. It didn't take a lot to bring one on, and that was the very last thing she needed to deal with at the present time. With Charlie trotting along silently behind her, Ginny allowed her mind to go back in time. Could it really be just a few short weeks since all their lives had changed so drastically? This time last year her mam had still been alive, and so had George, Betty and Tim ... but now they were all gone. Ginny still found it hard to believe that she would never see any of them again, and she struggled with the pain of that knowledge every single day. Strange how the one they had all feared for most, Charlie, was still there

24

– although she thanked God for it.

Her mind drifted to her mother's grave, right next to those of their three siblings in St Paul's churchyard. Now the farm labourer's cottage where they had always lived no longer rang with laughter and Seth Thursday had become a changed man.

'You'll have to be the woman of the house now,' he had told Ginny curtly the day following his wife's funeral, and she had never gone to school again from that day to this – apart from to explain to her kindly teacher why she was unable to continue. Ginny had officially left school at the age of fourteen but had stayed on, training to become a teacher. Emily Thursday had been so proud of her ... but that dream would have to be put to one side, for now at least.

Ginny sighed as her thoughts returned to her father. Seth had always been such a wonderful father, but these days he flew off the handle for the least little thing, only to sob helplessly and apologise profusely when the rages passed. On the rare occasions when he did go to work Wilf Jacobs had had to come to the cottage and practically drag him there, and Ginny was concerned that the farmer, never the most tolerant of men, was at the end of his patience. Ginny rightly guessed that it was only Blanche who had managed to keep Seth's job safe for this long, but it couldn't continue this way for much longer. Things had slowly gone from bad to worse but Seth had never stayed away from home before and now Ginny was really worried, especially after what Sally had said, although she didn't believe for one moment that her father was in jail.

By the time the farm cottage in Whittleford came into view, Ginny was having to almost carry Charlie. Her brother had no strength left.

'Nearly there,' she puffed keeping her eyes firmly fixed on their home. It was then that she saw the farmer and his wife emerge from the kitchen door, closely followed by a young man and a woman, and heedless of Charlie's protests, she ran ahead of him. What had those strangers been doing in their home? She saw the couple climb on to a small cart pulled by an old nag and then the farmer strode away. Blanche had spotted Charlie and Ginny by then and she waited by the door with an anxious expression on her face.

'What's going on?' Ginny demanded breathlessly when they were within earshot. 'What were you all doing in our cottage? Is me dad home yet?'

'Ah, that's what I need to talk to you about,' Blanche replied with a sad smile. She'd always had a soft spot for Ginny, and what she was about to do was almost breaking her heart but she daren't go against her husband. As she ushered them inside Ginny was pleased to note that the fire was still in. At least keeping warm was one thing they didn't have to worry about. There was an abundance of fallen branches in the nearby woods and every day she went out and dragged enough back to keep the fire burning. Also, Seth had kept a good supply of wood in the small shelter outside.

With the door closed against the biting wind, Ginny dropped the heavy basket on to the table and pulled the shawl from her head, revealing her long sheet of black hair. Blanche meantime stood nervously wringing her hands, saying, 'I'm afraid I have some rather bad news fer yer, pet.'

Ginny's blue-grey eyes stretched wide with terror. 'Why, has somethin' happened to me dad?' she asked.

Blanche, a rosy-cheeked woman who was almost as far round as she was high, shook her head. 'He's not hurt, if that's what yer askin' but...' She gulped before making herself go on. 'But he is in bother... What I mean is, he was in a fight a few nights back and the man he hurt is seriously ill in hospital.'

The colour drained out of Ginny's face as she listened.

'They've got yer dad locked up at the police station an' they're sayin' that if the chap he hurt should die, they could charge him wi' murder.'

Sally Moreton's words suddenly rang in Ginny's ears again. She asked in disbelief: 'B ... but what happened?'

Blanche sighed. 'It was some kerfuffle as they left the Inn, apparently. Yer dad hit the bloke and he fell an' cracked his head badly on a rock.'

'So what will happen now?' Ginny's voice was wobbly and Blanche took her hand and patted it as Charlie started to whimper. He didn't quite understand what was being said but he knew that something was badly amiss by the way his big sister was reacting.

'Even if the chap survives, yer dad is likely to go down fer a long stretch, an' the trouble is... Well, yer must understand we need a reliable worker at the farm. The people who you just saw leaving

27

will be movin' in here next week. He's to be the new farm labourer the mister's set on.'

'In here? Into *our* home?' Ginny was horrified. 'But then what will happen to me an' Charlie?'

'Aw, well...' Blanche looked towards Charlie and her teeth clamped down on her lip. She gently led him to the fireside chair and beckoned Ginny over to the deep stone sink out of earshot.

'The thing is,' she said uncomfortably, 'my Wilf needs to let whoever is workin' fer us live in this cottage. None o' this is easy fer us, pet. I hope yer know that, 'cos I fair thought the world o' yer mam, God bless her soul. An' Wilf were more than happy wi' yer dad an' all, when Seth were himself. But you know as well as we do how he changed after he lost yer mam, an' me an' Wilf have been all but carryin' him – turnin' a blind eye to the days when he didn't come to work an' what not. So now ... well, the long an' the short of it is we've decided you can move in wi' us. Yer a good little help about the farm an' I've no doubt you'll more than earn yer keep, lass.'

'But what about Charlie?'

Blanche avoided Ginny's eyes as she answered. 'I've had a word wi' the Guardians an' they're willin' to take him into the workhouse. It stands to reason he'd be no good on the farm, he's only a weak little chap an' sadly we can't afford to keep them as can't earn their keep. At least in there he'll get three square meals a day an' be looked after.'

'*What?* The workhouse? Over my dead body,' Ginny vowed, her blue-grey eyes flashing.

'I know it ain't ideal – but what else is to become of yer both?' Blanche was clearly upset but

28

nowhere near as much as Ginny was.

'And when is all this supposed to be happening?' The girl's eyes were as cold as black ice now.

'We thought the weekend comin' would be the best time. The Guardians said yer could take your brother to the workhouse on Saturday morning. They'll be expecting him. Meantime I'm sure if yer were to call at the police station they'd likely let yer see yer dad fer a few minutes.'

Drawing herself up to her full height, Ginny nodded, her mouth set. 'Thank you, I'll do that tomorrow.'

Feeling as if she was being dismissed Blanche backed towards the door, glancing about her as she went. Once there she paused to say, 'The folks as will be moving in here said to tell you they'd be more than happy to make you an offer fer the furniture an' yer pots an' pans. Unless yer want to sell 'em yerself o' course. They're newly-weds, see, so they ain't got much yet.'

Ginny did not respond. She turned towards Charlie without another word and, glad to make her escape, Blanche slipped away, tightening her shawl about her plump shoulders as the wind snatched at her skirts.

It was only when she was quite sure that the woman had gone that Ginny's shoulders slumped and feeling her way across the room she dropped heavily on to a chair. Her mind was in a whirl. In the space of just a few minutes her life had been turned upside down – yet again. She was to leave the only place she had ever known as home, and as for Charlie ... the thought of her dear little brother, the only sibling she had left alive, being shut away in the dark forbidding workhouse made a lump form in her throat that threatened to choke her. Everyone knew that most of the folks who were incarcerated in there never came out again.

Oh Daddy, what have you done? she cried silently as scalding tears began to slide down her cheeks. But then Charlie placed his small hand on her arm and she brushed them quickly away.

'What's happenin', Ginny?' His eyes looked too large for his pale face as she patted his bottom and forced a smile.

'Nothing fer you to worry about, pet. Now go back an' sit by the fire an' keep warm while I get these vegetables peeled.'

Docilely he did as he was told, but she could tell he knew that something was wrong. I'll wait until he's in bed before I try to have a proper think and make some kind of a plan, Ginny promised herself as she began to prepare their meagre meal.

Two hours later, when Charlie was snoring softly in his bed, his tummy full of wholesome soup and a bowl of stewed apple, and the cottage was tidy again, Ginny sat in her father's chair and looked around the room. An old dresser stood against one wall, covered in Emily Thursday's somewhat mismatched but treasured china, along with her best tea set, used only on high days and holidays. To either side of the fireplace were two wing chairs. If the girl closed her eyes, she could still see her parents sitting in them in happier times, her mother contentedly darning and her father reading the newspaper. The flagstone floor was covered in colourful peg rugs that Emily had worked on over many months, and in the centre of the room was a large scrubbed oak table surrounded by six wooden chairs. Gleaming copper pans were suspended above the fireplace and on another wall hung the mirror where her mother would stand each morning twisting her long blonde hair into a thick plait that hung almost to her waist. Charlie with his soft fair curls reminded her of their mother every time she looked at him.

She supposed that she'd had a happy childhood compared to the children like Sally Moreton who had been brought up in the tiny courtyards in town where rats were frequent visitors and illness was rife.

Out here in the countryside on the edge of Nuneaton she and her siblings had enjoyed clean fresh air and plenty of good, nutritious food. Their mother had always worked tirelessly to keep her five children respectably dressed too, and they had never been infested with head lice, or 'nitties' as they were known locally – Emily had made sure of that. She had also insisted on them all attending school, and would sit with them at night by the light of the oil lamp helping them to improve their reading and writing. But none of this had prevented the terrible disease from picking them off one by one, and now this business with her father was the final straw. *Murder* ... that was what Blanche had said; if the man her father had fought with died, Seth Thursday would be facing a murder charge. Ginny shuddered, for she knew only too well the sentence that was passed on murderers. They were hanged by the neck until they were dead! Ginny shook her head to try and rid herself of the mental image of her beloved father dangling there with his tongue lolling out and his legs jerking sporadically as the life oozed out of him. Then the tears came again – so fast that she felt as if she couldn't breathe. Eventually they slowed and, worn out, she threw some slack on to the fire and locked the cottage door. She was just too tired to think about anything any more tonight. She would try again in the morning.

Chapter Three

As always, Ginny was up at the crack of dawn, and while Charlie slept on, still worn out from his exertions the day before, she made her way to the farm to milk the cows. It was a job she normally liked but today she was so tired that it was an effort to put one foot in front of another. The little sleep she'd had, had been full of nightmares about Charlie being shut away and her father being hanged.

Blanche was in the farmyard when Ginny arrived, throwing down food for the squawking chickens that had just been released from their coops.

'Mornin', lass,' she said timidly, noting the dark shadows beneath Ginny's eyes and the stoop of her shoulders. 'Come into the kitchen fer a nice warm cup o' tea afore yer start. The kettle should be singin' be now.' It was a ritual they usually enjoyed together every morning but today Ginny shook her head.

'No thanks, missus. I want to get off soon as I've milked the cows, to find out if I'll be allowed to see me dad.'

'O' course.' Blanche Jacobs scuttled away from the accusation she saw in Ginny's eyes. But then this sad state of affairs wasn't down to her, was it? she said to herself. Her Wilf had been more than lenient with Seth Thursday since his missus had died, but this time he'd gone too far. At best he could be put away for months or at worst... She stopped her thoughts from going any further.

Blanche had never disliked Seth although she'd always felt that he wasn't good enough for Emily. He had been raised in the workhouse whilst Emily had been brought up in the parish of Coton, the only child of a couple who had had her in middle age. They had been a good, god-fearing pair but sadly they were both dead now. Up to a point Emily's genteel ways and soft-spoken voice had made the local people steer clear of her, for she didn't speak like them and they felt that they had nothing in common with her. Her house and her children were always spotlessly clean, and come rain or shine she would set off in her best bonnet for church every Sunday without fail. Not that Blanche found anything wrong in that. She had always found Emily to be a kindly, good-natured soul, but there were those about who were jealous of her and considered that Emily thought herself above them.

Blanche entered the farmhouse kitchen and lifted a heavy sooty-bottomed pan. It was time to start frying the bacon; her husband would be in for breakfast soon, once he'd got all the cows into the milking parlour. I'll do a bit extra and Ginny can take it back for her and Charlie, the woman thought to herself as she busily set to. She wasn't happy at all about what was to happen to the two poor children, but what option was there?

Two hours later, Blanche made her way to the milking parlour with a few nice thick rashers of bacon wrapped in a piece of white muslin, only to find that Ginny had already finished her chores and left. The cows had been let back out into the pasture, the floor was swept and washed down, and the fresh milk was standing in buckets in a neat row all along the back wall. With a sigh, Blanche turned and retraced her steps.

Back at the cottage, Ginny was brushing her long black hair before pinning it up as Charlie sat at the table with a bowl of porridge in front of him. He was strangely quiet and Ginny was concerned that he might be about to have one of the terrible breathless attacks that afflicted him. She wished that she didn't have to leave him, but she could hardly take him to the police station with her, and by now she was desperate to see their father – if the sergeant in charge would allow it, that was.

'Will you be all right on your own for a while, Charlie?' Her voice was laced with concern.

The child nodded, 'I'll be fine,' he assured her and a wave of protectiveness coursed through her. She was the only one Charlie had to look out for him now and she knew that she would rather die than let him go into the workhouse. But what was to become of them? She wished that her maternal granny and grandad were still alive.

They would have known what to do. It was clear that she and Charlie couldn't stay here any longer and she had precious little money – nothing but a few measly coppers, in fact.

Pushing the disturbing thoughts to the back of her mind, she wrapped her shawl about her shoulders and told him with a forced cheerfulness, 'You can work on your letters when you've finished your breakfast. I'll be as quick as I can, pet.' Dropping a hasty kiss on his springy fair curls she hurried from the room before she lost her courage. She wasn't looking forward to going to the police station one little bit, but it was necessary if she wanted to see her father.

The walk into town took her nowhere near as long as it had the day before without Charlie holding her back and eventually the stone steps leading up to the large double doors of the police station came into view. Taking a deep breath, she entered and made for the desk where a sergeant was bent across some paperwork.

As she approached, the officer recognised her instantly as Seth Thursday's daughter. A nice little lass she was, he thought. It was a damned shame, what had happened to her mother and the three little ones. Seth Thursday had been a good man until then, but grief had sent him off the rails. Truthfully, the sergeant wasn't at all happy about having to keep Seth locked up. From witness accounts it appeared that Seth had only got into a fight in order to defend himself because the other chap had thrown the first blow. Now the aggressor's life hung in the balance and Seth could be tried for murder if the man didn't recover. But then the law was the law and there was nothing he could do to change it.

'Hello, pet, how can I help you?' he asked in a friendly manner. The poor little lass looked as if she had the weight of the world on her shoulders – and her not much more than a child either. She wasn't as far through as a broom handle, but with her lovely thick coal-black hair and her blue-grey eyes it was clear to see that she was going to be a beauty.

'I ... I've come to see if I might be able to visit me dad.' Her tongue flicked out to moisten her dry lips as she shuffled uncomfortably from foot to foot. 'I'm told you're holding him here.'

'We are that,' he agreed solemnly. 'And strictly speaking he shouldn't be allowed visitors ... but seeing as it's quiet I dare say a few minutes wouldn't hurt.' He turned then and shouted through the open door behind him, 'Constable Watkins!'

A young policeman appeared.

'Take this young lady down to the cells and give her ten minutes with Seth Thursday, please.'

The young man looked mildly surprised as he glanced at Ginny but all the same he nodded towards a door on the other side of the room.

'Would you like to come this way, miss?'

No, Ginny wanted to shout, *I wouldn't like to come this way*, but she remained silent, and followed him all the same.

After fumbling with a huge bunch of keys, the constable unlocked the door and once she had passed through it he locked it behind her before beginning to descend some steep stone steps. She followed him down them with her heart in her mouth. The walls were stone like the steps, which were worn down in the middle from the countless feet that had passed up and down them over the years, and the air felt cold and damp.

At the bottom she was confronted by a line of cell doors on either side of a long corridor. After pausing in front of one, Constable Watkins unlocked it and told her, 'I'll wait here for you, miss.'

She nodded her thanks. Stepping inside the cell she started as she heard the door clang shut behind her, the sound echoing off the grimy walls. It was gloomy in there with the only light coming from a tiny window set high up in the wall. But then as her eyes gradually adjusted to the light she saw the shape of her father sitting on a low iron bed. Apart from a wooden chair and a metal bucket the room was bare, and as he looked up at her she wanted to cry. He looked dirty and unkempt and was in desperate need of a shave. But it wasn't just that which upset her; it was the look in his eyes. Helpless and hopeless.

'Oh, Daddy!' The words caught on a sob and before she knew it he was beside her with his arms strongly wrapped about her.

'Eeh, pet. I'm *so* sorry,' he gasped. His lovely black hair was greasy, his chin covered in stubble and he smelled of stale sweat, but Ginny clung on to him as if her life depended on it. He was still her dad, no matter what he had done.

'I didn't mean to hurt him, I swear it,' he told her. Then, with a hitch in his voice, 'But I've brought all this on meself. I should have been at home, taking care of you and Charlie. Are you both all right?'

He led her to the bed and they sat down together with their arms still wrapped around each other. She wished that she could just wave a magic wand and conjure everything back to the way it had been a few months ago, but she knew that this was impossible.

'Yes ... we're all right but...' Bracing herself, she went on to tell him about the visit from the farmer's wife and what Blanche had planned for her and Charlie, and when she'd finished, Ginny saw tears glistening in her dad's eyes.

'It's no more than I deserve,' he said brokenly. 'But you and Charlie shouldn't suffer for what I've done. The poor little chap wouldn't last no time at all in the workhouse. He's never been strong and I know all too well what it's like in that god-forsaken place.' He fell silent for a time but then turning to her he told her urgently, 'This is what you must do, pet. First off, go to Lamp Hill Hall and ask for the housekeeper. Her name is Mrs Bronson, and she'll know who you are. She will help you, but if for some reason she doesn't, then get yourself and Charlie away from Nuneaton as quickly as possible.' As he went on, Ginny began to cry.

'But if this housekeeper doesn't help us and we follow your last advice, how will you know how to find us when you get out of here? And how will we know what is happening to you? And who is this housekeeper to us anyway?'

He tenderly stroked a tendril of coal-black hair that had escaped from its knot from her cheek.

How could he tell her that he didn't expect to ever walk free again? That his life was going to end here, on the end of a rope?

'Don't you get worrying about that,' he told her softly. 'I'd walk to the ends of the earth if need be to find you, so you just look out for you and Charlie. Will you promise me that? At least I won't have you two to worry about then. And do it soon, eh, love? There's no point in tarrying.'

Too choked to speak, she nodded numbly, but then they heard the key in the lock and saw the young constable standing there. 'I'm afraid your ten minutes is up, miss,' he said.

Ginny rose unsteadily. She didn't even know when or if she would ever see her father again and her legs suddenly felt wobbly. She kissed Seth and clung to him wordlessly for a moment before walking away, and when the door once again clanged shut she was sure that her heart was going to break.

She and the young constable were halfway up the stairs when he paused, and bending to her ear he whispered, 'I couldn't help but overhear some of what you and your father were saying. I should head for Nottingham if I were you, if this house-keeper doesn't help you. The Goose Fair is on and there's always hirings there.'

She looked up at him warily but he smiled and promised, 'Don't worry, I'll not say a word. Good luck.'

They continued to climb in silence and once back upstairs, Ginny quietly left the station. It was almost lunchtime by the time she arrived back at the cottage to hastily check on Charlie, then after changing into her oldest clothes she made her way back to the farm; the pigsties were due to be cleaned out today and although it was a filthy job Ginny didn't mind doing it.

Seeing her cross the yard, Blanche hurried outside. 'Come in and have a warm drink afore yer start,' she invited and Ginny, who had had nothing to eat or drink for several hours, reluctantly did as she was asked. Deep down she knew that Blanche and her husband had always been good to her family and it was hard to feel resentful towards them for long. She needed to talk to Blanche anyway and she supposed that now was as good a time as any.

'I've been thinking,' she began cautiously as she sat at the kitchen table with a steaming cup in front of her. 'I think I will let your new tenants have all our stuff. It won't be any use to me, will it? But I'd like two pounds for everything. I'll even leave the bedlinen and the curtains for that. Do you think that's reasonable?'

'Aye, I'd say it was,' Blanche nodded. 'The young chappie is working here with the mister today as it happens, so I'll ask him later before he leaves, shall I?'

'Yes, please. And could you ask him to let me have it as soon as possible?'

When Blanche looked mildly surprised, Ginny hurried on: 'I'd like to buy some warm clothes for Charlie, you see, before he goes into the workhouse.'

Blanche flushed guiltily. 'Yes, of course.' She didn't like to tell the girl that new clothes wouldn't be necessary for where Charlie was headed. In that place the children were all dressed in the same drab brown uniform – but the subject was dropped.

Once all the jobs were finished Ginny headed for home, committing the surrounding trees and fields to her memory. She'd had some happy times there but once she left she was aware that she might never return and it was a sobering thought.

She found Charlie playing on the hearthrug with Ginger and her heart skipped a beat. She hadn't given a thought as to what might happen to the cat once she and Charlie left, but she hoped that the young couple who would be the new tenants of the cottage would adopt him. Charlie looked slightly better for having spent a day in the warm and Ginny smiled a greeting as she crossed to the fire and pushed what remained of the pan of stew they'd had the night before over it. While it was heating through she fetched what was left of the bread from the pantry and divided it equally between her and Charlie, then tipped some milk into a saucer for Ginger. Thankfully Ginger was a very good mouser so he didn't take a lot of feeding at all.

'Dad still hasn't come home,' Charlie remarked innocently and Ginny gulped as she wondered how she should answer him. She didn't want to tell him that their father was in jail, nor of the fact that very soon now they would be leaving their home. He was only a child, after all, and she was afraid that he might let their plans slip to Blanche.

'He's, err ... he's had to go away for a while,' she said. 'But he's fine – really.'

Charlie accepted what she said with a nod and

41

Ginny sighed with relief. After they'd eaten she dragged the tin bath in from outside and made Charlie sit in the hot water she'd heated while she washed his hair and every inch of him. He didn't complain. It was a ritual Ginny had carried on from the time his mother was alive and he was used to it. When he was as clean as a whistle she dried him thoroughly and sat him back in front of the fire to dry his hair, then after tucking him into bed and after tipping yet more boiling water into the bath she herself sank into it gratefully. There was so much to think about; so much planning to do and she felt slightly panicked.

'If this housekeeper doesn't help you, go to Nottingham Goose Fair,' the young constable had advised her, but if the couple who were going to live in the cottage didn't buy all the contents, how were they to get there? Ginny needed the money for their train fares and to tide them over until she could find a job and somewhere for them to live. And then she thought of what her father had first said. 'Go to Lamp Hill Hall and ask for the housekeeper.' But who was this woman, Mrs Bronson, to them – and why should she help them? Ginny didn't fancy the idea of approaching a stranger for help at all. *Stop it!* she scolded herself. They would manage somehow without having to resort to going to a stranger. The thought of Charlie being locked away in the workhouse was unthinkable.

'Always look on the bright side' had been one of her mother's favourite sayings, but right at that moment Ginny couldn't even imagine what a bright side would look like.

Chapter Four

Ginny was cleaning out the milking parlour after milking the cows the following morning when Blanche appeared in the doorway.

'I've come to give yer this, pet,' she said, holding out two crisp pound notes.

'Young Ted Williams an' his missus who'll be movin' into your cottage thought your price was more than fair an' he asked me to thank yer very much.'

As Ginny took the money without a word and stuffed it into the pocket of her apron, Blanche noted the dark circles beneath the girl's eyes and guilt washed through her again. Only the night before, she'd pleaded with her husband to let her take little Charlie in too, but Wilf had been adamant.

'We can't afford to take in anyone who won't earn their keep,' he'd insisted, and deep down she'd known that he was right, but it didn't stop her from feeling terrible about it.

'Will you be comin' in fer a drink?' she asked then but Ginny shook her head.

'No, thanks. I've all mine and Charlie's things to pack when I've finished here.'

'Of course. Well, in that case is there anything I can do to help?'

When Ginny again shook her head, Blanche pleaded, 'Then at least let me send yer back wi' some o' the joint o' beef I cooked last night, for yours an' Charlie's dinner. It'll only go to waste if yer don't take it. I baked a spare apple pie an' all. I know yer both partial to a slice o' that.'

Ginny's first reaction was to refuse. She'd inherited her proud streak from her mother but seeing that the woman was only trying to be kind, she nodded. 'Very well. Thank you, it'll save me cooking.' She didn't add that she and Charlie had precious little left to cook and there was no way she was going scrabbling under the market stalls again after what had happened with Sally Moreton the last time. Her cheeks still burned with shame every time she thought of it. It seemed that everyone had known about her father's arrest before she did. Thinking of him now, locked up in that bleak soulless cell, made tears prick at the back of her eyes again but she bravely held them at bay and went on with what she was doing.

'Right, I'll go and get you a basket made up then,' Blanche declared, and when she had bustled away, Ginny let out a sigh of relief.

As the girl paused to watch Blanche walk across the farmyard through a number of squawking chickens, she let her hand drop to the money she had thrust into her pocket before turning her attention back to the job in hand.

When she entered the kitchen shortly afterwards, she found that Blanche had packed a basket of food for her and Charlie.

'And while yer here yer can look at the room I've got ready fer you,' Blanche invited. She moved across the large kitchen to a door at the side of the enormous walk-in pantry and threw it open. The room had always been used as a storage cupboard before, but Ginny could see that despite it being small, Blanche had done her best to make it cosy for her. A narrow iron bed stood against one wall, all neatly made up with clean linen and blankets, and Blanche had squeezed a chair and a chest of drawers in there too. Pretty flowered curtains hung at the tiny window and a jug and bowl stood beside a pile of clean towels on the chest.

'It ain't very big, admittedly' Blanche said, 'but at least it's off the kitchen so it'll always be warm in there for you, and I got the mister to put some nails in the wall so's yer can hang yer clothes up.'

Under other circumstances no doubt she could have been very comfortable in there, but knowing that she was never going to sleep there made Ginny unsure of what to say.

'Thank you,' she mumbled, turning to lift the basket of food from the table. 'And thank you for this too.'

'You'll see this is fer the best eventually, pet.' Blanche could see how unhappy the girl was and felt heartsore for her. 'An' I'm lookin' forward to havin' you about the place all the time. You've done a grand job o' takin' on the jobs about the farm that your mam always did since she...' Her voice trailed away as she realised that she was just making things worse. She was aware of how much Ginny had enjoyed working at the school, and felt as if she might be rubbing salt into the wound.

Ginny knew that she was only trying to be kind, and that had Blanche known that she and Charlie had been struggling for food she would have provided them with some victuals before

45

now, but once again pride had reared its ugly head, which was why she had gone scrummaging around the market. But at least they would eat well tonight.

As she set off for home, Ginny realised with a sickening little jolt that she was about to spend her last night in her own bed. Tomorrow was Friday, so she and Charlie would have to leave under cover of darkness the next evening in case the Guardians came for him on Saturday morning. It was a daunting thought and her footsteps dragged.

Brother and sister dined like kings that evening. Ginny cut off some thick juicy slices of beef from the joint that Blanche had given her and fried some potatoes to go with it. They finished the meal with chunks of fresh baked bread and some of the creamy butter Blanche had supplied, along with a slice of apple pie, then curled up together in the chair by the fire. The wind had picked up and was rattling the windowpanes but inside all was warm and cosy and soon Charlie was yawning.

'Let's get you tucked into bed before you fall asleep,' Ginny chuckled.

'Can Ginger come to bed with me tonight? It's too cold to turn him out,' Charlie said sleepily.

'I suppose so,' Ginny answered indulgently. Soon her little brother was snuggled down in bed and he was asleep almost before she left the room. She then entered her parents' room and rummaged about in the bottom of their wardrobe until she came across her mother's old carpet bag, which she then took into her own room. She hastily filled it with the clothes that she would take with her. There were not that many and they were all well worn, but even so they were neatly stitched and spotlessly clean and ironed. She then crept along the landing and back into Charlie's room and silently packed his things too as Ginger stretched and eyed her warily.

Once she had everything she needed she took the bag back to her own room and pushed it as far under the bed as it would go. There was no point in worrying Charlie and telling him more than she had to until the next evening. Already she was dreading it.

At last she made her way back downstairs again and after throwing some more logs on to the fire she sat and stared about her. The cottage wasn't luxurious by anyone's standards but her mother had made it into a cosy home for them all. The chairs were covered with brightly coloured cushions that Emily had stitched from material she had left over after making the curtains and her little touches were everywhere that Ginny looked. Suddenly she thought back to the last Christmas they had all shared together before tragedy struck, and in her mind's eye she could see the Christmas tree her dad had fetched from the market standing in a sturdy bucket of earth at the side of the fire. She and her brothers and sister had spent a whole afternoon making decorations for it. On Christmas Day they had dined on the most enormous goose Ginny had ever seen, followed by her mother's delicious Christmas pudding that Emily had soaked in brandy for weeks before steaming it in a china basin covered with a clean piece of cloth tied with string. It had been such a happy day and it was heartbreaking to think that such a day could never come again. Sniffing, Ginny swiped a tear away and pulled herself together with an effort. There was no use in sitting feeling sorry for herself. From now on Charlie would rely on her and her alone, and Ginny Thursday was determined that, come hell or high water, she would not let him down.

The following morning, after giving Charlie another slice of Blanche's apple pie, Ginny set off bright and early for the farm. She was conscious that she must make this day appear as any other to the farmer's wife. It wouldn't do if she were to get an inkling that Ginny and Charlie were planning to run away. The girl knew it would be hard to act normal though, because her stomach was churning to such an extent that she hadn't been able to eat even a crumb of the delicious pie at breakfast.

She was milking the second cow when Blanche appeared in the doorway, enveloped in an enormous clean white apron, and holding a cup of tea in her hand.

'I thought I'd bring this out to yer seein' as yer didn't call in again afore yer started.' She placed the tea down on the floor out of reach of the cow's hooves and eyed Ginny with a frown. The girl was as pale as lint, but then that was to be expected. The poor lass would be kissing her little brother goodbye this time tomorrow, for the foreseeable future at least.

'I was thinkin', yer could bring yer things over tonight an' put 'em in yer room,' Blanche suggested then, but Ginny shook her head, just a little too quickly; it made the woman look at her suspiciously.

'No ... no, it's all right. I'll do that in the morning,' she stammered.

Blanche raised an eyebrow but then picked her way back across the farmyard to the kitchen without another word. The girl was as jumpy as a newborn kitten.

Wilf was there, waiting for his breakfast, and as she slammed some bacon into the frying pan his wife commented, 'I've got the funniest feelin' that young Ginny is up to somethin'.'

'Such as what?' The farmer took a slurp of tea as he gave his attention to his wife.

'I ain't rightly sure – but yer don't think she's plannin' on doin' somethin' silly, do yer? Like runnin' away, I mean.'

He shrugged. 'I don't see that there's much we can do about it even if she is.'

'But the pair of 'em wouldn't last two minutes if they had to fend fer themselves.' Blanche said worriedly as she cracked a freshlaid egg in with the bacon. When no answer was forthcoming she glanced towards her husband but his head was once again buried in the newspaper. So with a sigh she turned back to what she was doing.

When Ginny had finished milking Primrose, the last cow, she gave her an affectionate pat on the rump before leading her back out into the pasture. This will be the last time I do this, she found herself thinking and the thought brought her no joy. She had taken over the jobs her mother used to do on the farm shortly after Emily's death and

49

had become proficient at them; she also enjoyed doing them. But now was not the time for day-dreaming so she resolutely set about the cleaning up. Blanche was a stickler for cleanliness, which was why so many local folk came to her for their milk. She always insisted that the cow's udders were thoroughly washed before Ginny started milking them, and the buckets were scalded out each day. Then once the milking was done the whole milking parlour had to be scrubbed all over again, ready for the next time.

Once the job was finished, Ginny looked about to make sure there was nothing she had missed before heading for the dairy. Friday morning was butter-churning day, another job that she usually enjoyed but today she just wanted to get it over with. She found the large jug of cream that Blanche had skimmed from the top of the milk over the last few days waiting for her in the dairy, and after tipping it into the churn she rolled her sleeves up and began to turn the handle. Eventually the cream separated from the buttermilk and Ginny drained it off and laid the newly formed butter in a large dish. She then washed it a number of times, removing as much of the buttermilk as she could before folding salt into it. She'd worked up a sweat by then and was in the strangely satisfying process of shaping it into pats when Blanche once more appeared at the door with a steaming cup in her hand.

'To keep the cold out,' she said.

'Thanks.' Ginny took a sip as Blanche examined her work.

'You've gotten to be a dab hand at this,' she

praised. 'Just as good as yer mam were. She'd be proud o' yer, lass, if she could see yer now. I were thinkin' that once you move into the farmhouse, we could give you a regular wage. It wouldn't be much, o' course, 'cos you'll be getting yer board an' keep an' all, but a bit o' pin money to spend.'

When no response was forthcoming she went on awkwardly, 'I'm right sorry about what's happenin'. I just wish there were some other way but the mister can't afford to be a man down wi' this big place to run. Although the harvestin's out o' the way there's still a number o' jobs to be done before the really bad weather sets in. Walls to be repaired, all the animals to be brought in from the fields...' She spread her hands helplessly. 'Yer do understand, don't yer, pet?'

'It's all right,' Ginny answered. 'You're only doing what you think is best for us both.'

But it isn't! she told herself. There was no way on earth that she'd be separated from Charlie. She did feel guilty though at letting Blanche down, but unfortunately it was inevitable. The kindly woman would soon find someone else.

'Right, well ... I'd best get on then,' Blanche said. 'I've the pigswill to prepare before I get the dinner on.'

Ginny kept her eyes on what she was doing and eventually Blanche shuffled away. Ten minutes later, she was back to tell Ginny, 'I have a bit of extra work fer yer to do today, pet. I need yer to make a start on cleaning the front parlour. It's not been used fer a while so I'd like you to go in there and give it a good going over, polish the furniture an' what not.'

51

Ginny frowned. She'd been hoping to get home to Charlie but she didn't want to refuse so she nodded reluctantly.

Soon after, she called in at the farmhouse and Blanche sent her into the parlour armed with beeswax polish and dusters and a mop and bucket. As soon as Ginny had disappeared off along the narrow passage, Blanche hastened out into the yard again and over to the pigsties where fourteen-year-old Davey, the son of another of the farm labourers, was working.

'Davey ... here, lad,' she hissed. 'I've an errand I want yer to run fer me. Leave that fer now, you can finish off when yer come back – an' hurry now.' She then quickly told him where she wanted him to go and pressed a letter into his hand.

Davey was off down the farm drive like the wind and, feeling thoroughly guilty, Blanche slowly went back into the kitchen.

It was almost four o'clock in the afternoon when Ginny finally finished all the jobs that Blanche kept finding for her to do, but at last she was free to make her way back to the cottage, and the farmer's wife had given her an extra shilling for her trouble. The leaves on the trees were falling like confetti as she walked home and she thought how beautiful everywhere looked. She knew every inch of the surrounding countryside and had spent many happy hours playing in the fields and the streams as a child and she knew that she would miss the area. Even so, she felt that she was doing the right thing. She loved Charlie far too much to allow him to be put into the workhouse, and if it had to be a choice between him and her home, he would win every time.

When the cottage came into view she stopped to admire it for a moment. A small picket fence surrounded the front garden and smoke was curling lazily from the chimney. Unlike the other labourers' cottages, theirs was planted with flowers, and a few late-flowering roses were still blooming. Virginia creeper and ivy vied for first place as they clambered up the walls and Ginny stifled a sob as she remembered how much her mother had loved it. That little garden had been Emily Thursday's pride and joy, and in the summer it would be a profusion of colour: wallflowers, roses, hollyhocks, lavender – any cutting that she had been able to beg, borrow or steal had been planted and lovingly tended there. The back garden had been Seth's domain. That was laid mainly to vegetables with an ash path winding through it that led to the outside privy. Beyond that was a tiny orchard full of apple trees, and they had all, however small, helped to pick and gather the apples when they were ripe so that their mother could make pies and puddings with them. Unlike many in the town, Ginny had never known what it was to go hungry – until recently.

With a heavy sigh, she moved on. At least she would be able to take her memories with her and one day, hopefully, when Charlie was fully grown, they would be able to come back.

'I'm home, pet,' she shouted as she stepped through the door that led directly into the kitchen-cum-sitting room. There was no reply save from Ginger, who stretched and meowed then curled up into a ball again in front of the fire.

'Charlie...' Ginny's voice echoed through the cottage but still there was nothing. She wondered if he had felt ill and gone upstairs to lie down but a quick inspection of the bedrooms showed no sign of him. It was very strange. Charlie didn't usually venture off on his own but then again, she had been gone for a long time so perhaps he had got bored and taken himself off for a walk?

After making up the fire and pushing the kettle into the heart of it she crossed to the window. If he had gone out to play she would have expected to have seen him on her way back from the farm, but he must have decided to go in the other direction. She'd been hoping that he would rest up today so that he'd have more energy when they set off later that evening, but there was still plenty of time for him to rest. The light was only just beginning to fade so he was sure to be home soon. Meanwhile, Ginny decided to get their meal ready for when he came back. However, by the time the food was cooked, there was still no sign of him and she began to feel anxious. She glanced at the tin clock on the mantelpiece: it was now gone five o'clock. Where was he? It was so unlike him to just disappear like that.

Eventually she wrapped her shawl tightly about her shoulders and set off back to the farmhouse. If she was delayed, Charlie often came to meet her and she wondered if Blanche had let him wait in the kitchen. He had never been an adventurous child and rarely went anywhere apart from to the farm and to school, especially once the nights had drawn in, so Ginny still wasn't overly concerned as yet. The afternoon was dark but she knew her way like the back of her hand and she hurried sure-footedly through the dusk. Eventually the lights from the farmhouse kitchen pierced the gloom and, shivering, Ginny quickened her steps.

Blanche was in the process of dishing up the evening meal when Ginny entered and she turned startled eyes to her.

'Is Charlie here?' the girl asked.

Blanche nervously licked her lips and glanced towards her husband who was smoking his pipe at the side of the fire before answering. 'No, pet, he ain't. The thing is, the Guardians came an' took him to the workhouse this afternoon while you were workin'. We thought it would be easier fer you both if yer didn't have to say goodbye.'

'No!' Ginny swayed and clutched the back of a chair as Blanche's words sank in. She was too late. Charlie was already gone and at that moment she had no idea if she would ever see her little brother again.

Chapter Five

Seeing the stricken look on the girl's face, Blanche dropped the serving spoon and took a step towards her, holding her hands out beseech-ingly. 'Please try an' understand, pet. I did what I thought was fer the best. I was worried sick that yer were plannin' to run away an' yer'd have no one to look after yer. An' even if yer didn't, I

55

knew how hard the partin' was goin' to be fer you both an' I was tryin' to help you avoid it. One day you'll see it was easier this way.'

'No, I won't – and I'll *never* forgive you for this,' Ginny choked out, then she stormed out into the dark afternoon leaving the door swinging open behind her.

Deeply distressed, Blanche made to go after her but, holding his hand up, her husband stayed her. 'Leave her be, lass. She'll need a bit o' time to think things through,' he advised wisely.

Blanche went to close the door and nodded sadly. She supposed he was right and what was done was done now.

Meanwhile, Ginny was racing across the fields as if the hounds of hell were baying at her heels. Mixed emotions coursed through her. She didn't stop until she reached the cottage and then, dropping on to a chair, she lowered her head into her hands and sobbed as if her heart would break. She had always been fond of Blanche but at that moment she hated her with a vengeance. What must Charlie have thought when the Guardians of the workhouse turned up out of the blue to take him away? He was only a little boy, and not a very strong one at that, and he must have been terrified. She tortured herself with visions of him screaming for her to help her and the tears flowed even faster. At last they were spent and she wiped her streaming eyes and nose on the sleeve of her blouse, something her mother would never have permitted. But her mother wasn't there any more to scold her. No one was – and it came to the girl then that she was all alone in the world now.

Taking a deep breath, Ginny tried to think of what she should do next. She had never intended to go to the farm to live and leave Charlie to the tender mercies of the workhouse, and she was even more determined now that she would never cross Blanche's doorstep again. How could she live with the woman, knowing what she had done? But where did this leave her? What was she to do now? She shrank from the idea of approaching the housekeeper her father had told her to go to for help. This Mrs Bronson at Lamp Hill Hall was a complete stranger to her, after all, and Ginny was proud like her mother had been. The idea of going to the hiring fair had flown out of the window now too. It would mean leaving the area and her brother – but how was she to live, and where? The two pounds the new tenant of the cottage had paid her suddenly seemed very insignificant and she searched her mind for ways that she might raise some more money. It suddenly came to her. Her family's clothes were all still there, and if she was to bundle them up and take them to the rag stall in the market she would get money for them. Not much admittedly, but the way she saw it, every little helped.

Before she could give herself time to think about it, Ginny flew upstairs and began to bundle everything together. It was heartbreaking to handle her mother's and her siblings' clothes, but she hardened her heart. They had no need of them now but she did – if she was ever to raise enough money to get Charlie out of the workhouse. She would have to find a job and somewhere to live so that she could prove to the Guardians that she was capable of caring for him. It was a daunting thought for such a young girl but she knew that Charlie would be depending on her to help him and somehow she would do it.

Eventually everything was packed into her mother's shawl and Ginny hefted the big bundle downstairs to the small kitchen. Luckily it was market day the next day and she intended to be there at first light – before Blanche came looking for her. Knowing that she should sit down and eat, she tried to force down some of the meal she had made for herself and Charlie, but the food just seemed to lodge in her throat, so she placed it down for Ginger. The tears started again as she stroked his silky fur. After tonight she would lose him too and she suddenly felt very vulnerable and alone.

After tidying the room from habit and banking down the fire, she took herself off to bed, but sleep eluded her. It was still dark when she rose the next morning, and after washing in the jug of cold water she got dressed and went downstairs to gaze around the familiar room for the very last time. In just a few hours the young couple that Wilf had employed would be moving in and this would be their home then. Trying not to think of it, she brushed her hair and pinned it up before wrapping her warmest shawl about her shoulders and knotting it at the front.

'Goodbye, Ginger,' she said as she bent to stroke him with tears in her eyes. 'I hope the new folks will look after you.' Ginger purred and arched his back as he rubbed against her legs but then she resolutely lifted the bundle of clothes and the bag she had packed for herself and Charlie, and headed for the door. The two pounds and her mother's gold wedding ring were tucked safely away in her pocket and she didn't look back as she let herself out into the cold morning air. There was no point in prolonging the agony. Getting Charlie back must be her priority now.

As she trudged along Haunchwood Road she passed many miners on their way to their shift at the pit and a few of them glanced at her askance, wondering what such a young lass was doing abroad so early in the morning. Ginny, however, was so steeped in misery that she barely noticed them.

When she finally reached the marketplace she found a hive of activity. Men were setting up the stalls ready to display their wares and the sounds and smells of the animals over in the cattle market wafted on the air. Ginny made straight for the rag stall and found Maggie Drew already piling it high with secondhand clothes that the local women would sort through during the day to come.

'After a nice new outfit are yer, pet?' Maggie asked chirpily as she lifted a faded muslin dress. 'Happen this would be right up your street.' She sniffed and settled her old bonnet more firmly on her grey hair as Ginny shook her head.

'Actually I have some clothes that *you* might be interested in.'

Maggie looked her up and down. The girl's clothes looked clean and respectable as did the girl herself; so happen she might be able to make a few bob here. She wiped her nose along the sleeve of her old coat, leaving a shiny trail. 'Hmm, well, let's 'ave a look then. But I ain't makin' no promises. I only buy decent stuff, yer know.'

The assortment of clothes on the stall looked little better than rags to Ginny but she didn't comment as she handed the bundle over.

As Maggie sifted through the items, Ginny had to bite her lip to stop herself from bursting into tears again. There was Betty's favourite dress, and her mother's Sunday best bonnet. Ginny had contemplated keeping it but was wise enough to realise that she needed the money it would bring more at the minute. Everything was clean and ironed and the garments stood out from the others on the stall. She had even added her father's Sunday suit. There seemed little point in leaving it hanging in the wardrobe and she doubted he'd have need of it for a time at least.

'Well, I'll 'and it to yer, they's decent quality an' nice an' clean an' all,' Maggie admitted. 'How's about I give yer three bob fer the lot to take 'em off yer 'ands?'

'But they're worth much more than that!' Ginny objected and she began to draw them all together again.

'All right, all right, 'old yer 'orses.' Maggie stroked her chin thoughtfully and swiped a dusting of snuff from her top lip before saying reluctantly, 'How's about *four* bob? I 'as to make a profit, yer know.'

Ginny sighed. She'd hoped for more but four shillings would be better than nothing.

'Very well.' She waited while Maggie slowly counted the money into her hand, then without even thinking where she might be going, she found herself heading for the workhouse. Perhaps they might let her see Charlie? The sky overhead was overcast and a bitter wind was blowing as Ginny toiled up the hill from Coton to the Bull Ring. The bag containing her possessions was getting heavier by the minute and when the forbidding-looking building came into sight she let out a sigh of relief, making her breath hang on the air like lace in front of her. When she reached the large double doors at the centre of the property, pulling herself up to her full height, she lifted the heavy brass knocker and let it drop. The sound echoed hollowly inside but within seconds she heard footsteps and the door creaked open.

'Yes?' A woman in a drab brown dress stared at her coldly. A chatelaine hung about her waist from which dangled a number of keys. Her grey hair was scraped into a severe bun at the back of her head and her grey eyes were as chilly as the weather outside.

'Well, what do you want, girl?' she demanded impatiently. Ginny seemed to have temporarily lost the power of speech. 'I don't have time to stand here all day, you know.'

'Please, Miss ... Mrs ... I was wondering if I might be allowed to see my little brother? He was brought here yesterday but he doesn't need to stay now. I have money – look.' Ginny fumbled in her pocket and held out her fortune to the woman. 'I can take him and care for him myself.'

The woman scowled. 'How old are you, girl?'

'I – I'm almost seventeen,' Ginny stammered.

'And where would you take your brother to live?'

'Well, I haven't found anywhere yet but I'm sure I will and Charlie would be fine with me.'

The woman bestowed a scornful look on her. 'You're barely old enough to be looking after yourself, let alone a child – and you haven't even got anywhere to stay. Would it be Charles Thursday you're talking about?'

'Yes – yes, that's him.' Ginny nodded eagerly, but then saw a look of contempt flit across the woman's plain face.

'From what I understood from the Guardians, you were supposed to be going to live in the farm where your father was employed. That's why you weren't admitted here too. Is that right?'

Flustered now, Ginny nodded. 'Well, yes, but there's no need for either of us to be here. I can get a job and take care of us.'

'I suggest you come back in a couple of years' time, and meanwhile I should go back to the farm if I were you. It's doubtful that anyone will want to employ a girl whose father is in jail. You'd like as not both end up on the streets.'

Ginny's chin came up and she looked the woman straight in the eye. 'My dad didn't mean to hurt the man,' she said. 'It was the other chap who threw the first punch and I *can* take care of us.'

'All the same, I wish you to leave now. You've taken up quite enough of my time.' The woman was already in the process of closing the heavy door but Ginny put her hand against it.

'Then if I'm not allowed to take my brother out of here, may I at least see him?' she pleaded. 'He's only eight and he must be so confused and frightened.'

An angry flush had spread across the woman's cheeks as she slapped Ginny's hand away. 'Your brother is being fed and he has a bed to sleep in. You should be grateful,' she rasped. 'And visiting the inmates is not allowed during the week. They are all working. Idle hands make work for the devil.'

'What – even the children?' Ginny was horrified. 'Then when *may* I see him?'

'Sunday afternoon between two and three, although it would be better if you left him to settle.' With that she slammed the door in Ginny's face as tears began to stream down the girl's cheeks. She stared at the grimy windows. Each one was criss-crossed with metal bars on the insides and the whole place looked stark and uninviting. And to think that her poor Charlie was in there. Ginny could only hope that the rest of the staff had more compassion than the woman she had just spoken to, or she dreaded to think what would become of him.

She turned away disconsolately, realising that there was no way she would be allowed to see Charlie today. The woman she had just spoken to had probably got a swinging brick for a heart and not an ounce of kindness in her. Suddenly Ginny's stomach growled ominously and she recalled that she hadn't eaten since the night before – and that barely a few mouthfuls. She supposed that she should head back into town to get something to eat then try to find somewhere to stay for a few nights. There was no point in hanging around the workhouse. On feet that felt like lead she tramped back towards the market where she bought a tray of faggot and peas. She felt surprisingly better with something in her stomach but now she was faced with finding somewhere to lay her head and she didn't have a clue how to go about it.

'Excuse me, you wouldn't happen to know of a lodging house, cheap, would you?' she asked the man on the stall where she'd purchased her meal.

He raised an eyebrow. 'You're a bit young to be livin' away from home, ain't yer, pet?' he answered kindly, then pointing towards Stratford Street he told her, 'You could try Old Ma Bevins. She's got a cottage in Oaston Road by the cemetery over the Leicester Road Bridge, an' I've heard she takes in the odd lodger from time to time. You can't miss it, it's just past the gates o' the cemetery. It stands alone.'

'Thank you, I will.' Ginny smiled and moved on. She had barely got through Bond Gate when it started to rain and she hugged her shawl more tightly about her, feeling thoroughly miserable. When she reached the bridge on the Leicester Road she paused to peep over it at the trains in the Trent Valley railway station. They were belching smoke and steam and she likened them to the fire-breathing dragons her dad had used to tell her stories about. She had never been on a train – never been beyond her home town, in fact – and she had no desire to.

After a couple of minutes to catch her breath she moved on, and turning into Oaston Road she saw the enormous gates of the cemetery ahead of her. Hurrying past, she focused on a small cottage which stood alone on the other side of the gates. The windows were grimy and the small front garden was clogged with weeds. All in all, it didn't look too clean or inviting at all but it was raining harder than ever now so Ginny forced herself to open the small gate, walk up to the front door and rap on it. As she waited the rain trickled down her face and soaked through her shawl.

After a while she began to think that no one was in, but just as she was about to turn disconsolately away, she heard the sound of the bolts on the other side of the door being drawn and two beady black eyes peered out at her from a face that was as wrinkled as a walnut.

'What d'yer want?' she snapped.

'I er ... I was told that you might have a room I could rent.' Ginny clutched her bag as the old woman scowled at her.

'Were yer now? An' iffn I had, have yer the money to pay fer it, young woman?'

'Oh yes.' Ginny fumbled in her bag and produced the coins she had got for the clothes.

The woman stared at her suspiciously. 'Hmm ... yer ain't wi' child, are yer? 'Cos I don't take in no little 'uns 'ere!'

'No, I most certainly am *not*,' Ginny answered indignantly as two patches of colour stained her cheeks.

'Then yer'd better come in out o' the rain.' The old woman opened the door and Ginny stepped past her into a room that made her catch her breath with alarm. There were cats everywhere she looked, and the stench was overpowering. The sink was piled high with dirty pots and the windows were so filthy that she could barely see through them ... but a large log fire was roaring

65

up the chimney so at least it was warm in there.

'The room I let out is up there in the eaves,' the old woman told her, pointing to what was little more than a ladder stretching up into the ceiling in one corner of the room. 'I sleep in here wi' me cats now. Can't manage the steps any more.'

'May I see it?'

The woman pulled her faded shawl more tightly about her scrawny shoulders and curled her lip. 'Fussy, ain't yer – but yes, yer can if yer like. It'll probably need a clean but that'll be up to you if yer decide yer want to take it. My cleanin' days are over an' I just muddle by as best I can now. An' you'll need a candle. There ain't no winder up there.'

For the first time, Ginny felt some sympathy for the poor soul. She was clearly very old and it couldn't be easy for her living alone. Her clothes were so worn and faded that it was difficult to distinguish what colour they might once have been and Ginny wondered how long it had been since she had changed them. Judging from the stale smell that was emanating from her, it had been some long time.

Placing her bag on the floor and after lighting the stub of a candle that the old woman pointed to on the table, she headed for the steps and soon she found herself in quite a spacious room. The only place she could stand upright was in the centre, for the eaves sloped on either side of it, but there was room for an iron bed, a chest of drawers and a washstand which housed a cracked jug and bowl. Some nails had been hammered into the back of the door where she could hang her clothes too, so all in all there was everything she needed there, although as the old woman had warned, it was in desperate need of a clean. Festoons of cobwebs hung from the roof and clouds of dust rose from the floorboards as she crossed the floor. Briefly she thought of her cosy bedroom back at the cottage but she pushed the thought from her mind. Beggars couldn't be choosers.

'I'll take it,' she told Florrie Bevins when she clattered back down the stairs, and after negotiating the rent she paid the woman a week in advance and hefted her bag upstairs. It was still only mid-morning but suddenly Ginny was so tired that she was sure she could have slept for a week. She'd hardly had a wink the night before but now that she had secured somewhere to stay, she was keen to try and find some work. The money she had wouldn't last for long if she didn't add to it. While she was in the town she would buy some cleaning things too, she decided. Looking at the state of the cottage, she doubted Mrs Bevins set much store by such things. Then when she got back she could give her room a thorough clean. With a sigh, Ginny set off again, after telling the old lady what she was up to, and promising to bring back a few bits of shopping for her too. It was turning out to be a very long day.

Chapter Six

Thankfully the rain stopped falling on the walk back into town but even so by the time Ginny reached the marketplace she was so cold that her teeth were chattering and her hands were blue. She could feel blisters popping up on her heels too as her boots were far too tight. Her mother had intended to buy her another pair shortly before she had taken ill, but then Ginny counted herself lucky that she had any boots at all. Most of the children she had gone to school with went barefoot or wore wooden clogs.

As she neared the marketplace, which was busy now, she hesitated, wondering where she should start, and as she was standing there she noticed a tall figure in a dark uniform striding towards her. It was the young constable who had spoken so kindly to her in the police station so she waited until he was standing in front of her.

'Good day, Miss Thursday.' He doffed his cap, making Ginny feel very grown up. 'How are you?'

Ignoring his question she asked pointedly, 'How is my dad?'

'Well, it happens that there's good news on that front. It seems that the chap he hit is recovering.'

Ginny let out a sigh of relief. At least her father wouldn't be tried for murder now.

'In actual fact, your father is going in front of the magistrates on Monday morning,' he went on.

68

Ginny swiped the rain from her face as she peered up at him from her deep blue-grey eyes and the young constable felt an unaccustomed blush rise to his cheeks. He hadn't realised before just how beautiful Ginny was. Her skin was as smooth as silk and her glorious hair glistened like the feathers on a raven's wing.

Get a grip man, he silently scolded himself. She's barely more than a child at present. Even so, his heart was thudding so loudly that he feared she might hear it.

'What do you think will happen to him?' she asked a little shakily. Despite his uniform there was something about this young man that made her feel that she could trust him.

'I reckon he'll get five years at best,' he told her, his face sympathetic. 'But are you and your brother coping all right?'

Ginny gulped to stem the tears. 'They've taken Charlie into the workhouse,' she told him in a wobbly voice. 'So I'm looking about for work now and somewhere for us to live till our dad comes home.'

'I see.' He frowned, wishing that he could help her before asking, 'Have you been to the house-keeper at Lamp Hill Hall as your father suggested?'

Ginny shook her head. 'No, not yet. Not until I've tried to get some place on my own. I have no idea who this woman is anyway. I've never heard me mam or me dad mention her before so I'll only go to her if all else fails. And I certainly can't go to the hiring fair now without Charlie.'

The young constable nodded and sighed. 'Then

I wish you the very best of luck.' He turned to walk away, aware that he and Ginny were attracting some curious looks from the passers-by, but a gentle hand on his arm stayed him and his heart began to pound faster than ever.

'Is ... is there any way you might be able to let me know what happens to me dad?'

He cleared his throat. 'Well, I dare say I could if you let me know where you're staying.'

Ginny quickly told him and gave him directions to Mrs Bevins' cottage. She then stood and watched him melt away into the throngs of shoppers, suddenly feeling that she had one friend in the world at least.

For the next three hours she entered every shop she passed – the tailors, the bakers, the hardware store and many more, even the cobblers – to enquire if there was any work available, but the answer was always the same. There was nothing, and by then she was becoming thoroughly disheartened and the afternoon was beginning to darken. In the end, along with the parcel of fish-heads and twist of baccy requested by her new landlady, she bought a packet of soda crystals, a cheap broom and headed back to the cottage.

She found the old woman snoozing in front of the fire with one cat asleep on her lap and another on her shoulder. There was a pan of something simmering on the fire that smelled quite delicious and Ginny suddenly realised that she was hungry again.

'I was wondering if I might borrow a bucket and some rags to spruce my room up,' she said to the old lady. 'I've bought some soda crystals and a broom.'

Mrs Bevins nodded towards the small kitchen area. 'You'll find all yer need over there. This place weren't allus like this, yer know.' She looked around dejectedly as her hand stroked the cat sleeping on her lap. 'I used to 'ave this whole place gleamin' like a new pin but me old bones make it difficult fer me to get about now, let alone clean.'

'In that case perhaps I could do a little cleaning down here for you when I've finished upstairs?' Ginny offered.

'Well, I'll admit the place could do wi' a bit of a tidy-up,' the old woman said begrudgingly. 'An' if yer willin' to do it, then per'aps I could share me supper wi' you. The neighbour along the way fetched me some vegetables from 'is garden an' a nice bit o' beef skirt from the butcher's an' I've a stew cookin'.'

'That would be lovely.' Ginny flashed her a smile then shrugging off her wet shawl she headed for the sink. Behind the grimy curtain beneath it she found a bucket and after cleaning it out she filled it with hot water from the kettle before tipping some of the soda crystals in. Under the sink she also found a bar of carbolic soap. It had been there so long that it was as hard as a rock but she shaved a little from that too into the bucket for good measure. Finally, armed with everything she thought she might need, she set off up the ladder to make a start. First of all she stripped the grubby bedding from the bed, hoping that the old lady would be able to supply her with some that was slightly cleaner. The straw

71

mattress looked mucky too but there was nothing that could be done about that for now so she set about sweeping and scrubbing the floor with some rags that Mrs Bevins had supplied her with.

Ginny had to work by the light of a candle, and as the afternoon darkened it threw shadows across the walls and guttered in the draughts. At last she was finished, and dropping the filthy rags back into the bucket she sat back on her heels and looked about with satisfaction. It was still very basic but at least it was clean now, or as clean as she could make it. She hefted the bucket downstairs under the watchful eye of Mrs Bevins and after emptying it outside she tackled the mountain of dirty pots piled on the draining board. Luckily there was a kettle of hot water simmering on the range and once she'd used that she refilled it and set it on to boil again. When the pots were washed and dried she set about sweeping the floor. She would have liked to open the windows to let out the overpowering stench of the numerous cats but it was far too cold for that for now so she simply did the best she could. There was a hole under the back door where the animals could go out to use the garden and then come back in. Thank heavens for that, thought Ginny.

'Yer chokin' me,' the old woman complained as clouds of dust flew into the air but ignoring her, Ginny carried on. Judging by the state of the flagstones, the place hadn't been cleaned for weeks – months even – so if the old lady wanted it done she would just have to put up with a bit of inconvenience for now. Next she refilled the bucket with yet more hot water and soda and carbolic soap, and then got down on her hands and knees and began to scrub for all she was worth with an old brush she'd found on a wobbly old shelf beneath the sink.

'There!' she said, half an hour later as she surveyed her handiwork. There was still a lot to be done but already the room was looking much better and Ginny fancied the smell of cats wasn't so strong either.

'I dare say it does look a bit improved,' the old woman sniffed. 'But come an' have sommat to eat now. Me stomach feels as if me throat is cut.'

Ginny obligingly fetched two clean dishes from the dresser that stood against one wall, noticing that that too was in dire need of a good clean.

'You'll find some fresh bread in the crock over there,' Mrs Bevins told her as she ladled the stew into the dishes and soon they were seated at the table eating their meal. It was surprisingly tasty and Ginny had cleaned her dish in the blink of an eye.

'That was delicious,' she thanked her as she put down her knife and fork. 'My mam always used to make lovely stews...' Her voice trailed away as Florrie Bevins raised an eyebrow.

'Used to?'

Ginny could have bitten her tongue out. The less the old woman knew about her the better – and here she was already talking about her family to her. Mrs Bevins would probably turn her out in the cold if she got to find out that her father was in the nick. Hastily she snatched up the dishes and carried them to the sink as the old woman shrugged her shoulders.

'A cup o' tea wouldn't go amiss now,' she called over. 'Measure some tea into the pot, would yer? The kettle's almost boiled again.'

Ginny did as she was told. The room was warm and suddenly she felt so tired she could have slept on a broomstick. She thought of Charlie and wondered what he would be doing then and had to swallow the lump that rose in her throat. She doubted it would be warm in the workhouse after all the dreadful stories she'd been told about the place. The sooner she could find a job and get him out of there, the better.

'I was wondering ... do you have any clean sheets?' she asked when they had finished their tea.

'Clean sheets? Yer fussy, ain't yer? What were wrong wi' them that were on?'

'Oh, they were just a bit dusty.' Ginny was trying to be discreet and save the old woman's feelings. 'I've put them in to soak and I'll wash them and hang them out in the morning if it isn't raining.'

'Huh! I don't know about rainin', it's cold enough fer snow.' The old woman shivered as she pulled her shawl more tightly about her shoulders and pointed to the bed in the corner. 'I usually turn in early these dark nights. Per'aps yer'd like to take the coal scuttle outside to the coal store an' fill it up fer me. At least we can be warm in 'ere.'

Ginny obligingly did as she was asked and was surprised to see that the coal store was quite well stocked.

'Me husband were a miner. Killed down the mine he were in a fall, God rest 'is soul, so I gets a small pension an' a coal ration, which is somethin' to be grateful for I suppose,' Mrs Bevins explained when Ginny returned. She then pointed to a large wooden trunk and told her, 'You'll find some clean sheets an' blankets in there.'

Ginny lifted the lid to find the trunk was full of snow-white sheets and thick woollen blankets as well as a number of good quality towels.

'Well, don't look so surprised,' Mrs Bevins said haughtily. 'There were a time when my washin' were the best to be seen hereabouts. It's only since me old bones 'ave let me down that I've 'ad to let the place go.'

Ginny smiled apologetically, then after selecting what she needed she lit a candle and scuttled back up the ladder again with an armful of clean linen. In no time at all the bed was made up, and sitting on it, Ginny gingerly took her boots off, wincing as the heels of them rubbed against her blisters. She then undressed and by the light of the candle she tipped some of the cold water from the jug into the bowl and methodically washed every inch of herself from top to toe. She then slid into her nightgown and brushed her hair before shouting down the crude stairs, 'Good night, Mrs Bevins.'

'Hmph!' came the reply and Ginny grinned. Mrs Bevins was a crusty old so and so but Ginny had an idea that beneath her tough exterior she wasn't quite as hard as she made out.

She slipped into bed and sighed as she thought of Charlie and her father, but soon exhaustion claimed her and she slept like a top.

Noises from the kitchen woke her the next morning and for a moment Ginny lay there disorientated, wondering where she was. Then it all came back to her and leaping out of bed she shuddered in the icy air as she hastily washed and dressed.

'Ah, so you're up then, are yer?' Mrs Bevins commented as Ginny clattered down the wooden stairs.

'Yes. I thought I'd make an early start on finding a job,' Ginny answered.

'Well, get some o' this porridge down yer afore yer go.' Mrs Bevins carried a pan to the table. 'If yer give me an extra sixpence a week on top o' your rent I'll throw in breakfast and dinner of an' evenin'.'

Ginny thought that sounded more than fair, and nodded eagerly. She was young and optimistic and feeling much better after a good night's sleep. Surely she'd find herself a job today?

'Thank you.' She smiled as the old woman slapped a large bowl of steaming porridge in front of her before hobbling off to return the pan to the top of the range.

'It's really tasty,' Ginny told her appreciatively.

'So it should be. I used to be a cook in Lamp Hill Hall when I were younger, and me old man were the gardener there afore he went down the pit.'

The mention of Lamp Hill made Ginny think of what her father had said about going there and asking for the housekeeper.

'Did you enjoy working there?' Ginny asked conversationally.

''Twere as good a place as any, I dare say,' Mrs Bevins answered, slopping tea from the large brown teapot into a cracked mug.

'Was a Mrs Bronson the housekeeper when you were there?' Ginny asked casually and the old woman frowned.

'Aye, she was. If yer could call it that.'

'What do you mean?' Ginny paused with her spoon halfway to her mouth.

'Well, she were supposed to be the housekeeper but she were more like a member o' the family. Thick as thieves wi' the master an' the mistress, she were.' Mrs Bevins suddenly closed up like a clam and waved her hand airily. 'But never you mind about that, just get that food down yer while it's good an' hot. You'll need it if you're goin' out there. It's cold enough to cut yer in two an' everywhere is thick o' frost.'

Sensing that the old woman wasn't going to say any more, Ginny finished her meal before trotting off to the privy that stood at the end of a long path at the bottom of the garden. Just as Mrs Bevins had said, it was bitterly cold and she was shivering by the time she returned to the warmth of the kitchen.

Ginny quickly washed and dried the few pots that were in the sink, then after wrapping up in as many layers of clothes as she could, she set off on her job-hunt again, praying that she would have more success than she had the day before.

Chapter Seven

Ginny entered the cattle market to the sounds of raised voices as the farmers bartered over the animals they were selling. This, added to the frightened bleats of the penned sheep and the lows of the cattle, made it almost deafening. Indignant chickens trapped in cages squawked and flapped their wings as she passed them and Ginny tried to avert her eyes. In other pens were pigs; they would sell well this close to Christmas and she felt sad as she pictured them on a plate as someone's Christmas dinner. Moving hurriedly on, she came to the other part of the market where stalls sold everything from hardware to fancy ribbons. She stopped and chewed on her lip, wondering which way she should go. She'd tried most of the shops yesterday so she turned about and headed for Attleborough. Perhaps there would be jobs going at the mill there.

An hour later her spirits dipped as she was turned away. She had no experience of the machines and she was too big to go crawling beneath them to capture the loose cotton, so the gruff foreman she had spoken to had shown her the door in no uncertain terms even when she had pleaded that she was willing to do anything. The frost had melted now and a thick freezing fog was settling over the town. Ginny traipsed back to the marketplace and it was then that she saw the young constable again. He was talking to one of the farmers but when he saw her he hurried towards her.

'Is there any more news of my father yet?' Her eyes searched his face hopefully.

As he removed his helmet, the young fellow felt the colour rise in his cheeks. Ginny Thursday was little more than a girl as yet, but everything about her promised that in the not too distant future she would become a very beautiful young woman.

'As a matter of fact there is.' His face told her clearer than words that she wasn't going to like what she was about to hear. 'I just learned back at the station that your father was sentenced to seven years this morning.'

'*Seven years!*' The colour drained from Ginny's face. She had clung on to the desperate hope that he would be released without charge, but that hope was gone now. Somehow she was going to have to get Charlie out of the workhouse and care for him until her father returned. But *seven years* ... it sounded like a lifetime and she suddenly felt very young and vulnerable.

'I'm so sorry.' The constable's voice seemed to be coming from a long way off and Ginny pulled herself together with an enormous effort.

'Between you and me, the sergeant and the rest of the blokes at the station all thought it was a bit harsh but your dad was unfortunate enough to get put in front of the wrong judge. Are you going to be all right?'

She managed a weak smile. Somehow she sensed that she had found a friend in this young man. 'Yes ... thank you. Me and Charlie will be fine – when I can get him out of the workhouse and find us somewhere to live and a job, that is.'

'Have you tried the mill?' he enquired kindly.

Ginny nodded. 'Yes, but I've no experience so they wouldn't take me on.' Her lip quivered.

'Then what about trying some of the big houses in the posher areas? They're always looking for maids. That's if you don't mind doing that sort of work?'

'I'll do anything to keep us going till Dad comes home,' Ginny answered as she started to back away from him. She desperately needed to be alone for a while to think about what he had just told her, but his idea was a good one.

'Look, if you should need any help, just come to the station and ask for me. The name's Bertie, Constable Bertie Watkins.'

'Thank you, but I'm sure I shall be fine.' Ginny flashed another polite smile before turning about and hastening away, feeling more alone than she had ever felt in the whole of her life. And all Bertie Watkins could do was watch her go, feeling helpless.

Ginny went to treat herself to a hot cup of tea from the pie man in the market. She begrudged spending any of her precious pennies but she hoped it would warm her up. It did, and as the shock of what the young constable had told her began to wear off, she straightened her back and set off in the direction of Swan Lane. There were some very big houses there, owned by the wealthy; surely one of them would need some help?

As the day wore on, the fog thickened until Ginny could barely see her hand in front of her and she began to feel like she was the only person left in the world as she trudged from one house to another. Now and again people loomed up in front of her like spectres and she would start, but still she continued door-knocking. The answer was always the same and by late afternoon she was thoroughly disheartened and feeling hungry too. It had been a long time since she'd eaten the warming dish of porridge at breakfast. It was getting dark by then so reluctantly she headed for Mrs Bevins' cottage, trying to stay optimistic. Surely she would have better luck tomorrow?

Her heels were raw by the time she turned into Oaston Road and she was so cold that she'd lost all feeling in her hands. When Mrs Bevins answered her knock on the door and Ginny entered the kitchen, the heat met her and her nose began to glow.

'Lordy, look at the state o' yer!' Mrs Bevins exclaimed, ushering her towards the fire. 'Whatever 'ave yer been doin' all day? Sit yourself down an' I'll pour yer a cup o' tea. Yer dinner will be ready in no time. I've done us a cottage pie fer tonight.'

The unexpected words of kindness made tears spring to Ginny's eyes as she huddled in the chair, but she bravely blinked them away. There was no point in feeling sorry for herself. It was Charlie and her father she should be feeling sorry for.

'So, did yer 'ave any luck in findin' a job then?' Mrs Bevins asked as she pressed a steaming cup into her hand.

Ginny shook her head miserably. 'No. I've been trying the big houses today to see if anyone needed

81

a maid, but there was nothing. I've still got money to pay your rent though,' she added hastily.

Mrs Bevins sniffed. 'Aye, well 'appen sommat'll turn up soon, an' in the meantime yer comfy 'ere, ain't yer?'

'Very comfy,' Ginny said truthfully.

The old woman pottered away to check on the pie as Ginny stared into the fire. She wondered where her father was. She'd forgotten to ask the young policeman what prison he had been sent to, not that it made much difference. From what she'd heard, one was as bad as another and she asked herself how Seth would survive seven long years of being locked up. Her thoughts then turned back to Charlie. It seemed a lifetime until Sunday when she'd be allowed to see him, but she knew she must try to stay optimistic. She might well have found a job by then, and if she had, she would be able to take him out of that god-forsaken place.

'Right, get yerself to the table then.' Mrs Bevins' voice sliced through her thoughts and Ginny willingly did as she was told. It had been a long time since breakfast and she hadn't liked to waste any more of her precious pennies on lunch.

For the rest of the week, Ginny rose early every single day and after breakfast she set off in search of work, but as the week came to an end she was no nearer to finding anything, although she had tramped for miles. Still, at least she would be able to see Charlie soon, she told herself in a desperate effort to keep her spirits up. On Saturday she found herself heading towards St Paul's Church and once in the churchyard she stared down at the graves of her family, wishing she could have afforded some flowers to lay on them; however, she was aware that she must make every farthing count and hoped they would forgive her for coming empty-handed.

The wind was whistling through the leafless trees and as Ginny hugged her shawl tightly about her she suddenly became aware of someone standing behind her. She whirled about then let out a sigh of relief as she saw Father Mick, as he was known to everyone, standing there in his long black vestments.

'Ginny Thursday, I thought it was you. Wherever have you been, child? They're frantic with worry about you back at the farm. They said you'd run away without telling them where you were going.'

Ginny shrugged. She loved Father Mick, in fact all his parishioners loved him. He had a heart of pure gold and Ginny had known him all her life but she wasn't prepared to give away too much even to him.

'They put Charlie into the workhouse,' she said, eyeing him with a sullen expression on her face.

His eyes were full of sympathy as he nodded. 'I know,' he said. 'But Blanche was only trying to do what she thought was best. Between you and me, I think she would have taken both you *and* Charlie in like a shot, but she's governed by Wilf. But look ... why don't you come into the vicarage for a nice hot drink? You look frozen through.'

She stared at him suspiciously as he stroked his thick grey beard. If he thought he was going to persuade her to go back to the farm, he would be sadly disappointed. She believed what he had said about Blanche but would never forgive the farmer or his wife for what they had done, not if she lived for a million years.

Seeing her reluctance, he held his hand out although he made no move to come any closer. She looked like a frightened little bird that was about to take flight at any second and he didn't want her to be any more upset than she clearly already was.

'Just for a hot drink,' he urged gently. 'And perhaps a slice of Mrs Braintree's delicious fruit cake? I can thoroughly recommend it.' Mrs Braintree was his loyal housekeeper and Ginny was tempted. Her stomach was just beginning to rumble and a warm drink would be most welcome.

'All right, Father – but I won't go back to the farm!'

Seeing her mutinous expression, he nodded.

'I wouldn't dream of trying to force you,' he agreed, and so they began to walk across the churchyard, the wind slapping her skirt and his vestments against their legs.

'Here we are then,' he commented pleasantly a short while later as they entered the hallway of the vicarage. 'Now you go in there and sit down by the fire and I'll go and see what we can scrounge out of Mrs Braintree.'

Ginny entered the room he had pointed to as he hurried away and immediately the warmth wrapped itself around her like a blanket. There was a large log fire roaring up the chimney and the room was cosy and inviting although the furniture was slightly shabby. A threadbare rug which must once have been very colourful lay in front of the hearth, and on either side of it stood two worn but comfortable-looking wing-back chairs. Everything smelled of beeswax polish and Ginny imagined how lovely it must be to close the curtains and curl up in one of the chairs on a cold winter's night – not that she supposed Father Mick would have much chance to do that. He seemed always to be called out by one or another of his parishioners, although he never complained. She had just taken a seat in one of the fireside chairs when Father Mick reappeared and she made to rise.

'No, no, my dear. Stay where you are, please, and get warm,' he encouraged as he ran his hand through his shock of wiry hair. Like his beard it was grey. He was a tall, thin man with a ruddy complexion and Ginny wondered how old he might be.

'So,' he said, going to stand in front of the fire. 'Have you found somewhere to stay?'

As Ginny stared into his kindly blue eyes she sighed and nodded. 'Yes, I have.' That much she was prepared to tell him, although she wouldn't disclose exactly where it was. 'I have to find a job now, and then when I'm earning I intend to take Charlie out of the workhouse and look after him myself.'

'But you're very young to be thinking of taking on such a responsibility,' he remarked worriedly.

'I'll be seventeen just before Christmas,' she told him with her chin in the air. 'And I'm *perfectly* capable. I always helped me mam with the little ones.'

The conversation was stopped from going any

further when the door suddenly banged open and Mrs Braintree appeared carrying a laden tray. She was a short stout woman with white hair and a kindly face, and she beamed at Ginny as Father Mick hurried forward to take the tray from her.

'I've just been baking,' she informed her. 'So I've made a few sandwiches with some of the fresh bread and the ham joint left over from dinnertime. I know his lordship 'ere will eat it if you're not hungry. I swear this man has hollow legs. He never stops eating yet there's not a scrap of fat on him, whereas I only have to look at a slice 'o cake an' me hips 'ave grown an inch.'

'Rubbish, Mrs Braintree, you're a fine figure of a woman,' Father Mick teased and she blushed becomingly before wagging her finger at him. She then gave Ginny a friendly grin and ambled away as Father Mick began to pour tea into two delicate china cups and saucers.

'Sugar?'

When Ginny nodded he added two lumps and a dash of milk before handing hers to her, saying, 'Do help yourself to something to eat, Ginny. I shall have to finish it all if you don't. I'm afraid Mrs Braintree is a great believer in feeding people up. I ought to be the size of a house really. The only reason I do eat so much is because I don't like to offend her. Sometimes it takes me all my time to get upstairs, I'm so full up. I swear I shall burst one of these days.' Then on a more solemn note: 'We've missed you at Sunday school.'

Ginny began to relax; Father Mick was so kind it was hard not to do so in his company.

'I've missed coming,' she told him. 'And I've

missed going to the school too. But when Mam became ill, I...'

'I know,' he said gravely as he lifted the cup to his lips. 'Your teacher, Miss Timms, had great hopes for you. She said you were the brightest pupil she had ever had and she hoped that you'd become a teacher yourself one day; you were shaping up nicely. But life can be so cruel, child, and usually to those who least deserve it.' He coughed slightly to clear his throat then before saying tentatively, 'I heard about what happened to your father too, Ginny.' He let out a deep sigh. 'It's all very sad and very out of character for Seth. Before he lost your mother I'd never known your father to drink, apart from special occasions like the Harvest Festival and Christmas. His sentence was a little harsh, to say the least considering the circumstances – but now you must take good care of yourself.'

'Oh, I shall be perfectly all right,' Ginny said with a confidence she was far from feeling. Then, hoping to change the subject, she helped herself to one of Mrs Braintree's delicious ham and pickle sandwiches while Father Mick bit into some homemade shortbread. They sat in silence, listening to the logs spit on the fire and the ticking of the old grandfather clock that stood in one corner, and Ginny took comfort from the kindness in this place.

Chapter Eight

'Whatever's the matter wi' yer, girl?' Mrs Bevins said irritably on Sunday morning. 'Yer've been like a cat on 'ot bricks ever since yer got out o' bed this mornin'. You'll wear a hole in me floor if yer keep pacin' up an' down like that.'

'Sorry.' Ginny glanced at the old-fashioned wooden clock on the mantelpiece for the tenth time in as many minutes. In just two more hours she would be able to set off and see Charlie, and she could hardly wait. Throughout the morning she'd been doing jobs about the cottage for the old woman, and now it was scarcely recognisable as the place she'd walked into just the week before. The diamond-leaded windows shone, inside and out, and the curtains had been taken down and soaked, then washed and dried in front of the fire on a big wooden clothes-horse. Ginny had then pressed them with the hot flat-iron before hanging them back up. The floor was swept and scrubbed, the furniture gleamed with the polish Ginny had enthusiastically rubbed into it, and there was now no trace of the smell of the cats, even though they still lounged about the place as if they owned it. Mrs Bevins had been very sparing with her thanks for all that Ginny had done, but every now and then the girl would catch her looking about admiringly with a satisfied little smile on her face. The old woman had even washed herself and changed her clothes, and Ginny had washed and pressed those as well.

'Well, are yer goin' to just stand about day-dreamin' an' let me dish this dinner up all on me own?' Florrie Bevins' voice jolted Ginny back to the present and she scurried across the room to help her.

The meal as always was delicious and while she ate it Ginny tried not think what Charlie might be having. She'd heard that the food they served to the people in the workhouse was atrocious, barely fit for pigs, and she wondered if they would allow her to take him something in.

The minutes ticked away, each one seeming like an hour until at last it was time to go. Ginny had washed and dried the pots and Mrs Bevins was dozing in front of the fire with one of the cats on her lap and two more curled up at her feet. Even so, as Ginny wrapped her shawl about her, the woman opened an eye and asked, 'An' where might you be goin' in this? It's a real pea-souper out there.'

'Oh, I err ... just thought I'd carry on looking for work,' Ginny stammered. Over the last few days Mrs Bevins had become more curious about her and had questioned her about her circum-stances, but as yet Ginny still hadn't revealed where she had come from. She felt that the less Florrie – or anyone else for that matter – knew about her, the better for now.

'On a Sunday? I doubt folks will thank you for knockin' on their doors today.'

Ginny shrugged as she made for the door.

'I dare say the worst they can do is clear me off,

isn't it?' she said more sharply than she had intended to. Mrs Bevins might be a bit short and a bit slow with her praise but Ginny was already discovering that her bark was far worse than her bite.

'Go on then, but don't come moanin' to me if yer catch yer death o' cold,' the old lady grumbled, then snuggling further down into her chair she closed her eyes again as Ginny let herself out. The air outside was so bitter that it took her breath away for a moment but nothing would have kept her from seeing Charlie, so she set off at a good pace.

After walking through the town she took a short-cut over the Cat Gallows Bridge and along Greenmoor Road, and soon afterwards the grim façade of the workhouse loomed out of the mist. There were a number of people already queuing outside, no doubt here like herself to visit some-one, Ginny thought, and she joined the end of the queue. The seconds and the minutes ticked away, each seeming like an eternity as Ginny blew on her hands and stamped her feet to try and get some warmth into them. Then suddenly the faint chimes of the clock in the marketplace striking two sounded in the distance and the heavy bolts on the inside of the workhouse door were drawn open. Over the heads of the queue, she saw a pale-faced young woman in a shapeless grey dress stand aside to let everyone pass.

People surged forward and Ginny found herself being jostled along a dark corridor. She emerged into an equally dingy room that was full of old tables with mismatched chairs placed around them. People hurried forward and took a seat as the fearsome woman who had spoken to her on her last visit marched into the room, the keys on the chatelaine about her waist clanking together as she walked. The young woman who had admitted them hastily took her place at her side, and as people told her the names of the inmates they had come to see she marked them off on a clipboard she was holding. The young girl disappeared off, returning with people who were all dressed in the same drab grey uniform as herself: shapeless shift dresses for the women, baggy grey trousers and shirts for the men. The inmates all seemed to look the same: their eyes were without hope, their faces pale, and Ginny noticed that they were all painfully thin. She gulped to hide her distress as the woman finally reached her table.

'Name of the person you've come to see?' she barked without taking her beady eyes off the list.

'Charles Thursday.'

At this the woman raised her head and as she stared at Ginny recognition dawned in her eyes. 'Ah, so it's you again, is it? Go and stand out in the corridor. I'll talk to you when I've finished doing this.'

Ginny rose to do as she was told, feeling shaken and apprehensive. There were children appearing too now, no doubt to see parents who had been forced to place them here because they couldn't afford to feed them – but where was Charlie?

What if something had happened to him? Had he had one of his turns? Or worse still, had he met with an accident? All manner of terrible possibilities began to flash through her mind and

91

by the time the stern-faced woman finally joined her she was trembling with fear about what she might tell her.

'I'm afraid you're wasting your time coming here. Your brother is gone,' she told Ginny without preamble.

Ginny gasped as her hand flew to her throat. 'What do you mean ... *gone?*'

The woman frowned at her as if she was an imbecile. 'I mean exactly what I said. Your brother is no longer in the workhouse; he's been taken out of here.'

'*What?*' Things were getting worse by the second. 'B ... but where has he gone? And who's taken him?'

'I can only divulge that information to the child's parents,' the woman told her unfeelingly. 'Many of the children in here under the age of fourteen are often fostered or adopted, especially the boys. They are very popular with farmers to work the land.'

Ginny stared at her in stunned disbelief. 'But no one would choose Charlie for something like that. He's only eight years old, and small and weak for his age.'

'It's no concern of yours,' the woman snapped haughtily. 'All you need to know is that he's gone, so please leave now and don't trouble us again.'

'But can't you *please* just tell me where?' Ginny implored as tears sprang to her eyes.

'I've already told you *no*, I *cannot!* Now are you going to leave or do I have to have you forcibly removed?'

Ginny opened her mouth to protest again but

seeing the implacable expression on the woman's face she closed it. She seemed to be devoid of any natural kindness or human warmth. The woman continued to glare at her and Ginny half turned to go. Their altercation was attracting attention but suddenly all the heartache and pain that she had suffered over the last few months caught up with her, and before she could stop herself she whirled round and, raising herself up to her full height, her hands clamped into fists, she said boldly, 'My mother is dead and my father ... well, I'm sure you are aware where he is. Neither of them can be here so that makes *me* Charlie's next-of-kin, so I *demand* you tell me where he is – and I won't budge from this spot until you do!'

The woman's eyes seemed to almost pop out of her head and angry colour flooded into her cheeks. She was clearly used to being obeyed. No one in the workhouse was in a position to do otherwise.

'We'll see about that, young lady!' she sputtered and after clicking her fingers two men appeared as if she had conjured them up from thin air.

'Get this ... this *person* ... *out* of here this minute!' she spat and the men instantly caught hold of Ginny's arms and began to haul her towards the door.

Ginny fought them for all she was worth, digging her heels in and protesting loudly, but her strength was no match for theirs and minutes later they opened the door to the workhouse and she was thrown unceremoniously out on to the cold pavement. She landed painfully on her hands and knees and looked behind her just in time to see the door being slammed. Tears of frustration began to stream down her face as she picked herself up and brushed herself down with what dignity she could muster, beneath the curious gaze of the passers-by. She could only imagine what they must be thinking. Most people were dragged into that dreadful place kicking and screaming – not thrown out!

Deeply humiliated, she limped away. Charlie was all she had left now – until their father came home, that was – and that was years away – but how was she going to find out where he was now? She had never felt so utterly alone as she headed back to Mrs Bevins' cottage, too upset to even think about searching for a job. There would probably have been no point anyway, she supposed, with it being the Sabbath. The shops were all closed and she'd tried almost all of them anyway. But at least she still had some money, she thought, and tried to cheer herself as she felt the weight of the little pouch she had sewn into the waistband of her skirt. That would ensure that she could pay Mrs Bevins her rent for some weeks at least, and surely by then she would have found a position?

Back on the Cat Gallows Bridge that crossed the Coventry canal, she paused to stare down into the sluggish brown water and as she did so a dead dog, bloated and grotesque, floated by beneath her. Shuddering, she clutched her shawl about her and hurried on. Her hands and knees were skinned and she could feel blood trickling down her leg but she would clean the wounds when she got back to her lodgings. The sky was darkening now and as she moved on she saw some youths, three of them, coming towards her. They looked an unsavoury bunch and she kept her head lowered, hoping to avoid eye contact. But it wasn't to be. The youths clearly had other ideas.

'So who 'ave we 'ere then?' she heard one of them say when they were almost abreast of her. His friend's laughter egged him on as he stood in Ginny's path. She was suddenly aware how isolated she was. Even if she were to scream her head off, it was highly unlikely that anyone would hear her.

'Look ... I don't want any trouble,' she told him. 'Please just let me pass and go on my way.'

'*Ooh!* 'Ark at her then, lads. A right little lady, ain't she?' Then his tone becoming menacing, he leaned towards her and snarled, 'Think yer too good fer the likes of us, do yer? Well, per'aps it's time someone taught yer a little lesson. Whadda yer say, lads?'

His friends nodded eagerly. Ginny was a pretty girl and they were bored. The youth took a step closer and Ginny flinched. He was so near now that she could smell the rank stink of him. His hair stood out about his head like a wiry halo and his teeth were crooked and green. Just the thought of him touching her made nausea rise in her throat. But before she could do anything to prevent it, his arm snaked out and he pulled her roughly to him, clamping his disgusting mouth on hers. He had her firmly about the waist but he suddenly held her at arm's length. He had felt the coins in her little pouch as he'd pressed her to him and Ginny's hand automatically flew to it. 'Now, what 'ave we 'ere then?' his eyes glittered wickedly.

'N ... nothing,' she gasped. 'Now leave me alone and let me by.' But her words fell on deaf ears as he painfully twisted her arm with one hand whilst thrusting his hand into her waistband with the other.

'Well, blow me down wi' a feather,' he crowed as he yanked the stitches loose and held the treasure high. 'We might be able to afford a pot o' two of ale after all tonight, lads!'

Thankfully he was so busy undoing the pouch that he momentarily forgot all about Ginny and, taking advantage of the fact, she lifted her skirts in a most unladylike manner and ran as if the devil himself were snapping at her heels. She didn't pause to look round or draw breath until she was in Bracebridge Street where she leaned heavily against a wall with a hand pressed to the stitch in her side. She was sobbing now as despair washed over her and cursing herself for a fool. Why oh why had she carried all her money with her? It would have been safe back at Mrs Bevins' and now all she had left was her mother's wedding ring, which thankfully she had tied on a piece of string about her neck. Thankfully too she had paid Mrs Bevins another week's rent in advance that very day, so she was guaranteed shelter for another week but then what was she to do with not a penny in the world to her name?

Her future had never looked so bleak, and as Ginny Thursday dragged herself towards the cottage in Oaston Road her feet felt as if they were made of lead – like the weight in her heart.

Chapter Nine

'Good 'eavens, what's 'appened to you, lass?' Florrie asked, the moment Ginny staggered into the cottage looking bedraggled and miserable.

'Oh, I err ... slipped over,' Ginny mumbled, reluctant to tell the woman that she no longer had a farthing to her name. It had started to rain and now on top of everything else she was soaked to the skin.

'Well, you'd best go up to yer room an' get out o' them wet clothes,' Mrs Bevins said, eyeing her with concern. 'Else you'll be catchin' worse than a chill!'

At that moment, Ginny felt that would have been a solution to all her problems but she merely nodded, and lighting a candle, she made her way up to her room. Once she had stripped off, she bathed her sore hands and knees then put on some dry clothes before carrying the others downstairs to dry by the fire.

'There's a bit o' roast pork left from dinner an' a fresh loaf in the crock if you've a mind to cut yerself some bread,' the old lady told her when she came back downstairs but Ginny politely declined. She had lost her appetite and felt that if she tried to eat anything, it would choke her. Somehow she had to find out what had happened to Charlie and also get herself a job otherwise she too might land up in the workhouse.

Terror ran through her at the thought.

Mrs Bevins meanwhile was watching the girl and thinking that Ginny was something of a mystery. She was certainly very young to be caring for herself, and the woman had the feeling that she was in some sort of trouble. Perhaps she had run away from a bully of a father? Whatever, there was nothing she could do about it until Ginny confided in her, and up to now she had clammed up every time she so much as asked her anything about herself. With a shrug, Florrie put the big tabby on her lap on the floor, took up her old clay pipe and lit it with a spill from the fire as Ginny set about tidying the room.

As the days went by, Ginny became more and more frantic and frustrated. It would soon be time to give her landlady another week's rent but as yet she still hadn't succeeded in finding a job despite the fact that she had walked for miles. And then at last, late on Wednesday afternoon as the sky was darkening, Ginny entered the pie shop in town.

'I was wondering if there were any jobs going?' she asked half-heartedly. She had been turned away from so many places now that she had more or less lost all hope.

The middle-aged woman standing behind the counter narrowed her eyes and peered at her. The woman didn't look any too clean but Ginny knew that the shop did a roaring trade from the miners, who often called in on their way home from work to take a hot pie back to their families.

'There might be,' she said cautiously. The girl certainly looked respectable enough. 'As it so

'appens, we sent the last girl packin' only yesterday. Lyin' little toad she were. Reckoned my Bill
'ad got 'er belly up, she did, so we showed 'er the
bloody door.' She sniffed indignantly before
asking, 'So what experience 'ave you 'ad?'

'Well, I've never actually worked in a shop
before but I'm a good cook,' Ginny informed her
hopefully.

'Hmm, in 'ere my Bill does the main o' the
cookin',' the woman informed her. 'But we need
someone who can live in. You'd 'ave to be up at five
every mornin' to light the ovens an' get 'em 'ot fer
Bill to 'ave the first pies in by six.'

'Oh, that wouldn't be a problem,' Ginny answered immediately. Could the woman have
known it, this was the answer to all her prayers,
for even if she got a job she was still going to have
to find somewhere to live.

'Hmm.' The woman patted her chin thoughtfully with a grubby finger. 'In that case I'll show
yer down to the basement where the cookin' is
done an' tell yer what yer duties would be. Iffen I
did give yer the job, when could yer start?'

'Oh, just as soon as you like – tomorrow if you
want.' Ginny was trying not to appear too eager
and failing miserably as the woman took her to a
concrete staircase that led down to the basement.
As they made their way down it, the heat rose to
meet them and Ginny felt as if she was walking
into a furnace. She could only imagine how hard
it would be to work in such temperatures all day,
but then she was in no position to be picky. It
would be better than being out on the streets and
being cold, or having to go to Lamp Hill Hall and

throw herself on a stranger's mercy.

Eventually she found herself in a huge room with deep ovens taking up the whole of one wall. A man stood at a table in the centre of the room rolling pastry and he looked up as the woman told him, 'I've someone 'ere who's after a job, Bill. What do yer think?'

The man was enormous and appeared to be almost as far round as he was high. He wore a grubby white apron that strained across his huge stomach and his thinning hair was plastered to his scalp with sweat. He clapped his hands, sending a shower of flour floating into the air, and stared at Ginny with a grin displaying yellowing teeth.

'Well, she looks fine to me. 'Ave yer told 'er that we need someone to live in?'

The woman nodded. 'I 'ave that, an' she says it wouldn't be a problem. She can start straight away an' all.'

'Exactly where would I be living?' Ginny ventured and the woman pointed to a door on the opposite wall.

'There's a bed an' all you'll need in there,' she told her as if she was offering first-class accommodation.

'May I look?'

Again the woman nodded as Ginny crossed the room, which she saw with dismay was very dirty. There were what looked suspiciously like mice droppings all across the floor, and dirty pots, thick with grease, were piled on every available surface. The bedroom that she found herself in – if it could be called such – was little better. A tiny window high up on one wall let in the grey afternoon light and Ginny gulped as she stared at a metal bed on which lay a grimy straw mattress. Just as she had at Mrs Bevins' cottage, she would have to scrub the whole place down. The floor was filthy and the room was so tiny that she could barely turn around in it and she began to feel claustrophobic. But then she knew that it was better than nothing until she could find something more suitable.

'H ... how much are the wages?' she asked falteringly.

'Till you've proved yerself you'll get two shillin' a week an' yer keep.'

It wasn't much but again, it was better than nothing. 'Then I'll be happy to take it if you think I'm suitable.'

As the woman led her back towards the staircase, Ginny could feel the man's eyes burning into her back and she wondered if there had been any truth in the allegations made by the poor girl who had been dismissed. The way the man had looked at her had made her feel very uncomfortable but she was desperate: she would just have to take her chances.

Once they were back upstairs, Ginny stood aside as the woman served a customer with two hot steak and kidney pies.

'Right then, I'm Edith,' the woman told her when the door had closed behind the customer. 'Will yer be wantin' to move in tonight, ready to start in the mornin'?'

'Yes, I suppose that would be best,' Ginny agreed then said tentatively, 'What time off will I get?' It was best to get the questions out of the way.

'We open six days a week. We only 'ave Sunday

off but some o' that is spent gettin' the kitchen to rights so I dare say yer could 'ave Sunday afternoons off if yer've got all the chores done.'

Ginny was sure that the kitchen hadn't been cleaned for months but she was too polite to argue so she merely nodded in agreement.

'Me an' Bill live in the rooms above the shop,' Edith went on to tell her. 'An' you'll find a privy outside in the back yard. If yer turn up wi' yer stuff after six tonight, give our door a good knock an' me or Bill'll come down an' let yer in. But yer only on trial, mind! Shall we say fer a month?'

Ginny nodded, and as another customer entered she quietly left the shop. Back at Mrs Bevins' cottage, when Ginny explained why she was leaving, the old woman seemed genuinely sorry to see her go and even refunded a few pennies of her board money. It took Ginny only a matter of minutes to pack her few belongings and then she clattered down the wooden staircase to say goodbye to Florrie.

'Look,' the old woman told her hesitantly, 'ever since yer arrived I've 'ad the feelin' that you're in some sort o' bother.' When Ginny opened her mouth to deny it the woman held her hand up to silence her. 'O' course it's none o' my business, which is why I ain't pressed yer. But I want yer to know you've been a good lass fer me, an' if ever yer should need shelter, yer can always come back an' there'll be a bed 'ere waitin' for yer.'

Just as Ginny had suspected, it seemed that the old woman had a soft heart beneath her crusty exterior. Ginny bent to kiss her cheek, making colour flow into Florrie's wrinkled face.

'Now there's no need fer any o' that sloppy stuff,' she objected. 'Get off wi' yer ... but remember, I'm 'ere if ever yer should need me.' With that she turned her attention back to the newspaper she was reading, and with a last glance around at the contented cats who were curled up in balls and the now spotless room, Ginny promised her that she would visit when she could, and let herself out into the cold early evening air.

As she was heading for her next home she realised with a little jolt that it was now almost December. Christmas would be rolling around in no time. The first without her family. She thought of the loved ones lying in the churchyard in the cold earth, of her father who would be spending his Christmas in prison, and then wondered again where Charlie might be – and the pain stabbed at her heart as sharp as a knife. But then she pulled herself together with an effort. The sooner she could start to get some money behind her, the sooner she could employ someone to help her in her search for her little brother. The thought lent speed to her feet.

The pie shop was closed, its lights extinguished as she had expected when she arrived, so she knocked on the door that she assumed led up to the rooms above it. Within seconds she heard heavy footsteps echoing off the bare wooden stairs inside and as the door creaked open she saw Bill with a guttering candle in his hand staring out at her.

'Ah, so yer 'ere, are yer?' he said unnecessarily. 'Wait there while I goes back to get the keys to the shop,' he ordered her and she stood on the cold pavement stamping her feet to try and get warm. Bill reappeared seconds later and as she followed him to the door to the shop her heart started thumping. As before the way he looked at her was unnerving but Ginny tried her best to persuade herself that she was just being silly. Bill was almost old enough to be her grandfather – so what interest would he have in her, she asked herself. Once inside the shop he lit an oil lamp and by its flickering light she followed him down into the basement. When they entered, there was a scurry of activity on the floor and as he held the lamp aloft they were just in time to see a fat tail disappear into a hole in the wall. Ginny shuddered. Rats!

Seeing her unease, the big man laughed. 'They won't 'urt you if you don't 'urt them,' he told her with a throaty chuckle as he scratched his hairy armpit. Despite the cold he was wearing an old shirt. Ginny thought it might have been white once but now it was so grimy it was hard to tell. His braces dangled loose about his fat backside and she was sure she'd never seen such an odious-looking man in the whole of her life before.

'The missus said to tell yer you'll find some bedding in the blanket box in yer room.' He was eyeing her appreciatively again and Ginny backed away, keen for him to be gone.

'Thank you ... I'll err ... just get settled in then.'

He pointed to a door in the far wall next to the massive ovens. 'There's a yard out there wi' a privy an' a coalhouse. Make sure you 'ave the ovens goin' for when I come down at six in the mornin'.'

Ginny tensed as he slowly walked towards her.

Even the thought of being down here alone with the rats was preferable to being alone with him.

'It will be done,' she assured him, clutching her small bag of possessions in front of her for protection.

After placing the oil lamp on the table he turned to leave then and it was all she could do to prevent herself from letting out an audible sigh of relief.

'Good night, 'elp yerself to tea an' whatnot. You'll find some in the cupboard over there, an' there's some pies in there an' all if yer 'ungry.'

That's one consolation at least, Ginny thought as he clattered away up the stairs. At least I'm not going to die of hunger or thirst. When his footsteps had faded away and she had heard the sound of the shop door slamming, she lifted the lamp and gazed about in dismay, keeping a wary eye on the hole in the wall in case the rat should choose to make another appearance. She had thought Mrs Bevins' cottage was dirty when she had first arrived there but that had been nothing compared to this. The soles of her boots were sticking to the build-up of spilled food and filth on the floor, and the walls were covered in grease and grime. She noted there was a window in there but it was so filthy that it was impossible to see anything out of it, and it was covered in dead flies.

Feeling a little overwhelmed, Ginny wondered where she should start. She was suddenly terribly weary and decided that for tonight she would simply concentrate on getting her bedroom ready. She would begin to tackle this room the following day, in between doing her jobs. The bedding that

Bill had told her about left a lot to be desired but she would have to manage with it for now. As soon as she got her first pay she would treat herself to some cheap but clean bed linen from the rag stall in the market. She found a broom and a mop and bucket lurking in a corner of the kitchen and after boiling some water on the stove she swept the bedroom floor and washed it. It was a very small room, containing only a blanket box and a rather dilapidated chest of drawers, but at least there was room to put her things away. There wasn't even a jug and bowl and Ginny realised that she would have to wash in the kitchen sink each night after the shop had closed. It wasn't ideal, but once again she was grateful for small mercies. At least it was warm in here, which was more than could be said for outside.

Later that night, she stood back to survey her handiwork. The bedroom was as clean as she could make it now so she boiled another kettle of water to make herself a cup of tea and wash in. She felt rather vulnerable as she stripped her clothes off and kept a wary eye on the stairway the whole time she was washing in case Bill decided to put in another appearance. Thankfully he didn't, so once she was clean she made herself a hot drink and helped herself to a large slice of pie. She had taken an instant dislike to the man but she had to admit he was an excellent cook, which was probably why his pies were so popular. At last, with a full stomach and feeling reasonably clean, she slid into bed. She was tempted to leave the oil lamp burning to deter the rats, but was worried about using too much oil, so instead she lit the stub of a candle and placed it carefully on the chest of drawers.

It was only when she was tucked in that misery claimed her once more as she thought of her position. She didn't even know where her brother had been taken. Only now did she realise what a sheltered privileged life the little Thursday family had led – but that was all gone now. Tears trickled down her cheeks but eventually exhaustion claimed her and she slept.

Chapter Ten

For Ginny, the first few days of working in the pie shop passed in a blur. Her day began at five in the morning when she would rise and get the fires going in the ovens. Bill would then join her at six o' clock and she would carry out whatever orders he barked at her. Rolling pastry; preparing the meat for the pies, getting the pies out of the oven, running upstairs with whole trays of them to keep the shop supplied – and in between she would try to keep on top of the cleaning. Oh, the cleaning! It seemed endless, and this went on usually until gone seven o'clock at night when Edith and Bill would return to their rooms above the shop. By then Ginny would be so tired that every bone in her body would be aching. The young girl had almost forgotten what daylight looked like, for it was dark when she rose and dark when the shop closed. But even then her day was far from over.

There were all the trays that the pies had been baked in to be washed ready for the next morning and the floors to be swept and scrubbed. Only then would Ginny wearily strip off her clothes and wash every inch of herself in the bowl that she kept for that purpose. Afterwards she would wash through the clothes she had been wearing that day and hang them over a line she had strung up across the ceiling in one corner of the kitchen especially for that purpose. Luckily the heat in the room always ensured that they were dry for the next morning, otherwise she dreaded to think what she would have smelled like. The only consolation was that up to now, Bill had made no move towards her and Ginny was beginning to wonder if perhaps she might have misjudged him. Admittedly she often looked up to find his eyes tight on her but he had kept his hands to himself so she could cope with that, and her confidence was slowly growing.

And then at last Sunday morning dawned. Ginny awoke at five and automatically began to clamber out of bed before remembering that the shop would not be open that day. There was still the kitchen to clean admittedly, but after that the day would be her own – not that she had any- where special to go or anyone special to see. Just for now, she needed a little break from dear old Mrs Bevins. No doubt she should have spent the time searching for Charlie, but where should she start? Dropping back into bed, for a while she gave in to the loneliness that wrapped itself around her like a cloak. Then with an effort she got up and got herself dressed.

Because she had made such a huge effort over the past few days, there wasn't too much to do in the kitchen. As the cold, early-morning winter sunlight filtered through the newly clean window, she realised with a little shock that it was 1st December, her birthday. Today she was seventeen years old. However, this year, unlike the ones that had gone before, there would be no celebrations. Ginny thought back to her last birthday, when her mother had woken her with a kiss and a small gift – a heart-shaped box to put her ribbons in that she had bought from the market. Then at teatime the whole family had sat down to a special birthday meal. There had been ham sandwiches and a rich fruit cake that Emily had made especially for the occasion. Unexpectedly, the girl found herself smiling at the wonderful memories. No one could take them away from her and she knew that they would last for ever. Soon her arms were deep in water as she tackled the dirty trays before turning her attention to the floor – and by late morning, the whole room was spick and span.

'Hmm, I dare say it'll do,' Edith said ungratefully when she came down to check on her shortly before lunchtime. 'I were thinkin' that Bill could show yer how to make the soup this week. It'll be one less thing fer 'im to 'ave to worry about, bless 'im!'

Ginny had quickly discovered that the thick broth that Bill made was also very popular with the customers, especially with the women from the mill who would call in for a dishful during their breaks. She had also discovered that Bill could do no wrong in his wife's eyes. Edith worshipped the ground he walked on.

'I'd be quite happy to do that,' Ginny agreed, noting that Edith had on her Sunday best clothes, which were only fractionally better than the ones she wore in the shop.

'Right, well, I'm off out now fer a couple of 'ours,' Edith informed her. 'I likes to go an' see me old mum on a Sunday. She's in 'er eighties now, see? My Bill is upstairs 'aving a rest so see that yer don't disturb 'im. Tara fer now.'

Ginny smiled as Edith puffed her way back up the stairs, then helped herself to a pie for her dinner. By the time she had eaten it and washed and dried the pots she was beginning to feel a little restless and decided to get warmly wrapped up and go out for some fresh air. She'd had little enough of it since she'd been there and realised now that it was unlikely she'd get the chance again until the following Sunday. Back in her tiny room, she quickly changed into the Sunday blouse and skirt that her mother had made for her to go to church in. Then she slipped her shawl about her shoulders and picked up her straw bonnet. There was no mirror downstairs so she crossed to the window where she could see her reflection. It was as she was standing there, tying the ribbons under her chin, that a shape came up behind her. Whirling about, she found herself face to face with Bill, who had a lecherous smile on his face.

'Well, now, an' don't we look bonny,' he leered. 'Off out to meet our young man, are we? I'd be surprised if a pretty young lass like you didn't have an admirer.'

'No ... yes...' Ginny stammered, not sure what

110

to say for the best. Perhaps if Bill thought there was a young man it would make him keep his distance?

'Is it yes or no then?' He frowned now as Ginny began to inch around him towards the staircase.

'Err ... yes, I do have a young man and if I don't hurry he'll come looking for me.'

Bill looked far from happy but thankfully he did nothing to delay her so Ginny shot off up the stairs as fast as her feet would take her. Luckily Bill had given her a key to the shop door so that she could come and go without disturbing him. Once outside in the marketplace, she felt safer. Something about that man made her skin crawl and she decided that from now on, she would aim to go out on a Sunday before Edith left to visit her mother.

She wandered aimlessly about, staring in at the shop windows, and it was as she was gazing into one particular shop at the hats displayed there that she became aware of someone approaching. Thinking that it might be Bill come looking for her, she froze – but instead she saw a smartly dressed young man.

'Hello, Miss Thursday, we meet again.' He swept his cap off and gave a little bow. He clearly knew her and there was something vaguely familiar about him although for the life of her she couldn't think where they had met before ... and then suddenly she recognised him. It was Bertie Watkins, the young constable, out of uniform.

'Oh hello.' When she smiled, Bertie's heart did a little flip. He was sure that he had never seen a more beautiful girl in the whole of his life.

'I err ... don't suppose there's been any news of my father?'

Seeing the hopeful look on her face he wished that he could give her good news. But he didn't have any.

'I only know that he's been sent to Winson Green in Birmingham to serve his sentence.'

'Oh ... I see.' To Ginny, Birmingham sounded like the other side of the world

'Are you out for a stroll?' Bertie asked then, hoping to take her mind off her father and put the smile back on her face.

'Yes. You see, I've started work at the pie shop in town and thought I'd get out for a breath of fresh air. I only have Sunday afternoons off.'

Bertie frowned. 'Not Bill Parsons' shop?'

When she nodded, he sucked in his breath before saying, 'I've heard he and his wife are hard taskmasters.'

'I suppose they are. I certainly don't get a lot of time to stand about.'

'And Mr Parsons ... is he treating you all right?'

Now it was Ginny's turn to frown. 'In what way?'

'Well...' Bertie hesitated before going on. 'Young Cissie Marston from the street where I live worked for him and he sacked her. Cissie is in the family way and says the baby is Bill's – that he forced himself on her – but Parsons is denying it so it's her word against his. Poor kid.'

'His wife did mention something about that,' Ginny answered worriedly. 'But he hasn't touched me.' She would have liked to add 'as yet', for she wouldn't have trusted Bill as far as she could throw him. Strange how she couldn't bring herself to say that, especially to a policeman, even if he was off duty.

'Well, just keep your eye on him and try never to be alone with him,' Bertie warned with what seemed like genuine concern and Ginny felt warm inside.

'I can't avoid being alone with him,' she pointed out. 'I help him with the cooking down in the basement and Edith serves upstairs in the shop.' But it was nice to think that there was still someone who cared about her, at least. Her thoughts turned to Charlie then and she told the constable what had happened the week before.

'The housemother wouldn't tell me where he is because I'm not his parent,' she ended with a catch in her voice. 'Is there anything that you could do?'

Bertie sighed. 'In actual fact I believe she's within her rights,' he told her apologetically. 'But I'll tell you what, when I get in to the station tomorrow I'll have a word with the sergeant and ask his advice.'

'Oh, thank you.' Ginny gasped with delight and his heart did another little flip. 'That's the best birthday present you could have given me.'

'Birthday? Is it today?'

Ginny blushed, wondering why she had let that slip. 'Yes, it is,' she confessed. 'And it's the first I've spent away from my family. This time last year we were all together, everyone was well and none of us knew what lay ahead.'

'Look,' he said, seeing the haunted look in her lovely blue eyes. 'Why don't we go for a stroll by the river? It's a little cold standing about here. If

113

any of the eating houses were open I'd take you for afternoon tea as a birthday treat but I'm afraid that everywhere is shut – apart from the inns, and I don't suppose you'd fancy venturing into one of those, would you?'

Ginny shook her head and grinned. 'No, not really – but I'd like some company on a walk,' she said shyly. He was nice, was Bertie, and made her feel that she wasn't completely alone in the world.

'So where do you live?' she asked as they strolled towards the park.

'I'm still at home with me mam and dad, and me four younger siblings in North Street,' Bertie told her. 'And I don't mind telling you they're right little devils, especially me two little brothers. I swear those two could get up to mischief in a padded cell.' And then he could have bitten his tongue out. What a terrible choice of words that had been, considering that Ginny's father had just been locked away, but thankfully, a glance at her face showed that she hadn't taken offence.

'My little brothers were rascals too...' Her voice trailed away then as a picture of their tiny coffins flashed in front of her eyes and again Bertie felt sorry for her. What a rotten year this poor girl had had.

'So how old are you today then – if I'm allowed to ask, that is? I suppose a gentleman shouldn't ask a lady her age. If me mam were here she'd clip me round the ear for being so forward.' The young man was keen to channel her thoughts on to happier things.

'I'm seventeen.'

'Seventeen, eh? Then I'll seem very old to you because I'm almost twenty. The youngest at the station, I am, and they don't half give me some gyp I don't mind telling you. They're always pulling pranks on me but I take it in good part.'

Ginny could well believe it. Bertie seemed to be very nice-natured. He was quite nice-looking too, though not in the conventional sense. He was very tall and thin, lanky almost, and he towered over Ginny. His hair was a rich dark brown with a tendency to curl that no amount of Macassar oil seemed able to tame for long and his eyes were a lovely honey brown – and kindly.

They strolled on, their breath hanging on the air in front of them, and soon they came to the River Anker and wandered along the banks, watching the swans who glided gracefully on its glassy surface. The weeping willow trees dangled their leafless branches into the water and as Bertie told her all about his family Ginny felt herself begin to relax a little. She in turn found herself telling him all about George and Tim and Betty, and for the first time she was able to talk about them with a smile instead of tears as she relayed some of the antics they had used to get up to.

Before they knew it, the afternoon was beginning to darken and the couple reluctantly turned back.

'I've really enjoyed this afternoon,' Bertie told her. 'Perhaps we could do it again next Sunday?'

'I'd like that,' she said with a blush. He was nice, was Bertie.

'And in the meantime I shall make a few enquiries tomorrow to see if there's anything we can do about finding out where Charlie's gone.'

'I'd appreciate that.' Ginny gave him a grateful smile. They had almost reached the shop door when they saw Edith walking towards them from the opposite direction. When she caught sight of them her lips tightened, although she said nothing.

'Thanks for walking me home,' Ginny said awkwardly as Edith glared at her and stalked off through the door leading to the rooms above the shop.

'It was my pleasure.' Bertie took off his cap and gave a gallant little bow again before setting off for home.

Ginny quickly went through the shop and down the stairs that led to the kitchen and her tiny room. At least it was nice and warm down here, she thought to herself. It was also a lot cleaner than when she had first arrived, thanks to all her efforts. She took off her bonnet and shawl and had just put the kettle on to make herself a cup of tea when Edith appeared on the stairs, closely followed by Bill who was looking none too pleased.

'I was just checking that you hadn't brought your young man home with yer,' Edith said with a glance around the room. 'We don't want any hanky-panky going on down here.'

Ginny opened her mouth to tell her that Bertie wasn't her young man but just a friend, then thought better of it and clamped it shut again. She'd already told Bill that she had a young man and perhaps if he thought it was Bertie it would put him off laying his hands on her.

'I wouldn't dream of doing such a thing,' she said primly instead.

Edith nodded. 'Good! Just see that yer don't 'cos I ain't having it said that this is a knockin' shop,' then without another word she turned about and pushed Bill up the stairs ahead of her.

When they'd gone Ginny grinned as she spooned some tea leaves into the pot. Hopefully now Bill would keep his distance – and she had made a friend in Bertie. He might even be able to find out where Charlie had been spirited away to. Perhaps things were finally looking up a little.

Chapter Eleven

On Monday Bill barely said a civil word to Ginny all day apart from to bark orders at her – and that suited her just fine. As it was a market day, they were rushed off their feet; they even sold out of pies at one stage and had to wait for another batch to cook, so by the time they closed the door of the shop at six-thirty, Ginny was exhausted. They had been so busy that she'd had no time to do any cleaning during the day and once Edith and Bill had retired to their living accommodation she stared around with dismay. A mountain of dirty pots waited on the large wooden draining board, and every surface including the floor was covered in a fine layer of flour. Ginny glanced towards the holes in the skirting boards. She had blocked them up with old newspapers or anything she could find, and the rats only put in the odd appearance now that there wasn't so much food left lying about, but she was still nervous of them.

Deciding that she would have something to eat and drink first before she made a start on the cleaning, she cut herself a chunk of bread and a slice of pie and after her meal she laid her head on her folded arms on the table. I'll just have ten minutes' rest, she promised herself, and then I'll set to. It was some time later when something made her jump and she realised that she must have dozed off. As she raised her head and stretched she was shocked to see Bill standing there staring down at her.

'I thought I'd catch yer idlin',' he said nastily and Ginny bristled.

'Don't worry, everything will be done before I go to bed ready for morning,' she retorted. She felt hurt and angry. The kitchen even now in no way resembled the terrible mess she'd first seen it in, so what was he complaining about?

Looking at the clock, she saw with a little shock that it was gone eight o'clock.

Bill sidled up to the table and leered at her. 'Per'aps that young boyfriend o' yours 'as tired yer out,' he said suggestively.

'Bertie is a gentleman,' Ginny informed him with her nose in the air.

'Huh! Young chap like that don't know 'ow to show a girl a good time,' he said. 'Whereas an older bloke like me knows 'ow to please a woman.'

Before Ginny could say another word he suddenly reached out and pinched her bottom and she leaped away from him as if she had been stung.

'How *dare* you?' she spat, incensed. 'If you so

much as come near me again I shall tell Edith.'

He chuckled as he turned to leave. 'Think on what I've said, wench. I can be very generous to them as please me.'

With that he left, leaving Ginny quaking with fear. What chance would she stand against him if he were to come down here late at night? She set about her chores, keeping one eye on the stairs all the time, then carried a bowl of water into her room to wash in. She was too afraid to wash in the kitchen now in case Bill reappeared unexpectedly. Thankfully, there was no further sign of him but, all the same, when she went to bed Ginny heaved the chest of drawers across the door just in case, then huddled beneath the covers listening to every tiny sound until at last as the first signs of dawn crept through the tiny window, she slept.

The following day, Bill appeared downstairs to make a start on the baking as if nothing untoward had happened. Perhaps now that she'd shown him she wasn't in the least interested in him he might leave her alone. It was when the shop doors finally closed that Edith appeared on the stairs looking none too pleased.

'Here,' she said disapprovingly, holding out a small package wrapped in brown paper. 'A young copper come in earlier on an' asked me to give yer this. He said to tell yer Happy Birthday.'

Ginny flushed as she took the gift.

'Copper? Yer never told me yer boyfriend were a copper,' Bill muttered.

Ginny stared him in the eye. 'Oh, didn't I

mention it?' she said innocently, then taking her gift into her room she dropped it on to the bed to be opened later and went to start on the cleaning up as Bill and Edith bustled away.

When everything was done and she was finally washed and in her nightclothes she took the oil lamp into her room and after dragging the chest of drawers against the door again she sat on the bed to open her present. Inside was a brooch in the shape of a leaf with a crystal dew drop in the centre of it. She smiled at Bertie's thoughtfulness. She doubted the brooch would have a lot of monetary value but the thought that he had gone to the trouble of choosing it for her meant the world.

For the rest of the week, Ginny kept as far away from Bill as she possibly could. But on Thursday afternoon when they had yet another rush on, he asked her, 'Get that tray o' pies out o' the oven, would yer? I'm up to me neck in pastry fer the next lot 'ere an' they should be cooked be now.'

Crossing to one of the ovens, Ginny took a cloth and had just lifted the tray of pies out when a hand suddenly snaked around her and squeezed her breast. With a scream she dropped the tray and the freshly baked pies scattered across the floor.

'You clumsy little cow!' Bill shouted. 'What did yer 'ave to go an' do that for? I were only 'aving a bit o' fun wi' yer. Can't yer take a joke?'

'I didn't find it very funny,' Ginny snapped back, her hands clenched into fists.

At that second Edith appeared on the stairs. 'What the 'ell is all the shoutin' about?' she demanded. 'An' are them pies ready yet? I've got a queue o' folks up 'ere waitin' fer 'em.'

'This clumsy little mare just dropped 'em,' Bill announced spitefully. 'The next lot'll be a good ten minutes.'

'I dropped them because you handled me,' Ginny defended herself indignantly, pointing to the floury handprint on her blouse.

'I never did,' Bill denied innocently. 'I just brushed by yer on me way to the oven.'

Angry colour flooded into Edith's cheeks. 'Don't you *dare* go sayin' such wicked things about my 'usband,' she hissed pointing a shaking finger in Ginny's direction. 'Cissie, that last 'un that worked 'ere tried that, an' she soon got 'er marchin' orders, so if yer don't want to go the same way you keep your mouth shut, madam! An' 'urry up wi' them pies, will yer!' With that she strode away, leaving Ginny bristling as she glared at Bill.

'You'd best clean up the mess then, 'adn't yer?' he said, and returned to rolling the pastry.

Ginny took a deep breath and did as she was told. It appeared that she'd get no help from Edith. In her eyes Bill could do no wrong, so Ginny would just have to manage him as best she could herself. She needed this job. It would be Christmas in three weeks and where else did she have to go? *Nowhere,* a little voice in her head told her and once again the loneliness was almost painful.

Thankfully there were no further incidents with Bill that week, although Ginny would often catch him watching her with a sly grin on his face; however she ignored him as best she could. At

121

least I have Sunday to look forward to, she told herself. And Bertie might have some news of Charlie by then.

The thought kept her going and on Sunday morning she got through her chores as quickly as she could before going up into the shop to look out for a sign of Bertie. At last she saw him striding along the street, and she hurried out of the shop door, locking it behind her, and went to meet him. She had washed her hair that morning and was dressed in her Sunday best with Bertie's brooch pinned to her blouse, and he looked at her admiringly before saying, 'Why, Ginny, you look lovely, lass.'

Ginny smiled. The grey bombazine skirt that she was wearing had been made from a dress her mother had bought from the rag stall in town. Emily had sat up long into the night cutting it down and reworking it for her, and Ginny loved it. Her blouse had originally been two of her mother's best linen pillowslips, and now had pintucks all down the front of it and a little high ruffled collar. The sleeves had matching ruffled cuffs.

Bertie thought the girl looked beautiful. Her hair tumbled from beneath her only straw bonnet in a thick shiny black plait, and he wished then that he had bought her some flowers. He had been tempted to, but decided that seeing as they'd not long met it might not be appropriate. There would be time to woo her properly when she knew him a little better. Until then, Bertie was looking forward to getting to know her properly, for he had realised the moment they met that here was the girl with whom he wanted to spend the rest of his life. Could she have known that, Ginny would have been disturbed. She liked Bertie very much and was grateful for his friendship, but her thoughts were too full of finding Charlie for her to harbour any romantic notions towards him – or any other young man for that matter.

As they started to walk away from the shop Ginny pulled aside her shawl to show him the brooch and told him bashfully, 'Thank you so much for your gift. It's lovely and I shall treasure it.'

'Oh, it were nothin'. It just seemed sad that your birthday was goin' to pass without anyone acknowledgin' it.'

'Well, I love it,' she assured him. Then becoming solemn she asked, 'Did you manage to find anything out about Charlie?'

Bertie sighed and shook his head. 'I had a word with the sergeant as I promised, but unfortunately it seems that the housemother was within her rights to withhold the information from you. Lots of kiddies get fostered out and adopted from there by all accounts. Farmers tend to be keen to take the lads to help out on the farms and the girls usually go to the big houses to go into service.'

'To be used as cheap labour, you mean!' Ginny said bitterly. 'I know that goes on, Bertie. What I don't understand is, why anyone would choose Charlie if they wanted a worker. Surely they would choose a sturdier-looking lad? Charlie isn't the strongest of little chaps.'

'Then perhaps he was one of the lucky ones who got adopted because the couple who took him simply wanted a child. If that's the case, hopefully he'll have a good life. Sadly, the sergeant told me we're not allowed to intervene 'cos no rules have been broken.'

Ginny's breath came out on a hiss of frustration. 'In that case I shall have to carry on trying to find him by myself. And I will, don't you doubt it! Charlie is my little brother – he belongs with me and I won't rest until we are reunited.'

Bertie could have told her that he doubted there was much chance of that happening. Not until Charlie was old enough to come looking for her at least, but he didn't want to make her any more upset than she clearly already was, so he carefully changed the subject, asking, 'How have things been at the shop? Has Bill Parsons been behavin' himself?'

'Yes,' Ginny lied, seeing no sense in causing trouble.

The atmosphere lightened then when Bertie went on to tell her about the latest prank one of his brothers had pulled on their little sister.

'He caught a fish in the canal an' put it in me sister's bed! By, yer should 'ave 'eard her screamin' blue murder. She near on give me mam a heart attack.' He chuckled and Ginny found herself smiling too.

'Did he get into trouble for it?'

'Not 'alf. Me dad gave him a good clip round the ear an' told 'im if he does anythin' like that again, he'll take his belt off to him.'

Again they found themselves heading in the

124

direction of the river. There was little else to do on a Sunday afternoon but they chatted of this and that, and by the time they arrived back at the shop again, Ginny was in a happier frame of mind. It was nice to have someone to talk to.

'I don't suppose there's any chance of yer gettin' time off one night in the week, is there?' Bertie asked as they stood at the door. 'I could take you out for somethin' to eat then, or we could go to the music hall perhaps?'

Ginny shook her head regretfully. She had never been to a music hall and would have loved to go.

'I'm afraid it's usually going on for nine o'clock by the time I finish each night,' she explained. 'After the shop is shut at six-thirty I have to clean the kitchen and get everything ready for the next morning, you see.'

He nodded. 'Fair enough. Shall we say the same time again next Sunday then? If we're not knee-deep in snow, that is. I reckon it's on the way, lookin' at that sky.'

Ginny thought he could be right. It was certainly cold enough, and the heavens were a curious grey colour, low and leaden with not a cloud in sight. She hoped it wouldn't come yet though. She looked forward to seeing Bertie because he was the only one she ever got to talk to properly now. She didn't count Bill and Edith.

'Next Sunday then ... barring the snow.' Her eyes were twinkling as she said goodbye and let herself into the shop. She'd enjoyed her walk but she would be glad to get back into the warm now.

Once she'd locked the door behind her she

125

hurried down to the basement where she immediately began to take off her shawl and bonnet. It was then that she saw Bill leaning against the sink, observing her.

'Had a nice time with Lover Boy, did you?' he asked with a leer on his face.

Ginny was glad that the table was between them and intended to keep it that way.

'Was there something you wanted?' she asked sharply, ignoring his question. She was determined not to show him how afraid of him she was.

'Not really.' He shrugged his plump shoulders, setting his double chin dancing, and she had to suppress a shudder. She found everything about him repulsive. 'I just got a bit lonely as Edith's gone to see her ma an' I thought yer might want to be nice to me.'

'I have work to do now that I'm back,' Ginny answered coldly and he chuckled.

'Fair enough, but yer won't 'old out against me for ever. Like I said, I can be very nice to them as is nice to me.' As he spoke he opened his palm and she saw a number of shiny shillings there. More than she earned in a month, she had no doubt, but the thought of what he might want her to do for them nearly made her want to retch.

'I don't want you to be nice to me,' she growled. 'So kindly go away and leave me alone to do the job I'm paid for.'

He scowled for a moment but then threw back his head and bellowed with laughter. '*Ooh!* Hark at little Miss La-di-da!' He returned the coins to his pocket, then with a sneer told her, 'You'll change yer mind, they allus do.' With that, to her immense joy he turned and left the room.

Once he was gone, she sagged with relief. Had she had somewhere else to go she would have left there and then, but as it was she was reliant on this job for now at least. The problem was that she worked such long hours that she had no chance to try and find another job – and she wasn't sure how long she could hold off Bill's advances. Still, I've managed up to now, she told herself, trying to be optimistic – but the fear remained.

Chapter Twelve

Just as Bertie had prophesied the snow began to fall midweek and by the following Sunday it lay thick on the ground. There would be no chance of a walk that day and Ginny felt disappointed. Sunday afternoon was the only chance she had to leave the shop and now she would have to wait another whole week before she could venture out. She doubted very much if Bertie would turn up that afternoon but she got herself ready and stood waiting in the shop, peering from the window just in case. She'd had a terrible week with Bill trying to paw her with every opportunity he got and she would have been glad of a distraction to take her mind off it.

She had been standing there for fifteen minutes and was just about to give up on him and go back downstairs when suddenly she saw a snow-covered figure approaching the shop with his head down and his coat collar turned up. It was Bertie, she was sure of it, she would have recognised his lanky stride anywhere now. Risking a telling-off from her employers, she ushered him into the shop for a moment when he arrived, whispering, 'It's lovely to see you, Bertie, but we can't go walking in this. The snow is coming down thick and fast.'

He grinned good-naturedly. 'I know that and I was just sayin' the same to me mam. She suggested that you might like to come to our house fer Sunday tea. If yer don't mind bein' surrounded by a mob of unruly, noisy kids, that is?'

'Oh.' Ginny was taken aback but then as she thought of the lonely hours she would spend downstairs if she didn't accept his offer, she went on: 'That would be lovely, but only if you're sure your mam doesn't mind.'

'She wouldn't have offered if she did, would she?' He gave Ginny a cheeky wink. 'Now get yerself wrapped up warm an' we'll be off. It'll only take us a few minutes to get there.'

And so Ginny rammed her bonnet on, wrapped her shawl tightly about her and they set off.

Bertie's house was one of a terrace in North Street and she wondered how people could tell one from another. They all looked exactly the same with front doors that led directly out to the street.

'We'll go in the back way.' Bertie took her elbow and directed her down a long narrow entry. They then crossed a number of back yards before he flung open a door and told her, 'In yer go.'

128

Ginny found herself in a small kitchen. There was a woman slicing bread at a scrubbed oak table that stood against one wall and she smiled at her warmly. Ginny took to her instantly. Mrs Watkins was a small, plump woman, which made Ginny wonder where Bertie had come from. He certainly didn't take after his mother. She had dark hair that had a tendency to curl and her rounded figure was enveloped in a snow-white apron. Her eyes were blue and kindly, and she immediately welcomed Ginny, saying, 'Well, it's nice to meet yer, lass. Our Bertie's told us all about yer. Come on in an' shake the snow off that shawl. I'll dry it by the fire for yer then I'll make us all a nice cup o' tea. I dare say yer could drink one.'

There was the sound of laughter coming from the room next door and Mrs Watkins nodded towards it. 'I'm afraid the little 'uns are all a bit high-spirited today, what wi' bein' trapped inside.'

'Oh I'm used to it,' Ginny assured her as she thought back to happy times with her younger brothers and sister.

'Come and brave the clan then,' Bertie grinned when Ginny had handed her shawl to his mother and he led her into the next room. She immediately felt at home there and it very much reminded her of the sitting room she had lived in with her family back at the cottage. It wasn't overly large and the furniture was mismatched but it gleamed with polish and everywhere was clean and cosy. Four young people whose ages looked to range from about five to fifteen years old looked up curiously. Two of them were seated on a sofa, the other, younger two knelt on the brightly coloured rug playing with a board game. They all greeted her with cheeky smiles and Ginny saw at once that they were all miniature versions of Bertie.

'Are you our Bertie's girlfriend?' the youngest of the group piped up and his sister dug him sharply in the ribs with her elbow, bringing forth a cry of protest.

'Our ma said you wasn't to say that, our David, fer fear of embarrassin' 'er!' she scolded.

Ginny felt herself blush but Bertie saved the day when he said quickly to the two sitting on the sofa, 'Shove over then, you pair, an' let our guest sit down. She'll think we've no manners.'

They giggled as they quickly did as they were told and Ginny gingerly took a seat next to them. There was a man sitting quietly at the side of the roaring fire trying to read his Sunday newspaper and smoke his pipe, and he too smiled a welcome. Now Ginny saw where Bertie got his height from, for even sitting down the man was enormous.

'Take no notice o' this unruly lot, pet,' he advised her with a twinkle. 'They don't mean no 'arm. They're just tickled pink 'cos our Bertie ain't never brought a young lady home afore.'

'But I'm not his...' Ginny began to object and then thought better of it. She didn't want to embarrass Bertie after all when he had been kind enough to invite her there.

'Right, now that there is Ruby,' Bertie told her, pointing to the older of the two girls. 'David you've already met, unfortunately.' He paused to glare at David, who giggled. 'And the other two are Michael and Lily.'

Ginny inclined her head. 'And I'm Virginia, but

everyone calls me Ginny.'

'We already know that. Our Bertie never stops goin' on about yer,' David piped up again and earned himself yet another dig in the ribs from Ruby.

Mrs Watkins bustled in then with two cups of tea which she handed to Bertie and Ginny.

'Can't we 'ave a cuppa tea, Ma?' Michael asked and she wagged her finger at him.

'No, you cannot, young man. You can wait till teatime now, same as everybody else. I've made that fer Bertie an' Ginny 'cos they've been out in the cold.' She shivered as she looked towards the window where the snow was steadily falling.

Michael shrugged and turned his attention back to the book he'd been reading.

'Our Michael is a bit of a bookworm,' Bertie confided. 'He's off to the free readin' rooms every chance he gets. I reckon he's goin' to be a scholar.'

'That's as maybe but I doubt he'll do any better than you,' Mrs Watkins said. She was clearly very proud of the fact that her son was a policeman, albeit a fairly newly recruited one. She went on to ask Ginny how she liked working at Parsons pie shop and Ginny answered cautiously. She could hardly tell Mrs Watkins what a lecherous man Bill was in front of the children, so she merely answered politely saying that she was fine there until something better came along.

'Hmm, well, from where I'm sittin' you're wasted there,' the woman said forthrightly. 'Bertie tells me you're like our Michael, bookish an' so on, so I would 'ave thought an intelligent well-turned-out young lady like you could get a post as a governess or some such at least.'

'I do love reading,' Ginny said wistfully. 'My mother was very keen that we should all have the best education we could get.'

They chatted of this and that, and the minutes flew by; before they knew it it was time for tea.

Mrs Watkins placed a large plate of bread and butter in the centre of the table and the children helped themselves as if they hadn't seen food for at least a month. There was home-made bramble jam for the children and creamy local cheese for the adults, as well as ham and a variety of pickles, followed by a large sponge cake, still warm from the oven, that seemed to vanish in seconds. Although the fare was simple it was plentiful, tasty and filling.

'I swear this lot 'ave got hollow legs,' Mrs Watkins groaned and her husband laughed.

'Would you just listen to her, eh? She flies into a panic if they go off their food then grumbles when they eat everything she puts in front of them.'

Ginny saw the closeness between the couple, and once again she was reminded of her own parents. The afternoon passed by all too quickly and at six o'clock Bertie suggested that he should walk her home before the snow got any deeper.

Mrs Watkins hurried away to fetch Ginny's shawl, which she had dried by the fire, and as the girl was wrapping it around herself she clucked her tongue.

'You should have a warm coat on in this weather, pet,' she scolded. 'That shawl won't do you much good.'

'I intend to get one soon from the rag stall,'

Ginny told her.

Mrs Watkins nodded approvingly. 'Good, but now before you go, what are you intending to do on Christmas Day?' Bertie had explained about Ginny's circumstances and the kind-hearted woman didn't like to think of the girl spending the day on her own.

'I hadn't really thought about it,' Ginny said. She doubted very much whether Edith and Bill would invite her to share it with them, and if truth be told, she wouldn't want to anyway.

'Well if you've a mind to you're very welcome to come and have Christmas dinner with us. We're a bit squashed in here as yer can see an' we ain't grand but we can allus make room fer another little 'un.'

'Thank you.' Ginny was deeply touched. 'Can I let you know?'

'O' course yer can, pet.'

Ginny said her goodbyes and Mrs Watkins saw them to the door, and before she knew it she was feeling her way back down the dark entry behind Bertie. They said little on the journey back to the shop. They were too intent on keeping their heads down and lifting their feet out of the piling snow but at last they arrived.

'So will yer think on what me mam offered ... about comin' fer Christmas dinner, I mean?' Bertie asked eagerly.

A little wriggle of fear squirmed in Ginny's stomach. She liked Bertie and already considered him a friend, but she didn't have any romantic notions of him and hoped that he wasn't thinking along those lines. Her sole concern at present was

133

to find Charlie; she didn't have time for anything else. All the same she had no wish to hurt his feelings so she said softly, 'Yes, I will think about it – and thank you. It's been a lovely afternoon. But get yourself off home now, Bertie. You'll turn into a block of ice if you stand about here for long.'

He chuckled, then hesitated as if there was something else he wanted to say – but then, seeming to think better of it, he turned and disappeared into the snow.

Thankfully, a thaw set in over the next few days and the snow gradually disappeared although it was still bitterly cold. In fact, the newspapers reported that it was the coldest Christmas on record for fifty years.

After giving the matter much thought Ginny decided that she would take up Mrs Watkins' generous offer of spending Christmas Day at North Street. Anything was better than a lonely day in the basement beneath the shop, so when Bertie called for her on Christmas morning she was dressed in her best and ready to go.

'Eeh, yer look grand, lass,' Bertie told her as she slipped out of the shop door and closed it behind her. When he bent his arm she slipped hers into it and off they set, their heads bent against the cruel wind. They arrived at Bertie's to be greeted by the delicious smell of a roasting goose and shrieks from the youngsters who were in a high state of excitement after opening their presents. The drop-leaf table had been opened to its fullest extent and Mrs Watkins had laid it with her best white linen cloth and her special china kept only for high days and holidays. In the centre of it stood a bowl of holly with bright green leaves, heavy with red berries, and in her mind's eye Ginny saw again the table her mother always went to great trouble over at Christmas.

'It looks lovely, Mrs Watkins. Thank you so much for having me. I feel quite awful about intruding on your privacy on such a special day,' Ginny said quietly, but the generous-hearted woman flapped her hand at her, sensing the girl's pain. She could only imagine how hard this first Christmas without her family around her must be.

'It's a pleasure, lass,' she promised, and she meant it. 'Now go an' sit by the fire an' I'll make you a nice cup o' tea. The dinner will be ready in a jiffy. I'm just waitin' fer the sprouts to finish cookin' now.'

'Oh no, I'd much rather help.' Ginny slipped her shawl off. 'I always used to help me mam get the Christmas dinner.'

'Then in that case yer can drain these spuds and give 'em a good old bashin'.' Mrs Watkins handed her a potato masher and pointed towards a bubbling saucepan on the range and Ginny happily obliged. From that moment on her sadness eased somewhat as she was kept busy helping Mrs Watkins, and in no time at all they were sitting down to a delicious meal.

Mr Watkins sat at the head of the table and carved the goose whilst everyone loaded their plates with steaming vegetables, and crispy roast and mashed potatoes. This was followed by a Christmas pudding that Mrs Watkins had had soaking in brandy for months, swimming in thick creamy custard. It was Ginny who found the shiny threepenny bit in her helping and David instantly told her, 'Close yer eyes an' make a wish – but don't tell anyone what it is, else it won't come true.'

Ginny obediently closed her eyes and Bertie had no need to ask what she had wished for. It would be to find Charlie and have her father home. Poor lass.

Ginny became solemn as she thought back to Christmases past but she soon forced a smile on her face and overall it was a very happy occasion and she was glad that she had come.

'Oh, I don't think I could eat another mouthful,' she groaned when dinner was done, and they all laughed.

'It were a right good meal,' Mr Watkins praised his wife and she blushed prettily at the compliment.

'What are you after, yer old charmer,' she teased and the children giggled before shooting off to resume their games of Snakes and Ladders and Ludo.

Ginny insisted on helping with the clearing of the table and the considerable amount of washing up, and the afternoon was rapidly darkening by the time she and her hostess had finished at long last.

'It'll be time to think o' gettin' the tea soon,' Mrs Watkins sighed wearily as she and Ginny finally sank down at the side of the fire.

'I shall be seein' to that,' Mr Watkins insisted. 'You pair have done your bit. Me an' our Bertie are more than capable o' gettin' the tea.'

The next hour was full of fun and frolics as everyone joined in the parlour games with the youngest members of the family, then Bertie and Mr Watkins piled the table again with all manner of home-made sweet and savoury treats. David immediately loaded up his plate.

'I swear these kids o' mine would eat till they burst,' Mrs Watkins commented with a shake of her head as she looked on fondly at her brood, and again pain stabbed at Ginny like a knife. They were such a happy, loving family – just as hers had been.

And then, noting the darkness outside she told them regretfully, 'It's been a wonderful day but I really should be going now. Mr Parsons is opening the shop the day after Boxing Day so I need to get the kitchen prepared. Thank you so much for having me.' She had to shout to make herself heard above the children, who were loudly singing 'Good King Wenceslas'.

'It's been our absolute pleasure, pet. You're welcome 'ere any time.' Mrs Watkins gave her an affectionate hug and Ginny felt a little glow of pleasure. Without these dear people her day would have been very miserable indeed.

Bertie walked her back to the shop and she pecked him hastily on the cheek. 'You're so lucky to have such a lovely family,' she told him.

'I know I am. There are times when I could knock the little 'uns' blocks off, but I wouldn't be wi'out 'em. But now you get in out o' the wind. I wouldn't be surprised if we didn't have some more snow tonight. Happy Christmas, Ginny.'

He strode away with his hands in his pockets, whistling merrily, and as Ginny let herself back in and hastened down to the basement kitchen, loneliness closed about her like a shroud.

The next day she missed her family more than ever, and worried about her father and Charlie every minute of the day. She was glad when the shop reopened and she could finally get back to some sort of normality. A new year was just around the corner, and she prayed that it would bring news of her brother.

Chapter Thirteen

On New Year's Eve, Ginny stayed up late to listen to the chimes of the clock in the marketplace ring in the New Year. She'd been reading about the Queen and Prince Albert's Christmas, surrounded by their nine children and the host of servants who waited on them, in one of Bill's old newspapers, and she couldn't help but compare it to her own. Reading the newspapers and the one book that she had brought with her – *The Mill on the Floss*, which had belonged to her mother – was the only pleasure she had left now. The hours she worked ensured that she no longer had time to get to the free reading rooms, and so she would read and reread the newspapers and George Eliot's novel from cover to cover.

Giving her newspapers when they had finished with them was one of the very few kindnesses that

Bill and his wife showed to her. Thankfully, Ginny had seen precious little of either of them over the Christmas period – mainly, she suspected, because they'd spent it in a gin-sodden haze. Bill continued to make crude remarks and try to touch her whenever the opportunity arose, but Ginny felt she could handle that and every night just to be on the safe side she dragged the chest of drawers across her bedroom door.

Now, hearing the sound of revellers in the marketplace wishing each other a Happy New Year, the loneliness she felt was hard to bear as she thought back to happier times spent in Whittleford with her family. With a sigh she carried the oil lamp into her bedroom and after pulling the chest of drawers into place she cried herself to sleep.

A knocking on the shop door awoke her the following morning and she leaped out of bed wondering who it could be. On entering the kitchen she glanced blearily at the clock and was shocked to see that it was gone nine o'clock! She rushed upstairs, still in her nightgown with her shawl wrapped around her, and opening the door a couple of inches, was astonished to see Bertie standing there.

As he looked at her with her hair hanging down her back like a black silken waterfall, he was momentarily struck dumb. Bertie Watkins was in love.

'Why, whatever brings you here at this time in the morning?'

'Mam insists that you come to our place for dinner again. It's a crime to spend New Year's Day on yer own,' he told her pulling himself together with an effort. And when Ginny frowned uncertainly, still half asleep, he went on in a pleading tone, '*Please* say you'll come.'

Ginny pursed her lips, then with a bright smile she nodded. What harm could it do? She was tired of her own company and would be glad when the shop reopened the next day. 'In that case, thank you – I'd love to. What time do you want me there?'

'Dinner will be ready at two o'clock but I could come back and fetch you if you'd like?'

'No, you stay in the warm. I know where it is and I'll be there,' Ginny assured him, shuddering as she looked at the frost sparkling on the pavements.

'Till two o'clock then.' Bertie grinned from ear to ear before setting off with a spring in his step.

Ginny hastily closed the door to shut out the cold and as she skipped back down the stairs she found that she was looking forward to the outing. It would certainly beat spending another day with only herself for company.

I'll have a thorough wash and shampoo my hair, she decided rushing across the kitchen to fill the large kettle. And then I'll press my best blouse and skirt and polish my new boots. She had pleaded with Bill the week before to allow her to visit the rag stall as her old boots were crippling her. Luckily, she had dropped on a very nice pair that fit like a glove and had had very little wear. Admittedly, they had cost some of her precious wages but Ginny felt they were worth it. Humming merrily to herself, she set the iron to heat against the fire while she waited for the kettle to boil.

With the first kettle of water she washed her hair and wrapped a towel around it then she crept to the bottom of the stairs and listened intently. There was not a sound. Hopefully, Bill and Edith would be snoring still, sleeping off the effects of the gin they had drunk the night before. Satisfied that she would not be disturbed, she stripped off all her clothes and began to wash every inch of herself, enjoying the feel of the warm water on her naked skin. She was towelling herself dry and looking forward to the day ahead when a noise behind her made her wheel about to find Bill standing at the bottom of the stairs, a lascivious smile on his face.

'Well, well ... expectin' me, were yer? I wondered 'ow long it would be afore yer saw sense.' Licking his thick lips in anticipation he began to walk slowly towards her, dropping the pile of newspapers he was carrying on to the table on his way.

With a screech, Ginny wrapped the towel she was holding around herself to try and cover her nudity as she began to inch towards her bedroom door.

'Now don't go bein' coy.' Bill held his arms out to her and she shuddered. 'Yer know yer want it. That boyfriend o' yours is nowt but a lad. Let me show yer 'ow a *real* man can make yer feel. You'll not be wantin' 'im again when you've had a taste o' what I'm gonna give yer.'

To Ginny's horror she saw his hand drop to his flies and she stared in horrified fascination as he fumbled with the buttons and withdrew his manhood.

'G … get away from me or I'll scream,' she warned in a shaky voice. This was her worst nightmare come true.

His member was standing to attention and he was rubbing it suggestively, leaving her in no doubt whatsoever of what he intended to do with it. He was standing between her and her bedroom now and she felt like an animal caught in a trap.

'*Please,* just go away and we can pretend this never happened.'

He shook his head. His eyes had a glazed look to them now and Ginny had never been more terrified in her whole life. Then suddenly he lunged at her, covering the distance between them in seconds, and he had his arm about her waist as he ripped the towel away.

'Fine little pair o' tits,' he drooled as his hand closed about one and he began to pinch and rub her pert nipple, making her cry out with pain. He was trying to drag her towards her bedroom and she could see the sweat standing out on his brow and smell the stale odour of him. They were almost at the door now and she knew that once they were inside and he had thrown her on to the bed, she would be no match for him.

She threw her arm out, desperately trying to find something on the table that she could use as a weapon, and suddenly her fingers came into contact with a knife she had left there earlier after peeling some potatoes ready for the next day. She was struggling for all she was worth but somehow she managed to snatch it up just as he pushed her roughly through the bedroom door. He briefly released her then, knowing that she had nowhere to escape to, but she faced him holding the knife threateningly in front of her, painfully aware of her vulnerability.

'Touch me one more time and I'll use it ... *I swear it!*'

He paused momentarily then laughed and began to advance on her again. She had retreated and now her back was pressed against the wall. There was nowhere else to go and the knife was all that stood between her and being raped.

'You wouldn't have the guts to use it,' he scoffed.

'Oh yes, I would. Just try me!'

He looked uncertain now and held his arm out and quick as a flash Ginny slashed the knife through the air, catching his vein. Blood instantly spurted into the room and he howled like an injured animal as she continued to thrust the knife towards him.

'Why, yer fuckin' little whore,' he gasped as he stared at his arm in horror. 'Look what yer've done now!'

'I'll stick it in you good and proper if you come one step closer,' Ginny warned and he sensed that in her desperation she meant it. The blood was pumping faster now from a two-inch gash and the colour drained from his face as he suddenly turned and scuttled away, leaving a trail of crimson-red drops in his wake. For a few moments Ginny stood there shaking like a leaf in the wind. Thanks to finding the knife she'd had a lucky escape – but how long would it be before he tried it again? If he got the chance, that was. If Edith were to even have an inkling of what had happened, Ginny knew that the woman's loyalty would lie with her husband and she herself would be out on her ear.

I have to get out of here ... now! she thought. In a panic she began to drag her clothes on. Her hair was lying against her back in a long wet mass but she had no time to worry about that for now. She had to get away as soon as she possibly could. Dragging her bag from beneath the bed, she bundled her belongings into it, then snatching up her shawl and bonnet she hurried into the kitchen and feverishly pushed her feet into her boots. From the rooms above she could vaguely hear the sound of shouting and knew it was only a matter of time before Edith stormed down to question her about what had gone on. If she were to take the stairs, she might even bump into her!

Turning abruptly, Ginny clasped her bag and headed out into the little yard beyond the kitchen. There was a gate in the fence and after heaving it open she escaped into a narrow alley and started to run. She had no idea where she was going to go, she only knew that she had to get away. Had she been thinking clearly, the girl would have gone straight to the sanctuary of Mrs Bevins' cottage. But she wasn't. Blind panic ruled her tormented mind. She ran until her lungs felt as if they were bursting, and a stitch in her side made her slow her steps. Glancing about, she was shocked to see that she had run almost the whole length of Queen's Road and was almost at the Cock and Bear Bridge. A path ran down the side of the bridge and once she reached it, she slithered down it and huddled beneath the bridge that crossed the canal while she got her breath back. Only then did she allow herself to cry as she recalled the feel of his disgusting hands on her body. But even so, she knew that it could have been much, much worse. If she hadn't managed to grasp the knife, he would have ... she thrust the image away as she almost choked on her sobs.

And now she was faced with the dilemma: where was she to go? Bertie's family would be expecting her for dinner. Should she seek refuge there? She decided against it. There were bound to be questions asked about why she was so suddenly homeless and she just wanted to put the whole awful incident behind her. As she sat there, shivering with shock and with cold, hugging her legs, her chin on her knees, the tears flowed faster. It felt as if her whole life had started to fall apart on the day the first of her family had passed away, and she had been powerless to stop it. And then it came to her ... Father Mick! He might be able to help her.

Ginny crouched beneath the bridge for another half an hour in case anyone might be following her and then she ventured out into Croft Road and looked either way. She saw nothing untoward. A few people were out and about, but no one gave her a second glance so gripping her bag she began to head for St Paul's Church; because it was New Year's Day, Father Mick might be at the vicarage. On the journey there, Ginny's mind was in turmoil. If she had severely injured Bill, would Edith report her to the police? And what would Bertie and his family think of her when she didn't turn up for dinner? There were so many questions buzzing around in her head and she had no answer to any of them. She was still traumatised by the thought of what might have happened to her if she hadn't been able to grab the knife and ward Bill off. Tears flowed again at the horror of it, and by the time she rapped on the door of the vicarage, her eyes were red and swollen.

She heard footsteps approaching along the corridor and the next second the door opened and Mrs Braintree peered out at her. Recognising Ginny and then noting the state the girl was in, she sucked in her breath.

'Good Lord in heaven, whatever has happened to you, lass!' she exclaimed, then taking Ginny firmly by the elbow she hauled her over the step and led her towards the sitting room at the back of the house.

'I ... I would like to see Father Mick,' Ginny faltered, holding back the sobs that were threatening to erupt again.

'And so you shall,' Mrs Braintree soothed. 'But not yet a while. One of his parishioners is dying and he's gone to pray for him. Never mind though. You're safe here with me. Now tell me what's wrong.'

Ginny shook her head as fresh tears coursed down her cheeks. 'I ... I can't,' she gasped.

Mrs Braintree frowned. 'Well, something's clearly amiss, but you just sit there then while I go and make you a nice hot cup o' tea. You look perished.'

She gently pressed Ginny into one of the fireside chairs then bustled away, leaving the girl to try and pull herself together.

When the housekeeper returned with a loaded

tray, Ginny seemed a little calmer and after pouring the tea into a pretty china cup and saucer, Mrs Braintree handed it to her.

Ginny drank the scalding liquid in nearly one gulp then gave the woman a tremulous smile. 'I'm sorry to barge in on you like this. I think I'll go away and come back later. Father Mick might be home by then.'

'You'll do no such thing!' Mrs Braintree puffed her chest out indignantly. 'Father Mick wouldn't thank me for letting you go anywhere in this state. No, you just sit there till he comes back and get warmed through. He shouldn't be too much longer now.'

Ginny accepted a second cup of tea although she refused a slice of cake. She was so upset that she was sure if she tried to eat anything it would lodge in her throat and choke her. An awkward silence settled between them until Mrs Braintree eventually asked, 'Would you be all right on your own for a few minutes, pet? I have to go into the kitchen and prepare the vegetables for Father Mick's evening meal.'

'I shall be fine, thank you,' Ginny assured her and settled further back in the chair as the kindly woman lifted the tray and headed for the kitchen.

There was nothing but the sound of the grandfather clock ticking away and the logs on the fire spitting to be heard and as Ginny slowly unwound, she suddenly asked herself why she was there. What could Father Mick do, after all? This was her problem, not his. Quiet as a mouse, she picked up her bag and crept from the room. She could hear Mrs Braintree pottering about in the

147

kitchen as she slowly tiptoed towards the front door. Then she was through it, closing it quietly behind her – and then she began to run. For a moment she considered going back to Mrs Bevins but her pride stopped her. It wouldn't be fair to take her troubles to the old woman's door, even though she was fairly sure that Florrie would have given her shelter. She had no idea now where she was running to, but knew if she ran to the ends of the earth she would never be able to forget what had almost happened to her today. What a terrible start to the New Year of 1861 it had proved to be.

Chapter Fourteen

She had been wandering about aimlessly for over an hour with still no idea whatsoever of where she was going when she found herself in Whittleford, very close to her old home. Not wishing to be spotted by the farmer or his wife she set off across the fields until she found herself in a little wooded valley named 'Hollow Sticks' by the locals. It was a relatively unspoiled area of woodland with farms and cottages dotted here and there, and with a little start Ginny realised that she was very close to Lamp Hill Hall.

What was it her father had said to her? *'Go there and ask for Mrs Bronson, the housekeeper.'*

Up until that moment, Ginny hadn't even considered taking his advice, since she had been so sure that she could fend for herself – but now she was painfully aware that she didn't have any other options. The light was already fading from the afternoon and as yet she had nowhere to sleep that night and only a few shillings tucked into the pouch in her belt. It just might be that there would be a position there for her; at any rate it was worth a try.

Like most people in the town, Ginny knew that Lamp Hill Hall was owned by the Walton-Hughes family. James Walton-Hughes had commissioned Thomas Larkins Walker, the well-known architect, to design and have it built for him back in the 1830s in the style of an Elizabethan mansion, after demolishing the original building that had stood there. James and his family had lived there ever since. The Walton-Hughes family were said to be the wealthiest in Nuneaton. James had started off as a corn and cheese merchant but now he had a finger in almost every pie in the town. He owned shares in the local Haunchwood brickworks, in the Haunchwood pit, in the Windmill Hill Quarry – and he was also very astute at property speculation and owned many houses and farms about the town. It was rumoured that an army of staff kept the house running but only the tradesmen who delivered there ever got to have a glimpse of it as it was situated in sprawling grounds at the end of a very long drive.

At the entrance to the drive were two enormous, ornate wrought-iron gates and Ginny was relieved to see as she approached them that they were open. She slipped through them, noting that a small gatehouse surrounded by trees stood to one side of them. Through a window she could see a man whom she supposed was the gateman sitting drinking tea at a table in a kitchen with a woman, and she hurried silently on by. She found herself on a drive that twisted and turned. Yew, willow and oak trees grew in wild profusion on either side of it and today they acted as a tunnel; the bitterly cold wind sliced into her until her teeth were chattering. Through the trees she could see immaculately kept lawns and flowerbeds – although there were no flowers in them now, of course – and she imagined how beautiful it must be there in the spring and summer. She seemed to walk for miles until at last she rounded yet another bend and the Hall came into view. It was so immense that it almost took Ginny's breath away.

Lights shone from some of the windows and she gazed in awe at the immense chimney-stacks and the enormous porch which was held up with two magnificent marble pillars. The outer walls were a profusion of climbing ivy and Virginia creeper, and Ginny felt as if she could have stood there admiring it for hours. She was doing just that when a young man leading a spirited horse appeared around a corner of the house.

'Sorry, but this is private land,' he told her as he came to a halt at the side of her.

'Oh ... oh yes, I know. I was admiring the house but I'm here to see Mrs Bronson.'

'On New Year's Day?' The young man scratched his head then shrugged before saying, 'Follow that path there. It'll take you round to the servants' quarters.'

Ginny flashed him a smile that, unbeknownst to her, made the young man's heart skip a beat, before heading in the direction he had pointed. She came to a large yard at the back of the house where there were a number of outbuildings but she recognised the kitchen entrance immediately by the sounds and the delicious smells coming from one particular door.

She tapped on it tentatively and it was opened by a girl with deep brown hair who looked to be about her own age. Inside, Ginny could see people flying about ladling food on to big silver salvers, and into porcelain dishes, and her stomach rumbled in protest; she'd eaten nothing since morning.

'I'm here to see Mrs Bronson,' she told the girl, mustering every ounce of courage she had.

The girl raised her eyebrows but then told her, 'Wait 'ere a minute.'

The door was shut firmly in Ginny's face and just as she was beginning to think that she was being ignored and had raised her hand to knock again, it was opened once more, this time by a plump, harassed-looking woman in a mob-cap and a huge white bibbed apron, holding a large wooden spoon in her hand.

'Well?' she questioned, staring at Ginny.

'I'm here to see Mrs Bronson,' Ginny repeated, holding her head high.

'At this time on a New Year's Day? We're in the middle o' preparin' the meal fer the family an' their guests. Do you 'ave an appointment? She ain't said nothin' to me about anyone callin'. What do you want wi' her?'

'That's my business – and no, I don't have an appointment,' Ginny answered sharply.

'Then in that case go away an' come back when we ain't so busy!' The woman began to close the door again but Ginny was desperate now and she flung her arm out to stop her.

'Please – I know she'll see me!' She didn't know any such thing and was well aware that Mrs Bronson might in fact send her away with a flea in her ear, but she wasn't prepared to give up so soon now that she was finally there. 'Tell her that Virginia Thursday is here to see her and that it's important,' she rushed on.

The woman paused and eyed her thoughtfully up and down then somewhat reluctantly she held the door wide.

'You'd best come in. But I can't spare anyone to go lookin' for her till I've got this meal served. You'd best sit over there an' wait a while an' be patient.'

Ginny followed the woman's pointing finger to a long wooden settle that was placed to one side of an inglenook fireplace and she walked unsteadily towards it through the most enormous kitchen she had ever seen in her entire life. The whole of our cottage in Whittleford could have fitted into this one room, she thought wonderingly as she took a seat, painfully aware that a number of eyes were staring at her with curiosity. Maids in starched white caps and frilly white aprons were snatching up the dishes that had been filled and were carrying them away through a green baize door at the far side of the room as Ginny sat patiently waiting. The woman who had admitted her was now standing over a huge range stirring something in a pan as she shouted orders at the rest of the women; Ginny realised that she must be the cook. A massive oak dresser stood against one wall covered in pretty china cups, saucers, plates and dishes. Every piece was gilt-edged, covered in tiny pink rosebuds, and Ginny guessed it must be worth a fortune. Unlike the kitchen she had become used to working in beneath the pie shop, this one was spotless and everything her eyes settled on gleamed, from the copper pans suspended above the inglenook to the flagstones on the floor.

The young red-haired girl who had first opened the door to her was standing at a huge stone sink scrubbing pans; glancing over her shoulder, she gave Ginny a shy smile. The table that took pride of place in the centre of the room was surrounded by rows of matching ladder-back chairs. The staff scurried about like little ants, each person seeming to know exactly what they were doing, and eventually the last dish was snatched from the table and borne away, and the ruddy-faced cook sighed and stretched her back. Then, as if she'd suddenly remembered that Ginny was there, she looked again at the lass at the sink and told her, 'Nancy, dry your hands an' go an' find Mrs Bronson, would yer? She'll probably be in 'er room, if she ain't up with the mistress. Tell 'er she 'as a visitor.'

The girl instantly did as she was told and then the cook seemed to forget Ginny's existence again as she sank into a chair at the table and reached for a teapot.

The minutes ticked away but eventually Nancy returned to say, 'She's comin', Cook. But she weren't none too pleased. She said as she weren't expectin' anybody.'

Shortly afterwards the green baize door opened and a smart-looking woman appeared. She appeared to be in her middle to late fifties and was wearing a very full-skirted dress that swished as she walked. It was navy blue with a white lace collar and cuffs, and tiny pearl buttons ran all the way up the front of the bodice. Her hair was very fair and pulled into a neat chignon on the back of her head, and her eyes were a deep blue. Ginny guessed that she must have been quite a beauty in her younger days. She was still a very attractive woman now.

'So, Cook, who is this visitor that insists I must see them?' the woman asked, looking put out at having her peace disturbed.

The cook took a slurp of her tea and thumbed towards Ginny, who had risen to her feet.

'It's the lass over there. She said you'd see 'er. Her name's Virginia Thursday.'

For an instant Ginny could have sworn she saw the woman start, but then composing herself, Mrs Bronson approached Ginny to say, 'You'd better come along to my office.'

The cook looked mildly surprised. She'd expected the housekeeper to give Ginny her marching orders but then she shrugged and turned her attention back to her mug of tea.

Ginny followed Mrs Bronson through the green baize door into a corridor that had her eyes almost popping out from her head. Highly polished parquet tiles were covered by rugs dotted here and there which had colourful flowers woven into them, with deep fringes at either end. Ginny was sure she had never seen anything quite so grand. A heavy crimson flock paper covered the walls and huge gilt-framed pictures awed the girl. Ginny was so taken with looking at her surroundings that when the woman stopped in front of a door, Ginny almost ran into the back of her.

Stepping to one side Mrs Bronson ushered the girl ahead of her into a room with a large polished desk at the centre. An oil lamp stood on one end of it, casting a warm glow about the walls, and Ginny noted that the curtains were now tightly drawn against the late afternoon.

'So ... Miss Thursday, how may I help you?'

Gulping, Ginny dropped her bag to the floor before saying falteringly, 'My ... my father said to come to you... He said you might be able to help me. I need a job, you see. I was working at the pie shop but then today Mr Parsons tried to ... to...' Tears threatened to choke her then but she rushed on, 'Dad's been sent to prison and the farmer's wife he worked for got Charlie my little brother put into the workhouse. And now they're saying that he's not there any more and I don't know how to find him or what to do.' Suddenly she could hold the tears back no longer and they spurted from her eyes, temporarily blinding her.

The woman stood patiently, her hands clasped neatly at her waist until the storm of weeping had passed, and then without a word she handed Ginny a white handkerchief that she took from one of the pockets of her full skirt.

'Th ... thank you.' Ginny noisily blew her nose and mopped her tear-drenched face as she made a huge effort to compose herself.

155

'Right, well, where a job is concerned I may just be able to help you,' the woman informed her. 'As it happens, one of our laundry maids has just left. Have you ever done that sort of work before? I'm afraid it's very back-breaking.'

Ginny shook her head. 'No I haven't, but I'm a fast learner and I really don't mind what I do.'

'If I gave you the job – and I do say *if* – you need to know that you would be responsible for what we call the rough laundry. In other words, you would be washing the staff uniforms. We have another laundry maid who takes care of the family's laundry. You would work from six o'clock each morning until seven o'clock each night. On Sunday mornings you will be allowed time off to attend church should you so wish.'

Ginny felt a little guilty. Her visits to church had been few and far between since losing her parents, for sometimes she had questioned a God who could allow such terrible things to happen but she wisely didn't comment and the woman went on, 'You would get every other Sunday off. Your pay would be three shillings a week paid quarterly, and your board. You would share a room with one of the other staff up in the staff quarters. As for your brother's whereabouts, I may be able to help you there too. I sit on the Board of Governors at the workhouse so I can make some enquiries for you.'

Ginny was hardly able to believe her luck. At least she would have somewhere to stay – and nothing could be harder than working in the pie shop, surely? And the thought that this woman might be able to track Charlie down was an added bonus.

'I'll take it, and thank you,' she said gratefully in case Mrs Bronson should change her mind.

'Very well, you may start in the morning. I shall see that you are issued with your uniform then. Follow me and I'll get one of the staff to show you to where you will be sleeping.' And so it was decided.

Chapter Fifteen

'Cook, Miss Thursday will be joining the staff,' Mrs Bronson informed the woman when they arrived back in the kitchen a short time later. 'Would you get someone to show her to her room? She will be taking Katie's place in the laundry.'

The cook looked slightly surprised but simply said, 'Right y'are, Mrs Bronson, leave 'er wi' me.'

Mrs Bronson nodded and turning, she swept from the room without giving Ginny so much as a second glance.

'Well, I don't know how yer managed that, lass,' Cook said bemused when the woman had left. 'No interviews, nothin'! She must have took a fancy to yer – but are yer sure yer up to it? You ain't as far through as a broomstick an' the rough laundry maid is the lowest of the servants here.'

'I shall be fine,' Ginny assured her proudly. 'I'm not afraid of hard work.'

'Hmph! Well, we'll see if yer still singin' from the same hymn-sheet come the end o' your first week.' Then, addressing another young woman she told her, 'Nancy, take Virginia up to her room, would yer? She'll be sharin' wi you.'

As the girl turned towards her Ginny said quietly, 'Everyone calls me Ginny.'

'Then Ginny it will be,' Nancy declared with a kindly smile and she began to lead her to yet another door off from the kitchen. There were so many, Ginny wondered if she would ever find her way about the place.

This door opened on to a steep narrow staircase that led up to the servants' quarters in the attics, and their footsteps echoed hollowly off the rough wooden treads. There were no fripperies here, Ginny noticed, and the higher they climbed the colder it seemed to get.

'Yer need yer thick underwear on up 'ere in the winter,' Nancy told her. 'Then in the summer it's swelterin'.'

Ginny was pleased that Nancy seemed friendly at least, especially as they were going to be sharing a room. She was a tall, slim girl, at least half a head taller than Ginny, and she had lovely deep brown hair that she wore in a bun in the nape of her neck.

'I'm surprised they've taken anyone on so quickly to fill Katie's place,' she said conversationally as they continued to climb. 'I didn't think Mrs Bronson would start looking for a replacement until after the holidays. Katie left to get married, you see. She wed one of the junior grooms and they've moved away so Mrs Bronson will be advertising for someone to take his place too.'

'Well, I just heard about the vacancy by chance,'

Ginny told her cautiously. She didn't know the other girl well enough to go into details about her personal life or what had happened with Bill Parsons yet. They came to a long corridor with doors on either side of it, and halting at the third one along on the left, Nancy threw it open and turned to Ginny.

'This is the room you'll be sharing with me,' she said. 'Excuse the mess, won't you? I overlay a little this morning and didn't have time to tidy up. It's a good job it isn't the day for Mrs Bronson's room check. She comes up once a week to make sure everywhere is spick an' span and if it isn't you lose your Sunday off.' Rushing forward into the room she began to gather up the clothes that were scattered on the bed, pointing to another on the opposite wall.

'That will be yours and that chest of drawers there. We'll have to share the jug and bowl.'

Ginny shuddered as the cold crept into her bones. It had been warm down in the basement beneath the pie shop with all the ovens going, but she supposed she shouldn't grumble. At least here she was safe from Bill's groping hands – and if she had to share a room, Nancy seemed nice.

With the clothes all collected, Nancy bundled them unceremoniously into a drawer before saying, 'I'd better get back down then and leave you to settle in. I'll come up and fetch you for supper, shall I? We eat last. The family first, then the housemaids and finally the laundresses and the general maids. Mrs Bronson has a tray in her room. I'll fill you in on who everyone is later but I must go now else Cook will have me guts fer

159

garters. Oh, and by the way, there's a chamber pot under the bed should yer be took short.'

When Ginny wrinkled her nose, Nancy giggled. 'Don't worry, you'll probably not have to use it very often. The servants' privy or the "water closet" as they call it 'ere, is out in the yard next to the laundry. If yer get into the habit o' using it afore yer come to bed you won't need the pot. If you should though, Mrs Bronson insists we empty 'em first thing afore we start work. You just follow the cinder path behind the stable block an' empty it into the cesspit. Now I really *am* goin' this time. Will you be all right?'

'I shall be fine.' Ginny smiled at her, suddenly realising what a long day it had been. She would have liked nothing more than to curl up in the bed but knew that she ought to get her things put away first and tidy herself up. She had escaped from Bill's advances with her hair dripping down her back and now it was in need of a good brush and plaiting. She could only imagine what a sight she must look.

Nancy left then with a last cheery grin and Ginny began to unpack her bag, not that she had much to put away. There would be room to spare in the chest of drawers but then she wouldn't need many clothes anyway if she was to be issued with a uniform. In no time at all she had done, and crossing to the window she peered out. She found that this room looked down on the stable block and she saw some fine-looking horses being led around the yard. Everything felt so strange but she supposed she should be grateful that she'd found somewhere safe to stay. Dropping on to the bed she hugged her shawl about her and sat shivering as she waited for Nancy to come back and fetch her.

Ginny was dozing the next time Nancy appeared and found herself in pitch darkness.

'Sorry,' the girl apologised. 'I never thought to leave a candle up here fer you.'

'It's all right, I've been napping.'

Ginny followed her back down the stairs to find a number of people already seated at the big table in the kitchen. A leg of pork and a bowl of potatoes was placed in the middle of the table and Ginny thought what a pleasant change it would be from pies. They had been her staple diet whilst she'd worked at the pie shop.

'Sit yourself down then,' Cook ordered as she began to carve the meat.

Ginny obeyed, glancing around at the people seated at the table.

'How d'you do,' one young man said with a friendly smile as he held his hand out. 'I'm Johnny Grady, one of the junior grooms. I live here with my family and usually eat with them, but seeing as Cook's done one of my favourites and I wanted to meet you...'

Ginny solemnly shook his hand. He seemed friendly enough. She had already met Nancy – and the cook, of course.

There was another young lady present and she too seemed pleasant. 'I'm Phyllis, you'll be working with me in the laundry. I do the washing for the family.'

'There's some others you'll get to meet,' the

cook informed her then. 'There's the rest o' the Grady family, they live over the stable block. Jim is the head groom and coachman. Then there's his wife, Molly, and their sons Will and Johnny 'ere – they're the junior grooms. Molly works in the dairy here supplyin' us wi' all our butter an' cheese, and although Will is the youngest junior groom he also helps out Ted Ventriss, the gardener, when they ain't too busy. Ted lives in a little cottage in the grounds and he tends to keep himself very much to himself, especially since he lost his wife, God bless 'er soul. Lovely woman Thelma was, but that's life, ain't it?'

'Yes, then there's Barbara and Millie, they're the house-maids, the ones you saw wi' the fancy aprons and mob caps.' Nancy sighed longingly. 'They get all the nice jobs to do like waitin' on table an' answerin' the door to visitors an' so on, while I get all the mucky jobs like cleanin' out the grates an' relightin' the fires each mornin'.'

'Yer should just think yerself lucky you've got a job,' Cook scolded, waggling a wooden spoon at her. 'There used to be a boot boy, a valet an' a butler 'ere an' all, but the master got rid of 'em. He said there weren't no need fer so many staff since the mistress rarely leaves her room any more. He never wanted a valet in the first place an' said he were more than capable o' dressin' 'imself.'

Ginny would have liked to ask more about the family but was too polite to do so. No doubt Nancy would tell her all about them when they were alone in their room later that night.

They all tucked into their meals then and Ginny had to admit that the food was delicious. The main meal was followed by an apple pie and a jug of thick creamy custard, and by the time she'd finished Ginny was so full she could barely move.

Nancy immediately began to clear the table and Ginny insisted on helping.

'I do all the washin' up. That's my job,' Nancy informed her proudly as she loaded the pots on to the draining board.

Millie and Barbara appeared then with yet more trays of dirty pots from the dining room. Millie gave Ginny a warm smile but Barbara barely glanced at her.

'She can be very stuck-up,' Nancy whispered when the housemaids had disappeared back through the green baize door. 'Thinks she's it, she does! You'd do best to keep out of her way. She's got the hots fer Master Giles, not that he'd ever look the side she's on except fer a bit o' you-know-what.'

'That will be quite enough o' that sort o' talk in my kitchen, young lady!' Cook scolded and Nancy instantly looked contrite and turned her attention to the job at hand.

'Sorry, Cook.'

'And so yer should be.' Despite her harsh words she winked at Ginny and the girl wondered if perhaps the woman's bark was worse than her bite.

'You shouldn't be doin' this – it ain't your job,' Nancy pointed out then and Ginny shrugged as she lifted a cloth and began to dry the pots that the girl had washed.

'It's all right. I haven't got anything else to do, have I?'

The two housemaids were still coming in and

163

out bearing trays full of dirty dishes and cutlery, and Ginny noticed that Nancy took especial care with them. The china was so fine that Ginny could see through it when she held it up to the light and she was almost afraid to touch it. Meantime, Cook had retired to her chair at the side of the fire to read her newspaper with a pair of spectacles perched on the end of her nose, and Nancy was making her a fresh pot of tea. Cook's job was done now until the following morning.

'There's not usually this many pots, but Master Giles an' Master Sebastian 'ave friends stayin' over the holidays,' Nancy confided then. Ginny didn't like to ask who they were and just got on with her drying up.

Once Nancy had served Cook with a steaming cup of tea she then changed her apron and began to collect the coal scuttles from the various rooms and refill them but at last all the jobs were done and she asked, 'Is there anything else yer want doin', Cook? If not I'm off to the water closet an' then I'm up to me bed.' She gave an enormous yawn.

'No, that's all fer tonight. G'night, lass,' Cook said.

Ginny rose to follow her. The thought of using the chamber pot while Nancy was in the room with her was more than she could bear. It was bitterly cold outside and as she followed Nancy across the yard she wished that she'd thought to put her shawl on. It was very quiet out there with nothing to be heard but the sound of the wind sighing in the trees and the whinnying of the horses from the stables. The girls hastily did what they had to do then rushed back to the warmth of the kitchen. After lighting a candle, Nancy led her upstairs to their room. Cook had dozed off and was snoring softly and the two girls were as quiet as they could be so as not to disturb her.

'Phew, that's another day over with,' Nancy said tiredly when they were in their room. The wind was battering at the window as if it was trying to gain entry and Ginny was sure it was almost as cold in there as it was outside. Nancy quickly slid out of her clothes and folded them ready ready for the next day, then slipped a long linen nightgown over her head. Then taking up a brush she released her hair from its pins and began to brush it as Ginny started to undress too.

'So who are Master Sebastian and Master Giles?' she asked as curiosity got the better of her.

Nancy hopped into bed and pulled the covers up to her chin. 'Master Giles is the son o' the house.' She grimaced. 'I'd give 'im a wide berth if I were you. He's a nasty piece of work though he's got the looks of an angel. The mistress 'as spoiled 'im rotten, see? Apparently, 'er an' the master wanted a large family but there were complications at their son's birth an' they were advised not to 'ave any more children. Then when their son, Timothy, was in his early twenties he had a riding accident and broke his neck. His young wife was seven months pregnant with Master Giles an' the shock of losin' her husband sent her into early labour. Master Giles survived against all the odds but his mother died havin' him, poor soul, so the master an' mistress 'ave brought him up as their own. It fair broke the mistress's heart

165

by all accounts, an' healthwise she ain't been the same since. Master Sebastian an' his sister, Miss Diana, are the mistress's nephew an' niece. They were orphaned at an early age an' the master an' mistress took 'em in an' they've brought them up as their own an' all.'

'And what are they like?'

Nancy leaned up on her elbow in bed and grinned. 'Master Sebastian is lovely, always got a smile fer you an' no airs or graces whatsoever, he an' Master Giles go to a school in Rugby. But Miss Diana ... Ugh, she's a right little madam. The mistress always wanted a daughter so Diana can wind 'er around 'er little finger. Miss Diana had a governess until recently. Or should I say a number o' governesses. None of 'em stayed fer long 'cos o' Miss Diana's tantrums. The master were on about sendin' 'er away to a finishin' school in France but it seems the mistress won't 'ear of it. She'd wrap 'er in cotton wool if she could. Miss Diana is deaf as a doorpost, see? An' the mistress is fiercely protective of 'er.' She gave another huge yawn then and dropped back on to the pillows.

'And what about Mrs Bronson? Has she been here long?'

'Longer than me,' Nancy said sleepily as she snuggled further down under the blankets. 'She's officially classed as the housekeeper but her an' the mistress are as thick as thieves. She's more like a lady's maid or a nurse to 'er.'

'And is Mrs Bronson a kind person?' Ginny was aching to know more about her now and why the woman might have helped her. And how had her father known her? There were so many un-

166

answered questions.

'Nancy ... did you hear me?'

She was answered with snores coming from the other bed. The questions would have to wait for another day.

Chapter Sixteen

'Wake up, sleepy 'ead! It's time to start work.'

At the sound of Nancy's voice, Ginny started awake and scrubbed at her eyes with her knuckles. She had slept badly and would have liked nothing better than to turn over and burrow beneath the covers again. All the same she scrambled out of bed and felt in the gloom for her clothes, which she had folded across the brass footboard at the end of the bed. She then quickly brushed and plaited her hair, hastily washed her hands and face in the bowl of cold water and, still barely awake, followed Nancy down the back stairs to the kitchen. Phyllis, the other laundry maid, was already there and she smiled at them cheerily.

'Right, you come wi' me,' she told Ginny. 'I need to show you 'ow to get the fires goin' under the coppers in the laundry room so we can heat the water for boilin' the whites. By the time we've done that, young Nancy 'ere will no doubt 'ave a nice cup o' tea on the go.'

Ginny reluctantly followed her from the kitchen and across the yard and on the way they passed Johnny, who was heading for the stables.

'Mornin', ladies,' he greeted them pleasantly, but Ginny could do no more than raise a weak smile in response.

It was bitterly cold in the laundry room. Buckets with various garments soaking in them were standing in a row all along one wall and Ginny was shocked to note that there was ice floating on some of them.

'Don't worry, it'll warm up by the time we get the fires goin',' Phyllis promised. 'An' by lunch-time you'll be sweatin' cobs, believe you me.'

Ginny watched her closely and eventually the fires were all burning brightly beneath the enormous coppers. 'Now you only use these for the towels and the whites,' Phyllis explained. 'The coloureds are done in those big dolly tubs, then you take them to the sink over there and rinse them thoroughly before feeding 'em through the mangle. On a good day there are lines strung across the yard where you can hang 'em out to dry. In this weather you have to use the lines in 'ere.' She pointed up to the ceiling and Ginny saw a number of wooden struts that were lowered with ropes.

'You'd be surprised 'ow quickly the things dry once it warms up in 'ere,' Phyllis chattered on. It was all going in one ear and out of the other by now and Ginny had to stifle a yawn.

'There then, that should do it,' Phyllis said after a while, wiping her hands down the coarse linen apron that covered her plain grey dress. 'Now let's 'ead back to the kitchen an' see if Nancy's got that tea ready. I don't know about you but I'm ready fer one. We've got to get you your uniform an' all. We 'ave breakfast about nine o'clock after Cook 'as seen to the family. By then we should 'ave the first load strung up.'

They found Mrs Bronson in the kitchen waiting for them with a number of clothes folded across her arm.

'Your uniform and underclothes,' she informed Ginny without a hint of a smile as she held them out to her. 'There are two of each. I trust that they will fit you.'

'Thank you, Mrs Bronson.' Ginny meekly took them from her.

'You are to wear them at all times whilst you are in the house,' Mrs Bronson told her. 'And you are only to wear your own clothes when you have time off. You never, under any circumstances, go beyond the green baize door unless summoned. Are there any questions you would like to ask me?'

'I don't think so,' Ginny answered coolly.

'Good. Should you ever wish to speak to me for any reason, you may inform Cook.' She then inclined her head and left the room without another word as Ginny turned her attention to the clothes over her arm. There were two grey dresses that appeared to be identical to the one Phyllis was wearing, and two enormous coarse bibbed aprons as well as two plain white petticoats and two pairs of cotton drawers. They had clearly been worn before but at least they were clean, Ginny found herself thinking.

'You'd best go up and get yerself changed,' Cook advised her. 'An' when yer come back down yer can 'ave a nice cup o' tea afore yer go to start work.'

'Thank you.'

Ginny dashed up to the room she shared with Nancy and hastily changed into her uniform. The dress was slightly big but after tying the apron tightly about her waist it would do. It was an unbecoming shade of grey with a high neck, long sleeves and a fairly full skirt.

Once back downstairs she swallowed the tea Cook put in front of her in one gulp then hurried out to the laundry again. It was still dark, so for a time they would have to work by the light of an oil lamp.

'Now first you have to sort yer washin' into piles,' Phyllis explained, sorting through an enormous stack of dirty laundry. 'The dresses will be done in the sink, the aprons and drawers can go into the coppers to be boiled, apart from the frilly housemaid ones; they have to be done separately.'

Ginny's eyes strayed to two large buckets that appeared to be full of blood.

'Ugh! And what are those?'

'Mmm, that's your worst job I'm afraid,' Phyllis said. 'That's all the monthlies. Yer know? From the women's courses.'

Ginny looked horrified. 'Surely I haven't got to wash those?' she gasped.

Phyllis sniffed. 'I'm afraid someone 'as to, an' unfortunately the rough laundry maid is the lowest in the 'ouse. Sorry, pet, but you'll soon get used to it. Use the wooden tongs to fish 'em out, an' the soap an' washboard to get the worst of the stains out of 'em, then throw 'em in the copper last of all when you've done all the other whites.'

Ginny turned away in disgust and started to

sort through the pile as Phyllis had shown her. Within minutes of standing over the steaming coppers and dunking the aprons and drawers into the boiling water sweat was standing out on her brow and she rolled up her sleeves and undid the top buttons of her dress. Then began the laborious task of transferring everything from the coppers to the deep stone sinks and rinsing every item by hand. She frequently swiped the sweat away as it dripped into her eyes, but by the time Phyllis told her to stop for breakfast she had managed to get the first load slung over the lines.

'When we come back yer can tackle the uniform dresses,' Phyllis told her. 'An' that ain't easy either 'cos they all have to be scrubbed by hand in the sinks.'

She held up the dress she had been working on then. It was a lovely shade of sky-blue satin with an enormous skirt and lace about the cuffs and the neckline, and Ginny thought she had never seen anything so pretty.

'This is one o' Miss Diana's. I don't actually wash it. Once a week I wipe round the hems then clean under the arms wi' rosewater,' Phyllis explained. 'Some of 'em are made of silk so they ain't made to stand up to a lot o' washin'.'

'I can't imagine wearing a dress like that,' Ginny said dreamily.

'Well, they ain't made fer the likes o' you an' me, are they?' Phyllis headed for the door, closely followed by Ginny, and within no time they were sitting at the kitchen table eating bacon and thick juicy sausages. Well, I can't deny that there's plenty to eat here, Ginny thought as she helped herself to more tea from the pot. Breakfast was a hurried affair, however, and no sooner was it over than everyone scuttled back to their jobs as little Nancy made haste to clear the dirty pots away.

The morning seemed to last for ever, and by the end of it Ginny felt as if her back was breaking. Her arms ached too from lugging the wet washing from one place to another. She had thought that working at the pie shop was hard graft but she soon discovered that it was nothing compared to this. Her hands were sore too from the laundry soap, but she battled on, determined not to complain. They stopped at one o'clock for a brief lunch break then during the afternoon all the things that were dry had to be pressed. By the time they returned to the kitchen that evening for supper Ginny could scarcely put one foot in front of another and all she wanted to do was sleep.

'It'll get easier,' Cook informed her kindly as she placed a plateful of cottage pie in front of her. 'You get used to it after a time.'

Ginny doubted that she would ever get used to it and kept her head down, fighting the urge to cry.

At last she trudged upstairs with her first day behind her, and this time it was she who fell asleep before Nancy, even though there were still many questions that Ginny had wanted to ask her.

The next morning when she woke, Ginny instantly became aware of how sore her hands were. During the night they had cracked and swelled and the skin was a horrible red colour. It was painful even to get dressed and she struggled with the buttons on her dress.

'Goodness me, they're a mess, ain't they?' Cook declared when Ginny went downstairs and showed them to her. 'It's 'cos they ain't used to bein' in water fer so long but they'll harden up. Meantime I'll give yer a little tip.' She lowered her voice. 'Soak 'em in yer chamber pot.'

'*What?*' Ginny couldn't believe her ears. Nor could she think of anything worse.

Cook nodded her head wisely. 'It's sommat in the urine that hardens 'em an' I know it works from other laundry maids 'ere as 'ave tried it.'

Mrs Bronson entered the kitchen then and seeing the state of Ginny's hands she clucked her tongue. 'Oh dear. They look rather sore. Don't you have any cream you can use on them?'

When Ginny shook her head, looking thoroughly miserable, the woman turned her attention to Cook. 'Could you have one of the maids bring a tray of tea up for the mistress, please? She's had a very bad night, I'm afraid.'

And with that she strode from the room, her skirts rustling about her, without giving Ginny a second glance.

Fat lot she cares! Ginny thought resentfully and accepted the tea Cook was holding out to her, wondering how on earth she was going to get through another back-breaking day.

By lunchtime, even though she had been repulsed by Cook's suggestion of dipping her hand in a chamber pot, she was in so much pain that she would have tried anything. But she didn't complain. She merely got on with her work as best she could.

It was as she was making her way back to the laundry with Phyllis after lunch that she got her first sight of Miss Diana. She was on her way to the stables dressed in a stylish dark green riding habit trimmed with black braid, and Ginny was sure she'd never seen such a beautiful girl in her life. Diana's hair was a rich golden colour and her eyes were as blue as the sky. Tall and slim, she carried herself majestically and the four young men who were with her all appeared to be listening to her raptly. However, when she spotted Ginny and Phyllis she came to an abrupt stop, and pointing her riding crop towards them she laughed gratingly.

'Boys – look. The peasants are on their way back to work.' She spoke in a harsh voice that Ginny found rather strange.

The tallest of the young men looked at her reproachfully. He too had blond hair and blue eyes and Ginny wondered if this was Sebastian, Diana's brother.

'There was no need for that, Di,' he scolded, taking her arm and looking directly at her. 'They're not doing you any harm, are they?' The girl shook him off and flounced away, and as he glanced towards Ginny their eyes momentarily locked. He smiled at her apologetically and she looked away flustered as she hurried to keep up with Phyllis. The next second they were inside the laundry with the door firmly closed behind them.

'Ooh, there are times when I'd like nothin' more than to give that young madam the good slap she deserves,' Phyllis fumed.

'Is she always like that? Rude, I mean.'

Phyllis nodded. 'Yes, more's the pity. Except for when the master is about, that is. She wouldn't dare talk to the servants like that in front of him. Trouble is, the mistress has ruined her from the day she stepped through the door.'

'Well, the young man who told her off seemed nice enough.'

Phyllis nodded again. 'That's Master Seb and he *is* nice. Different to his sister. I sometimes wonder if they both came out of the same womb. Another one to look out for is Master Giles. Keep away from him, Ginny. He's no good, an' I reckon the master despairs of him at times. The mistress is a gentle soul and lovely but she's spoiled him an' all. The master's allus up an' down to his school gettin' him out o' some bother or another.'

Ginny crossed to the sink and, grimacing, she plunged her hands into the water again. 'So what is wrong with the mistress?' she asked. 'Nancy mentioned that she was an invalid.'

'That's right, she ain't never been the same since she gave birth to Master Timothy, from what I can gather. She nearly died havin' him by all accounts. Then when he was killed an' his young wife died, she took to Master Giles. Soon after that she took to her sister's children when their parents died. She's treated them as her own. Trouble is, she's been far too soft wi' 'em if you were to ask me. Spare the rod an' spoil the child an' all that.'

'And what's the master like?' Ginny was highly intrigued to hear about the family she was now working for.

'Good as gold. He's a self-made man, not one

175

o' these that were born wi' a silver spoon in 'is mouth, so he's very down to earth.'

'Do he and his wife have a good relationship?'

'Oh yes, he dotes on her. So does Mrs Bronson for that matter. Her official role is that of house-keeper but she spends as much time lookin' after the mistress as she does runnin' the house.'

Her words echoed what Mrs Bevins had once told her. 'I see.' Ginny sighed as she turned her attention back to the job in hand. Did it really matter what the family were like? She wasn't likely to see much of them, was she, shut away in the laundry all day. Her thoughts turned to Charlie again and hot tears ran down her face and dripped into the soapy water. Somehow she just had to find him.

It was later that afternoon as Phyllis and Ginny were still busily working away that the door opened and Master Sebastian appeared.

Removing his hat, he addressed Ginny, saying, 'I'm so sorry for my sister's behaviour earlier on. I'm afraid she can be rather rude at times.'

'It's all right, sir.' Ginny flushed as she straightened from the sink, and for a moment a silence hung between them, then with a last smile he turned and strode away.

Ignoring Phyllis' knowing grin, Ginny quickly turned back to what she had been doing. Perhaps it wouldn't be as bad working at Lamp Hill Hall as she had thought.

Chapter Seventeen

Ginny had been working at the hall for three days when Mrs Bronson suddenly appeared in the laundry. Phyllis had come down with a heavy cold and wasn't working that day, so Ginny glanced up from the sink with surprise when she heard the door open wondering who it might be. When she saw Mrs Bronson she hastily dried her hands on her apron and looked at her apprehensively. Perhaps she had come to dismiss her because her work wasn't satisfactory.

'Cook tells me your hands are still paining you,' the woman said, and when Ginny nodded she asked, 'May I see them?'

When Ginny held them out towards her she saw the housekeeper visibly wince. She then took a little pot from her pocket and pressing it into Ginny's hand she advised, 'Rub this salve into your hands each night before you go to sleep. Hopefully it will help.'

At this unexpected gift, Ginny was momentarily rendered speechless, but then she said thickly, 'Thank you. You're very kind.'

The woman stood staring at her, her hands clasped before her as if there was something else she wanted to say, but then she turned abruptly and made for the door where she paused to ask, 'Are you settling in here, Virginia?'

'Yes, ma'am, thank you.'

'Good.' She was gone then, leaving Ginny to stare down at the little pot of cream in her hands.

By the time Ginny's first Sunday off rolled around she was so tired that she was minded just to spend the whole day in bed sleeping. But then she decided that it seemed a shame to lose what little free time she had lying about and she felt she really ought to go to Bertie's house to apologise for disappearing as she had and to explain where she had been. The Watkins family would no doubt have been worried about her. She'd also try to find time to give Mrs Bevins a quick visit. She didn't much fancy the thought of going into the town centre in case she bumped into the Parsons, but knew that she would have to face up to them at some point so she may as well get it over and done with. With a sigh she rolled off the mattress and began to get dressed at almost the same time as Nancy stirred.

'So what are you doing today?' Ginny asked as she tipped water from the jug into the bowl.

'Oh, I shall walk into town and spend the day wi' me family.'

'How lovely, where do they live?'

'In Swan Lane.'

'Really?' There were some very smart houses there and Ginny hadn't imagined Nancy coming from anywhere quite as grand.

'Oh well, the thing is, me dad's a banker. I don't even really need to work if I don't want to, but I ain't one fer bein' idle.' Nancy grinned. 'Me dad weren't none too pleased at all about me takin' this post, not when we 'ave maids of us own at 'ome.' She giggled, and it was so infectious that Ginny smiled too.

'In that case we could walk into town together,' Ginny suggested and after Nancy had agreed, they each got busy putting on their Sunday best. It seemed that life was full of surprises.

At that moment in Celia Walton-Hughes' bedroom, Mrs Bronson was plumping up the pillows on the woman's bed and making her comfortable before placing the breakfast tray across her lap.

'Now,' she encouraged gently, 'I've got Cook to do you a nice soft-boiled egg just as you like it. Do try to eat a little at least.'

'I'm not really hungry.' Celia's face was as pale as the pillow slips she reclined on and her fingers fidgeted nervously. 'I can't believe the boys are going back to school tomorrow,' she said then with a catch in her voice. 'The Christmas holidays just seem to have flown by.'

'Ah, so that's what you're fretting about, is it?' Anna Bronson reached out and stroked the stray curls from the woman's forehead as a mother might have done to a child. 'But what you're forgetting is that when they come home in September they won't be going away again – unless they decide to go on to university, that is.'

'Even so, it's a long time between now and then and I'm not getting any stronger–'

'Nonsense!' Anna said sharply. 'You'll be fine again when the spring comes. You know you always feel better when the sun shines.'

'What's this about the sun shining?'

Both women's heads turned to the voice to see Celia's husband striding across the room with a smile on his face.

'I was just telling Celia that she'll feel better again when the warm weather arrives,' Anna explained and he nodded heartily in agreement as he stared down affectionately at the woman on the bed.

'Of course you will, darling. But for now is there anything I can get you?'

'No, dear. I have everything I need,' she assured him as he took her hand and kissed it. 'You and Anna take such good care of me. I'm afraid I've become a frightful burden to you both.'

'No, you have not!' Anna and James said in unison and they all laughed.

'Right, well, I'll just go down and have a word with Cook about this week's menus,' Anna said tactfully then, wishing to give husband and wife some time alone together, and she discreetly hurried from the room.

'Sebastian informs me we have a new laundry maid,' Celia said as James took a seat at the side of the bed.

'Yes, I believe we do, although I haven't met her. I leave all that side of things to Anna, as you know.'

'Hmm, well, I think I would like to meet her. It's always nice to know who is living in our house,' his wife said.

'Is that really necessary, dear? What I mean is – she's only a laundry maid.'

Celia shrugged, setting the feathers on her silk bed-jacket fluttering, and seeing the determined set of her chin he gave in, as he always did.

'Very well. If that's what you want, I shall get Anna to arrange it.'

She smiled at him – and just for a second he had a glimpse of the pretty girl he had once fallen in love with. Pain had ravaged her features and prematurely aged her, but surprisingly her hair was still the soft blonde colour it had been all those years ago and her eyes were still a lovely deep blue.

'Have the boys packed their trunks ready for going back to school yet?'

He laughed. 'Hardly. If it were left to them they'd forget half of what they need. But never fear, Barbara has done it for them. She's very efficient and I shall be travelling with them tomorrow. Don't worry, sweetheart. I shall make sure that they come and say goodbye to you before they leave.'

He crossed to the window then and stood with his arms joined behind his back as he stared out across the grounds. Watching him with his head of thick dark hair and his muscular physique, Celia thought what a fine figure of a man he still was. Many of their friends of the same age had run to fat and had paunches, but James was still as attractive as the day she had married him.

'So will you ask Anna to arrange for me to meet the new laundry maid? Perhaps tomorrow afternoon. I might feel well enough to come down to the drawing room for a time then. No doubt Diana will be in a fret because the boys have gone back to Rugby. Bless her, I think she gets lonely with no one of her own age to speak to, apart from the maids.'

'All the more reason for her to go to a finishing

school,' James remarked but Celia shook her head.

'No, she would be at too much of a disadvantage with her deafness and you know how embarrassed she gets if anyone comments on it.'

'But how is she ever going to meet a suitable young man to marry if she is never allowed out of the house?'

Celia shrugged. 'No doubt someone will come along. Perhaps one of the boys' friends that they bring here in the holidays? Anyway, I'm in no rush to get her off our hands. She is only seventeen, after all. There's plenty of time to be thinking of that in a few years' time.'

James sighed but didn't argue. He knew how his wife doted on her niece and he did sympathise with the girl's condition although there were times when he was tempted to put her across his knee and tan her backside for her when she flew into one of her tantrums.

'Ah well, I suppose I should leave you to your breakfast,' he said, changing the subject. Crossing to the bed he bent down and kissed his wife softly on the cheek. 'I've got some paperwork to do so I think I'll go and lock myself away in my office for a while and get it done out of the way.'

'All right, darling.' She watched him leave the room and as soon as he was gone she closed her eyes, the breakfast tray forgotten, and was almost instantly asleep.

Nancy and Ginny had almost reached the bottom of Tuttle Hill by then and as they approached the entrance to Swan Lane, Nancy told her brightly, 'My house is just down here. I'll see you later,

182

shall I? I'd ask yer to pop in but Mam an' Dad will want me to 'emselves for a bit.'

'That's all right,' Ginny answered with a smile as she eyed the huge houses curiously. She envied Nancy going home to visit her family and was intrigued to learn that the girl had come from such a privileged background. As Nancy set off, Ginny hurried on to North Street, keen to let the Watkins family know that she was safe.

It was Bertie's mother who answered the door when Ginny arrived and she instantly took her arm and drew her inside, saying, 'Oh, luvvie, we've been worried *sick* about yer. When you didn't show up on New Year's Day fer dinner, Bertie went round to Parsons an' that Bill Parsons sent him away wi' a flea in his ear. He just said as you'd took off an' left 'em in the lurch wi' no warnin'.'

'It wasn't quite like that,' Ginny said cautiously as her eyes settled on Bertie, who was grinning from ear to ear. 'And I'm so sorry I let you down. It was very rude of me.'

'Don't get worryin' about that fer now,' Bertie said, leading her to a chair. 'Just tell us where you've been an' if you're all right.'

'I'm fine,' Ginny assured him, undoing the ribbons of her bonnet. 'I've been working up at Lamp Hill Hall as a laundry maid, and this is my first day off so I had no way of letting you know where I was.'

'Lamp Hill Hall!' Bertie was astonished. 'But why did yer leave the pie shop so suddenly?'

Ginny was reluctant to tell him the truth for fear of more trouble so she just shrugged and said, 'I decided on the spur of the moment that I'd had enough of working there. I never really got on with Bill and Edith as you know so I just packed up and went off to try my luck elsewhere.'

'Eeh, but look at yer poor hands,' Mrs Watkins said, clucking her tongue.

Ginny glanced down at them. They were still red and chapped, but they'd hardened up considerably now and were nowhere near as painful as they had been when she'd first started in the laundry. 'They're not too bad now,' she assured the kindly woman. 'Mrs Bronson, the housekeeper, gave me some salve to put on them and that helped a lot.'

Bertie's siblings, who had watched her arrival, lost interest now and went back to what they'd been doing while Mrs Watkins pottered away to make some tea. Mr Watkins was dozing in the fireside chair with a newspaper covering his face, and now Bertie leaned forward and whispered, 'I think there's more to this than what you're tellin' me. You're not the sort to just up an' clear off like that. If he tried to 'urt yer, you should tell me an' I'll go round there an' knock 'is block off!'

Ginny giggled. 'Oh, and I'm sure your sergeant would love that.'

Thankfully Mrs Watkins bustled back in then to place a large ginger cake on the table and the children instantly clustered around it like bees around a honey pot. She urged Ginny to join them at the table and for now the reason she had left the pie shop was dropped, much to Ginny's relief.

After the tea and cake she spent another pleasant hour with the family until Mrs Watkins

184

asked tentatively, 'Have yer had any luck yet in trackin' down yer little brother, pet?'

Ginny's face fell. 'No, not yet, but the house-keeper at the Hall told me that she'd make some enquiries for me. She's on the Board of Governors at the workhouse so if anyone can find out what's happened to him, she can.'

'That's grand then,' Mrs Watkins said as Ginny glanced at the clock on the mantelpiece.

'I really ought to be going now,' she told them and Bertie instantly rose.

'I'll walk you back,' he offered but Ginny firmly shook her head.

'Thanks, but I shall be fine. I want to pop in and check that Mrs Bevins is all right on my way home.'

'But when will we see you again?'

'I could come on my next day off in four weeks' time?' She said goodbye to the rest of the family and Bertie saw her to the door.

'Are yer sure that yer all right up at the Hall?' he asked worriedly and Ginny felt so happy to have a friend like Bertie.

'I'm fine. It's hard work,' she confided, 'but then they do say that good honest work never killed anyone, don't they? And I'd rather be there than in the pie shop.' She shuddered involuntarily.

'Well, just keep yer eye out fer that Master Giles, the son o' the house,' Bertie warned. 'He's got himself a bit of a reputation fer gettin' into trouble.'

'Oh, he and the nephew are going back to school tomorrow, so it's not likely I'll see any more of him till the next holiday,' Ginny said, then with a little wave she set off for Mrs Bevins' cottage as Bertie stood and watched her until she turned the corner and was out of sight.

Chapter Eighteen

'Hello, Cook, am I the first one back?' Ginny asked when she breezed into the kitchen at the Hall that afternoon. Her cheeks were glowing from the fresh air and her eyes were sparkling.

'No, Nancy's upstairs in 'er room. Gone up fer a rest afore tea,' the cook informed her as she fetched a batch of scones from the oven.

'Already? She didn't spend long with her family then, did she?' Ginny remarked innocently.

The cook raised an eyebrow. 'It wouldn't be the family in Swan Lane in the posh house yer talkin' of, would it?'

Ginny placed her shawl over the back of a chair. 'Well, yes. Why do you ask?'

Cook sighed, then after glancing towards the stairs door to make sure there was no one there she confided, 'There ain't no family in Swan Lane. There *ain't* no family for Nancy anywhere, if it comes to that. The poor little lass were brought 'ere from the workhouse, same as Nancy. She were left on the doorstep there as a baby an' I think she's made this family up to feel she belongs somewhere. We all just go along wi' it rather than 'urt her feelings.'

'How awful for her.' Ginny felt tears sting at the

186

back of her eyes as she thought of Nancy's plight. She was feeling the loss of her own family but at least she still had a father, even if he was locked away for now, and a little brother, somewhere. To never have known them was infinitely worse than worrying about them now, surely?

'Phyllis ain't back yet,' Cook went on. 'She's gone to see 'er young man. Between you an' me I reckon we could be hearin' wedding bells there soon. It'll be a good thing for you if we do, 'cos then you'd take over the family's washin' an' someone else would be appointed to see to the roughs. That's 'ow it works here. Yer have to work yer way up. Millie an' Barbara both started in the laundry.'

'Really?' Ginny opened her mouth to ask more then closed it abruptly when Mrs Bronson breezed into the room.

'Ah, Virginia, you're back.' She smiled. 'Would you come through to my office, please?'

Ginny glanced nervously at Cook, wondering what she had done wrong as she followed the woman from the room. Once again she found herself in the beautiful hallway before Mrs Bronson ushered her into her office.

'Do take a seat, Virginia.'

The girl wished that she would call her Ginny as everyone else did. The only time she had ever been called Virginia before was by her mother when she'd been up to some mischief.

Ginny obediently perched on the edge of a chair and folded her chapped hands neatly on her lap.

Mrs Bronson began to pace up and down as if

187

she was choosing the words she was about to say.

'I'm pleased to tell you, my dear, that I have news of your brother.'

Ginny's back instantly stiffened as she stared at the woman expectantly before stuttering, 'I ... is he all right?'

'He is very well.' The woman nodded gravely. 'I visited the workhouse this morning for a meeting with the governors and I can now tell you that an elderly gentleman in Hull has taken him under his wing. The gentleman in question owns a thriving shipbuilding business there, so Charles will have the best of care, I assure you.'

Ginny's head was swimming as she tried to take it in. 'And will I be able to see him?' she asked eventually.

'I don't think that would be a good idea. Charles needs to settle with his new family for now, but perhaps when he is older it might be arranged if he wishes it.'

Ginny's heart plummeted although she was relieved to at least know where her dear little brother was now. And then something occurred to her and she said: 'But why would someone come all the way from Hull to adopt a child? Surely there are workhouses and orphanages closer to him.'

'It is not for us to question that. I'm sure the gentleman had his reasons. It should suffice to know for now that Charles is safe and well,' Mrs Bronson answered primly.

'Oh, it does! I mean, of course I am relieved to know he's all right,' Ginny said hastily. 'And I'm very grateful that you took the time and trouble to enquire for me, Mrs Bronson... I just wish he wasn't so far away, I suppose.'

The woman's expression softened as she saw the longing on Ginny's face and unconsciously, she put her hand out towards her, but then seeming to think better of it, she quickly withdrew it.

'Well, you may go back to whatever you were doing now,' she said. 'I'm aware that it's your day off and I have no wish to take up any more of your free time. How are your hands, by the way?'

'Oh, they're toughening up, thank you.' Ginny rose and made for the door in a whirl of emotions. She was relieved to know where Charlie was, and that he was safe – but it was a blow to discover that she couldn't see him. Still, it won't be for ever, she told herself as she hurried back to the kitchen. She'd decided that she'd spend a few hours in there. It was much warmer than up in her bedroom and she could read the old newspapers that Cook kept in a cupboard there. She wished she had another book to read; she knew *The Mill on the Floss* almost word for word now, but there was no time to visit the free reading rooms. Perhaps she could get Mrs Watkins to take out some books for her?

It was the middle of the following afternoon when Mrs Bronson made an unexpected appearance in the laundry. Phyllis and Ginny immediately stopped what they were doing and stood to attention.

'Ah, Virginia, would you come with me, please?'

Ginny glanced at Phyllis before following the housekeeper across the yard, wondering what was going on.

189

'There is nothing wrong,' Mrs Bronson said to reassure the girl, noting her worried expression. 'But the mistress has expressed a wish to meet you. She likes to know her staff.'

'Oh I see.' Ginny's breath hissed out on a sigh of relief. Once again she found herself in the family's part of the house and she stared in awe at an enormous crystal chandelier that hung at the bottom of a sweeping staircase leading up to a galleried landing.

'The mistress is in here in the drawing room.' Mrs Bronson stopped outside a door. 'I shall wait here for you, but do be sure to dip your knee and address her as ma'am.'

She opened the door and gently nudged Ginny inside. Ginny instantly forgot why she was there as she found herself in the most beautiful room she had ever seen. Dark green velvet curtains topped by ornate fringed swags in a lighter green hung at a window that overlooked the gardens, and a fire burned brightly in a tall marble fireplace. But then her eyes fell on a number of books lying on a small table and without thinking she crossed to them and leaned over to read the title of the top one.

'You must be Virginia.'

The voice made her start and she swung about to see a woman sitting in a chair next to a large bookcase on the other side of the room.

'Err ... yes, miss ... I mean ma'am. Sorry – I saw the books and quite forgot myself.' Ginny remembered to curtsey then and hastily dipped her knee as colour flooded into her cheeks.

Well, I made a right mess of that, she silently

scolded herself. However, to her relief she saw that the mistress looked amused rather than annoyed. She was quite beautiful but very fragile-looking, almost ethereal, Ginny thought.

'Come over here, my dear, and let me look at you.'

Ginny obediently crossed the room, her knees knocking and her feet sinking into the luxurious carpet. The whole place was like another world.

She stopped in front of the woman and they eyed each other.

Why, she's beautiful, the woman thought. And nothing like I expected, and then aloud, 'Do you like looking at books?'

'I like reading them.' Ginny smiled now, and once more the woman felt strangely drawn to her. 'I notice that you have *Adam Bede* over there. It's one of my favourites. I like George Eliot. Have you read *The Mill on the Floss,* ma'am?' Then realising that she might have overstepped the mark, she clamped her lips together.

'You can read ... *and* write?'

'Oh yes, ma'am. My mother and father always taught us and encouraged us. We three older ones went to school, and I had hopes of becoming a teacher one day, until...' Ginny's voice faded away and she wished that she could just come in and start all over again. She'd certainly bungled the introduction, that was for sure.

Mrs Walton-Hughes looked slightly surprised. Most of her staff signed for their wages with a cross.

She eyed Ginny silently for a few moments before saying softly, 'You are a very beautiful girl,

Virginia. And intelligent too, by the sounds of it. How are you settling in at Lamp Hill Hall?'

'Very well, ma'am ... thank you.'

'Good. Well, it's been lovely to meet you but I shan't keep you any longer. Should you ever have anything you are concerned about, please speak to Mrs Bronson or myself. I like my staff to be happy.'

'Thank you, ma'am.' Ginny dipped her knee again and began to back towards the door, and within seconds she was out in the hallway where Mrs Bronson was waiting for her. Without saying a word, the housekeeper led her back to the kitchen and then returned immediately to her mistress while Ginny hurriedly returned to the laundry. She had a pile of sheets to feed through the mangle.

'Goodness me, Anna. The girl was nothing like I expected,' Celia said the instant Anna joined her. 'Did you know that she can read and write? Whatever is she doing working in the laundry? She is totally wasted there. And she's so beautiful. Can you imagine what she would look like, dressed in the right clothes? I'm sure she would be quite stunning.'

'I think she might well be,' Anna answered as she tidied the magazines her mistress had been reading into a pile. 'But do you think you ought to go up and have a rest now? You're looking rather tired.'

'I am a little,' Celia confessed. 'I'm afraid the tantrum Diana threw this morning after James left to take the boys back to school in Rugby has quite drained me.'

'I think a lot of her ill temper stems from frustration and boredom,' Anna remarked. 'After all, she has no one of her own age here when the boys are away, and it must be difficult for her.'

'If you are trying to persuade me to send her away to a finishing school again you can forget it,' Celia said stubbornly as Anna helped her out of the chair, but as they made their slow way upstairs, the housekeeper's words played on her mind all the same. Anna was right. Diana was locked away in a world of silence when her cousin and her brother were absent.

'Do you think I should consider getting Diana a companion?' They had paused halfway up the stairs for Celia to get her breath back when she made the suggestion and Anna put her head to one side.

'That's a very good idea, but you would have to be careful whom you chose. An older woman might only seem like another governess to her, and most young people wouldn't care to take on such a post. Diana can be quite demanding, as we all know.'

'Hmm, perhaps you're right ... but I think I shall put the proposition to James and see what he has to say about it.' And so they continued to her room as the idea buzzed about in Celia's head.

Chapter Nineteen

'Do you think it would help Diana if we were to employ a companion to keep her company?' Celia asked her husband that night. She was sitting at her dressing table as Anna brushed her hair and, just as he did each evening, James had come in to spend some time with her before she retired to bed. It was a long time since they had slept together and Celia missed the closeness they had once shared, but James had been so afraid of the consequences of another child that he had moved into a separate room shortly after Timothy's birth.

'Do you mean another governess?' He was sitting in the armchair next to her bed reading a newspaper, but at her words he looked up and gave her his attention. 'I don't really think that would gain anything. Diana has had a whole string of governesses, hasn't she, and none of them have lasted for long.'

'No, no.' Celia flapped her hand at him. 'I was thinking of someone closer to her own age with whom she could perhaps form a friendship. She has had nothing in common with any of the governesses because they've all been so much older than her. Think about it ... the only time she ever comes into contact with anyone her own age is when the boys are home from school, and it's not quite the same as her having another girl to confide in, is it?'

'I suppose not,' James said hesitantly. 'But Diana can be ... shall I say, very trying? How long do you think a young girl would put up with her tantrums, dear?'

Anna kept her head down and remained silent. She never made comment unless asked to, when husband and wife were together. After a moment, she stood back and laid the silver-backed hair-brush down on the dressing table before murmuring, 'Is there anything else you would like me to do?'

'No thank you, Anna. That will be all.'

Anna inclined her head. 'Then I shall go and make your cocoa.'

Once they were alone Celia resumed: 'But I'm sure if we were to find the right person it would do Diana good. Won't you at least consider it, darling ... for me?'

James sighed. Celia knew that he found it difficult to deny her anything.

'Very well, I'll consider it – but I'm not making any promises, mind. The boys will be home for good in the summer and she'll have a lot more company then anyway.'

Deciding not to push it any further for now, Celia nodded then changed the subject. 'Have you met the new laundry maid yet?'

'Err ... no, I haven't. Why do you ask?'

'Because I met her today and she is really quite a charming girl – not at all what I expected. She can read and write and seems very intelligent too. She's also quite beautiful.'

'Well, as long as she does her job and doesn't cause any trouble, I tend to leave that sort of thing up to you and Anna.' He rose then to help her to the bed, and once she was sitting up against the pillows, he carefully pulled the covers over her.

'Anna tells me that you got up for a couple of hours today. I hope that means that you're feeling slightly stronger?'

Hearing the concern in his voice she gently squeezed his hand. She knew how much he worried about her. 'Yes, I have felt a little stronger these last few days. I hope I shall feel better still when the spring comes and I can go and sit outside in the sunshine. But now, read me some juicy bits from the paper, darling. You know I always enjoy this time of the evening.' And so her obliging husband did just that.

Over the next few days, Celia toyed with the idea that was growing in her mind but then that – and everything else for that matter – faded into the background when James came storming into the bedroom one morning brandishing a letter.

'It's from the school,' he spluttered, trying his best to control his temper. 'It appears that Giles is in trouble again and they are asking if I will attend the school as a matter of urgency. What the hell do you think he might have been up to *this* time? It was drinking last term, fighting the one before that. I sometimes despair of that grandson of ours, I really do!'

Without waiting for an answer from his wife, James paced up and down, fuming, 'I suppose I shall have to go today.' Then, turning to Anna, who was laying out her mistress' clothes, he said,

'Would you mind asking Millie or Barbara if they could prepare an overnight bag for me, please, Anna? The roads are so icy it will take me twice as long as it should to get to Rugby, and I may have to stay in a hotel for the night before setting off back.'

'Of course, sir.' Anna hurriedly left the room and went to track down one of the maids.

'I'm sure things won't be as bad as you think, once you get there,' Celia told her husband timidly, when Anna had gone.

He looked at her and sighed with exasperation. 'I might have known you would try to make excuses for him.'

She smiled sheepishly as she held her hand out to her husband. 'All I'm saying is, try not to think the worst,' she urged. 'But now come back and talk to me for a while before you leave.'

Forcing a smile, he went to sit in the chair at the side of her bed.

'Seems Master Giles is in bother at school again,' Cook whispered to Nancy later that morning. 'Mrs Bronson has Barbara packin' a bag for the master as we speak. He's to go to the school straight away, by all accounts.'

'I'm not surprised.' Nancy tossed her head. 'It beats me how anyone who's had so many privileges can be so selfish. He only ever thinks of enjoyin' 'imself.'

Cook nodded in agreement just as Ginny and Phyllis entered the room for their lunch, drying their hands on the huge calico aprons that enveloped them. Ginny's face was glowing from the hours she'd spent leaning over tubs of hot water and her back was aching, but she rarely complained. She had just taken a seat when a commotion in the hall reached them and they all looked towards the green baize door.

'That sounds like Miss Diana,' Cook said, and the two girls looked at each other. Out in the hallway, Diana was building herself up into a right old tizzy.

'*Want to come with you!*' she shouted at her uncle in the over-loud voice to which the whole household had become accustomed.

'Now, Miss Diana, that wouldn't be seemly at all,' Mrs Bronson mouthed as she caught the girl's cheeks and forced her to look at her. Diana had become quite adept at lip-reading. 'How can your uncle let you accompany him to a boys' school?'

Diana pouted as she slapped the woman's hands away.

'Want to GO!'

Her uncle sighed as he lifted the overnight case Barbara had packed for him. He was in a bad enough mood as it was without having to endure one of his niece's tantrums.

'May I leave you to deal with her, Anna?' he asked as he strode towards the door and Anna quickly nodded as she held fast to Miss Diana's arm.

Diana lashed out, but once the door had closed behind her uncle she gave a strangled cry and dashed towards the kitchen.

The women in there watched in horrified silence as the girl tore across the room and out into the yard.

'Best leave her be till she's come out of her mood,' Cook advised Ginny, who had just risen from her seat to follow her. 'There ain't no use tryin' to reason wi' her when she's in one o' her states. She'll come out of it eventually an' it ain't likely she'll want to stay outside fer long in this cold, is it?'

Ginny supposed she was right but felt sorry for the girl despite her tantrum. She was clearly very unhappy, and Ginny herself could only imagine how awful it must be, to be locked away in a silent world.

'Has she always been deaf?' she asked the cook as she poured herself and Phyllis a cup of tea from the sturdy brown teapot.

The woman continued to carve a fresh baked loaf as she answered. 'No, she ain't. Her parents died in an accident when their coach overturned goin' home from a party one night. They were killed outright, as was the driver, an' Miss Diana an' Master Seb were trapped beneath the carriage for hours till the staff at their house started to get worried 'cos they hadn't come home and went lookin' for 'em. Master Seb were unconscious, an' it were touch an' go whether he'd survive or not when they finally found 'em. Diana was in shock – an' from that day on she ain't been able to hear a thing, though the master an' mistress 'ave paid numerous doctors to look at her. It's a damn shame 'cos she's a pretty girl – an' wealthy an' all. Her parents left 'er an' Sebastian very well provided for, though their money is in trust for 'em till they each reach the age o' twenty-one. I don't mind bettin' there'll be a few gold-diggers sniffin' around her then, deaf or not!'

'How sad,' Ginny stared thoughtfully at the door as she absent-mindedly spooned sugar into her tea. Despite all her wealth it appeared that Diana had had a lot to contend with. First her parents' death, then the deafness. It was no wonder she could be difficult, shut away here in this big house with no one her own age to keep her company, apart from the young men when they were home from school. Not that it was any of her concern, she told herself. She'd had more than enough heartache in her own life to cope with and all she was centred on at present was to try and locate the whereabouts of Charlie.

Ginny was counting off the days until she was paid and intended to save every single penny until she had enough to make her way towards Hull. Surely once she got there it wouldn't be too difficult to find her brother? After all, how many shipbuilders could there be, living in the town? She would have liked nothing more than to have been able to set off on her search there and then, but common sense told her that it would be very difficult if not impossible with not a penny to her name and in these weather conditions. So swallowing her frustration, she forced herself to count her blessings. The work she was doing was laborious and back-breaking, but at least she had a roof over her head and good food in her belly, which was a lot more than many could boast. Her thoughts strayed to Sebastian then. She had bumped into him in the yard the day before he had returned to school and he had spoken to her so nicely that for a moment she had almost forgotten that she was a mere maid in his aunt and uncle's home. He was nice, Sebastian was ... and quite handsome too.

Her thoughts were interrupted when Ted Ventriss the gardener joined them as they were finishing their meal.

'The poachers have been busy again,' he informed them, taking off his flat cap and shoving it into his pocket. 'I've set more traps in the woods. That should slow the buggers down!'

'The master won't be none too pleased,' Cook warned him as she placed the meal she had kept warm for him on the table. 'Yer know 'e don't approve o' traps.'

'Well, it's either that or we'll not have a bit o' life left in the woods.' Ted scratched his head. 'I don't mind 'em takin' the odd rabbit or two, but they're stealin' the pheasants an' all now. I heard tell they're even stealin' the sheep from the neighbourin' farm. Farmer's out wi' his gun most nights now by all accounts, tryin' to catch 'em.'

Ginny shuddered as she rose from the table. She'd seen someone in Whittleford once when she was a little girl who had been caught in a trap and she'd never forgotten it. The man's leg had been mangled and had had to be amputated – but she'd heard her father say that it could have been far worse. He would have bled to death if someone hadn't come across him when they had.

'Ready to go back to the grindstone, lass?' Phyllis asked and Ginny straightened her aching back and nodded. There was still a long afternoon to get through before her work was done.

The master arrived home late the following afternoon with a face like a thundercloud and Master Giles slouching behind him.

'Go to your room until I send for you,' he told the boy sternly as Nancy hurried forward to take his hat and coat in the hallway.

Giles threw his own coat towards the girl and stormed upstairs without a word. The master then took the stairs two at a time and headed for his wife's bedroom.

'Oh darling, I've been *so* worried. Is everything all right?' she asked the second he set foot through the door. Anna was hanging the mistress's freshly laundered clothes away but she tactfully hurried out of the room to give the couple some privacy.

'No, I'm afraid it isn't,' he replied as he began to pace up and down with his hands clasped behind his back. 'Giles has been expelled.'

'*Expelled?* Celia was horrified. 'But whatever has he done that could be so bad they would expel him?'

James stopped his pacing long enough to tell her, 'He and another boy had been sneaking out during the night to visit some girls in the village and the girls' parents have put in a complaint to the school.'

'Is that all?' Celia smiled with relief. 'But darling, that's not so very terrible. Giles is a young man. It's natural at his age to want the company of pretty girls, and the girls must have been willing. Surely you can talk to the headmaster and ask him to give Giles another chance?'

'Don't you think I tried that?' James said tiredly. 'I even offered extra money for his fees but they've had enough of his behaviour.' What he didn't tell his wife was that Giles had raped one of the girls, and it had cost him a pretty penny to persuade her parents not to report his grandson to the police.

'Then we shall just have to find him another school to attend,' Celia said placidly, but James shook his head.

'There would be no point. He will be eighteen in a few months' time and I doubt any other school would take him with his reputation. I'm afraid this will also scupper his chances of going to university, so whether he likes it or not, as soon as he reaches his birthday he'll have to come with me and start work in one of my businesses.'

Celia's face clouded. 'But he was hoping to travel the world before he went to university and settled down to a job.'

'Then he can hope on,' her husband said shortly. 'Surely even you who have ruined him would not want me to reward his bad behaviour? What sort of a man will he become if we go on giving him all his own way?'

Celia's eyes filled with tears and her hands began to tremble on the quilt. She could never remember seeing James quite so angry and wisely decided to let him calm down before saying any more on the subject.

'Why don't I ring for a nice cup of tea for us both?' she suggested, hoping to defuse the taut atmosphere.

But James headed for the door, saying, 'Not now, my dear. I have pressing matters to attend to. I've wasted quite enough time on our grandson's escapades ... *again!'*

And with that he was gone, leaving her to stare worriedly at the door.

Chapter Twenty

The following day Phyllis came down with a terrible hacking cough and Mrs Bronson ordered her to rest.

'You can't work in that sweaty atmosphere with your chest like that,' the woman told her. 'You'll end up with pneumonia.' And Phyllis was only too happy to take this chance to stay in bed.

'Do you think you might manage to do the family's laundry as well for a few days until Phyllis is better?' Mrs Bronson asked Ginny and the girl agreed immediately.

'Oh yes, ma'am. I've seen what Phyllis does so I'm sure I'll manage.'

Mrs Bronson stared at her strangely for a moment then before leaving said quietly, 'You're a good girl, Virginia.'

Ginny crossed to the other side of the laundry where the family's clothes were dealt with. It would be nice to handle pretty things for a change. Humming to herself, she started to sort the different fabrics into separate piles. First, all of the mistress's fine silk negligees and underwear. She knew that Phyllis always washed those carefully by hand. An hour later she was squeezing the water from them after rinsing them thoroughly in one of the deep sinks when a shadow blocked out the light in the doorway.

Glancing up, Ginny saw the grandson of the house standing there watching her.

'Busy, are you?' he asked unnecessarily but he sounded friendly enough.

Ginny hastily straightened and swept a lock of her jet-black hair behind her ear, aware of what a mess she must look. She was soaked in sweat and her sleeves were rolled up to the elbows.

'Yes, sir. Phyllis and me are always busy,' she answered politely.

'Hmm.' As he stared at her he felt a twitch in his breeches. Despite being hot and sweaty Ginny was a beautiful girl and he decided there and then that it might be a good idea to get on the right side of her. He certainly wouldn't mind a roll in the hay with this one, and she was only a servant, after all. Just so long as his father didn't find out. He was in enough trouble as it was at the moment.

'I err ... ought to be getting on,' Ginny said then, interrupting his thoughts, and he nodded.

'Of course. I didn't mean to disturb you. Don't get working too hard now.' Then with a smile that could have charmed the birds off the trees he was gone.

Ginny frowned as she stared after him. There was something about that young man that she couldn't take to. Still, she consoled herself, she wasn't likely to see much of him anyway and resuming her humming she started to drape the clean washing along the lines strung across the ceiling to dry.

During the rest of the week, Giles stuck his head around the laundry-room door each morning on his way to the stables to say good day. He was very pleasant and never said a word out of place so Ginny wondered if she might have misjudged him and said as much to Cook one day as she was having her morning break.

'Huh! I wouldn't trust 'im anywhere near a pretty lass like you,' Cook replied shaking the wooden spoon she was using in her direction as a dire warning. 'You just take my advice an' steer well clear of 'im, pet. Oh, an' by the way, Mrs Bronson said to tell you that Phyllis will be well enough to start back again tomorrow. That should take a load o' work off yer shoulders.'

'Actually I've quite enjoyed doing the family's washing,' Ginny confided. 'Some of Miss Diana's dresses are so beautiful it's a pleasure to handle them. I can only imagine what it must be like to wear them.'

'Mm, well, imagine is all you're ever likely to do. Them sorts o' clothes ain't fer the likes o' workin'-class people like you an' me.'

'I suppose not, but it does no harm to dream, does it?'

Ginny answered with a cheeky grin and Cook smiled.

At last Sunday rolled around and Ginny set off to see the Watkins family as she usually did now on her day off. She was carrying a basket of lavender scones that Cook had made especially. Bertie had taken to coming to meet her, and sure enough she found him waiting at the end of the drive.

They had just set off down Tuttle Hill when they saw a rider galloping towards them; as he drew closer, Ginny recognised Master Giles. When he came abreast of them, he yanked the beast to a halt and called down to Ginny, 'This your young man, is it?'

Before Ginny could answer, Bertie drew himself up to his full height and said coldly, 'I am, as a matter of fact, and if I were you I'd slow down. That poor beast is frothing at the mouth.'

The smile vanished from Giles' face. He glared at Bertie and pulled on the reins, making the horse start. Its eyes were wild and rolling in its head and Ginny nervously took a step back.

'How I treat my horse is no concern of yours,' Giles spat, then lifting his whip he cracked it down on the poor creature's shank, making it rear with pain before it galloped away.

'Cruel sod,' Bertie said with disgust as they watched Giles disappear off into the distance in a cloud of dust. 'People like him shouldn't be allowed near animals if you ask me.'

They fell into step again and continued on their way, but for Ginny the afternoon was spoiled. She'd hoped that she'd made Bertie aware that they were no more than friends, but it seemed he had other ideas – unless he had said what he had just to upset Master Giles. Now Giles might blame her for the way that Bertie had spoken to him, and that could only cause unpleasantness at Lamp Hill Hall – not that she could do much about it now. In fairness, Bertie had been perfectly justified in complaining about the way Giles was riding the horse. The poor animal had

207

looked exhausted. She'd often heard the grooms complaining that Giles mistreated his mare, but she doubted that anything she or Bertie said would change this, so perhaps it would have been better if he had kept quiet. However, his police training had taught Bertie about the Cruelty to Animals Act of 1849; he had witnessed Giles committing a crime.

Bertie was still fuming when they reached his home, and after greeting his mother, he burst out: 'We just met Giles Walton-Hughes on the road and you should have seen the lather his poor horse was in. The vicious swine doesn't deserve such a splendid animal.'

Mrs Watkins tutted as she placed the tea cosy over the pot and left it to mash. 'Ah, well, that's the way of the world, I'm afraid, lad,' she said matter-of-factly. 'We don't always get what we deserve, an' often them that don't deserve it do! But now stop your moanin'. Young Ginny didn't come to hear that, did yer, lass? Tell me all about what you've been gettin' up to.'

So Ginny did just that, and laughed at the antics of Bertie's younger siblings who were play-fighting on the mat in front of the fire. It was a very pleasant afternoon, but then the shadows began to lengthen.

'I think I ought to be heading back now,' she said regretfully, then rose to collect her bonnet and her warm shawl. It always felt nice to be at the heart of a loving family again; it brought back happy memories of her own loved ones. All afternoon she had been grappling with an idea and now she plucked up the courage to ask, 'Mrs Watkins, on my next afternoon off, would you mind very much if I brought a friend along to meet you? I share a room at the Hall with her and she has no family of her own so she usually just walks about aimlessly on her afternoon off.'

'Eeh, poor lass, why is that then?' Mrs Watkins asked as she reached across to clip the ear of Bertie's younger brother who was getting a little over-zealous.

'Her name is Nancy and she was raised in the workhouse.'

'Why, of course yer must bring the lass along, she'll be more than welcome,' the kindly woman said in her usual big-hearted manner, although Ginny couldn't help but notice that Bertie didn't look any too pleased at the idea. Ginny said her goodbyes then and agreed to let Bertie walk her part of the way home. She would be glad of his company today as she had no wish to bump into Giles while she was on her own, not after the way he had behaved earlier.

'I don't know why you'd want to bring your roommate along,' Bertie grumbled as he strolled along with his hands in his pockets, kicking at the loose stones in the lane. 'We get little enough time together on our own as it is.'

That was exactly why Ginny had suggested that Nancy should come along although she didn't tell him that, of course. She had no wish for their relationship to go beyond friendship, but she didn't want to offend him.

'Well, let's just see how it goes,' she said tactfully and Bertie was obliged to agree as he didn't want to appear churlish. He insisted on walking her all the way to the huge gates of Lamp Hill Hall, and once there, Ginny leaned across and pecked him on the cheek.

'Take care then till the next time I see you,' she called as she tripped quickly away down the drive. She turned just once when she'd run some distance and was relieved to see that Bertie had gone. Now she could slow her steps and make the rest of the journey in a more leisurely fashion. She had almost reached the turn in the drive that led to the servants' entrance when a sound made her stop in her tracks and the hairs on the back of her neck stand up. It sounded like an animal in pain. With her heart in her throat she croaked, 'Is anyone there?'

Nothing but silence answered her and she began to think she had imagined the noise and was about to move on when it came again – from a cluster of ash trees at the side of the drive.

Approaching cautiously, she peered into the gloom and then started as she saw a shape lying on the ground. It wasn't an animal at all but a person, if she wasn't very much mistaken. Hurrying now, she rushed towards it and dropped to her knees heedless of the dirty ground. It was a man. He was lying in a foetal position and he was groaning.

'What's happened to you?' she asked, placing her hand gently on his arm. Another groan was her only answer but she sensed that he was seriously hurt.

'Just lie there while I run to get help.' She knew that she would never be able to move him on her own and in a second she was racing across the lawns with her skirts bunched in her fist.

Cook looked up, startled, from her seat at the side of the fire when Ginny burst into the kitchen. It had been a rare old afternoon one way and another, what with Master Giles coming back bloodied after a fall from his horse. Not that it didn't serve him right. She was only surprised that the mare hadn't thrown him before, the way he laid that blasted whip on the poor creature.

'Whatever's wrong, lass?' she asked. 'Yer look like death warmed up.'

'Th ... there's a man ... he's lying injured at the side of the drive,' Ginny gasped breathlessly.

'What do yer mean, injured? What's up wi' him?'

'I can't see, it's too dark in the trees, but he needs help.'

'Right.' Cook looked towards Nancy, who was thumbing through an old magazine of the mistress's in a rare quiet moment, and ordered, 'Nancy, run across to the stables an' tell Ted an' some o' the stable lads that their help is needed. You'll have to go along of 'em, Ginny, to show 'em where he is.'

'Of course.' Ginny dumped her empty basket and tore back to the drive, waiting impatiently for Nancy and the men to join her. Whoever the stranger was, he had seemed to be gravely injured.

Ted Ventriss had been enjoying a quiet Sunday-afternoon nap at the side of the fire but had come immediately and was snapping his braces into place as he demanded, 'So what's to do then, lass? Can't a soul get a bit o' peace round this place even on the Sabbath?'

Ginny haltingly told him and the stable lad he'd

brought with him about the man she had found injured and while she spoke, she led them towards him. 'He's in there,' she said pointing a wavering finger towards the ash trees.

She stood there while Ted went in to take a look. He quickly reappeared, to tell her: 'Me an' Johnny are goin' to carry him round to the kitchen. It's too dark to see what's up wi' him out 'ere so you go off, young lady, an' tell Cook to stand by.'

Ginny obediently raced away again and Cook began to cover the old overstuffed sofa that stood to one side of the fire with a clean but tattered sheet. Minutes later, puffing and panting, Ted and Johnny appeared. Ted had the man beneath the arms and Johnny was holding his legs. Between them they managed to get him laid on the sofa.

Cook looked sombrely down at the dark red stain on his shirt. 'He's bleeding badly,' she said. 'Johnny, you'd best ride for the doctor, lad, though I doubt this poor fellow will last till he gets here, lookin' at the state of him.'

Johnny hastened away to saddle a horse and do as he was bid, while Cook ordered Nancy to fetch her a bowl of hot water and some clean rags. The stranger was mumbling incoherently by now.

'We'd best get this shirt off him an' look at the damage,' Cook said. 'Help me, would yer, Ted? We need to keep him as still as we can till the doctor gets 'ere.'

Ginny chewed nervously on her lip as she stared down at the stranger. He was a good-looking young man, about twenty years old, she gauged,

212

but she couldn't remember seeing him hereabouts before. He looked to be quite tall with thick brown hair that curled about his head, and he was well built.

Cook undid his shirt and with Ted's help the women managed to peel it off him, moving him as least they could.

'Christ,' Ted choked when his bare chest was revealed. 'The poor bugger's been stabbed!'

They all stared in horror at the wound on his chest, which was pumping blood, and Nancy began to cry softly.

'Go to your room,' Cook ordered her sternly as she lifted a rag and pressed it on the open wound. Somehow she had to stem the flow. 'I can't be doin' wi' your hysterics at the minute, girl. An' you, Ginny, run through an' tell the master what's happened. We should let him know, seein' as this poor chap were found on 'is land.'

Ginny was back with the master within minutes and he looked gravely on as Cook valiantly attempted to stop the bleeding.

'Do any of you have any idea who he is or what he was doing on my land?'

They all shook their heads and a tense silence settled on the room. Ginny kept glancing anxiously at the clock on the mantelshelf, every minute feeling like an hour, but at last the kitchen door opened again and Dr Gifford appeared.

'Right, give me some space, please,' he commanded as he threw his coat haphazardly down and opened his black bag, and they all stepped back, only too pleased to hand the responsibility of the wounded stranger to him.

'Well done, Mrs Martin,' he told the cook eventually. 'If you hadn't slowed the flow of blood down, I reckon this young fellow would have been a goner by now.'

Ginny was surprised. She had grown accustomed to knowing the woman simply as 'Cook'; it had never occurred to her that she might have a name.

'From what I can see, this chap has been very lucky indeed. Had the instrument that stabbed him gone another couple of inches to the side, it would have entered his heart and that would have been the end of him. As it is though, it may have pierced his lung. It's too soon to tell.'

'Should we get him to the hospital?' Mr Walton-Hughes asked. 'We could take him there in the carriage.'

'Thank you, but no. He needs to be kept as still as possible, for now at least,' the doctor advised. 'Would it be possible to keep him here? I'm afraid it's going to be touch and go for a while.'

'Of course. Ginny, would you go and ask Barbara to prepare a bedroom?'

Ginny nodded and shot off to find the girl. What a day it had been, one way or another. She certainly wouldn't be sorry when it was over.

Chapter Twenty-One

For the next twenty-four hours the stranger's life hung in the balance and he lay in a fever, with Barbara and Millie taking it in turns to nurse him. Then finally, in the early hours of the morning, his eyes fluttered open and he asked croakily, 'Wh ... where am I?'

'Shush now an' rest,' Barbara told him kindly as she continued to bathe his forehead with cool water. 'You're safe now. Just try to sleep.'

The young man looked around at the unfamiliar room and frowned. What was he doing here? Then slowly everything began to come back to him and he screwed his eyes tight shut. It was that bastard Giles Walton-Hughes who had done this to him. There and then, he vowed to get well – and then he would make Giles pay.

Barbara had skipped away to inform Mrs Bronson that the stranger was now conscious, and a few minutes later she returned with the housekeeper who smiled at him.

'Ah, so you're back with us then. You gave us quite a scare for a time. How are you feeling?'

'Not so good,' he croaked truthfully, but then what could he expect, after Giles had nearly done for him?

Mrs Bronson gently lifted his head from the pillow as Barbara poured a trickle of water into his mouth. He swallowed some then began to choke, sending waves of hot pain through his chest.

'That's enough,' the older woman warned as she laid him down. Then, softly: 'Can you tell us your name?'

He opened his mouth to answer her but then clamped it shut again. For now he preferred to remain anonymous.

'I ... I can't seem to remember.'

'Don't worry,' the woman soothed. 'Your body has had a terrible shock. I'm sure it will all come back to you in time. The doctor will be in to check you again this afternoon. But for now, try to get some sleep.'

That, he discovered, was a very easy order to follow ... within seconds he was sound asleep again.

'Well, at least he's come round,' Mrs Bronson muttered to Barbara. 'Let us hope he'll start to recover now.'

She left the room then, leaving Barbara to watch over the patient, and once out on the landing she almost collided with Master Giles who was in a right old temper.

'I don't know why we have to have that stranger here in the house,' he raged. 'He could be anybody. Why – he might try to slit our throats while we sleep.'

'I doubt there's much chance of that, Master Giles.' Mrs Bronson stared at him primly. 'He is so weak he can barely lift his head from the pillow at present, let alone murder us in our beds. And it was your grandmother and grandfather's express wish that we should tend to the young man until he's able to be moved. He was found on their pro-

216

perty, after all, so they feel they have an obligation to him.'

'Rubbish!' Giles made to open the bedroom door but Mrs Bronson laid a restraining hand on his arm.

'I'd rather you didn't go in there just yet,' she said firmly, wondering why Giles should have such an interest in the patient. 'The young man is sleeping at present and he must not be disturbed.'

Giles glared at her but stomped away like a sulky child as she heaved a sigh at his retreating figure.

Dr Gifford called as arranged later that afternoon and expressed his satisfaction at the patient's progress. Like the housekeeper he wasn't overly concerned about the temporary memory loss.

'Try to get him to take a little thin chicken soup and make sure he has plenty of fluids,' he advised before he left, and Mrs Bronson hurried away to instruct the cook.

Meanwhile, in the bedroom the doctor had just left, the patient lay admiring his surroundings. The room was decorated in a soft silver grey with dark blue velvet curtains that brushed the darker grey and blue Turkey carpet on the floor. The bed was a four-poster with a deep feather mattress, and he had never seen anything quite so grand, apart from in illustrations.

I could get used to this way of life, being waited on and pampered, he thought to himself. And why not? Giles owes me now after what he's done to me. Unaware that his enemy had been lurking nearby, a smile played at the corners of his mouth as he began to devise a plan.

At that moment, Ginny was being shown into the drawing room where the mistress was waiting for her. Celia was sitting at the window with a thick rug across her legs, staring out towards the lake.

Ginny's heart was in her throat as she wondered what she might have done wrong. She had not seen the mistress since their first meeting a little while ago, and when Mrs Bronson had come into the laundry to inform her that she was wanted, she'd flown into a panic.

'Don't look so worried, my dear,' Mrs Bronson told her as Ginny followed her through the enormous hallway. 'I'm sure there is nothing amiss.' She paused then at the wide double doors and after knocking she entered and Ginny heard her say, 'Virginia is here to see you, ma'am.'

'Ah, thank you, Anna. Do send her in.'

Mrs Bronson beckoned to her and once Ginny had gone inside, the housekeeper discreetly took her leave.

'Virginia, do please come over here where I can see you,' the mistress said, patting a chair at the side of her.

Ginny crossed the room and perched gingerly on the edge of the chair like a little bird which might take flight at any second.

Celia eyed her thoughtfully for a moment before saying, 'I have a little proposition I'd like to put to you, dear. You see, the thing is, I've been thinking for a while about getting a companion for Miss Diana. Someone round about her own age to keep her company and act as a lady's maid to her. She's coming to the age where she needs someone to help her with her hair and her dressing. I had thought of advertising the post but then Anna – Mrs Bronson – suggested you, Virginia. You are clearly a very intelligent girl. You can read and write and I think you would be good for her. As you are aware, Diana is handicapped in as much as she is deaf and that can lead to frustration, so she can often be difficult. Do you think you could handle her moods, and is the position something you would consider?'

Ginny was so taken aback at the prospect of the job being offered to her that her mouth gaped and she was rendered temporarily speechless.

'Well, I don't know,' she stammered honestly. 'I've never done anything like that before so I'm not sure if I would be any good as a companion.'

'On the contrary, I think you would be very good at it,' Celia said. 'Diana has a limited vocabulary as you are aware, because of her deafness, but if she were to have a full-time companion I'm sure her speech would improve. She can lipread and enjoys reading so there is something you have in common to start with.'

'But I don't have much idea of what is fashionable and I've never dressed anyone's hair in my life. Apart from my little sister's when she was alive...' Ginny ended with a catch in her voice as the memories flooded back. She had used to love plaiting little Betty's hair.

Celia smiled at her sympathetically. Anna had told her something of the girl's background and she felt sorry for her. Meanwhile Ginny's mind was working busily as she stared down at her work-reddened hands. What the mistress was offering her was a rare opportunity and she would be a fool not to accept it – but what about Charlie, she asked herself. She had planned only to stay long enough to save up her train fare to Hull, but it wouldn't be so easy to walk away from this job, would it?

'Of course, your wages would increase commensurately,' Celia went on temptingly, 'and naturally we would have to get you some new, more suitable clothes. So what do you think, my dear? Is it something you would consider?'

'But what about my work in the laundry – who would do that?' Ginny fretted.

Celia smiled. 'Oh, I'm sure we could soon find someone suitable from the village to take over that job,' she assured her. 'But I think it would be a lot harder to find someone as suitable as you for the post I'm offering. Please do say you'll give it a try at least. We could perhaps say a month's trial?'

'Very well, ma'am, and thank you,' Ginny said, making a hasty decision. At the end of the day, this was just too good an opportunity to miss and the thought of not having to spend any more time sweating in the laundry was welcome indeed. 'When would you like me to start?'

'Well, I've already spoken to Diana about it and she seemed quite taken with the idea,' Celia confessed. 'Mrs Bronson suggested that if you agreed to take the post, you could start straight away. She is willing to take you into town this afternoon in the carriage to have you fitted for some new outfits, and whilst they're being made I'm sure Diana could find you some gowns that you could borrow. You would also be sleeping on the same floor as my niece in a room adjoining hers, so that you can be on hand whenever she needs you. But one word of warning: as I told you, Diana can be difficult so you must be firm with her from the start otherwise she'll walk all over you.'

A little grin played at the corners of Ginny's mouth. That didn't frighten her, not after all she'd been through during the last few months. But it was all happening so fast she could scarcely take it in.

'I'm sure I shall be fine,' she said with a confidence she was far from feeling. It wasn't the thought of being Diana's companion that scared her, it was the prospect of the complete change in status that she was about to face.

'Then if we've decided, I suggest you go and get your things from the room you share with Nancy, and then Mrs Bronson will show you where you will be sleeping from now on. Then after lunch she will take you off to the dressmaker.'

'Yes, ma'am.' Ginny dipped her knee and left the room in somewhat of a daze to find Mrs Bronson waiting for her.

'So what has been decided?' the housekeeper asked as they walked side by side towards the kitchen.

'I've agreed to give the post a month's trial.'

'A very wise decision, I'm sure,' Mrs Bronson told her, looking quietly pleased.

Then Ginny changed the subject when she asked, 'How is the man I found injured?'

'Coming along slowly.' Mrs Bronson pushed the green baize door open and they walked into the heat of the kitchen. 'He is conscious now and the doctor hopes that he will make a full recovery in time. All thanks to you, of course. If you hadn't found him when you did, he might have died from exposure, let alone from loss of blood.'

Ginny shrugged, feeling she deserved no credit at all. Anyone would have run for help as she had.

Cook was rolling pastry at the table and almost dropped her rolling pin when Mrs Bronson informed her, 'Virginia is to become Miss Diana's companion as of today, Cook, so she will be collecting her things and moving to the room adjoining Miss Diana's immediately.' Then turning to Ginny, she said, 'I shall be back here shortly when you've collected your things together, to show you to your new room.' And then she left.

'Well, I'll be!' Cook looked quite astounded. 'You've dropped on yer feet, ain't yer, me gel? Though I doubt it will be all plain sailing. Miss Diana's got a rare old temper on her when she's a mind.'

'I can handle her,' Ginny answered, while still trying to take it all in. 'But I hope I'll still be able to have my meals down here with all of you.'

'Bless your 'eart,' Cook beamed. 'Yer a good gel, Ginny, an' yer deserve to go up in the world. Yer were wasted in that laundry wi' a mind like you've got. But now run upstairs an' get yer stuff together. Yer don't want to keep Mrs Bronson waitin', now do yer?

And so Ginny did as she was told, with very mixed feelings. It took her no time at all to bundle up her few belongings. She wished that she could have seen Nancy to explain personally but supposed that the cook or one of the other staff would have told her what was happening by the time she herself got to see her.

Mrs Bronson was waiting for her when she returned to the kitchen and instantly began to lead her through the main house and up the sweeping staircase. It was like entering another world and Ginny could only stare about in awe.

'Your room is along here,' Mrs Bronson said, stopping halfway down a long landing on the first floor. She threw a door open and Ginny's jaw dropped. This was easily twice the size of the room she shared with Nancy up in the servants' quarters, and there was a fire burning in the grate.

'Either Barbara or Millie will see that the fire is kept alight for you,' Mrs Bronson explained. 'Cleaning out grates is not part of a companion's job.' She then pointed to a door. 'That leads into a bathroom, then into Miss Diana's room,' she told Ginny. 'You will be allowed to use the facilities in there.'

Ginny could hardly believe it. An indoor bathroom! All she had ever known was a tin bath in front of the fire once a week or a strip wash in cold water since she had come to the Hall. She stared about her. A highly polished brass bed covered in a floral bedspread stood against one wall and the long window was covered in curtains in the same material. A huge rug took up most of the floorspace and around the edges of it the wooden floor was so shiny that she could almost see her face in it. There was a wardrobe, a chest of drawers and a small desk and chair set in front of the window, and Ginny thought it was one of the most beautiful rooms she had ever set eyes on.

She sensed the housekeeper watching her closely and forced a wobbly smile.

'Right then, I'll leave you to get settled in.' The woman smiled at her kindly. She was always polite to Ginny, although the girl had noticed that she could be quite short with the rest of the staff if they so much as put a foot wrong. 'Then after lunch I'll get Mr Grady to drive us into town.' With that, she quietly left the room, leaving Ginny looking stunned at this change in her fortunes.

Chapter Twenty-Two

It was mid-afternoon. Giles had prowled about his bedroom for most of the day, hoping for an opportunity to get into the wounded man's room unnoticed. The housekeeper and the girl had gone off in the carriage somewhere and the doctor was presently examining the patient under Barbara's watchful eye. The physician seemed to have been in with him for ages, but at last Giles heard the bedroom door open further along the landing, and peeping through the gap in his own door he saw the doctor leaving. Thankfully, Barbara was with him. This was his chance. He waited until he heard their footsteps receding on the stairs then scuttled along the landing and slipped into the man's room.

The patient was propped up on pillows with his chest heavily bandaged; his face was a ghastly white from losing so much blood. He was exhausted following the doctor's examination but even so his eyes flickered open when he heard someone enter the room – and on seeing Giles, he sneered: 'I wondered how long it would be before you turned up to see what damage you'd done.'

Giles' hands clenched into fists at his side. 'I obviously didn't do enough if you're still here,' he spat. 'What the hell do you think you're playing at?'

'Just enjoying a bit of mollycoddling,' the man replied with a sardonic grin. 'And you need to be nice to me, otherwise I might regain my memory and tell your grandfather who did this to me.'

'*You swine!*' Giles was trembling with temper but now the man's face became hard.

'No, it's *you* who is the swine,' he said hoarsely. 'How would your grandparents feel if I was to tell them the reason why I was coming to see you, eh? That you raped my sister when she came to inform you that she was carrying your child! You did it to terrify her into keeping quiet – then when I come to confront you, you do this to me! You try to murder me – and damn nearly succeed, you devil! I don't think they'd be very pleased, do you?'

'So what exactly do you want, Peters?'

The young man winced as he shifted slightly. He was still in a great deal of pain. 'I want justice,' he hissed, gritting his teeth, 'for my sister and for me. And I intend to get it, one way or another.'

Giles took a threatening step towards him but

at that moment they heard footsteps outside on the landing and Giles halted, his face showing his frustration. It would be so easy to finish the bloke off at the moment in his weakened state. A cushion over his face and it would all be over in a matter of minutes. It was getting him alone for long enough to do it that was the problem.

'I know what you're thinking,' the sick man gloated, 'but don't even think of trying it. I asked the maid for a pen an' paper earlier on an' I'm going to write a letter telling why I'm here and what you did to me. I shall ask her to keep it safe then and should anything happen to me, to hand it to your grandfather.'

'Why, you low-life bastard, I've a good mind to—' Giles' cry of rage halted abruptly when Barbara breezed into the room with writing materials in one hand and a number of clean towels in the other. She bobbed a curtsey when she saw Master Giles there, but ignoring her completely he pushed past her and left the room, slamming the door resoundingly behind him.

Barbara shivered. What disgraceful behaviour in a dangerously ill man's room. 'What did Master Giles want?' she asked the young man in the bed.

He shrugged, sending waves of agony through his chest. 'I ... I think he just wanted to meet me,' he croaked as sweat stood out on his forehead and Barbara rushed forward to gentle him back on to the pillows.

'You know what the doctor said,' she scolded. 'You're to rest and speak as little as possible. You still have a long way to go if we're to get you back on your feet.'

He gave a small nod, and before she'd put the clean towels away had drifted off to sleep again.

His next visitor was Diana. She had seen everyone speaking of the young man who had been found injured on their property and was curious to see him for herself. Just before dinnertime that evening she made her way to his room, knocked and quietly entered.

Millie was sitting at the side of his bed feeding him spoonfuls of chicken broth, and glancing at the latest visitor she then looked directly at Diana and mouthed, 'Good afternoon, miss.'

Diana inclined her head then pointed at the man in the bed. 'What is his name?' she asked in her harsh voice.

The stranger frowned. She was a pretty enough lass admittedly, and beautifully dressed, but there was something about her voice that wasn't quite right. She was almost shouting and her words all came out in one tone.

Again Millie looked directly at her. 'We don't know what his name is, miss. He's lost his memory.'

Diana regarded him steadily from her violet-blue eyes before turning abruptly and leaving the room as suddenly as she had entered it.

'Who was that?' Peters' eyes were fixed on the door and he could still smell her perfume.

'That's Miss Diana, the mistress's niece. She came here when she was still small after her parents were killed. She's deaf, as you probably noticed, so when we speak to her we have to look directly at her so she can read our lips.'

'I see. That must be quite a handicap to cope with.'

Millie nodded. 'I suppose it is, though I doubt it will prevent the gold-diggers from seeking her out. When she reaches twenty-one she's going to be one of the wealthiest women in the county, from what I've heard. Her parents left a fortune in trust for her and her brother, although I suppose she'll be able to claim hers earlier if she marries. But hush now and eat some more of this broth. Cook made it specially for you and you'll never get strong again if you don't eat.'

Peters obediently opened his mouth like a little bird but his mind was otherwise engaged. So Giles' cousin was set to inherit a fortune, was she? There and then he began to form a plan. The information Millie had unwittingly given him could just prove to be the making of him. He'd already realised that it would be in his own interests to put on a show if he was to milk this situation for all it was worth, and that wouldn't be difficult. He had spent long enough with the toffs from the boarding school in Rugby to mimic how they talked and behaved, and he intended to do just that. If he played his cards carefully this could prove to be a very interesting interlude indeed. With a weak smile he once more submitted to Millie's nursing. Yes, despite his sufferings and those of his dear sister, what had happened to him at Lamp Hill Hall could prove to be very advantageous indeed!

In the town Ginny's head was spinning as she watched the dressmaker jot down a list of all the clothes she had been measured for. She dreaded to think how much they were all going to cost, but Mrs Bronson had insisted she should have everything she might need.

'After all, as Miss Diana's companion you will be expected to accompany her when she goes out, and the mistress is keen to get her out and about visiting now,' the woman had told her firmly. And so they had spent the whole afternoon choosing materials for various gowns and Ginny felt as if she had been measured from head to foot.

She was to have two day gowns, to be worn over a modest cage crinoline. For these they had chosen a light silver-grey, very fine wool material. Mrs Bronson had then decided that one should be edged with cream and pearl buttons, the other with burgundy braid. Then there was a day dress suitable for visiting in a striking shade of blue. There was underwear, petticoats and stockings as well as new nightwear and a thick warm cloak that would have a fur lined hood. A beautiful Paisley shawl, in rich tones of russet, blue and amber, was chosen to keep her warm in the house. Mrs Bronson seemed to have a far better idea of the fashions than Ginny did, so she was happy to leave the decisions to her for the most part, although she had enjoyed choosing the material for her best gown. Then had come the shoes, soft leather lace-up boots for walking out in the day, satin slippers for more formal occasions and even a pair of soft house shoes that made her feel as if she was walking on air. Ginny knew that she was going to feel like a princess in all her new finery and had to keep pinching herself in order to believe that this was really happening.

'So when do you think you can have all this ready, Mrs Docherty?' Mrs Bronson enquired, pulling her gloves on when at last they had done.

The plump dressmaker scratched her chin thoughtfully. 'Well, if me and my seamstress both work on them I should say around two weeks. Will that be acceptable?'

'Very,' Mrs Bronson replied. 'Just send your bill to Mr Walton-Hughes. Good day to you.' She then beckoned to Ginny and the girl followed her from the shop and over to the carriage where young Johnny Grady was stamping his feet to try and keep warm as he waited for them.

It was on the way back to the Hall that Ginny ventured, 'Mrs Bronson, have you had any news of my brother?' Despite the excitement of the new job and the pleasure of choosing all her new clothes, she would have given them all up in a sigh if it meant being with Charlie again.

A closed look came down across the woman's face and she pointedly looked away out of the carriage window. 'Not yet, I'm afraid, but be assured that he is being well cared for.' Then, keen to change the subject she went on, 'Diana recently went through her clothes and discarded some gowns that she no longer wears. As you have probably noticed, she's rather spoiled so she has many others and I'm sure there will be some amongst them that will fit you for now until your own are ready. We will look through them as soon as we get back so that you can begin your new job tomorrow suitably attired.'

Ginny nodded, feeling subdued. The thoughts of Charlie and how much she missed him had taken the shine off the day. Even so she was aware that, with the rise in her wages, she would be able to go and find him all the sooner so she tried to quell her impatience.

When they arrived back at the Hall, Mrs Bronson led Ginny up to the attics where she opened a large trunk of clothes.

'This one is a bit summery for the time of year but it should do you for now,' she commented as she passed Ginny a pretty pale green muslin dress sprigged with tiny rosebuds. 'And your shawl will keep you warm. Here is another, thicker one. Why don't you go and try them on? You and Miss Diana look to be about the same size so they should fit. Whilst you do that I'll go and borrow a cage and a few petticoats for you, I'm sure she won't mind.'

They made their way back through the attic, past furniture covered in dust-sheets and trunks of long-abandoned objects. Once in her lovely new room Ginny tried on her recently acquired finery. Although the items were second-hand they were still by far the finest clothes she had ever owned and she gazed at her reflection in the mirror that hung above her chest of drawers in astonishment. The green gown was fractionally short but other than that it fitted her perfectly, and she could soon let the hem down when she got a few spare minutes. She ran her hand across the pretty material wonderingly before then slipping on the other gown, which was blue. The bodice had a row of tiny silver buttons running all up the front of it, and full sleeves. The material was so soft after the coarser linen that Ginny was accustomed to wearing, and the skirt showed off her slender waist before flowing out over the cage. She then wiggled her feet into the soft suede house shoes that Mrs Bronson had insisted she should have. A quick tidy of her hair and she was ready to go down to the kitchen to show off her new finery.

'Well I'll be! I scarcely recognised yer,' Cook gasped when Ginny appeared looking slightly embarrassed. The girl could only imagine what the rest of the staff would think about her promotion; she was still shocked about it herself. 'I don't reckon Barbara's going to be any too pleased about this,' the older woman added. 'She's allus had ideas above her station.'

Ginny had dreaded this kind of reaction. 'I didn't ask for the post,' she muttered defensively.

'Hmm, well, I fully approve of it. To my mind yer far too pretty an' clever to be shut away in the laundry, an' havin' someone her own age might do Miss Diana the power o' good.' Cook paused. Then: 'Though I wouldn't want to be in your shoes when she 'as one of her tantrums.' She chuckled. 'She's been known to wallop more than a few o' the governesses the master employed to look after 'er, and on more than one occasion. So take a word of advice, pet. Start as yer mean to go on, an' if she clobbers yer – why, clobber 'er one back.'

Ginny looked horrified. She could never imagine herself doing that. But then she'd never imagined herself being employed as a lady's companion. It just went to show, you never knew what life had in store for you, and she began to think about the following day with very mixed emotions.

Chapter Twenty-Three

Joe Peters woke that evening to find himself alone. Now that his fever had broken, the maids had been instructed to go about their duties when they were not needed. Glancing around the comfortable room, he smiled and stretched without thinking – then winced with pain. It was then that the door opened a fraction and he saw Diana solemnly peeping in.

'Come in, I was just getting lonely,' he called out, making sure she could see his lips.

As she approached the bed, he studied her. The young woman was actually very pretty, which he considered a bonus if the plan he was hatching was to come to fruition. She was an heiress, and should he charm her into falling in love with him, everything she owned would be his if they married. He would never have to work again and would live in luxury for the rest of his life. The thought was appealing, although he felt no physical attraction towards her, despite her pretty face. From the odd comments he had gleaned from the maids she was a spoilt little bitch – and then, of course, there was the handicap of her deafness. But he was sure that he could cope with that. After all, once they were married he didn't have to see that much of her and he could live the life of Riley with money in his pocket.

Diana stopped at the side of the bed and looked at him shyly. Apart from her brother and her cousin and the occasional friend they brought home from school, she had mixed with very few young people and was fascinated by this young man. He was very handsome and she found herself blushing at the thought. Everything about him was intriguing. Who was he? Where had he come from? What had he been doing on her uncle's land?

'You are looking very nice,' he said, and was gratified to see her blush deepen. This was going to be even easier than he had thought. With a smile he patted the side of the bed, inviting her to sit down next to him, and she willingly did so.

'Well done, my dear. You look just right,' Mrs Bronson commented approvingly when Ginny appeared in the kitchen the next morning ready to start her new job. Ginny had taken Miss Diana's cast-off clothing into the laundry room the evening before and had pressed it all, and now in her new blue gown and with her shining hair neatly pinned she did indeed look very tidy.

'You can begin by taking Miss Diana's breakfast tray up to her,' Mrs Bronson went on. 'She informed me last night that she didn't wish to sit at table with her father this morning. But seeing as it's your first day in your new role, I shall accompany you. She is, of course, aware that you will be looking after her as of this morning, but it might be easier for both of you if I do the formal intro-

234

ductions. After all, she has only ever seen you when passing the laundry room before, and I imagine this will be as awkward for her as it is for you.'

'Thank you.' Ginny was grateful for the offer. She'd wondered what she should say, or whether she should just walk into the young woman's room unannounced.

The cook quickly prepared a tray and when it was ready Mrs Bronson nodded to Ginny to pick it up and follow her.

'As soon as Miss Diana has been served and the introductions have been made, you can come down and have your own breakfast,' she informed the girl as Ginny carefully followed her up the stairs with the heavy tray, intent on not dropping it or spilling anything. She heaved a sigh of relief when they reached the landing with no mishaps. As she had quickly discovered, the wide skirt, cage crinoline and layers of petticoats were all well and good, but climbing stairs with a loaded tray was no easy task whilst wearing them. When they reached the door to Miss Diana's room, Ginny was surprised when Mrs Bronson opened it a fraction and wafted it to and fro before entering the room.

'It's to give her fair warning that we are coming in,' the woman explained. 'It's no good knocking, is it, if she's unable to hear us.'

'I see.' Ginny nodded, understanding the sense in what the housekeeper said. She also understood more than ever then that it would be strange getting used to working and spending time with someone who was deaf.

As Ginny hovered in the doorway, Mrs Bronson crossed to the enormous sash-cord window and swished the curtains aside, and as light flooded into the room, a lump beneath the blankets of a beautifully carved four-poster bed gave a low groan.

'What time is it?' Miss Diana grunted as she emerged bleary-eyed from beneath the covers.

Mrs Bronson turned to face her full on and mouthed, 'It's time for your breakfast. Your new companion has it here for you.'

The girl's eyes flicked towards Ginny, who hurried forward as Diana pulled herself up on to her pillows.

'I'll put it here for you, shall I?' Ginny said, then flushed as she realised that she hadn't looked directly at Miss Diana as she said it. This was going to be even harder than she'd imagined. Looking the girl full in the face she repeated herself and this time Diana nodded and allowed Ginny to place the tray across her lap. There was no word of thanks but then Ginny knew that as she was still only a servant she should expect none.

'Ginny will be back to help you dress and do your hair when you've finished with your breakfast,' Mrs Bronson mouthed at her and Diana nodded again. As Ginny followed Mrs Bronson from the room she could feel Diana's eyes boring into her back and her nervousness increased. Perhaps she would have been better off staying in the laundry, after all. At least Phyllis had been easy to work with. She had a vague feeling that Miss Diana wasn't going to be so amenable.

'In future when you excuse yourself from Miss Diana or leave the room you should dip your knee,' Mrs Bronson scolded gently. 'After all, you are still only her companion and you must remember at all times that she is the mistress's niece.' Her face softened somewhat then as she saw Ginny's dismay and she went on, 'However, that doesn't give her licence to bully you. Should she raise her hand to you, come and find me immediately and I shall talk to her.'

Raise her hand to me! Ginny gulped in shock and suddenly her old job in the laundry was even more appealing. What have I let myself in for? she asked herself. But it was too late to go back now and she knew she should give it a try, at least.

When she and Mrs Bronson arrived back in the kitchen they found Cook preparing another two breakfast trays.

'This one is fer the mistress, an' this one here is fer the young man.' She shook her head disapprovingly then before confiding, 'Though I can't understand why he's still here. After all, he's out of danger now, so surely he's well enough to be moved to the cottage hospital?'

'The crisis may have passed, but our guest is still very far from well – and he still can't even remember who he is,' Mrs Bronson said sternly. 'It wouldn't look very charitable of the master and mistress if they were to just turn him out, especially as he was found on their property, now would it?'

'I suppose not,' Cook said grudgingly. 'But we should at least give him a name till he remembers his own, surely? I never know how to refer to him. An' how long does Dr Gifford reckon it will be afore his memory does come back anyway?'

'He has no idea. It could be a day, a month or even longer,' Mrs Bronson sighed. 'But you do have a point about calling him something. I'll suggest it to the mistress when I take her tray up to her and see what she thinks.'

Slightly mollified, the cook returned to what she was doing as Ginny sat down to help herself to a dish of thick creamy porridge.

When she'd finished, she hurried back upstairs and wafted Diana's door to and fro as she had seen the house-keeper do, and was rewarded when Diana grunted, 'Come!'

Closing the door behind her, Ginny remembered to bob her knee as the girl watched her warily. She was standing at an armoire that was crammed with all manner of delightful dresses ranging from day wear, to riding habits and ballgowns.

'May I help you choose?' Ginny asked, remembering to wait until the girl was looking directly at her.

They stood side by side as Diana discarded one outfit after another, then she dragged one out. It was a soft burgundy wool trimmed with cream piping, with a very full crinoline skirt, and Ginny guessed that this one gown alone had probably cost more than she could earn in a whole year.

'Petticoats are in there.' Diana pointed towards another smaller armoire on the opposite wall and then disappeared off into the bathroom, leaving Ginny to choose what she should wear underneath it.

It took Ginny almost half an hour to get her new mistress into her clothes. Diana had insisted that

Ginny should pull her stays as tight as they would possibly go until Ginny began to wonder how the girl would possibly manage to breathe. She did have to admit that her waist was tiny, however, when she had finally buttoned up Diana's dress for her. The girl then plonked herself down at her dressing table, and taking up an ornate silver-backed brush Ginny began to brush her hair for her. It was thick, with a tendency to curl, and the most glorious shade of golden-blonde that Ginny had ever seen. She felt quite envious as she glimpsed her own poker-straight jet-black mane in the mirror. Miss Diana's hair was so much more fashionable than hers.

'Shall I put it up for you?' she mouthed, staring at her new mistress in the mirror. Diana had lifted a magazine by now and was already glancing through it. She merely nodded, so Ginny began. She soon found that dressing hair wasn't as easy as she had thought and she was all fingers and thumbs as the hair pins flew everywhere. The silky strands seemed to possess a life of their own. But then at last she was done and she stood back for Diana to examine herself. It was far from perfect but then it was her first attempt so she didn't consider she'd done too badly.

Diana gazed at it critically for a second then grunted before turning her attention back to her reading, so Ginny took that as a sign that it was acceptable and set about tidying the room. There seemed to be clothes flung everywhere. She sorted them into piles. One for the laundry, one for those items that needed pressing. The others were carefully hung away – and not once did

239

Diana even glance towards her. Ginny began to feel as if she was invisible but then Diana suddenly flung her magazine aside and motioned Ginny to follow her.

When Diana marched up to a bedroom door and opened it, Ginny was confronted with the grievously injured stranger she had found in the grounds some days before. She recognised him instantly – although he, of course, didn't know who she was. He was propped up on pillows with his empty breakfast tray laid across his lap and he smiled at Diana as she entered. But then he caught sight of Ginny behind her and interest sparked in his eyes. He wondered who she was. This girl was nowhere near as fashionably dressed as Diana, but there was something about her that appealed to him instantly – not that he would show it in front of Diana.

'Good morning.' He held his hand out and Ginny was shocked to see the change in Diana as she hurried towards him. She was positively simpering, and a blush had spread across her cheeks.

'This is my new maid,' Diana told him with a careless gesture in Ginny's direction. 'She is the one who found you on the night you were attacked.'

'Then I must thank you.' The young man then held out his hand to Ginny. Unsure what to do, Ginny reluctantly moved towards him. She didn't care for the way his eyes raked her from top to toe; it reminded her of Bill Parsons leering at her while she was working at the pie shop. She shook his hand briefly and was dismayed when he held it for a fraction longer than was necessary. Diana seemed oblivious to her discomfort and Ginny moved away from the bed again just as soon as she was able to.

'Go and tidy my room,' Diana commanded airily without glancing at her. She was far too busy keeping her eyes firmly fixed on the young stranger and Ginny could see that she was smitten with him.

Despite the offhand way her new mistress had addressed her, Ginny was only too happy to oblige and she scuttled away. Up until now Diana had done nothing to endear herself to her. In fact, she had spoken to Ginny as if she was of absolutely no consequence – but Ginny couldn't help but feel a little sorry for her. It couldn't have been easy for her, growing up in a silent world after the trauma of her parents' death and Ginny was determined to try her best to make the girl's world a little easier even if Diana was hell-bent on making things as difficult as she could.

It was almost an hour later when Diana reappeared, and by then Ginny was going through her chest of drawers, sorting out the contents. Everything had been thrown haphazardly into them and it would take her weeks to work her way through the muddle. There were so many drawers that Ginny was sure Diana could have clothed the whole village of Whittleford with the contents. The girl was smiling dreamily, and at sight of her new companion she said, 'He is very handsome, don't you think?'

Ginny gulped and looked away, not knowing quite how to answer. 'I'm not sure, miss. I didn't really take that much notice.' Suddenly realising her mistake again, she looked back at Diana who was glaring at her, and repeated what she had said. This, she thought wryly, was going to take some getting used to, and suddenly it felt like it was going to be a very long day.

That afternoon, following Dr Gifford's visit, James strode into the invalid's bedroom and told him, 'The doctor is very pleased with your progress, young man. It appears you have been extremely lucky. The knife that stabbed you missed your major organs by a whisker.'

Joe laid a hand across the bandages still tightly wound about his chest and offered a weak smile. 'Yes, I suppose I was.' He wiped his brow dramatically. 'But if only I could remember how it happened and who I am!'

'I'm sure it will come back to you, given time,' James said kindly. 'But in the meantime the staff think it might be a good idea if we gave you a temporary name till you can remember your own. How would you feel about that?'

Joe nodded. 'I think it's an excellent idea. Did you have any in mind?'

'Hmm.' James stroked his chin thoughtfully before suggesting, 'How about Ben? That's a pretty straightforward sort of name. Unless you'd prefer something else, of course? It is only temporary, after all.'

'Ben is fine,' Joe assured him. He quite liked it: Ben, Benjamin, had a nice ring to it. 'And thank you, sir, for all you are doing for me. I do appreciate it.'

'Think nothing of it. Just concentrate on getting well. And now I'll bid you good afternoon. I'm going to take tea with my wife. Is there anything you would like?'

'Oh no, sir ... thank you. You've done quite enough for me as it is.'

James nodded and strode from the room, and once the door had closed behind him, Joe smirked. He was actually feeling much better – to the point where he felt he might have been capable of getting up and dressed. But he had no intention of doing that yet. He was quite happy where he was for now, lying in bed and being waited on hand and foot, thank you very much, and he had every intention of dragging it out for as long as he could. Not long after, Millie appeared with his afternoon tea tray. The cakes and little savouries on the china stand looked delicious and he could quite easily have eaten the lot, but it wouldn't do to appear to have his appetite back so he waved them aside and instead took little sips of his tea, aided by Millie who held the cup to his lips.

'It is so frustrating, feeling so weak,' he croaked and she instantly smiled sympathetically at him.

'Don't you worry now. We'll get you back on your feet, but you mustn't try and rush things.'

'I suppose you're right but I do *so* hate being such a burden on everyone.' He sighed dramatically and dropped back against the pillows and was gratified when Millie gently stroked his arm.

'That's enough of that silly talk. You're no such thing. Now you have a little nap and I'll be back later with some nice chicken broth for you.'

'Very well.' He obediently closed his eyes as Millie crept from the room.

In her sitting room at that moment, Celia was asking after him.

'He's doing as well as can be expected,' James informed her, helping himself to a generous slice of Cook's delicious fruit cake, 'but it's going to take some time I think. We've decided to call him Ben until he remembers who he is. The staff were finding it difficult, not knowing what to call him.'

'Mm, I can understand that. And is there still no sign at all of his memory returning? No snippets from his past that have come back to him?'

'Not as yet, but Dr Gifford says it is still very early days. Physically he should make a full recovery now but his memory loss is a different thing entirely.'

'I see. Then we must keep him here as long as it takes,' she said quietly and her husband nodded in agreement.

Chapter Twenty-Four

By the end of the first week in her new job, Ginny was beginning to wish she had never accepted it and would have gone back to her old job in the laundry like a shot. Anything was better than the way Miss Diana treated her. The problem was, Mrs Bronson had already taken on a girl from the village who came in each day to do the rough laundry now so she was stuck with her role as companion.

'What's happened to yer eye, lass?' Cook asked horrified when Ginny came down with Miss Diana's empty breakfast tray early one morning.

Placing the tray on the table, Ginny raised her hand and touched her face.

'I was clumsy enough to spill a little tea on to the tray as I placed it on Miss Diana's bed for her, and she lashed out,' Ginny said. She had no doubt her eye would be black by lunchtime – and this wasn't the first time, although thankfully she had been able to hide the other bruises. The first had come when Diana had been looking for a handkerchief in her drawer, only to find that Ginny had moved them to another one when tidying so that they were all neatly together. She had turned and pinched Ginny's arm spitefully as a torrent of abuse that could be heard all over the house had streamed from her lips. Ginny had been shocked speechless. Diana had then yanked the drawer out and thrown the whole of its contents across the floor, screaming at Ginny to do what she was paid for before she stamped off to see Joe – or Ben as he was known to her. The second time had come when Ginny was lacing her stays one morning.

'Tighter!' she had yelled, and when Ginny had tried to explain that they would go no tighter, the girl had punched her, catching Ginny just above the wrist.

Now Ginny slumped miserably down on to one of the kitchen chairs and rested her chin on her hand as she confided, 'I wish I'd never agreed to do this job. Miss Diana talks to me and treats me like I'm dirt on the bottom of her shoes and I don't know how much longer I can take it. I mean, I know that I'm there to look after her and I'm happy to do that, but ever since I started she's not lifted a finger to help herself. She'll be expecting me to wipe her backside next,' she ended dismally.

Cook tutted in disgust. 'You shouldn't have to put up with that sort of behaviour!' she exclaimed. 'Why don't you have a word with Mrs Bronson?'

'What would be the point?' Ginny sighed.

'The point in what?'

The pair of them started. They hadn't heard anyone come into the room but as they glanced towards the green baize door they saw Mrs Bronson standing there.

'Look at Ginny's eye,' Cook said hotly. 'Miss Diana just did that to her – an' it ain't the first time she's lashed out neither! It ain't right. The little madam wants her backside tannin', if yer were to ask me, an' I'd like to be the one to do it.'

Crossing over to Ginny, the housekeeper put her hand beneath the girl's chin and lifted her head, and as she saw her swollen eye she winced before telling the cook, 'Get some raw steak on that immediately, please. It's supposed to be good for bruising. Meanwhile I'm going to have a word with the mistress. You should have told me about this before, Virginia,' she scolded Ginny. 'I did ask you to let me know if she raised a hand to you. It appears to me that Miss Diana is treating you more like her own personal slave than a companion, and it's high time she was put in her place. This sort of behaviour is totally unacceptable.'

'Oh no ... *please*. It will just make things worse,'

Ginny cried but Mrs Bronson was adamant.

'No one gets paid enough to be knocked about, Virginia,' she said resolutely. 'So now if you will excuse me.' And with that she sailed grim-faced from the room with her back as straight as a broom-handle, leaving Ginny to bite her lip with anxiety. What if the mistress took her niece's side? She could find herself out of a job – and then how would she ever earn enough to go and search for Charlie?

The cook interrupted her gloomy thoughts when she bustled over with a lump of raw steak dripping blood.

When Ginny looked at it doubtfully the older woman waggled a finger at her. 'Are you goin' to start bein' difficult an' all now? This is fer your own good, so hold still, will yer?'

Tipping Ginny's head back, the woman slapped the steak none too gently on her eye. Well, if it wasn't bruised before it certainly will be now, Ginny thought to herself. She was still in the same position some minutes later when Mrs Bronson reappeared.

'I've spoken to the mistress,' she informed her, 'and Mrs Walton-Hughes is in total agreement that Diana must not be allowed to treat you like that. She has promised to have a word with her, but meantime, should this happen again I want you to come to me *immediately*. Is that quite clear?'

'Yes, Mrs Bronson,' Ginny agreed meekly as Cook lifted the disgusting lump of bloody meat from her eye and gently wiped the area clean with a cold wet cloth. The day certainly hadn't got off to the best of starts and all she could do now was hope that it was going to improve.

When Ginny returned to Diana's room late in the afternoon to help her change for dinner, she found the girl in a strange mood. Glancing furtively at Ginny's eye she flushed but said nothing as she sat down at her dressing table for Ginny to dress her hair. This was one of the things that Ginny was still struggling with. Practice makes perfect, she consoled herself, but all the time she was working she was aware of Diana's eyes on her in the mirror. Perhaps she's feeling guilty – and so she should, she thought, but she made no comment. With luck it would be the last time the girl raised her hand to her.

Along the landing in the small sitting room attached to her bedroom, Celia was telling her husband about what had gone on and he tutted with annoyance.

'I hope you gave Diana a good telling-off,' he said as he stretched his legs out towards the fire. He had spent a long day at the quarry going over the books with the manager there and he was dog tired. The last thing he needed was to come home to trouble.

'I did,' Celia said gravely. She adored Diana but she was well aware of her faults and was not prepared to allow her to be violent towards a member of her staff. 'And to be honest her attitude towards Ginny isn't the only thing that's troubling me.'

'Oh?' James raised his eyebrows as he sipped at the glass of whisky in his hand. He wasn't a great drinker but he always enjoyed one before dinner.

'It's the young man we are caring for,' Celia told him gravely. 'Ben, I believe you decided to call him, didn't you?'

James nodded. 'Yes, we agreed on that name just until he remembers his real one. But what has he done? He hasn't even been able to get out of bed yet, as far as I know.'

'It isn't what he's done exactly, it's Diana. According to Anna, she's spending a fair amount of time in his room each day. It concerns me, James. After all, we have no idea who he is or where he has come from and Diana is so innocent. She's led such a sheltered life. I fear that when he's recovered and he goes back to wherever he came from, she's going to be broken-hearted.'

'Hmm, I see what you mean,' James admitted. 'But what can we do about it? I can hardly ban her from his room if he is happy to see her, can I? He must get very bored lying there and he's probably just glad of the company.'

'I suppose so,' she agreed slowly. 'But I thought I'd just express my reservations so that you can keep an eye on things. Giles is clearly not happy to have him here either, although I have no idea why he should feel that way. It isn't as if he's having to look after him, is it? Yet he asks me daily if Ben is well enough to leave yet. Don't you find that strange?'

James sniffed. 'Giles is in a permanent bad humour since he was expelled from school. Probably because he knows that in a few months' time he is going to have to start to work for his living. What does he expect me to do? I can hardly turn the poor chap out into the cold in the state he's in, can I? I'm afraid the problem is that both he and Diana have been thoroughly spoiled, and now we are reaping the rewards.'

'They've been treated no differently to Sebastian – and he isn't giving us any trouble, is he? And I've told Diana in no uncertain terms that if she so much as lifts her finger to Ginny again, she will find herself in serious trouble.'

Her husband's lips twitched with amusement. 'I think you've rather taken to that girl, haven't you, my dear?'

Celia shrugged her frail shoulders and he suddenly noticed that she seemed to have lost yet more weight and decided to have a quiet word with Anna about it at the first opportunity. Perhaps she would be able to coax her mistress to eat a little more.

'Will you be coming down to dinner this evening?' he asked then.

Celia shook her head. 'I think I'll just have a tray up here tonight if you don't mind, darling. It quite upset me having to chastise Diana and I feel drained.'

'Very well. I'll just pop along and get changed then, but I shall be back up to see you after dinner. We might have a game of chess if you're not too tired?'

She nodded and gave him a gentle smile as he strode from the room, but once out on the landing the answering smile slid from his face and he decided to pay their guest a visit. Celia did have a point. They had no idea who Ben truly was or where he had come from – and the very last thing he wanted to do was place Diana in any danger.

When he tapped on Ben's bedroom door and entered his room, it was to find Diana sitting at the side of his bed with a wide smile on her face. The couple had clearly been laughing at something but Ben nodded respectfully towards him as Diana rose to her feet.

'Good evening, sir. Diana was just telling me some amusing tales about some of the governesses she has had.'

So it's Diana now, is it? James found himself thinking as alarm bells went off in his head. Celia was clearly right. The girl's cheeks were flushed, her eyes were shining and she seemed to be having trouble dragging her eyes away from the invalid.

'Was she now?' James' smile gave nothing away. 'So how are you feeling today?'

'A little better, thank you, although the doctor did say when he called this afternoon that he thought it was too soon for me to think of getting out of bed until the wound begins to heal. He's afraid I'll start the bleeding off again.'

'Then of course you must follow his advice,' James stated. 'And is there still no sign of your memory returning?'

Joe raised a hand to his forehead. 'Nothing as yet, I'm afraid. Everything is just a void.'

'Ah well, I'm sure it will come in time.' Then turning to Diana, James suggested, 'Isn't it time you were making your way down to the dining room, my dear?'

The smile left her face but after glancing at Joe one last time she obediently left the room, leaving a waft of expensive French perfume behind her.

'I hope my niece isn't troubling you,' James said then but the young man carefully shook his head.

'It's quite the reverse, sir. She is wonderful company and she helps to pass the time away. It can get very lonely lying here all day... Not that I'm not grateful to be here,' he ended quickly.

'Hmm!' It wasn't quite the answer James had been expecting and he began to wonder if the young man wasn't smitten with Diana too. The problem was, what could he do about it if he was? But then deciding that he was worrying over nothing, James too turned to follow his niece. The chap would likely be gone in no time once he'd recovered; no doubt they would never see him again, so there was no point in looking for trouble. As Celia had mentioned, Diana had led a very sheltered life so she was probably just glad of a diversion and happy to have someone close to her own age to spend time with. In a slightly more settled frame of mind he made his way down to dinner.

Chapter Twenty-Five

At last it was Ginny's day off and she had promised to walk into Nuneaton with Nancy. Shortly after lunch, as she was getting ready to go to the Watkins', she asked Nancy, who had come into her new bedroom to wait for her, 'Were you thinking of visiting your family today? If not, you might like to come along with me. Mrs Watkins is a dear soul and I know you'd be more than welcome.'

Nancy, who had been in the process of looking around the lovely room, glanced at Ginny warily, wondering if she had guessed her secret – that there was no family and never had been. She had no idea that the cook had already told Ginny of her circumstances. Her first instinct was to refuse the invitation but then, without warning tears welled in her eyes and she bowed her head.

'Yer know, don't yer?' she said in a choked voice. 'That I've been fibbin' about me family I mean.'

Ginny instantly crossed to her and draped her arm about her shoulders, but she said nothing. If Nancy wanted to confide in her then she would. The girl was crying properly now and Ginny could feel her shoulders shaking.

'Me mam an' dad don't really live in Swan Lane,' she confessed eventually. 'I just said that 'cos I was embarrassed to tell yer that I were brought up in the workhouse. I don't even know who me mam an' dad was, but when I were a little girl I used to dream that they'd come fer me one day. They never did, o' course, so I made a family up in me head.' She looked at Ginny to judge her reaction before saying timidly, 'I bet yer think less o' me now, don't yer. I'm just a foundlin'.'

'I don't think less of you at all,' Ginny said with complete sincerity. 'I just feel very sorry that you had to go through that and I'm flattered that you confided in me. But now dry your tears and say that you'll come, won't you? The Watkins are a lovely family and I don't like to think of you sitting here on your own.'

253

Nancy sniffed and swiped at her nose with the back of her hand before smiling through her tears.

'All right then – if yer quite sure they won't mind? And Ginny, yer won't tell 'em what I just told yer will yer?'

'I wouldn't dream of it,' Ginny promised, although she had already mentioned the workhouse to Mrs Watkins. Nancy began to tidy her hair with a beaming smile on her face. Ginny's invitation had been totally unexpected and very much appreciated.

'I'm so excited,' she chattered as they eventually set off down the drive in their Sunday best. The clothes that Mrs Bronson had ordered for Ginny had duly arrived and she felt very grand in her smart new day dress and the warm fur-lined cloak the woman had insisted she should have. Nancy looked very pretty too in her straw bonnet and warm coat but Ginny was feeling increasingly guilty. Her reasons for inviting the other girl along had not been entirely selfless, after all. If Nancy was present, she would not have to spend any time alone with Bertie, for as much as she liked him and greatly valued his friendship, she had no romantic inclinations towards him whatsoever. She sometimes wished that she did, for Bertie would make someone a wonderful husband one day. He was kind, dependable and hardworking, but she knew that that someone would never be her.

'So what are Bertie and his family like?' Nancy asked yet again.

'You'll love them. They're a very happy, normal

254

family, and great fun,' Ginny told her.

Nancy was almost skipping along in her excitement. 'The only family I've ever known have been Cook and the people at the Hall,' she sighed. 'Not that I'm complaining, of course. I was very lucky to be chosen to work there. The master and mistress are very fair compared to how the servants get treated in a lot of the other big houses.' The confession had cemented their friendship and now Ginny felt very protective towards her, even though Nancy was only a year younger than she herself was.

They walked on until they came to the four-sailed windmill perched on the top of Tuttle Hill, then began to follow the edge of the deep quarry that led down to Abbey Green, at which point Nancy suddenly asked, 'Is Bertie your young man, Ginny?'

Ginny laughed and shook her head. 'No, not at all, although I like him very much. The only young man I want in my life at present is my little brother – when I can find him that is.' Thoughts of Charlie turned to thoughts of her father and she suddenly wondered how he was. Tears clogged her throat for a few moments. As they walked along she told Nancy a little of her past, but rather than feel sorry for her the girl was envious.

'You may have lost a number of your family,' she said quietly, 'but you were so lucky to have had them, if only for a time. I don't even know who my ma and pa were, and it wasn't much fun growin' up in the workhouse, believe you me. But then you'd know that, wouldn't you, if your dad grew up in there too. I dare say he told you how gruesome it was.'

Ginny had felt guilty then and supposed that Nancy was right. At least she had fond memories of happier times when the family had been all together whilst poor Nancy had nothing. Ginny had been shocked to discover that Nancy was only a year younger than herself, for she was so small. Now that she was seventeen, Ginny felt very grown up. Charlie would be a year older too, she suddenly realised, and felt an ache of longing. If only Mrs Bronson could find an address for him, she could at least write to him but as yet the woman had offered her no further information on his whereabouts...

Her gloomy thoughts were interrupted then when she saw Bertie waiting for her at the end of Swan Lane. She waved and he hurried forward to greet them.

'Hello, you must be Nancy. Ginny's told us all about you.' He stuck his hand out and as Nancy solemnly shook it, her cheeks flooded with hot colour. 'I'm Bertie.' He then turned his attention to Ginny but Nancy was unable to tear her eyes away from him and found that her heart was beating like a drum. He was simply the most handsome young man she had ever seen – and a policeman into the bargain!

'Come along then, ladies, Mam's got the tea ready,' he told them cheerily as he stepped between them and held his arms out for them to slip theirs through. They then went on their way with Bertie and Ginny chattering away nineteen to the dozen.

Nancy hardly said a word but when they

arrived at Bertie's home she stared around at the family in awe. Their home was far from stylish but it was spotlessly clean and there was a large fire roaring in the grate and laughter in the air.

This is just how I imagined family life would be, Nancy thought wistfully as Mrs Watkins took her hat and coat and gave her a pleasant smile.

'So you're Nancy, Ginny's little friend, are you? I'm Bertie's mother – you can call me Esther. Well, you're very welcome, lass. Come over to the fire and warm your hands now,' the kindly woman invited, then wagging a finger at the youngsters she warned them, 'Pipe down, you lot, afore I bang your heads together.'

Nancy couldn't help but smile. The children took not a blind bit of notice of her, which told her that their mother's bark was far worse than her bite. They all sat around the fire then, eating hot buttered crumpets washed down with sweet tea, followed by slices of a delicious walnut cake that Cook had given the girl to bring. Nancy felt as if she had died and gone to heaven and wished that the afternoon would never end, but it did, all too soon, when Ginny told her, 'We ought to be going now. Cook will only fret if we're out after dark.'

Nancy took her hat and coat from Mrs Watkins. 'Thank you so much for inviting me,' she told her fervently. 'I can't remember when I last enjoyed meself so much.'

The woman was touched. Ginny had told her that the poor lass had been brought up in the workhouse and she felt heart-sorry for her. It must be terrible to have no idea where you had come from and she was a comely little thing. Not as strikingly pretty as Ginny, admittedly, but there was something about her that Mrs Watkins found strangely endearing.

'You just come along of Ginny whenever you've a mind to,' she told her, planting a kiss on the girl's cheek. 'It's been a real pleasure to meet you and I hope these little tearaways haven't put you off.'

'Oh no, they haven't – not at all,' Nancy told her hastily. 'And I'd love to come again, if you'll have me.'

She and Ginny said goodbye to the rest of the family and soon after they were plodding back up Tuttle Hill. Ginny decided that it was too late in the day to pay Mrs Bevins a quick visit this month. A thick fog had come down and they could barely see a hand in front of them so Bertie insisted on walking them all the way back to the gates of the Hall again.

'And just remember what I said,' he instructed Ginny once they were there. 'If that spoiled little madam raises her hand to you again, you just make sure you give as good as you get and whack her one back!'

Ginny giggled. 'I don't think that would go down too well. After all, I am only her maid.'

'That still doesn't give her licence to thump you!' Bertie replied angrily. 'It seems to me she needs bringing down a peg or two.'

He said his goodbyes then and the girls set off along the drive.

'Bertie is ever so nice, an' ever so handsome, ain't he?' Nancy sighed dreamily.

Glancing at her, Ginny grinned. 'I've got a feeling you've taken a fancy to him,' she teased, causing the other girl to blush.

'No, I ain't,' she denied hotly. 'I were just sayin' he's nice. You must think so too, else why would you go to see him on yer day off?'

'Yes, he is nice,' Ginny agreed. 'But I promise you, Nancy: I could never feel anything more than friendship for Bertie.'

'Well, that's a shame then, 'cos from the way he looks at you, he clearly thinks of you as more than a friend.'

They fell silent then as they continued on their way.

At that moment, Giles was standing at the side of Joe's bed with his teeth bared in aggression. Just the sight of the scoundrel could send him spiralling into a rage. He'd been waiting for over an hour for his cousin Diana to leave the room, and he was none too happy about this development. She seemed to be spending more and more time with Peters.

'You are well and truly getting your feet under the table, aren't you?' he spat.

Joe grinned lazily as he swallowed the last piece of the delicious cake Millie had brought to him earlier and slowly licked his fingers.

'Just makin' the best o'things,' he drawled with a grin. He didn't have to put on his posh voice in front of Giles.

'Not for much longer you won't, because the doctor told my grandfather today that you're well on the mend now.'

'Physically maybe,' Joe mocked him. 'But there's still no sign of me *memory* returnin' – an' I don't think your grandparents would be heartless enough to turn me out when I don't even know who I am or where I'm from.' The smile slid from his face then and his eyes hardened as he ground out, 'Grow up, man. This could work to your advantage too.'

Giles frowned. 'How?'

Joe rolled his eyes to the heavens. 'Don't yer see? If I can get your cousin to marry me, her inheritance will become mine. Now I happen to know that as well as gettin' my sister into trouble you also have a few chaps from school who are baying for yer blood because of unpaid gambling debts. Is the penny dropping now?'

When Giles stared at him vacantly, Joe sighed. 'For God's sake, man! I could make sure that you were comfortable too then. Unlike your cousins who will inherit when they're twenty-one, you have no inheritance to come for years ... possibly until something happens to yer grandparents. Do yer *really* want to have to work for a livin'? Married to Diana, I could make sure that you had enough to do what yer liked. Are yer gettin' the picture now?'

When Giles still looked doubtful, Joe laughed. 'I can be very generous when I have a mind to be,' he said. 'But it would mean us working together. So – what do yer say? I'm prepared to keep me mouth shut about why I was here an' the fact that it was you who stabbed me, if you're prepared to play the game. And think of the scandal if it were to come out that it was you who

260

stuck me. Attempted murder, that was. Death by hanging, I don't doubt. Or you'd be shipped off to Tasmania. What would people say if they knew that I was only coming to defend me poor sister's honour? What would *that* do for yer family's reputation, eh?'

As much as he hated to admit it, Giles knew that Joe was right. His grandfather would never forgive him, and the idea of having more money in his pocket was appealing. He was dreading starting work, especially as James had warned him that he would receive no special treatment just because he was the boss's son. 'You'll start at the bottom and work your way up as I had to,' he had told him sternly. 'That way, you'll appreciate what you have.'

Giles shuddered as he pictured himself with the labourers working knee-deep in sludge in the bowels of the quarry with his hands blistered and his back breaking. Perhaps what Joe was suggesting wasn't such a bad idea, after all. It wasn't as if Diana was going to be forced into anything, was it? She was clearly infatuated with Joe – that was as clear as the nose on his face. But then he doubted it would all be as straightforward as Joe assumed it was going to be. He couldn't see his grandparents being very enamoured of her marrying someone who didn't even know where he belonged, for a start-off. They'd always harboured hopes that she would marry someone wealthy who would keep her in the manner to which she'd become accustomed, and spoil her as they had. He doubted Joe would do that. In fact, his reputation went before him in his home village and he was known to chase anything in a skirt, which made Giles all the more indignant that he was defending his sister's honour. Still ... it was worth considering.

'I have to go now or I'll be late for dinner,' he informed Joe, turning on his heel.

Joe smirked. 'You do that. And think on what I said.'

Stepping out on to the landing, Giles shuddered as he pictured the filthy cottage Joe had come from. Diana would be appalled if she could see it, but then she was never likely to, was she? And at the end of the day it wasn't him who would have to live with Joe, was it? Thoughtfully he straightened his cravat and headed for the stairs.

Dinner was a solemn affair. Celia had chosen to eat in her room as she wasn't feeling well again and Giles appeared preoccupied. For her part Diana seemed intent on getting away from the table as soon as possible and her uncle suspected it was so that she could hurry back to the young invalid's side. He had other plans for her, however, and as soon as Barbara began to clear the table, he told his niece, 'I would like to speak to you in my study, my dear.'

The girl looked vaguely surprised but rose and followed him all the same, wondering what he might want.

Once in his study he motioned her to a chair and when she was seated he snipped the end from a cigar and lit it, blowing a ring of blue smoke into the air. He then took a seat directly in front of her where she could clearly see his face and began: 'Diana, I am concerned about the amount of time you are spending in the young stranger's bedroom. The maids cannot always be present and it doesn't seem er ... correct.'

'What do you mean?' Her face had taken on the sullen look that usually preceded a tantrum.

Struggling to choose the right words and finding this extremely uncomfortable, James blustered on, 'He is a young man, my dear. And you are a young lady. He seems pleasant enough, admittedly, but it isn't right that a young lady should spend so much time in a young man's bedroom unchaperoned. So perhaps in future if you must visit him, you could make sure that someone is in the room with you. Your new maid, perhaps?'

'*Bah!*' Diana bounced out of her chair, setting her golden ringlets dancing, a sulky expression on her pretty face. 'But he gets lonely. What is wrong with me going to see him?'

James sighed as he ran his fingers through his hair. 'As I've said, it's not seemly for a young girl of your age to spend so much time in a man's sickroom. I'm not saying that you shouldn't go at all... Just take Ginny with you when you do, there's a good girl.'

With a face like a black thundercloud, Diana twirled about and left the room in a swish of satin skirts, slamming the door resoundingly behind her. The last thing she wanted was to have her rag-tag maid in attendance every time she visited Ben!

James blew out a long plume of smoke. Women! 'That was a disaster,' he whispered to the empty room.

Chapter Twenty-Six

'You are to come along to Ben's room with me *right now!*'

Startled, Ginny glanced up from the book she was reading to see Diana standing in her bedroom doorway. She looked to be in a rare old mood but Ginny's face remained calm as she answered, 'Sorry, miss, but this is my day off unless you'd forgotten. I was planning to have a quiet evening reading.'

'*I don't care!*' Diana stamped a daintily shod foot.

Ginny hesitated. She knew that she had every right to refuse the girl. It was her day off, after all, as she'd pointed out. And yet she had endless patience with Diana despite the way the young madam treated her. However she had no desire to enter the stranger's room any more than she had to. There was definitely something about him that made her skin crawl. Perhaps it was the way his eyes seemed to undress her – but only when Diana was occupied, Ginny had noticed. She'd been looking forward to a lazy evening curled up with *Mary Barton* by Elizabeth Gaskell, one of the books that Mrs Watkins had borrowed from the free reading room for her, but it looked like Diana had other plans for her. Even so, Ginny decided that it was time she stood her ground.

'I shall be quite happy to come with you in the

morning, but as you can see I'm reading at present,' Ginny said politely but firmly.

Diana's face was suddenly suffused with colour and she seemed to swell to twice her size.

'You will do as you are told and come with me instantly!' she screamed in a voice that could be heard all over the house. She wasn't used to not getting her own way as was more than evident as she advanced on Ginny threateningly.

'No, I'm sorry but I shan't.' Ginny returned her attention to the page that she was reading, hoping that Diana would storm away, so she was taken by surprise when she saw the girl sweeping towards her from the corner of her eye.

'How dare you defy me! You will look at me when I am speaking to you and you will do as you are told, damn you!'

Ginny raised her eyes but she had no chance to say a word before a resounding slap on her cheek made her head snap back on her shoulders.

For a moment she saw stars but then she leaped to her feet, as angry as Diana was – and before she could stop herself, she returned the blow.

Diana squealed like a scalded cat as Ginny's palm connected with her cheek and for a split second it was hard to say who was the more shocked of the two of them. At that moment, Mrs Bronson appeared in the doorway and demanded, 'Whatever is going on in here? We can hear you on the other side of the house!'

'Sh ... she hit me!' Diana sobbed as she pointed a trembling finger at Ginny whilst holding her stinging cheek with the other hand. She was almost bursting with indignation. It was the first

time in her whole life that anyone had ever laid so much as a finger on her in anger.

Mrs Bronson's mouth opened and shut like a goldfish's. 'But why ever would she do that?' And then as she looked towards Ginny she had her answer. The girl had gone unnaturally pale, which made the livid red marks of a hand-print stand out on her cheek all the more.

'Did you hit her first, Miss Diana?' Holding the girl's arm firmly she forced her to look at her.

'She wouldn't do as she was told,' Diana answered sullenly.

'I see. Then I think we had better discuss this with your aunt,' Mrs Bronson told her as she almost dragged her towards the door.

Left alone, Ginny sank back on to her chair, tears rolling unchecked down her cheeks. She already deeply regretted what she had done but it had been an instinctive reaction and there was nothing she could do about it now. She had no doubt at all that very shortly she would be summoned to the mistress's room and dismissed – and then where would she go? And just when she'd begun to think that she might soon be in a position to go and search for Charlie. She picked up the book she had been reading when Diana struck her from the floor where it had fallen and placed it neatly on the small desk, wondering if she should start to pack. At least then she could leave with a little dignity rather than have everyone know she'd been dismissed. Crossing wearily to the wardrobe, she removed her bag and began to pack only the clothes she had arrived with.

She didn't want to be accused of theft on top of

everything else. She had almost finished when Mrs Bronson appeared, stopping short when she saw what Ginny was in the process of doing. She looked shocked but then said calmly, 'Would you come with me, Virginia? I would like a word with you in my room.'

Ginny didn't see much point in it, but she followed her all the same. Mrs Bronson had always treated her fairly – more than fairly if truth be told – and she didn't want to upset her as well before she left.

Once downstairs, Mrs Bronson ushered her ahead of her into her tiny sitting room but before she could say anything, Ginny began, 'I know why you have brought me here but I shall save you the embarrassment of having to dismiss me. I've almost finished my packing and I shall be gone before–'

Mrs Bronson held up her hand to stem the flow of words and Ginny clamped her mouth shut. The redness was fading from her cheek now and a large purple bruise was already beginning to form.

'Would I be right in thinking that Diana struck the first blow?' the woman asked gently.

'Yes, she did. It was because I told her I wouldn't go to Ben's room with her as it was my evening off. Even so, I realise I shouldn't have hit her back but I'd had enough of her bullying ways, and...'

Her voice trailed away as she saw a wide smile on Mrs Bronson's face.

'Between you and me, you have just done what every single member of staff here has yearned to do for a very long time,' she confided. 'And I certainly hope you won't be going anywhere. I am not condoning your use of violence, of course, but because it was done in self-defence it can be excused. The mistress feels exactly the same and has asked me to apologise to you for Miss Diana's unforgivable behaviour. Mrs Walton-Hughes is with her now and she is none too pleased with her, believe me.'

'You mean, I'm not going to be dismissed?'

Mrs Bronson shook her head. 'Not at all, although I wouldn't recommend doing it again. The problem is, Miss Diana has no idea of how to behave, which is why the mistress employed you to be her companion. I am not making excuses for her, far from it, but she has rarely mixed with anyone apart from the members of this household and she has a very great deal to learn before she is introduced into polite society. I fear you shall have your work cut out trying to tame her, my dear, but I hope you are still willing to try. She isn't all bad, I assure you. She just gets very frustrated.'

Ginny felt ashamed. 'So what will happen now?' she asked meekly.

'The mistress has told Diana that she must apologise to you and warned her in no uncertain terms that if she ever lays a hand on you again, she will be in very grave trouble indeed. Can you be gracious enough to accept an apology?'

'Of course.'

'Then let this be an end to it. But now I think we need to attend to that cheek. I'm afraid you're going to have a terrible bruise and possibly another black eye as well. Come along. Cook seems to have a cure for all ills.' And then suddenly she did something completely unexpected. She placed her arm about Ginny's slim shoulders and gave her an affectionate little hug.

'You've had an awful time of it lately,' she said, 'but let us hope that things will start to improve for you from now on.' Then turning back into the efficient housekeeper that Ginny had come to know, she stepped aside, folded her hands primly at her waist and beckoned Ginny to follow her into the kitchen.

'So what was all the palaver earlier on about?' Joe asked Giles when he entered his room later that evening.

'It was Diana,' Giles answered. 'Apparently she struck that little maid of hers and the maid slapped her back. It was all hell let loose for a time there.'

Joe chuckled. 'She's a right little hell-cat, ain't she? But I'll soon tame her. I wouldn't mind taming that maid of hers either – she's a right tasty little piece – but not until after I'm married, o' course. Have you thought on my proposition?'

'I have, as it happens, but I think there is a major problem,' Giles answered glumly. It went seriously against the grain to have to be civil to this lowlife but he supposed he had no option.

'Oh yes?' Joe cocked his head to the side and peered at him as Giles strode to the window and stood looking out into the dark night. Barbara or Millie would be here at any moment to close the curtains and build up the fire, so he'd better say what he'd come to say as quickly as possible.

'The thing is, how can you marry anyone if you keep up the pretence of not knowing who you are or where you came from? You could already be married, as far as anyone knows. Surely you would have to have a legitimate name on a marriage certificate?'

'Hm, yer have a point there,' Joe agreed, as his forehead creased into a frown. 'I hadn't thought o' that. What do yer suggest we do about it?'

There was no time for Giles to answer for at that moment Barbara tapped on the door and entered the room breathlessly carrying a large scuttle fill of coal. Giles made no move to help her. Toting coal was a servant's job and he had never got his hands dirty – with work, at least – in his whole life.

The girl's eyes briefly rested on him but then as they flicked to Joe, her face lit up. She was more than a little taken with him – and she was sure that he was taken with her too, if the way his hands strayed across her backside every time she went to straighten his bed was anything to go by.

'Evening, sir. How are yer feelin' tonight?' The words were addressed to Joe so with a curt nod, Giles strode from the room. The conversation they had been having would have to wait for another time.

Back in her room Ginny was feeling mixed emotions: relief that she hadn't been dismissed, shame because she had retaliated to Diana, and regret that she had ever agreed to take the post of the young woman's companion in the first place.

The work in the laundry had been backbreaking, true, but everything had been so simple there and she'd quite enjoyed sharing a room with Nancy. It staved off the loneliness, having some-one to talk to, and sometimes they had chattered away to each other for hours. She knew she could never have that sort of a relationship with Diana. Any attempt at a conversation with her was hard work because the girl couldn't hear what she was saying and Ginny often had to repeat herself two or three times, which always made Diana frustrated.

A tear trickled down her cheek as she thought of her father and Charlie. Rarely an hour went by when she didn't think of one or the other of them. She worried about how her father was coping in prison and prayed that Charlie was being taken good care of. And now she had something else to fret about, for she couldn't see Diana being in a very good mood when she reported for duty to-morrow. The girl would no doubt be angry because her aunt and uncle had scolded her for being violent. Diana seemed to think she could behave any way she chose and Ginny dreaded how she might treat her the following day. Still, there was no point lying sleepless worrying over something that couldn't be changed so Ginny got undressed, wincing when her hand caught her cheek. Despite the salve Cook had dabbed on it, it was swollen and extremely painful and would probably be even worse by morning. With a sigh she clambered into bed, lay on her uninjured side and tried to sleep.

Chapter Twenty-Seven

Despite being advised by the housekeeper to take the following day off and rest, Ginny was up and dressed at her usual time the next morning. After dragging a brush through her thick black hair she twisted it into its usual plait then surveyed herself solemnly in the small mirror. Just as Cook had warned, one of her eyes was almost closed, encircled by a black and purple bruise. She raised her hand to gently touch it and sighed. She had slept little the night before as she deliberated on what she should do. Suddenly she didn't want to be here in the Hall any more, and the thought of just taking off and going in search of Charlie was sorely tempting. Even so, the people in the house, apart from Diana, had been kind to her and she didn't like the thought of leaving until they had at least found someone to replace her.

I'll talk to Mrs Bronson about it the first opportunity I get, she promised herself as she positioned the full skirt of her dress over the crinoline cage, then reluctantly turned and left the room. It was time to face Diana.

When she had made her way down to the kitchen to prepare the girl's breakfast tray, Cook gasped the minute she set eyes on her.

'Eeh, lass, are yer quite sure you feel up to workin' today? No one would blame yer if yer spent the day in bed. I could get Nancy to bring

272

yer meals up on a tray.'

Ginny smiled at her. 'Thank you, Cook, but I'll be fine. And Nancy has more than enough to do as it is without waiting on me. It's not as if I'm ill, although I admit I feel as if I've been in a boxing ring. But never mind, staying busy will keep my mind off things.'

'Well, if yer sure.' Cook sniffed and went back to the pan of kidneys she was preparing for the master's breakfast. He always liked a good meal to set him up for the day.

Nancy was at the sink washing pots and she smiled sympathetically at Ginny as she said, 'Well, at least you walloped her back – and serves her right! She hit me once when I dropped some toast off her breakfast tray on to her bedroom floor.'

Ginny shook her head. 'I think a lot of her trouble is frustration.'

'Huh! Don't you go makin' excuses fer her poor behaviour now,' Cook said, waggling a spatula in Ginny's direction. 'If yer ask me, the little devil could do wi' havin' her arse slapped.'

Nancy and Ginny exchanged an amused glance as Ginny set about preparing Diana's tray. When it was ready, she lifted it and said, 'Well, wish me luck then. I have a feeling I'm going to need it this morning.'

'Don't you go taking none of her mouth now,' Cook warned her sternly. 'If she starts her games again just drop her tray on her table an' go an' fetch Mrs Bronson. She won't stand no nonsense off her.'

'I will,' Ginny promised as she sailed from the

273

room balancing the contents of the tray ahead of her.

Outside Diana's door she transferred the tray to one hand then after cautiously wafting the door to and fro she entered the bedchamber and placed the tray down on a small table before crossing to the window and swishing aside the curtains.

Here we go then. She prepared herself as if she was going into battle but surprisingly there were no muttered curses from the direction of the bed this morning. Instead Diana emerged from beneath her blankets and eyed her warily.

'I'm sorry, Thursday,' she muttered as she saw the state of Ginny's eye. She herself had not escaped unscathed. Ginny noticed a faint bruise staining her pale cheek although it was nothing like as bad as the injury she had inflicted on Ginny.

'Let's try and forget about it, shall we, miss?' Ginny waited for Diana to pull herself up on to the pillows then placed the tray on her lap and went to throw some coal on to the fire. Barbara obviously hadn't been in there as yet and the fire was almost out. That job done, she brushed the dust from her hands and catching Diana's eye she told her, 'I'll go through to the bathroom and draw your bath for you now, miss, while you have your breakfast.'

'Thank you, Thursday.'

Ginny was stunned. It was the first time Diana had ever bothered speaking to her as if she was a person rather than a slave. Perhaps the day wasn't going to turn out to be as bad as she had expected.

Once everything was ready in the bathroom she

then went back into the bedroom and asked, 'What would you like to wear today, miss?'

Again very meekly, Diana answered, 'You choose, Thursday. Something warm, I think.'

Ginny selected a fine gown in a pretty shade of green trimmed with lace, then held it up for Diana's approval. 'Yes, perfect, thank you.'

Swallowing her surprise, Ginny said, 'I'll leave you to finish your breakfast in peace then, miss, and I'll come back in about fifteen minutes.'

When Diana nodded she hurried from the room and headed back down to the basement kitchen where Cook looked at her searchingly. 'She ain't had another go at yer, has she?' she asked.

Ginny laughed. 'Quite the opposite. She actually apologised and she's said thank you to me *twice* this morning. I don't think she's *ever* done that before?

'About bloody time an' all,' Cook grumbled as she laid some slices of crispy bacon on to a silver salver. 'Per'aps you've knocked a few manners into her. It's a pity yer can't do the same fer Master Giles. Now there's another one who's goin' to get his comeuppance one o' these days, you just mark my words. But now come to the table, lass, an' get somethin' inside yer. You look right poorly. Get a nice cup of hot tea down yer fer a start-off.'

Ginny did as she was told and surprisingly found that she did feel a little better with a hot drink and some food inside her.

'I'd better get back up there,' she said, the instant she had drained her cup. 'I don't want her snapping back into another bad mood, do I?' The words had barely left her lips when Mrs Bronson entered the room, and just as Cook had been, she was visibly shocked by the state of Ginny's eye.

'My goodness, Virginia. Why ever haven't you stayed in bed as I suggested?'

'Because I'm not ill, ma'am,' Ginny answered politely as she made for the door. 'And now if you'll excuse me, I must get back upstairs to Miss Diana. But, oh...' She paused then. 'Might I have a private word with you later when you have a moment to spare, please?'

'Yes, of course,' Mrs Bronson said and Ginny hurried past her without another word.

Diana was already in the bathroom when Ginny got back upstairs and once she had dried herself following her bath, Ginny helped her dress. There was not a single word of complaint this morning even when tightening her corsets, but now Ginny had made up her mind and once her mistress was seated in front of the dressing table she caught her eye in the mirror as she styled her hair and told her, 'I shall be giving notice later today, miss. I thought it fair that I should warn you that I shall be leaving when a replacement for me can be found.'

'Oh no!' Diana looked genuinely distressed. 'It is because of what I did last night, isn't it?'

'Not entirely,' Ginny answered truthfully as she continued to brush the girl's silky hair. 'I had been considering leaving before that incident occurred.'

'B ... but why?'

'I have personal matters that need attending to. A relative that I am keen to find.'

Diana shook her head. 'Please don't go, Thursday. Uncle will employ another old harridan to

276

accompany me everywhere and I couldn't bear it. I will never raise my hand to you again, I swear!'

Ginny concentrated on what she was doing, unwilling to give an answer as yet. This was going to take some thinking about so instead of replying she remained silent as Diana continued to avidly watch her face in the mirror.

Once the room was tidy again Diana then asked tentatively, 'Would you come along to Ben's room with me, please? My aunt and uncle don't think it is correct for me to spend time alone with him.'

Ginny's heart sank. She had been about to put away the clean clothes that had been delivered from the laundry room, but then Miss Diana had asked very politely and she was paid to be her companion, after all. Even so, the thought of having to spend time in that young man's company made her squirm.

'Very well, miss.' Ginny folded Diana's nightgown and tucked it beneath one of the lace-trimmed pillows on the bed, then unwillingly followed the young woman from the room.

Joe made a great show of welcoming Diana when they arrived. Barbara was in there dusting and Ginny seated herself discreetly as far away from the bed as she could. Even so, every now and then, his eyes would greedily seek hers. Ginny had an idea that he was actually a lot better now than he made himself out to be, but it wasn't her place to say it so she kept quietly in the background as Diana chattered away to him like a little sparrow. Dr Gifford confirmed her suspicions when he called later that day and declared that the patient was now well enough to get out of bed each day and sit in the chair by the fire or the window for an hour.

'And is there any sign of your memory coming back, young man?' the doctor asked but Joe shook his head solemnly.

'Not a thing yet, sir. Everything is just a blank.' He raised his hand to his forehead for effect as he said it, and the doctor hastily patted his arm.

'Well, don't get worrying about it. It'll all come back in its own good time.' He then nodded towards Diana and after snapping his black bag shut he strode from the room.

'I shall get Barbara to help you into the chair after lunch,' Diana told him as she sat down beside him on the bed and gently took his hand.

A flash of irritation crossed his face but it was gone so quickly that Ginny wondered if she had imagined it.

'Very well, but I have to tell you I'm not sure that I'll manage it,' he answered weakly. 'I still feel very shaky when I sit up.'

In actual fact he had no intention of getting out of bed just yet. He wanted to prolong his recovery for as long as he could, although he had no idea how he was going to cope with Diana's incessant chatter. She was getting on his nerves fawning all over him and despite the fact that she was a very pretty girl there were times when he just wanted to scream at her to shut up – although he wouldn't, of course.

'I ... I think I might manage some coffee now,' he said, and instantly Diana turned to Ginny.

'Would you go and get some please, Thursday.

278

And perhaps some of Cook's home-made biscuits? We need to build Ben's strength back up.'

Joe stifled his irritation as Diana began to fuss about him, straightening the eiderdown and plumping up his pillows. He had hoped that Diana would go for the snack, if only so he could have a break from her monotonous droning voice, but he plastered a smile on his face as Ginny rose and left the room without a word. Now had Ginny been the one with the money, he fancied he would have enjoyed what he was planning a whole lot more, for even with her black eye he still felt drawn to her. Still, he consoled himself, once he had got a ring on Diana's finger he wouldn't have to see that much of her.

With a little smile that turned Diana's heart to mush he looked directly into her face and whimpered, 'I'm afraid I am being a terrible trouble to you. Perhaps it would be better if I was transferred to the hospital until I can remember who I am? I am not your responsibility, after all.'

'Oh no, no! I wouldn't dream of having you moved,' she said with genuine distress and he felt a little thrill. She was like putty in his hands and everything was going exactly as he had hoped. It was just a matter of time now before he could put his plan into action.

Chapter Twenty-Eight

It was later that evening when she went down to the kitchen for a cup of tea with Cook and Nancy before retiring to bed that Ginny got a chance to speak to Mrs Bronson. Her eye had pained her all day and she had developed a headache so she wasn't in the best of humours and had suddenly decided that the sooner she left to search for Charlie, the better.

'Ah there you are, Virginia.' The woman stepped from her room as Ginny was heading for the kitchen. 'I believe you wished to speak to me?'

'Oh yes.' Deciding that she might as well get it over and done with, Ginny followed the house-keeper into her small sitting room. It was very warm and cosy, with a huge fire crackling in the grate.

Ginny sat down when asked and folded her hands in her lap as the older woman took a seat opposite her.

'So what can I do for you, my dear?'

'Erm...' Ginny cleared her throat. 'The thing is, Mrs Bronson, I'm very grateful to you for employing me, but I feel I really must leave to search for my brother now. I have enough saved up for the train fare to Hull and I can't rest until I've seen that he is safe.'

'I see.' The woman rose and headed for a tray of coffee that she had just brought from the kitchen. Without asking she poured two cups and added sugar before handing one to Ginny and taking her seat again.

'I can understand your concerns,' she said gravely. 'But what would you do when you got to Hull if you only have enough for the train fare? You will need a job and somewhere to stay while you search for him. You can't live on the streets.'

'I'll manage,' Ginny said as her chin rose. 'Charlie is all I have left now – until my father comes home, that is, and that could be some long time away.'

The woman nodded before asking, 'Has Miss Diana been horrible to you again? Is that what has brought this on?'

'No, not at all. If anything she's been very pleasant today but I never intended to be here for a long time. Obviously I have to find my little brother.'

Mrs Bronson stared thoughtfully into the flames roaring up the chimney then shocked Ginny when she asked, 'Would you be prepared to stay for a little longer if I were able to find out more about where your brother has gone?'

Ginny ran her tongue along her dry lips. 'Well, yes I suppose I would, but how will you manage that if the people at the workhouse won't give you the address?'

'Let me worry about that.'

A silence settled between them for a time as they both sipped at their drink, then, plucking up every ounce of courage that she had, Ginny blurted out, 'How did you know my father, Mrs Bronson, and why have you been so kind to me?'

A hint of colour flared in the woman's cheeks before she answered cautiously, 'As I told you, I am on the Board of Governors at the workhouse and as your father spent his childhood there I came to know him and quite a few of the other children quite well over the years.'

Why do I get the feeling that there's something she isn't telling me? Ginny mused silently. She then considered what Mrs Bronson had said and came to a decision. 'If you think you can find out where Charlie is, then yes,' she said, 'I would stay on for a while longer and I would be very grateful.'

'Excellent.' The housekeeper looked vastly relieved. 'I'm sure you are exactly what Miss Diana needs,' she said softly. 'And I would worry about you if you were to go off on a wild-goose chase. It isn't safe for a young woman alone to go gallivanting off to areas unknown. But now I have a present for you. I believe you like to read so while I was in town today I picked up a couple of books for you.'

Crossing to a small table that stood to one side of the window she picked up a brown-paper parcel and handed it to Ginny and when the girl opened it she gasped with delight. The first book was *Cranford* by Elizabeth Gaskell and the second was *Wuthering Heights* by Emily Brontë.

'I hope you haven't already read them?'

Ginny was rendered temporarily speechless and could only shake her head as she looked in genuine pleasure at the two volumes.

'Oh no, ma'am, I haven't read either of these,' she managed to stammer. 'I have read Mrs

Gaskell's *Mary Barton,* and loved it. I'm sure I shall love them both. Thank you very much.'

The woman's expression was kindly as she saw the joy on the girl's face. 'Good. And when you have finished them I shall enjoy hearing what you thought. Then you are more than welcome to borrow some of mine.' She gestured towards a tall mahogany bookcase that was groaning with a variety of books and Ginny could hardly believe her ears. The staff had warned her on arrival that Mrs Bronson could be quite aloof and yet Ginny herself had received nothing but kindness from her. But why? she asked herself. Why has she gone out of her way to be so obliging to me if she isn't like this with the rest of the staff?

It was all very confusing, but then, not wishing to overstay her welcome she rose from her seat, placed her cup and saucer back on the tray and said, 'Thank you again, ma'am. I shall treasure them you can be sure and I shall look forward to hearing news of Charlie's whereabouts. Good night.' Then clutching the precious presents to her chest she bobbed her knee respectfully and hurried from the room.

Once she was gone, the housekeeper's chin drooped to her chest as tears ran unchecked down her cheeks. 'I must ask Celia for some time off and pay a visit as soon as I possibly can,' she said aloud to the empty room. And once again she prayed to God for forgiveness for the terrible thing she had once done. It seemed that the consequences of that wrongdoing were to haunt her for ever.

'But of course you may have some time off, Anna

dear,' Celia told her later as Mrs Bronson helped her into bed. 'Are you planning to go somewhere nice? A little holiday would do you the power of good, although I believe you might have waited for better weather.'

'It isn't a holiday,' Mrs Bronson replied as she settled the blankets gently across her fragile legs. 'I have to visit an elderly relative. I've been putting it off. Oh dear, I hope you will manage without me,' she fretted.

Celia squeezed her hand affectionately. 'Of course I shall manage. Barbara and Millie will help, although I shall miss you, of course. How long do you plan to be gone for?'

'Oh, no more than a week at most,' Mrs Bronson assured her as she passed her the latest copy of the monthly *The Englishwoman's Domestic Magazine,* and turned up the lamp at the side of the bed.

'Then go as soon as you please and don't get worrying about anything here. Oh, and by the way, how is our patient doing?'

Mrs Bronson shook her head. 'Actually the doctor did say that he was well enough to start getting out of bed to sit in a chair for short periods today but when Barbara attempted to get him up this afternoon he insisted that he was too weak to manage it.'

'And don't you believe him?'

'No, I don't,' Mrs Bronson replied abruptly. 'Just between you and me there's something about that young man that I can't quite take to. I can't put my finger on it but I don't like the way he looks at Diana for one thing. She seems to be completely smitten with him, which doesn't help matters.'

Celia grinned, transforming her pain-wracked face for a few seconds. 'But isn't it quite normal for young girls to develop crushes? I remember I did when I was her age. I was totally in love with my maths tutor at one stage, or at least I thought I was. And James and I have told Diana that she is not to go into his room and be alone with him any more, so they can't get up to much, can they?'

'I suppose not,' Mrs Bronson agreed reluctantly. 'But I won't be sorry when he's recovered and away from here all the same. He could be literally anyone!'

'I'm sure you are worrying unnecessarily,' Celia said kindly. 'But now away with you and start planning your trip, and we will manage without you, have no fear.'

Mrs Bronson smiled and slipped from the room just in time to see Diana creeping out of Joe's bedroom. The girl's hair was loose about her shoulders and she was wearing a long pink dressing robe.

The girl started guilty when she saw Mrs Bronson. Then, covering the distance between them in seconds she said, 'Don't look so angry, Bronny.' It was an affectionate nickname she had used when she was younger. 'I only popped in to give Ben Father's yesterday's newspapers. He gets so bored lying there all day. You won't tell my aunt, will you? Please, Bronny!'

Mrs Bronson's expression softened. 'All right then, I'll overlook it just this once, but if I see it happen again I *will* tell her, do you understand,

Miss Diana? It really isn't seemly for a young lady to drift about the house in her nightclothes and *especially* not into gentlemen's bedrooms!'

Diana nodded and flitted away like a beautiful butterfly as Mrs Bronson frowned. Yes, the sooner that young man was gone from the house the better.

Anna Bronson set off from Lamp Hill Hall two days later. Jim Grady had been about to drive her to the railway station, but as Mr Walton-Hughes was passing it on the way to one of his factories at that time he offered to give her a lift in his carriage instead.

Johnny, who would be driving them, assisted her into the carriage and once the master was seated beside her the young man clucked at the horses and they set off at a trot.

Once they had passed out of the estate and on to the road, James took her hand and asked worriedly, 'Are you quite sure you are doing the right thing, Anna?'

'What other option do I have?' she asked miserably. 'If I don't go and check on Charles, Virginia will go in search of him – and God knows what might happen to her, a young woman on her own. Surely I owe her this much at least?'

'Of course ... but if Celia should ever find out...' As his words trailed away she stared at the man whom she loved more than life itself. The trouble was, she also loved his wife as a sister and so theirs was a love that was doomed never to amount to anything. They both cared far too much for Celia and would never do anything to cause her pain.

'Don't worry, I shall be very careful,' she promised and he nodded as he stared glumly from the carriage window at the passing fields. Their love affair had begun shortly after Celia had become unwell when the family had lived in Hull. Anna had joined the household as house-keeper at his former home and one night she had found him crying. The doctor had just informed him that Celia must never bear any more children and out of consideration for her he had moved into his own room. But a man has needs and eventually it was Anna who had fulfilled them. And so, ever since, they had snatched what little forbidden time they could together, always being careful to protect Celia, for James still loved her and over the years Anna had come to love her too.

'You don't deserve any of this. It would have been better for you if I had never met you,' James said bleakly.

'Nonsense,' Anna replied. 'I knew what I was entering into and I have no regrets, so stop worrying. Things will work out, you'll see.'

He nodded but deep inside he wondered if they ever could.

When they reached the railway station James helped her down from the carriage and shook her hand formally. 'Goodbye, Mrs Bronson,' he said as Johnny Grady lifted her small case down from the back of the carriage. 'I do hope you have a good trip.'

'I'm sure I shall, thank you, sir,' she replied as she took her case from Johnny. Then with a nod to them both she turned and went to catch her train.

It was late that afternoon when the cab that had brought her from the railway station pulled up in front of a huge terraced house on a hill in a smart area of the town. She paid the driver then stood for a moment looking over the rooftops to the ships that bobbed on the sea in the harbour as she breathed in the salty air. It felt like such a long time since she had last been here – a lifetime, in fact – and yet everything looked exactly as she had remembered it.

After a while, she drew herself up to her full height and climbing the steps to the front door, she lifted the highly polished brass knocker and rapped on it. Almost instantly she heard footsteps approaching and the door was opened by a young maid with rosy cheeks dressed in a frilly white apron and matching mob cap.

'Ah, you must be Miss Anna,' the maid greeted her with a broad smile. 'The master said to expect you. Won't you come in?'

Anna stepped past her into the hallway and quickly glanced around. Here too everything was just as she remembered; it was as if time had stood still in her absence.

The young maid was hovering as Anna removed her hat and coat and handed them to her. She said, 'The master is in the drawing room, miss. Shall I tell him you're here.'

'Yes, please do,' Anna answered briskly. She wasn't looking forward to the meeting that lay ahead one bit, and was impatient now to get it over with.

The maid scuttled away, only to return seconds

later to tell her, 'The master said to go right in, miss.' She then bobbed her knee and disappeared off in the direction of the kitchen as Anna took another quick look around. The parquet floor gleamed in the glow of an oil lamp, and everywhere smelled of beeswax polish. She had grown up with that smell in her nostrils and even now after all this time it still reminded her of this place. This had been the only home she could ever remember until she had decided to stretch her wings, and it still held many happy memories for her.

Crossing to the mirror, she tidied her hair as best she could, then taking a deep breath, she approached the door and opened it quietly. The smell of fine cigars and brandy reached her instantly and her eyes immediately found the figure sitting in his favourite chair at the side of the fireplace. Some things, it seemed, never changed.

'Hello, Uncle.'

As Anna crossed the room, he smiled at her.

'Hello, darling Anna. It's been a long time. I haven't seen you since your father's funeral.'

'I know, and I apologise. I kept meaning to come and see you, but somehow there always seemed so much to do and...' Her words trailed away as she stared down at the shrunken figure in the chair. It was ten years since she had last seen her uncle, and during that time his hair had turned from dark brown to a silvery grey. He seemed thinner too and so much older. He must be at least seventy-five now, Anna thought, trying to calculate his age in her mind. And she had neglected him terribly. Shame washed over her.

She wished now that she had made more of an effort, but James and Celia needed her and there had never seemed a right time to leave them... Stop it, she scolded herself. You're just making excuses. But I'll make it up to him. I will!

She took a seat in the chair opposite him and he pulled on the bell-rope dangling at the side of the fireplace.

'You must be hungry and thirsty after your long journey. I'll get Lucy to bring you some tea and cake. That should keep you going until dinner-time, my dear.'

A lump formed in her throat as she nodded. There were no recriminations but that was his way. She had always been dear to him; in fact, looking back, she realised that she had always been closer to him than to her own father.

Seeing her distress, he reached across a gnarled hand and gently rubbed her arm. 'We'll talk later, shall we?' he suggested and she nodded again, too full to speak.

Chapter Twenty-Nine

'Is Charles not eating with us, Uncle?' Anna asked as they seated themselves at the dining-room table.

'Not this evening. I thought it might be better if he ate in the nursery with his nanny, so that we can talk.'

'Of course.' She folded her hands in her lap as

Lucy ladled soup into their dishes, then when the young maid had left the room she asked, 'How is he?'

'Oh, he's fine and a grand little chap,' her uncle replied as he lifted his spoon and took a mouthful of the soup.

Anna stared at him for a moment before saying, 'I shall never be able to thank you enough for taking him in as you have.'

He brushed aside her thanks with a wave of his hand. 'I would have helped out a long time ago if you had allowed me to. What has happened to his parents is most unfortunate.'

Anna stared down at the soup cooling in front of her. Suddenly she had completely lost her appetite – but then this house had always had that effect on her. It had been her childhood home and every time she stepped through the door she was assailed with memories and guilt. This was only the second time she had visited for many years. The time before had been for her father's funeral and as she remembered, the sense of guilt became acute. If only they could have become reconciled before he died, but it was too late for regrets now.

As if he could read her mind her uncle stretched his hand across the table and patted her shoulder.

'You do know that your father never stopped loving you, my dear, don't you?'

Anna shrugged. 'I don't know why. I let him down badly.'

'Perhaps he thought that at the time, but when he had had the chance to cool down, he realised that he had been a little hard on you. If he could

291

forgive you, surely you can forgive yourself?'

Anna had been just a small child when her mother had died and so her father had brought her up single-handed with the help of his loyal staff and a governess. Now, Anna's mind drifted back over the years to the day she had informed her father that she wished to take up the post of a housekeeper for the Walton-Hughes. She had still been in her teens and he had begged her to at least wait until she was twenty-one. After all, she had been raised as a lady, and as he had pointed out, there was really no need for her to work. 'One day when I am gone you will be a very wealthy woman,' he had told her. But Anna had been young and headstrong and insistent. And so she had left home with bad feelings between them, although she had missed him dreadfully.

And then a few years later she had discovered she was with child. Not knowing what to do she had gone to her uncle for advice and it was he who had persuaded her to pay her father a visit. The visit had not gone well. He had been bitterly ashamed and disappointed in her and so once again they had parted on bad terms and she had stayed with her uncle until her child was born.

James Walton-Hughes had been distraught, for the child she had carried was his, although he could never lay claim to it whilst his wife was alive. He cared for her too much, as indeed Anna did, and so they had reluctantly abandoned the child shortly after its birth and Anna had gone back to resume her post of housekeeper in Lamp Hill Hall. Thankfully over the years Anna had been able to see her child from time to time and as her grandchildren had been born she had deeply regretted that she was unable to be a part of their lives. And then their mother had died and their father had wound up in prison, and so now at last she was doing what she could for the two of them that were left, although it seemed pathetically little. Even now she could not disclose her true identity to them and it hurt to have to keep them at arm's length.

'How is Virginia doing?' Her uncle's voice disturbed Anna's thoughts and she sighed.

'She is now acting as a companion to Diana and she has absolutely no idea who I am,' she confided. 'But I know she misses her little brother terribly.'

'Then bring her here to join him,' he suggested. 'This is your house, after all. When I moved here to stay with your father it was only meant to be a temporary measure. I don't know why you asked me to stay on really. Do you have plans to move back here?'

'No, and I don't know why I hang on to it really,' she admitted. 'Perhaps it is still a link to my father and after all, you would have had to find somewhere else to stay had I decided to sell it. No, it suits me to keep it – stability for the future, I suppose. But now tell me how the business is doing.'

'Very well. I'm afraid I am far too old to play an active part in it any more but I have an excellent manager overseeing everything and he brings me the accounts to look through every month. Trouble is, he's no spring chicken now either so in the not too distant future I shall have to find someone suitable to train to take his place – but that's not a priority just yet. Your profits for your half of the business are paid into a separate account quarterly, and with that alone you could afford to retire and live comfortably for the rest of your life. But you won't, will you...'

She smiled wistfully at him. 'No, my future is mapped out and I have to be there for James for as long as he needs me. If only we could choose who we fall in love with, eh? My life might have been so different had I not met him – but I did. As for bringing Virginia here, it would be very risky. Were she to discover who I am, it might get back to Celia and it would break her heart. Charles is not old enough to understand, but she is.'

'Hmm.' Her uncle sat back in his chair, steepled his fingers and stared thoughtfully off into space. 'And is there no chance of getting their father out of jail?'

'James is doing what he can behind the scenes,' she answered. 'But of course there can be no guarantee, so it's up to me to see that both of them are all right for now at least. Virginia believes that you came to the workhouse and took Charles out of the goodness of your heart. Even so, she is keen to see him and assure herself that he is safe and happy – and I fear that if that doesn't happen, she may run away and come to Hull to try to find him. Oh Uncle, everything is such a mess. What am I to do?'

Her uncle's eyes were sad. 'My poor girl, what tangled webs we weave.' He knew now that if he were to support her, he too must become a party to the deceit – but what alternative was there? He had loved Anna as his own since the day she had drawn breath, and there was nothing that he would not have done for her.

'You must go back and tell her that you have located Charles and that she is welcome to come and visit him.'

Her startled eyes flew to his face. 'You would allow me to do that without disclosing my secret?'

He nodded, suddenly feeling terribly weary, then became silent as the maid re-entered the room to clear the first course.

'You can stick to your original story,' he told her. 'Tell Virginia that I was a lonely old man seeking the company of a child and I promise I will not disclose the truth to her. I know that your father bitterly regretted your parting. Had you let us know where you were before he became so ill, I am sure he would have been in touch and you would have been reconciled.'

'But won't she become suspicious when she discovers that your name and mine are the same?'

'Ah, you have a point. I hadn't thought of that.' He patted his chin thoughtfully for a moment, staring off into space before saying, 'I am afraid there is no alternative but to admit the truth to her about our relationship. You could say that you had heard of their dilemma and mentioned it to me and that I had taken pity on the child. At least that way there is a chance of her learning no more, although it must be hard for you each day not to be able to admit that you are her grandmother.'

'Oh, it is.' Tears started in Anna's eyes. 'It was

295

even worse when she first came to the Hall and I had to watch her toiling in the laundry each day. Sometimes I just wish I could turn the clock back to when I was a girl. How naïve I was back then and how determined to go against Father's wishes. I wished with all my heart to spread my wings. It was by pure chance that I went to work for the Walton-Hughes family, and then when Celia became ill, it was our mutual concern for her that drew James and me together. I know that is a poor excuse for what we have done, but I cared about them both by then and I wanted to comfort him.'

'You have no need to explain yourself to me, my dear. I have no doubt that you have suffered every single day since the moment you were forced to give your child away.'

'I have,' she almost sobbed and then they fell silent again as the maid carried in the main course and placed it in the middle of the table. Anna sliced the succulent joint of beef that was sizzling on the silver salver and placed some on her uncle's plate along with a selection of vegetables, but he noted that she herself ate barely enough to feed a bird although he made no comment on it.

They were both relieved when the meal was finally over so that they could retreat to the drawing room. It was then, after she had refused a small sherry, that he asked, 'Would you like to see Charles now? I've no doubt Nanny will have him ready for bed.'

She nodded eagerly as he waved her towards the door. 'Then off you go. You know where the nursery is, or at least you should do, seeing as you spent your first few years up there. Introduce yourself as my niece.'

She smiled at him, then made her way upstairs. The maid had placed her bag in her old room and she glanced in as she passed. Once again everything was just as she had left it and a wave of nostalgia passed through her. Upstairs on the nursery floor she paused, then after tapping lightly on the door she entered to find the nanny sitting in front of the fire reading Charles a bedtime story. His hair shone in the light of the oil lamp that stood in the centre of the table as she introduced herself.

'Hello, young man. My name is Anna and my uncle has sent me up to meet you. I shall be staying for a few days and I hope we can be friends.'

The nanny, who was much younger than Anna had expected her to be, leaped to her feet and bobbed her knee.

'I were just reading young Master Charles a bedtime story, ma'am, though if truth be told, he can read almost as good as me even if he is only nine years old.'

'That's because me mam an' dad taught me to read,' Charles said solemnly.

'Why, that's wonderful.' Anna crossed to look down at the book they were reading.

'Oh, *The Children of the New Forest* by Captain Marryat. What an excellent choice. Perhaps you would like to read a little to me, Charles?'

Charlie was only too happy to show off his reading skills and as he read she kept her eyes fixed on his face, thinking what a lovely child he was. It came home to her again then just how much she had missed – and yet she knew that she could have done no other.

'Goodness me, what a clever young man you are!' she exclaimed when he came to the end of a section.

'That's what Uncle Edward says,' he told her proudly.

'I'm sure he does. But how are you settling in, Charles?'

His lip suddenly trembled and he gazed towards the fire. 'Uncle Edward is very kind to me, but ... but I miss me mam an' dad an' our Ginny. She's me big sister, an' I haven't seen her for ages. I don't even know if she knows where I am. They took me from the workhouse an' brought me here, an' I never even got to say goodbye to her.' The little boy looked absolutely distraught.

'Ah well, it just so happens that I may be able to do something about that.' Anna gave him an encouraging smile as he blinked to hold back tears. 'Virgini ... Ginny, your sister, works at the same place as me and when I go back I'm going to tell her where you are and bring her to visit you. Would you like that?'

'*Not half!*' The child's face lit up like a ray of sunshine. 'An' is she all right?'

'She's very well,' Anna assured him. Then, conscious of the nanny hovering in the background: 'But now I think your nanny is ready to put you to bed. Perhaps we could go for a walk together tomorrow if it isn't too cold and if Nanny doesn't object?'

The young woman smiled affably. 'That's fine by me, ma'am,' she said, as Charlie nodded his head vigorously.

'Excellent, then I shall say good night, Charles, and look forward to seeing you in the morning.'

'All right but ... well, do you think you could call me Charlie? It was my name till I came to live here. When I was at home I only got called Charles when I'd been a naughty boy.'

'Then in that case I shall do my best to remember to call you Charlie.' Anna stood and looked at him awkwardly for a moment. The urge was on her to give him a hug but thinking better of it she extended her hand and he shook it solemnly.

'Good night, Charlie.'

'Good night, Miss Anna.'

Anna left the nursery but once out on the landing she gazed down at the hand that Charlie had just shook. She could still feel his fingers in hers, so small and warm, and they had felt so right – which only went to press home just how much she had missed over the years.

Chapter Thirty

'When will Anna be back?' Celia asked her husband before he left the house one morning. The housekeeper had been gone for four days and Celia was missing her. They had become like sisters over the years, and although Barbara and Millie were doing a sterling job of meeting all her needs it wasn't the same somehow.

'She did say before she left that she would be

no more than a week at most so she could return any time now,' James said as he bent to kiss his wife's pale cheek. She looked even more fragile than usual and he wondered if he should call the doctor in to check her over. 'But now I must be going, darling. I have a meeting at the factory in town in an hour's time. Is there anything I can get you before I go?'

'No, I have everything I need, thank you.' She gave him a warm smile and returned his kiss before saying suddenly, 'You have been a marvellous husband, James. There are not many men who would have put up with me as you have.'

'Nonsense,' he spluttered with a frown but she shook her head.

'No, it's true. I have spent most of our married life confined to a sickbed. Many men would have been long gone.'

'But I am not many men and I consider myself very fortunate to have you as my wife, so we'll have no more of that silly talk, do you hear me?' His voice was stern but his eyes were soft as he straightened. 'Now be sure to ring the bell if you need anything and I'll be home as soon as I can.'

He left the room and closed the door softly behind him. Poor Celia. She couldn't help being an invalid. She had never been strong and giving birth to their son had robbed her of what little strength she had possessed. Unlike some women who took to their beds for the least little niggle, her weakness had been genuine and he blamed himself for that. But she had longed for a child so much that he had done nothing early in their marriage to prevent it despite the fact that the doctor had warned them that her heart was not strong. With a sigh he set off down the stairs. He too was missing Anna. The house didn't seem the same without her, for to all intents and purposes she had been more of the mistress at the Hall than Celia had, organising the staff, looking after his wife, planning the menus each week. It was only now that she was absent that he realised just how much she did do, and he silently prayed for her swift return.

The mood in Lamp Hill Hall lightened somewhat the next day when Sebastian paid an unexpected visit.

'It's only for one night,' he warned his aunt as he leaned across the bed to give her an affectionate kiss. 'I just suddenly got the urge this morning to come home, so I popped on the train and walked from the station. I shall have to go back tomorrow though because I have exams on Monday, but how is everyone? I've been worrying about Uncle James. He was in a tearing rage when he came to fetch Giles after he was expelled from school. Is Giles behaving?'

'Chance would be a fine thing,' his aunt answered with a wry smile. She then went on to tell him of Ginny's promotion and he smiled as he thought of the pretty little laundry maid. If truth be told he'd found himself thinking of her often since he'd returned to school.

'And how does my sister like having a companion?'

Celia chuckled. 'Well, there have been a few teething problems but Diana seems to be getting

used to it now. I just thought being around another girl of a similar age might be good for her.
And the thing is, Ginny is actually a very bright
girl so she might be good for her in more ways
than one.'

'I think it's an excellent idea,' Sebastian told her
approvingly. 'But now if you'll excuse me I'm off
to see if I can scrounge something to eat from
Cook. I'm starving! But I'll be back to see you
later.'

Celia smiled indulgently as Sebastian hurried
from the room and settled back to the volume of
Tennyson's poems she had been reading.

It was a little later when Sebastian bumped into
his sister and Ginny. He was heading for the
stable block to saddle his horse and the girls were
taking a leisurely walk about the gardens, well
wrapped up against the cold.

When Diana spotted him she whooped with
delight and flew into his arms, and he laughingly
lifted her from her feet and swung her about with
a wink at Ginny, who instantly blushed. He
always had that effect on her, although she had
no idea why.

'What are you doing home?' Diana asked and
he again explained that he had felt the sudden
urge to visit as they all fell into step together.

'And how are you enjoying your new position?'
he asked Ginny as they approached the stables.

'Fine, thank you, sir.' Her voice came out as a
croak and he laughed.

'Oh please, call me Seb or Sebastian,' he urged,
which only made her blush an even deeper shade
of red. Diana demanded his attention again then

so Ginny quickly excused herself and fled back to the house, feeling like a complete fool, and as he watched her go, Diana looked on with a grin on her face.

They didn't cross each other's paths again before he returned to school the next day and Ginny was relieved about it. For some reason she became tongue-tied if he so much as looked at her.

'Sebastian said to say goodbye to you,' Diana informed her after he had left the next afternoon, and then she giggled. 'I think he's got a soft spot for you,' she teased.

'Don't be so ridiculous.' Ginny was so flummoxed that she forgot to look at Diana as she said it and had to repeat herself before hurriedly getting on with what she had been doing.

As the train trundled along the track, Anna stared from the carriage window at the rolling fields beyond. For the first time in her life she had mixed feelings about returning to Lamp Hill Hall. She had enjoyed the time she had spent with Charlie, as he had insisted she should call him, more than she had ever thought possible, and it had been a real wrench to leave him. Over the years since abandoning her newborn child she had tried to push thoughts of that traumatic episode to the back of her mind, but now that she was in such close proximity to both her granddaughter and her grandson, she was finding it impossible. She sighed. Of course she was greatly looking forward to seeing James and Celia – and Ginny too, if it came to that – but she wished more than ever now that things might have been different. Inside her valise was a letter that Charlie had written to Ginny with her help, and she knew that Ginny would be overjoyed to hear from him and even more delighted when Anna informed her that she would be allowed to visit. The spring might be a good time to arrange it, she thought – if she could get Ginny to wait that long that was.

Her thoughts moved on to Celia as she wondered how she would find her. The sick woman had given Anna cause for grave concern lately. She seemed to be shrinking by the day and had started to insist that she didn't need help with bathing any more. Anna wondered why, and the thought of what she might be trying to hide filled her with dread. But then she pushed the gloomy thoughts aside. She might have left Charlie behind but at least she would soon see Ginny again. She was shocked to realise that she had actually missed the girl and had grown more than fond of her without even realising it.

And how would the young man be, who had lost his memory? she wondered. Surely his physical wounds should be healing by now? There was something about the stranger that made her feel uneasy. He was always polite and grateful for everything that everyone did for him, but Anna didn't like his over-familiarity with Diana, nor the way he encouraged the girl to fawn all over him. Then Anna scolded herself mentally. Here she was fretting and she wasn't even home again yet. Forcing herself to relax back in her seat, she closed her eyes and tried to rest as the train chugged along. She would be forced to take the responsibilities of the household back on to her slim shoulders again soon enough.

'Anna, you're home!' James exclaimed as he came out of the dining room that evening. It was hard to bide his delight at seeing her. 'You should have let us know you were coming and I could have sent Grady to fetch you from the station.'

She smiled as she removed her coat and bonnet and handed them to Millie, who was hovering close by. 'By the time a letter had reached you I would have been back anyway,' she pointed out. 'And it was no trouble to hop in a cab. But how is everyone?'

'Come through to the drawing room and I'll tell you. Oh, and Millie, could you bring a tray of tea through to us, please? I'm sure Mrs Bronson will be ready for one after her journey.'

'Certainly, sir.' Millie smiled obligingly and hurried off to the kitchen as James shepherded Anna ahead of him into the drawing room where a fire was crackling up the chimney.

'I've missed you,' he said quietly once the door had closed behind them.

'I have missed you too,' she murmured, 'but how is Celia?'

He crossed to the fire and stood with his back to it. 'Not good, to be honest, although she flatly refuses to let the doctor take a look at her. She's barely left her bed since you went, and I am feeling very concerned. But now tell me about the boy. Is he all right?'

'Oh, he's grand. He and my uncle have taken a rare shine to each other,' she told him, before adding quietly, 'He's a lovely little boy, James. He has a look of you about him.'

James lowered his head as pain throbbed through him. How he longed to lay claim to the child, and Ginny, but what would it do to Celia if he did? Everything was a mess and he could see no end to it. Anna had sacrificed so much for him all of her adult life and sometimes he could barely live with himself.

'And how is our wounded young gentleman?' Seeing James' pain, Anna was keen to change the subject.

'Oh, Ben's coming along nicely according to the doctor. Barbara even managed to coax him out of bed for an hour or two yesterday and today, but he still maintains that he can remember nothing.'

'And do you believe him?'

James bit on his lip for a second before shrugging. 'I'm not sure, to be honest. Doctor Gifford seems to think he should have remembered something by now, even if it was only in fits and starts.'

'Hmm, I would have thought so too.'

The conversation was interrupted then when Millie wheeled a trolley in. There was a selection of sandwiches and cakes on it as well as the tea that James had ordered.

'Cook thought yer might be peckish, Mrs Bronson,' the girl told her cheerfully. 'An' she said it'll be no trouble at all to sort yer a proper dinner out if you'd like one.'

'Thank her for me, Millie, but tell her that won't be necessary. This looks more than adequate.'

'Yes, ma'am.' Millie slipped away as Anna poured tea into two delicate china cups and helped herself to a sandwich.

'And how is Virginia,' she asked then. 'Are she and Diana getting along any better?'

'She's absolutely fine and as a matter of fact she and Diana are getting along swimmingly. Diana is even allowing Ginny to help her improve her reading and writing, would you believe? She's still spending more time than I'd like her to in Ben's room, but at least Virginia stays in there with her now.'

There was so much more he would have liked to say to her but they had both learned over the years that some things were best left unsaid. Even so, when she glanced up to find his eyes on her she saw all she needed to know reflected there, and she knew that given the chance, she would do everything all over again just to be near him.

'Right, I must get up to see Celia,' she said eventually when she had eaten a couple of the tasty ham sandwiches and had drunk two cups of tea. 'I have a letter for Virginia from Charlie too. I'm sure she'll be so relieved to know that he is well and happy. I've promised him that I shall take his sister to visit him – I thought perhaps in the spring if you have no objections?'

'Of course not.' He watched her leave the room and wished again that things might have been different.

Upstairs, Anna tapped and entered Celia's room, but she found the bed empty. She must be in the bathroom, she thought as she crossed to the door and inched it open. Celia had just climbed out of the bath and was in the process of wrapping a towel about her – but not before Anna noticed the swelling on her stomach.

'Oh Anna ... you're back.' Celia draped the towel about her as quickly as she could. 'How lovely it is to see you.' She was clearly all of a fluster. 'I've missed you greatly.'

'Thank you, I've missed you too. But may I help you to get dried and ready for bed?' Anna asked.

'No, no ... I shall be fine. Barbara has laid everything out already for me – look.' She waved her hands towards her nightclothes placed neatly across the towel rack and feeling that she had no choice Anna reluctantly backed out of the bathroom to wait for her. Eventually Celia joined her, and after helping her across to her dressing table, Anna lifted the tortoiseshell and mother of pearl backed brush and began to brush her hair.

'Did you have a good visit with your uncle? Did you find him well?'

'Very well, thank you. But Celia, I couldn't help but notice just now that you have a swelling on your stomach. Has it been there for some time?' Anna asked anxiously. Celia had refused her help in the bathroom for some weeks now and Anna wondered if this was the reason why.

Celia waved aside her concerns. 'Oh goodness me, that's just too much dinner I've eaten, that's all,' she said airily and then swiftly went on to tell Anna all that had been happening while she was away.

'It was lovely to see Sebastian, even if it was only an overnight visit, but I'm afraid James is getting very frustrated with Giles,' she confided. 'He has shown no interest at all in learning anything about any of the businesses and James is beginning to lose patience with him. All he seems to want to do is go off out and enjoy himself.'

'He's still very young. He'll settle down in time,' Anna said kindly, hoping to allay her mistress's concerns. 'And once Sebastian finishes school and comes home no doubt he will set a good example for his cousin and shame him into pulling his weight.'

'Let's just hope you are right. It's funny, isn't it? James always hoped that both the boys would go on to university, but Giles wouldn't be able to do so now and Sebastian has no wish to. He just wants to help his uncle to run his businesses.'

Anna noted that Celia looked tired and laying down the hairbrush she assisted her across to the bed and tucked her in, suggesting, 'Why don't you have a little rest before supper? I dare say James will be coming up to see you shortly.'

'I think I will.' Celia stifled a yawn with her hand as Anna swept back into the bathroom to collect her discarded clothes. When she emerged some minutes later, Celia was already fast asleep, so Anna laid them on a chair and tiptoed from the room, not wishing to disturb her. The rest of the tidying up could be done later.

Once out on the landing, Anna took a deep breath. She still had to face Ginny and give her the letter that Charlie had written to her. That would be the easy part. The hard part would be trying to explain why Charlie was living with her uncle, and Anna prayed that she would be able to do it in such a way that Ginny's suspicions were not aroused. Suddenly, as if by magic, the girl she had been thinking of emerged from Diana's bedroom with a pile of dirty clothes across her arm and Anna knew that the time had come.

'Mrs Bronson ... you're back – I didn't know,' Ginny exclaimed.

'That's because I only arrived a short time ago,' Anna could see the expectation in the girl's eyes.

'And did you get to see Charlie?' the girl blurted out before Anna had a chance to say another word.

'Yes, my dear, I did – and he looks wonderful, I assure you.' Anna fumbled in the pocket of her dress where Charlie's letter lay and handed it across to Ginny, whose eyes were alight. 'He wrote this for you, and I will explain everything to you this evening when I have finished all my duties. Perhaps you could come to my room at around eight o'clock?'

Ginny nodded but her eyes never left the precious letter she was clutching and it was obvious she could barely wait to read it.

'Yes, ma'am. Thank you.' She scooted away so quickly that she almost tripped on her skirts and Anna suppressed a smile. Ginny reminded her of herself at that age. She was strong-willed and eager to prove that she could be independent. Anna just prayed that things would turn out better for her than they had for herself. Ginny meanwhile was opening the door to her room. Diana was in Ben's room – again – but Millie was in there tidying up so she didn't need to be present. She would use this time to read Charlie's letter. Dumping Diana's laundry on to a chair on the landing she went into her room, turned the oil lamp up, then seating herself in the chair by the bed, she slit open the envelope, removed the letter and began to read it.

Dear Ginny, it began, and tears sprang to her eyes as she pictured her little brother writing it, leaning over the paper with his tongue in his cheek as he concentrated. *I am very well and hope you are too. Mrs Bronson said you were working for her and she seems very nice. I am happy living with Uncle Edward but I miss you.*

Ginny paused there as a sob rose in her throat. *His name is Mr Bronson too.* Ginny frowned here before continuing.

Will you cum and see me soon? Uncle Edward tuk me to see the botes at his bote yard the other day and it was gud. I like living here, he is kind to me but I wish you were here too. I have a nanny now, she is kind too but she makes me do my sums and my leters. She says my speling is geting a bit beter. Have you heard from Dad? When will he cum home? Mrs Bronson seys she will bring you to see me. Toomorow I am going to see the botes in the doks with Nanny if I am gud. I think about you all the time and I miss you very much,
love
Charlie Thursday XXX

Ginny smiled through her tears as she kissed the precious letter. At least Charlie sounded happy, but hopefully she would hear more about him later that evening from Mrs Bronson. Better still, it sounded like she might be allowed to visit him. But it did seem strange that the man who had taken him in had the same name as the housekeeper. It wasn't a common name – in fact, Ginny had never come across it before she had worked at Lamp Hill Hall. Tucking the letter into her pocket she hurried back out on to the landing and scooped up the dirty clothes before hastening away to deposit them in the laundry.

Chapter Thirty-One

'Come in,' Mrs Bronson said when Ginny tapped on her door later that evening.

Ginny quickly checked that the lace collar on her dress was lying flat before entering. Mrs Bronson was seated at a table poring over the household accounts but she gave her a welcoming smile.

'Ah, here you are, Virginia. Do sit down. I feel I need to explain a few things to you.'

Ginny sat down and folded her hands sedately in her lap as the woman came to sit opposite her. Anna remained silent for a while but then said quietly, 'I dare say that Charlie told you he is staying with Mr Bronson?'

Ginny nodded.

'And no doubt you found it strange that he and I share the same surname?'

Another nod.

'Then I should explain that Edward Bronson is actually my uncle. He is my father's younger brother and they started a very thriving business together many years ago. When my father passed away some years since, his half of the business and the house we lived in in Hull was left to me, but seeing as I didn't wish to return there my uncle moved into the house and he manages my side of the business in my absence.'

Two red spots of colour flared in Ginny's cheeks. 'So if you knew all along that Charlie was with your uncle, why didn't you tell me?' she said, hurt and annoyance sharp in her voice.

Mrs Bronson dropped her eyes. 'I should have told you,' she said in a low voice. 'And I'm sorry now that I wasn't honest with you from the start, my dear, but I assure you I had your brother's best interests at heart.'

Another thought occurred to Ginny then and her frown deepened. 'But why did you get your uncle to take Charlie from the workhouse in the first place?'

Anna gulped. This was the moment she had been dreading and she knew that she would have to answer the question very carefully.

'I suppose it was because I watched your father grow up in the workhouse,' she said cautiously. 'And I thought it would be so sad if the same thing happened to his son.'

'If you felt so sorry for my father, why didn't you help him then?' Ginny snapped, throwing caution to the winds.

'Because I was much younger then and it didn't occur to me.' Anna spread her hands helplessly. 'There were so many children in the workhouse, still are for that matter, that I would dearly like to help, but I'm only one person. I kept track of your father when he grew up and left the workhouse, and when I heard that he had married I rejoiced for him. I believe he was a good man until tragedy struck?'

'He still is a good man,' Ginny said defensively. 'But he couldn't cope with the loss of three of his children and my mother and he didn't know how to get through it. I know he wouldn't have meant to harm the man he fought with. My dad was never a violent man – never!'

'I believe you,' Anna said hastily. 'And I'm truly sorry that I didn't explain all this to you from the very beginning. When you turned up here with nowhere to go, the only way I could think of helping you was to offer you a position. But at least now you know the truth.' Or some of it, she thought. 'And when the weather improves, perhaps you would allow me to take you to visit Charlie so that you can see for yourself how well he is getting on. Alternatively, I have another suggestion to put to you...'

When Ginny gazed mistrustfully at her, Anna hurried on, 'My uncle has offered to have you there too. Think of it, Virginia – you and Charlie could be together again.'

Ginny stared at her in shock. '*Me*, go to live in Hull? But why would your uncle want *me* there? He doesn't even know me. And how would I earn my keep?'

'There would be no need to worry about that. You would be doing him a favour, as it happens. He's elderly now and he gets quite lonely, you see. I think that's why he's enjoying having Charlie there, because he breathes a little life into the place.' She watched Ginny closely, waiting for a reaction – but when it came, it was not what she had been hoping for.

'It's out of the question,' Ginny said decidedly. 'I need to be here so that my father can find me, and I couldn't put on someone I don't even know. I would appreciate you taking me to visit Charlie though, although I have to be honest and tell you that I have no intentions of letting Charlie stay in Hull indefinitely. Just as soon as I've saved enough up, I intend to get a job and rent somewhere to live so that I can have him with me until our dad comes home.'

Anna swallowed her disappointment. 'In that case, why don't you continue to work here and I'll ask the master if you couldn't rent one of the cottages in the grounds?' she suggested.

Ginny considered it for a moment but then shook her head. 'Thank you, but I am employed as Miss Diana's companion-cum-maid. What will happen when she decides to get married or leave home? There would be no position here for me then, and Charlie and I would be homeless again. I appreciate the offer but I think it would be better if I were to get somewhere where we can put down roots. Dad will need a home to come out of prison to.'

Anna was full of admiration for her grand-daughter. Ginny clearly had even more pride, loyalty and spirit than she had given her credit for. 'Let's not worry about that just yet,' she said encouragingly. 'At least for now you know that Charlie is being well taken care of.'

Ginny rose from her seat and bobbed politely. She was vastly relieved to know that Charlie was safe and happy in a decent home but still baffled and furious with Mrs Bronson for not putting her mind at rest long before this. All those sleepless nights, all those tears... Somewhere in the back of her mind things still didn't quite add up. But she'd had more than enough to cope with for one day.

'Thank you, Mrs Bronson,' she said quietly and then turned and left without another word.

Back in the sanctuary of her room, Ginny crossed to the window and stared sightlessly across the grounds. The only sound was the sighing of the wind in the leafless trees and the barking of a dog fox from the nearby wood.

Why would Mrs Bronson be working for a living as a lowly housekeeper if she was a woman of means? And why had she singled Charlie out for special attention – and herself, if it came to that? There were so many children incarcerated in the workhouse, so why them? And why had her father told her to go to Mrs Bronson for help in the first place? None of it made any sense, and the more she tried to figure it out, the more bewildered she became.

Heaving a sigh, she let herself out of her room and went to see if Diana needed any help undressing. At least they were getting along well now, which was something. In actual fact, Ginny was growing to be quite fond of her charge.

Diana was waiting for her and her eyes were glowing as she caught Ginny's hands and shook them up and down, telling her, 'The doctor says that Ben may get dressed for a while tomorrow.'

With Ginny's help her speech was improving. She didn't tend to shout every word now, and the words were more evenly spaced out, thanks to Ginny's patience.

'Oh, but what will he wear?' Ginny asked in surprise. As far as she knew, Ben only had the clothes he had been wearing on the night she had found him.

'He and Giles are about the same size so Giles will lend him some.'

'I see.' Ginny forced herself to look pleased but wished with all her heart that Ben might leave soon. Diana was absolutely besotted with him and Ginny dreaded to think how the girl would cope with his going. She helped her to undress and hung her clothes away, and was just about to leave the room when Diana suddenly said, 'Oh dear! I forgot to take this book along to Ben.' She made for the door, but Ginny gently took her arm and shook her head.

'You can't go dressed in those.' She pointed at Diana's nightdress and robe, and mouthed, 'Here, give it to me and I'll drop it into his room for him.' It was the last thing she wanted to do. As far as she was concerned, the less she saw of Ben the better, but she didn't want Diana to get into trouble with her aunt.

'Very well.' Diana reluctantly handed the book over and after saying good night, Ginny slipped away, not relishing having to spend even one second alone with Ben.

She found him comfortably settled, dozing when she tapped and entered his room. Keen to get away, she stated briefly, 'Diana asked me to bring this in for you.'

He grinned at her. 'Thanks very much. It's nice

to see you on yer own. I don't get much chance with Diana being here all the time.'

'Where would you like me to put it?' Ginny asked, ignoring his comment.

'Oh, I reckon I might start it right now if you'd bring it over here.'

She approached the bed reluctantly and was just about to lay the book on the cover when he suddenly sat upright and grabbed her arm in a strong grip.

'Don't be frightened.' He leered at her as he ran his finger up and down her wrist. 'I won't hurt you. In fact, I could be very nice to you if you'd let me. You're a welcome change from Diana. Her voice sets my nerves on edge, between you an' me.'

Ginny flung the book down and snatched her arm away. 'You are disgusting!' she spat. 'And pretending you can hardly move – you made a good job of it then. I wonder how ill you really are? As for Diana, she thinks the sun rises and sets with you, more's the pity! What would she think if I were to tell her what you just said about her?'

'Oh, I don't think you'll do that,' he drawled, dropping back on to the pillows. 'I would just deny everything – and who do you think she'd believe? I'd tell her that you've been making cow eyes at me when she wasn't about – and how long do you think you would keep your job then, eh, Miss Snooty Drawers?'

Ginny's skirts rustled and flared as she whirled around and started to stride from the room, intent on putting as much distance as she could between them – but Ben wasn't done with her yet.

'You'll be back,' he taunted. 'You want me – I can see you do.'

'When hell freezes over,' she ground out as she passed through the door and slammed it behind her. Leaning heavily against it then she took a deep breath and was just about to head off to her room when Mrs Bronson appeared around the corner.

'Why, Ginny, whatever is the matter?' she asked.

'Oh er ... nothing, ma'am,' Ginny muttered tiredly, then lifting her skirts she fled. She'd had just about all she could take for the time being.

Anna watched her go with a troubled expression on her face before making her way to Celia's room. James was downstairs in the study with Ventriss, who was still having problems with poachers, so Anna wanted to ensure that her mistress was made comfortable for the night. She was disturbed to see Celia's supper tray untouched when she entered the room, but keeping her voice light she crossed to the bed and asked, 'Do you have everything you need before I retire?'

'Perhaps just a few drops of laudanum in a glass of water please, my dear,' Celia replied. 'But don't tell James about it. You know how he frets.'

Anna carefully measured a few drops into a water glass. It seemed that Celia was needing more and more of the stuff to keep the pain at bay, yet she still stubbornly refused to see the doctor.

'I wish–' Anna started.

Celia cut her off. 'I think we both know that I am beyond wishing now, don't we?' she said softly. 'It's just a matter of time.' She looked so weary and frail that Anna could have wept for her, but still she refused to believe that there was nothing that could be done.

'At least let the doctor look at you,' she pleaded, with tears in her eyes. 'I could arrange for him to call when he comes to see Ben, and James need never know about it.'

Celia was silent for a moment but then she nodded resignedly. 'Very well, but I really don't think it will do any good.'

'Even so, it's worth getting his opinion,' Anna stressed as Celia gulped at the water. The effort of drinking exhausted her. She lay back against her pillows when it was gone and in seconds she was fast asleep while Anna crept from her room with a sorrowing heart.

Chapter Thirty-Two

It was at the beginning of April when James tapped on Joe's bedroom door one morning before going down to breakfast. Joe had just finished dressing in yet another of Giles' smart outfits and when James entered the room he said politely, 'Good morning, sir, and it looks set to be a fine one.'

'It does indeed.' With his arms behind his back, James strode across to the window and after a while he said, 'I was wondering how you are feeling now?'

Joe was well aware that the doctor would have informed him that the wound was fully healed, so he said truthfully, 'Much better, thank you, sir. I think I am recovered physically, it's just my memory loss that is the problem now.'

'I see ... and is there still no sign of it returning as yet?'

Joe sighed. 'To be honest, I get these feelings, as if it's all there ready to come back to me but is just beyond my grasp. It's very frustrating.'

'I can imagine it is, but let us hope it happens soon.' James regarded him solemnly. 'Meanwhile you may stay for a little longer, of course.'

This is it, Joe thought, the beginning of the end. He'd wondered how long it would be in coming.

'That's very generous of you, sir. You've been so good to me. I don't know how I can ever repay you.'

'There will be no need for that. It will be enough to see you well again and returned safely to wherever you came from. But now if you will excuse me I must get off. Good day, Ben.'

'Good day, sir.'

As the door closed behind James, Joe frowned. Although his host had been polite, Joe sensed that he was beginning to outstay his welcome. He had hoped for a little more time but things could be delayed no longer. It was time to start putting his plan into action properly now.

Walking with Diana in the garden later that day, he craftily said, 'I fear I am beginning to be a burden on your family, Diana. Perhaps it is time I moved on?'

Deeply distressed, she said immediately, 'Oh no, you mustn't! Your body may be whole again,

321

but you still don't know who you are. Where would you go?'

He shrugged. 'I could go and find work somewhere... We must face facts. After all, the doctor said my memory may never return, then again it could come back at any minute. But I admit that I ... that I will miss you.'

She stopped and said passionately. 'No, you *must* stay. Please. For a little while longer at least.'

'My dear girl.' He reached out and stroked her hair, causing her to flush with pleasure. Then, tucking her hand into the crook of his arm, he led her towards a summerhouse that stood amongst a little group of trees. Once inside he bowed his head as he told her, 'I really think I must go, sweet Diana. You see, I have developed feelings for you.'

'Oh, Ben, but I have feelings for you too!'

'Really, my love?' He opened his arms and she went into them willingly, and when he kissed her lips she made no objection; in fact, she clung to him. Then suddenly he held her at arm's length and stepped away from her.

'I'm sorry,' he muttered, running a hand distractedly through his hair. 'I shouldn't have done that. It was so wrong of me. I don't even know who I am. I could be a penniless beggar with nothing to offer you!'

'It wouldn't matter to me even if you were,' she said fervently.

'But your guardians wouldn't agree with that,' he told her, playing the hard-done-to fellow to the hilt. 'You have been brought up properly and no doubt your family hope you will make a good marriage. We must stop this – until my memory returns, at least.'

'It is too late to stop my feelings for you now!' the girl insisted, throwing her arms about his waist. With a sigh he lowered his lips to hers again and kissed her until she felt quite dizzy.

It was at that same moment that Nancy and Ginny happened to walk down the drive following a visit to Mrs Bevins and the Watkins family. It was a Sunday and as was his custom now, Bertie had walked them to the gates of the Hall.

'Eeh, but the gardens are looking lovely, ain't they?' Nancy said as she admired the daffodils bursting through the earth. 'I don't know how Ventriss manages all this lot with just a lad to help him.'

Ginny smiled. She had a feeling that it was Bertie rather than the garden that had put Nancy in such good spirits. She chatted on about him every opportunity she got and it was obvious that she was very smitten with him. Ginny just hoped that with time, Bertie would realise it too. Whenever she saw them together she couldn't help but think what a perfect couple they made. She herself was very fond of Bertie and his family, but she still could think of him as nothing more than a very dear friend and she knew that it would always be so. All her thoughts were focused on seeing Charlie again, which shouldn't be too far away now that the weather had suddenly improved, and if Mrs Bronson kept her promise.

The two girls walked a little further and suddenly Nancy caught Ginny's arm and dragged her to a halt, saying, 'Isn't that Ben with Miss Diana over there?'

Ginny's eyes followed Nancy's pointing finger and sure enough there they were, coming out of the summerhouse arm-in-arm for all the world like lovers.

Then suddenly, Joe pulled Diana into the shelter of a tree and kissed her soundly.

'Oh my goodness!' Nancy's hand flew to her mouth. 'What's the chap thinkin' of? The master and mistress 'ud have a fit if they saw them goin's-on.'

'Hmm, I've been expecting it, to be honest,' Ginny answered, hauling Nancy along. 'I reckon he's set his cap at Miss Diana.'

'Then why is he so free with his hands towards the rest o' the staff?' Nancy enquired indignantly. 'He's always tryin' to feel Barbara and Millie's arses when they're in his room. I bet Miss Diana would be none too pleased to hear that!'

Ginny shrugged. 'I suppose it's none of our business,' she said. 'But now come along. We don't want to be accused of spying on them.'

Seeing the sense in what Ginny said, Nancy hurried her steps to match Ginny's and soon the two love birds were out of sight.

'It might be best if we kept what we saw to ourselves,' Ginny said thoughtfully as they walked around to the servants' entrance at the back of the house. 'The master and mistress are so excited about Master Sebastian coming home, it would be a shame to spoil it for them.'

'Aye, happen yer right,' Nancy agreed. 'An' happen they'd never believe us anyway even if we did say sommat, so it's a case of least said the better, eh?'

After dinner that evening, Ginny went into Diana's bedroom. She was entitled to take the whole day off but the two girls had become closer over the previous weeks so Ginny didn't mind helping her to get ready for bed.

'Ah, Ginny!' Diana was seated at her dressing table taking the pins from her hair and Ginny noticed that her cheeks were flushed and her eyes were shining.

'You'll never guess what has happened.' She was so happy that her words were almost tripping over one another.

'Your brother is coming home tomorrow?' Ginny said immediately, without thinking, and then felt embarrassed to have mentioned it – and confused to realise that it had been on her mind. What difference would it make to her, after all?

'Pah.' Diana waved her hand impatiently. 'That's all Uncle James could talk about at dinner. I shall be happy to see him, of course. But it's something even better than that!'

'Really?' Feigning ignorance, Ginny crossed to her and began to unclip her hair, avoiding her eyes in the mirror. She had a terrible feeling she knew what was coming and could only see heartache ahead for her young mistress.

'Ben has told me that he loves me. And I love him too. Isn't that wonderful?'

At a loss for words, Ginny gulped before saying eventually, 'Isn't it all rather sudden? What I mean is, you haven't known him for very long and you don't really know anything about him or even where he comes from. None of us do.'

'I don't care!' Diana tossed her head impatiently. Ginny hadn't responded in the way she had hoped she would. But then, Diana thought, perhaps she was jealous? It would be quite understandable. Ben was very handsome, after all, and he loved *her*. Unable to stay in a bad mood she hugged herself.

'I don't care who he is or where he is from. I just know that we were meant to be together.'

'Have you spoken to your aunt or uncle about this?' Ginny questioned.

'Not yet.' Diana became a little more subdued. 'Ben thinks we should wait a while to see if his memory returns. But even if it doesn't, I still intend to marry him,' she finished defiantly.

Ginny collected up the hairpins and dropped them into a dish before beginning to brush Diana's hair but she could sense the girl was waiting for a response, so she said politely, 'Then I really hope it works out for you both. Now shall I go and take out your warming pan?'

With that she dived under the covers of Diana's bed before she put her foot in it and said something she shouldn't.

Chapter Thirty-Three

'Why, my darling, I'm sure you've shot up another six inches at least since the last time you were here. Welcome home, dear boy!'

'Thank you, Aunt. It's good to be back but

strange to think that I won't be going off to school any more.' Sebastian leaned down to kiss his aunt's cheeks, appalled to see how thin she had become in the few short weeks he had been away. She was so frail now that her body barely made a dent beneath the bedclothes, and the skin on her face looked as if it had been stretched across her cheekbones. Her eyes were sunken, with dark circles beneath them, but it didn't stop her being overjoyed to see him. She had always had a huge soft spot for Sebastian and had greatly looked forward to his homecoming.

'Your uncle and I are thrilled with your grades, dear,' she gushed on. But then becoming solemn she asked worriedly, 'But are you *quite* sure that you wish to work in the family business? I mean ... I know your uncle is thrilled at the idea, and Giles certainly doesn't seem very interested. But should you wish to go on to Oxford or Cambridge, we would understand perfectly.'

Sebastian patted her hand fondly, saying, 'I'm more than happy to help Uncle. In fact, I'm looking forward to it – although I don't know what he'll make of some of the ideas I've had, especially regarding the farms.'

Celia grinned. 'I'm sure he'll be more than happy to discuss new ideas. Someone young with fresh eyes is always a good thing. Times are changing and dear James is a reasonable man, as you know. But have you seen Diana yet?'

He shook his head. 'Not yet. I literally dumped my bags in the hall and came straight up to see you. Why? Is there a problem with her?'

'Not a problem exactly...' Celia bit on her lip.

'But I fear she has formed a romantic attachment to the young man Ginny found wounded in the grounds some months ago.'

'What? You mean to tell me he is still here?' Sebastian looked shocked. He had expected Ben to be long gone.

His aunt nodded. 'Yes, he is. His physical injuries have healed, of course, but he still hasn't regained his memory and I think your uncle is too kind to cast him adrift when he has no idea where he came from. Diana has been spending a great deal of time with him, although I have insisted that Ginny stays with them. Do you remember Ginny? Well, as I told you on your last visit I have appointed her as Diana's companion-cum-lady's maid, and the arrangement is working really well. Diana has calmed down considerably under Ginny's influence. It's just this attachment to Ben we are concerned about. He could be anyone, after all. A prince or a perfect scoundrel.'

'Quite,' Sebastian replied as a picture of Ginny's coal-black hair and sparkling grey-blue eyes flashed into his mind. He'd thought of her often.

'And what is Giles up to now?' he asked then, changing the subject.

'Not a great deal,' his aunt answered with a wry smile. 'I hate to say it for I love him dearly, but I'm afraid your cousin has never been very keen on work. But enough about that for now. I know your uncle intends you to have a few months off to get over all your studying before you start work with him, then I believe he's going to crack the whip at Giles too, which won't go down well at all if I know my grandson.'

'There's really no need for a vacation on my account,' Sebastian assured her. 'I'm looking forward to starting work.'

'Well, we'll see.' Celia sometimes guiltily wished that Sebastian had been her grandson rather than Giles. 'But now you run along to the kitchen and see if you can't cadge a piece of pie or something off Cook to see you through to dinnertime. It shouldn't be too hard; you were always able to wrap the poor woman around your little finger.'

He grinned as he lifted her hand and kissed it, then turning about he went to do as he was told. He was feeling quite peckish as it happened but then that was nothing new. The food at the school had been quite inedible at times so he always enjoyed being at home where Cook spoiled him with all his favourite dishes.

'Ah, here you are, Master Seb,' Cook said delightedly when he breezed into the kitchen. 'No doubt you've come to see what you can scrounge. Well, it just so happens that bein' as I knew you were comin' home, I baked a tray o' those drop scones yer always liked. How would one or two o' them go down with a nice bit o'jam an' cream?'

'Oh, if only you knew how I've *dreamed* of your scones,' he teased, placing an arm about her plump waist and planting a kiss on her cheek.

'Get off wi' you,' she scolded, although she was beaming all over her face. She had a mighty big soft spot for young Master Seb and always had had, since he'd been knee high to a grasshopper. 'Go an' sit yerself down at the table,' she ordered as she waddled off to the pantry to get the scones that had been cooling there.

Within minutes Sebastian had downed four of them, rolling his eyes as if he was in heaven.

'You're havin' no more, else yer won't have room fer your dinner an' I've done yer favourite fer tonight. Roast beef wi' all the trimmin's,' she told him indulgently. It was then that they heard someone come in at the front door and he rose hastily.

'I bet that's Diana,' he said. 'I haven't seen her yet so I'd best go and say hello, but I'll look forward to that dinner, Cook.'

She watched him go with a twinkle in her eye then returned her attention to the batter she was beating for the Yorkshire puddings.

It was Diana who had come in and Sebastian saw that she was with Ginny and a young man. Just for a second he had the idea that he'd seen the chap somewhere before, although for the life of him he couldn't think where. And then Diana spotted him and came running towards him, her crinoline flying behind her like sails in the wind.

'Oh Seb, you're home! I'm so pleased, especially as you won't be going away again!'

He caught her around the waist and twizzled her about as he had when she'd been a young girl, and she giggled with delight as Joe and Ginny looked on. Ginny was smiling but the young man looked less than pleased to see him, Sebastian noted. Now why would that be?

Placing his sister back down on the floor, Sebastian took her hand and approached the two standing by the door.

'Good day, sir.'

Ginny bobbed her knee but Sebastian frowned and said, 'Oh, please, Ginny. I told you to call me Seb.' Then, turning his attention to the young man – who, he noted, looked fit as a fiddle – he extended his hand and said politely, 'How do you do, Mr er...'

'It's just Ben for now,' Joe replied as he grudgingly shook his hand. 'Just until I get my memory back.'

'Ginny and Ben have been for a walk down to the lake with me,' Diana gabbled.

'It must be looking very pretty now with all the flowers springing back to life.' Her brother made a little bow then and excused himself, saying, 'If you'll forgive me I ought to go and do my unpacking. I've brought rather a lot of stuff back with me, seeing as I won't be going back to school again. And of course I'm rather keen to get round to the stables and see my horse, but I'm sure I shall see you all at dinner.'

As he collected two of his bags and carried them upstairs he marvelled at the change in Ginny. She looked very different from the girl he had first seen leaning over one of the dolly tubs in the laundry room with her hair tumbling from beneath her mob cap. Today she had looked very demure – more of a lady than his sister, in fact, with her shining hair woven into a smart fold on the back of her head and in her neat blue dress. Personally, Seb thought it was a wonderful idea of his aunt's to appoint her as Diana's companion. Ginny had been wasted in the laundry. Diana had never really mixed with young people near her own age apart from himself and Giles, and he was well aware that that wasn't quite the same as having another young lady to gossip to about all the things that were important to their sex.

Ben was another matter entirely though. Sebastian had sensed that the fellow's guard was up and again, he wondered why. However, he was soon involved in his unpacking and he didn't give the young man another thought until they were all seated at the dining table together that evening. Even his Aunt Celia had made an effort and had been helped downstairs to celebrate his homecoming, although he noted that Ginny wasn't present. No doubt she would be eating in the kitchen with the rest of the staff, which he thought was rather a shame. He had an idea she would prove to be very good company.

The first course was served – stuffed mushrooms grown at the Hall, one of his favourites, followed by Cook's promised roast beef, which had been cooked to perfection. Sebastian noticed that his aunt merely pecked at her food like a little bird but he himself did justice to everything that was placed in front of him and even had seconds. The next course was one of Cook's special trifles, a delicacy she usually kept for only very special occasions, and finally a cheese-board and a selection of fresh fruit was placed in the centre of the table.

By then his aunt was looking very pale so as soon as everyone had finished, James said, 'Would you like me to help you back up to your room, dear?'

'I'll take her up,' Anna offered. She always sat at

her mistress's side during mealtimes downstairs and Celia nodded gratefully.

'If you wouldn't mind, Anna dear. I'm sure James and Sebastian have a lot to talk about.'

Everyone else stayed in their places as Anna tenderly helped Celia from the room then James suggested, 'Shall we go through to the library for a glass of port and a cigar, Sebastian? I shall have to get used to treating you as a grown up now, especially if you're going to be my right-hand man.'

This earned a glare from Giles but the pair ignored it as they went out of the room, leaving Diana, her cousin Giles and Ben at the table.

'Your aunt tells me you are brimming with ideas. I'd like to hear them,' James said when they were sitting comfortably in the soft leather wing chairs either side of James' desk. Sebastian had accepted a glass of port but politely refused the offer of a cigar. One of the chaps at school had smuggled some in the year before; Seb had tried a puff or two and hadn't stopped coughing for an hour after.

'I'm not so sure you'll agree with all of them,' Sebastian commented with a grin. 'For a start, the last time I was home and went out for a ride on Flyer, I couldn't help but notice that some of the tenant farmhouses are in desperate need of updating and I think we ... you, that is, Uncle – owe it to your tenants to get the renovations done.'

'Hmm, it's certainly something I'll consider,' James said thoughtfully. 'Perhaps when you start work that could be one of your first jobs? Visiting each of the farms and making a list of what needs doing. Then you might price up what it's going to cost and we'll take it from there.'

'Gladly,' Sebastian agreed. 'Most of them, for instance, still have earth floors inside, and I think we should fit flagstones or possibly even wooden floorboards. We could keep the cost down if we used some of the flat stones from the quarry and got some of your workforce to fit them rather than employ firms from outside. Also, I noticed that the labourers who live in the quarry cottages in Tuttle Hill all share an outside well. What about if we piped water into each home and had a pump installed on their sinks?'

James was impressed with his nephew's ideas and soon the two of them were deep in discussion.

At that moment Ben and Diana were leaving the dining room and Diana said impulsively, 'Why don't we slip out for a walk before Ginny appears? No one will miss us. Uncle is in with Seb, Giles has gone off somewhere and Mrs Bronson will be getting my aunt ready for bed.'

Truthfully, Joe would have liked nothing more than to escape to his room for an hour's peace. He had spent most of the day with Diana and now her possessive behaviour and her grating voice were getting on his nerves. Even so he plastered a false smile on his face and said, 'That would be lovely, to have you all to myself for a little while. It's so frustrating having to have Ginny tag along all the time.'

He then tucked her arm into his and they made their escape through the front door. They raced to the summerhouse, breathless and panting, and Diana giggled as she drew Joe into the shadows. Within seconds she was in his arms and as his hand played across the bodice of her dress as he kissed her passionately, she swooned with ecstasy. Earlier in the day when they had managed to give Ginny the slip for a few minutes, he had tried to put his hand up her skirt but she had gently pulled away. He wasn't overly concerned. Slow and easy would win the race and soon it would be time to take things a stage further, for once he had taken her virginity the family would be only too grateful for him to wed her. The way he saw it, once she was soiled goods no one else would.

Chapter Thirty-Four

'Virginia, may I have a word, please?'

'Yes, Mrs Bronson.' Ginny bobbed her knee and quickly followed the housekeeper into her room.

She stared at her expectantly and was not disappointed when the woman asked, 'I was wondering if you would like to make the trip to Hull I promised you to see your brother.'

'Oh, yes, ma'am ... I'd *love* to!' Ginny's beautiful eyes were sparkling with pleasure at the thought of seeing Charlie again and Mrs Bronson smiled to see her so happy.

'I thought that we might leave next Monday. If that suits you, I shall make all the necessary travel arrangements.'

'You could stop the cost of mine out of my wages,' Ginny offered instantly but Mrs Bronson shook her head.

'There will be no need for that, my dear. The master has already offered to cover our travelling expenses.'

Ginny was touched. The family had been very kind to her and recently she had on occasion been summoned to read to the mistress of an afternoon when Mrs Bronson was busy with housekeeping duties. Sometimes they looked at Mrs Walton-Hughes' fashion magazines and Ginny had been able to practise some of the most recent hairstyles on Miss Diana. All in all, she was much happier these days although she still missed her family every single day. She and Diana were getting along famously now but Ginny did worry, for she had somehow become the girl's confidante. Diana was quite convinced that she was truly in love with Ben and this disturbed Ginny, for he still gave her the eye every chance he got – and surely he wouldn't have done that if the feelings he professed to have for Diana were real? All these thoughts were pushed far to the back of her mind for now though. All she could think about was seeing her little brother again.

'Do you have everything you need for the journey?' Mrs Bronson asked and Ginny nodded happily. She would quite willingly have gone dressed in rags as long as she got to see Charlie.

Once Mrs Bronson dismissed her, Ginny tore

upstairs to tell Diana her good news.

'Mrs Bronson is taking me to visit my little brother next week and so I shall be gone for a few days,' she blurted out breathlessly. She had spoken so quickly that Diana had been unable to understand her so Ginny had to repeat herself more slowly.

'Why, that's wonderful!' Diana was genuinely pleased for her. She had heard so much about Charlie that she almost felt she knew him. She went on: 'But you should have some new clothes to go in.'

Ginny frowned as she looked down at the skirts of her crinoline. The clothes she had now were the best she had ever owned and were more than respectable.

'But what is wrong with this one?'

'Pah!' Diana waved her hand. 'What if you have to dress for dinner? That dress is far too plain. So is your other one, for that matter. Let's see what we have in here that might be suitable.'

She hurried across to her armoire and began to rummage about, tossing certain gowns out on to the bed. They were all the colours of the rainbow but she leaped on one in a soft cream satin, saying, 'Ah, now this one would be perfect with your colouring.'

Ginny's mouth gaped open as she fingered the fine guipure lace about the neckline.

'I could *never* wear something like that,' she mumbled.

'Of course you could,' Diana insisted. 'Come on, let's try it on you. We are about the same size, but if it's a little large on you, you'll have time to alter it.'

Blushing deeply, Ginny slowly undressed as Diana tapped her foot impatiently. Once she was standing there self-consciously in her shift, Diana deftly slipped the dress over her head and began to lace it up the back. Ginny stifled a giggle. It was as if their roles had been reversed and suddenly she was the mistress and Diana was the maid.

'Look in the mirror,' Diana ordered then and when Ginny turned and caught sight of herself she was shocked. The dress fit perfectly and she barely recognised herself. Her hand flew to the small partly exposed cleavage. She'd never worn a dress like this in her whole life and her blush deepened.

'But I ... I couldn't wear this,' she mouthed to Diana.

'Of course you could!' Diana was in her element. 'But now we must find you some suitable shoes to wear with it.' Crossing once more to her wardrobe, she produced several different pairs of shoes. Unfortunately, Ginny's feet were at least a size larger than Diana's and none of them would fit.

'Oh well,' Diana said resignedly, 'it won't really matter with the dress being slightly too long. No one will notice.' Her mood brightening again, she tapped her lip with her finger as she studied Ginny before deciding, 'We should do something with your hair now. It's too severe like that. Sit down here.'

Ginny obediently sat down at Diana's dressing table and the girl took the pins from her hair. She then shook it out and began to brush it vigorously, clearly enjoying herself immensely.

'You must wear it loose,' she commented enviously. 'It's so beautiful.'

The black silky locks fell like a silken sheet almost to Ginny's waist and she raised her hand to touch it doubtfully. 'Do you really think so?'

'Oh yes. But now come along. We must show Aunt Celia how you look in all your finery. She won't recognise you.'

Taking Ginny's hand, she hauled her to her feet and dragged her protesting towards the bedroom door. Ginny still had doubts on whether she would ever even get the opportunity to wear such a dress, but she didn't want to spoil Diana's good mood. She was being very kind to her, after all.

They had only just stepped out on to the landing when Ben's bedroom door opened and he and Giles appeared.

'What's this then?' Ben was hardly able to believe his eyes. He'd always thought Ginny was a looker but now she was positively stunning. He'd not even recognised her for a second, for she looked more of a lady than Diana did.

Ginny squirmed with embarrassment as his eyes fastened on the neckline of the dress. And then suddenly Sebastian joined them too when he appeared at the top of the stairs. He had been out riding; his hair was tousled by the wind and his cheeks were rosy.

'Why Ginny, you look quite charming,' he said, his eyes openly admiring, but somehow Ginny could accept a compliment from him. She'd seen very little of him since he'd arrived home but whenever she had, he'd always been pleasant and polite and spoken to her as an equal.

'Come on,' Diana said, dragging Ginny along by the hand, and Ginny, who wasn't used to being the centre of attention, was only too happy to go.

Shortly afterwards when they were back in Diana's room and the girl was helping Ginny to take the dress off, Ginny told her, 'It's very kind of you to lend it to me, Diana. If I do get the chance to wear it, I shall take care of it, I promise.'

Diana frowned and her hands became still for a moment. 'But I'm not loaning it to you. It's a gift. It looks far better on you with your colouring than it ever did on me anyway.'

'Oh! Thank you so much.' Ginny's eyes filled with tears at the girl's kindness and generosity. They were getting along so much better now and Ginny was becoming genuinely fond of her.

But soon it was back to reality when Diana said, 'I think we'll go and see what Ben is up to when you've fastened your hair back up.'

Ginny's heart sank. It was as if Diana couldn't bear to be apart from him for more than an hour or two and Ginny could see nothing but heartache ahead.

Could she have known it, at that very moment as Joe and Giles strolled along the drive, Joe was telling him, 'I've decided it's time to let Diana think that my memory is coming back, and here's what I'm going to tell her...'

Giles listened intently, his brow furrowed. He had no option but to go along with Joe's scheme, for Joe could get him into deep trouble with his grandfather if he had a mind to, and lately Giles had felt that James was becoming increasingly impatient with him.

'So now what I want you to do is find Diana and send her to the summerhouse for me. She'll likely be lookin' for me already. She's like a bitch on heat followin' me about all the time. Tell her I wasn't lookin' too grand, eh?'

Giles nodded and, turning, strode back along the drive. He didn't feel as if he had much choice. He was just about to enter the house again when Ginny and Diana emerged and he gruffly told his cousin, 'Ben was heading for the summerhouse the last time I saw him. He didn't look too well.'

'Oh.' Diana was instantly concerned as she set off across the lawn, telling Ginny, 'Would you mind very much just giving us a few moments alone? You could take a stroll around the lake perhaps?'

Seeing Ginny's expression, Diana rushed on, 'I know Uncle James said Ben and I shouldn't be left alone, but I'm only asking for a few minutes. Oh *please*, Ginny!'

'Very well, but only for a few minutes, mind. I don't want to get into trouble with your aunt and uncle.' Ginny reluctantly turned towards the woods through which the lake lay as Diana scooted off in the direction of the summerhouse. She felt as if she was being pulled in two directions. Half of her wanted to obey her employer's orders, the other half of her felt that Diana, who was now almost eighteen, should be allowed some freedom. Not that she approved of Ben. She was so lost in thought that when she eventually emerged from the trees and moved towards the lake, she didn't immediately see the figure sitting there with his back against the bark of a tree.

'Hello, Ginny.'

When the girl turned startled eyes towards the voice, she saw Sebastian smiling at her.

'Are you looking for a bit of peace and quiet as well?' he asked.

'Er ... yes – no. What I should say is I'm just killing a few minutes before I meet Diana again. She's talking to Ben.'

'I see.' Even in the short time he had been home Sebastian could see how the land lay in that direction. Diana couldn't complete a sentence without mentioning the chap and Sebastian was somewhat concerned about it. They didn't know the bloke from Adam, after all, but he had clearly got his little sister Diana eating out of the palm of his hand.

'Come and sit by me,' he invited then. 'It's very peaceful here. I often come when I want to think.'

'I shouldn't, sir. I told Diana I would only be a few minutes.'

He laughed. 'Oh, Ginny, there's really no need to be so formal. Can't you please call me Seb?'

'Oh, I ... I'm not sure that that would be right,' Ginny faltered. He was the master's nephew, after all, not that he ever put on airs and graces, mind. Not like Master Giles.

He patted the grass at the side of him. 'Well, come and sit down for a moment at least. I promise I won't bite.'

Feeling that it would be churlish to refuse, Ginny slowly approached him and sat down, deliberately leaving some distance between them.

'To tell you the truth I shall be glad to start work with my uncle now,' Seb confided. 'He insists that I have a rest first but my head is so full of ideas.'

'What sort of ideas?' Ginny was curious now.

Sebastian quickly told her about the ones he had already put to his uncle, then went on, 'Another thing I'm very keen on is schooling. I know at least half of the local children don't attend school because their parents can't afford the pennies to send them. I think it's a crying shame. Oh, I'm well aware that some bosses prefer to keep their workers in ignorance, but times are changing. Everyone should be allowed the chance to read and write. I feel it's appalling that some workers can only sign with a cross, don't you agree?'

Ginny was warming to him by the second. 'Yes, I do agree. My parents were very strict about us going to school and they both used to teach us our letters and numbers at home as well.'

'So you enjoy reading, then?'

Ginny smiled and reeled off a list of some of the books she had read. 'Mrs Bronson is kindly allowing me to read some of hers now,' she told him animatedly. 'And sometimes in the afternoons I go in and read to your aunt. She really seems to enjoy it.'

'I'm sure she would.' Sebastian studied her for a moment. It seemed that Ginny Thursday was fairly well educated as well as being kind and pretty. 'I'd love to set up some sort of a little school for the children of Uncle's workers,' he went on. 'Nothing grand you understand? But somewhere to enable them to have at least a few hours' schooling a week.'

Ginny's eyes shone at the prospect. Like Sebastian, she believed that everyone should be allowed the chance to make the best of themselves.

'I think it's a wonderful idea, and as your uncle seems to be a very reasonable man I hope you'll be able to persuade him to go ahead with it. I've been helping Diana, as it happens. She confided that because she didn't much like most of her governesses she didn't really try to learn, but she's trying now.'

'I've noticed a big change in her,' Sebastian agreed. 'She seems much calmer, and not so keen to fly off into one of her tantrums.'

Ginny giggled as she confided, 'It hasn't always been like that but I think we've reached an understanding now. I just wish she wasn't so besotted with...' Feeling that she might have overstepped the mark, her voice trailed away.

'"With Ben", you were going to say, weren't you?' Sebastian probed.

Ginny nodded miserably. Then getting to her feet she hastily brushed down her skirts and told him, 'It's been lovely to speak to you and good luck with your ideas. But now I really ought to go and find Diana.'

'Of course. It's been really good to speak to you too, Ginny.'

He made no effort to stop her leaving but as she walked away she felt his eyes boring into her back and a little smile played about her lips. He was nice, was Master Sebastian, and handsome too! She blushed at the thought.

Chapter Thirty-Five

'Oh, darling, at last you're starting to remember again. That's wonderful!' Diana squeezed Joe's hand as they sat close together side by side in the summerhouse.

'It's only coming back in little flashes,' he told her dramatically as he sighed. 'But I'm sure my name is Joseph. I haven't remembered my surname yet though, and I have a feeling I was on my way back from a funeral when I was attacked – but I can't remember whose funeral it was.' His voice broke deliberately.

'*Please* don't distress yourself,' Diana begged. 'Your memory will come in its own good time. And you say your name is Joseph.' She rolled the name around her tongue. She was so used to calling him Ben that it would be strange to change that now – although of course she must if that was his name.

'It's a grand name.' She smiled at him encouragingly but then he wrapped her in his arms and it really didn't matter what his name was – he was just the man she loved. His kisses were becoming more ardent when she felt him pull away, and glancing towards the window of the summerhouse, she saw the reason why. Ginny was advancing across the lawn.

Quickly disentangling herself from his arms, Diana hastily straightened her hair and smoothed her skirts as Ginny appeared in the doorway.

'Good news,' Diana told her. 'Ben has remembered his first name. It's Joseph. How strange it will be for us all to get used to calling him something other than Ben.'

Ginny nodded. 'Yes, it will,' she said politely, then looking pointedly at Joe: 'But it's good that he's starting to remember.'

His eyes were mocking as he stared back at her. He'd sussed that Ginny didn't believe a word he said, but he wasn't too much bothered.

'I gather you're going away for a few days early next week?' he said insolently. 'It's to stay with Mrs Bronson's uncle, isn't it? How very strange for her to take such an interest in a *mere servant.*'

Ginny flushed. Diana must have told him, and it made her feel at a disadvantage to know that they'd been discussing her. No doubt he would be glad to see the back of her for a while if it meant him being able to spend more time with Diana. As things were, the couple never got too long to be alone together but while she was away, Diana would be at his mercy. It came as a little shock to realise that she'd grown protective of Diana. Ginny did not trust Joseph, as he now admitted to being called, as far as she could throw him, but while she was away there was nothing much she could do about it.

'Your aunt will be expecting you now, Diana,' she said, expressly ignoring him as she looked directly into the young woman's face.

Diana pouted for a moment but then throwing a dazzling smile at Joe, she told him, 'Ginny is right. I should go, but I'll see you later.'

He made a great show of taking her hand and kissing it gallantly. Ginny knew that it was for her benefit but she didn't comment on it. Just being this close to him made her skin crawl and she couldn't wait to be out of his presence.

He watched the two girls stroll away across the lawn then with a grin he went in search of Giles. It was time to inform him that he was ready to put the next part of his plan into action.

On Sunday morning after breakfast, Ginny and Nancy set off to see the Watkins as usual. There was a spring in Nancy's steps and Ginny noticed that she had trimmed her old bonnet with blue ribbons that matched the colour of her eyes. She had bought them off the tallyman who called at the back door of the Hall from time to time. She'd also washed her hair and brushed it until it shone and Ginny had no doubt that it was all for Bertie's benefit.

'I wonder if Bertie will come to meet us,' Nancy mused, peering hopefully ahead as they approached Abbey Green. Then on a more solemn note she asked, 'Are you and Bertie really only friends, Ginny?'

'Yes, we are,' Ginny answered without hesitation. It was clear that Nancy was as enamoured of Bertie as Diana was of Joe, although to her mind, Bertie and Nancy were far more suited.

'So ... you wouldn't mind if he had a proper girlfriend then? I mean, if he was to start walking out with someone?'

'I'd be delighted for him,' Ginny said with all sincerity. 'Especially if that someone was you.'

347

Nancy blushed to the very roots of her hair. 'I *do* like him,' she said shyly, 'but I'd never do anything to spoil it for you if you had feelings for him.'

'I don't, I promise you, so feel free. Bertie would be a very lucky chap indeed if he were to find someone as nice as you, and I think his mother would approve as well. It's clear that she's taken to you. The whole family have, in fact.'

Nancy let out a sigh of relief. 'But how do I let him know how I feel?'

'Just carry on being yourself and I don't see how he can fail to grow to like you,' Ginny advised.

Nancy smiled then changed the subject when she asked, 'Are you packed ready for your trip?'

'Just a few more things to pop in my bag to-night then I'm all ready to go in the morning.'

'Hmm ... don't you find it a little strange that Mrs Bronson has gone to so much trouble for you and your brother?' Nancy asked. 'What I mean is, she usually keeps herself very much to herself and doesn't have any more to do with the staff than she has to. Why do you think she's taken such an interest in you?'

Ginny found it uncanny that her friend was echoing the exact same words as those used by the repulsive Joseph. 'I think it's because she knew my father when he was in the workhouse as a child. She watched him grow up so I suppose she's just being kind,' she said. Ginny had asked herself the same question many times, but now she was just looking forward to seeing Charlie again.

'I notice you and Master Sebastian are gettin' on very well,' Nancy said innocently then, peep-

348

ing at Ginny from the corner of her eye. And Ginny, much to her friend's amusement, was instantly on the defensive.

'Sebastian – I mean *Master* Sebastian – is friendly to everyone,' she said rather sharply.

Thankfully the conversation was stopped from going any further when Nancy noticed Bertie striding towards them, and almost forgetting Ginny in her pleasure at seeing him, she darted ahead to greet him. The girls spent a pleasant day with the Watkins family. Esther had prepared dinner for them and Cook had sent over a huge apple pie with raisins and cloves, as well as a basket of eggs, a pat of butter and a dozen flap-jacks. When the meal was over, Ginny helped Mrs Watkins with the washing up, leaving Mr Watkins to have a doze in the chair whilst the children scampered off outside to play. Bertie and Nancy sat at the table to enjoy a game of cards. Ginny and Esther could hear them laughing from the kitchen, and Mrs Watkins commented, 'They seem to be gettin' along well.'

Ginny nodded as she placed the plate she was drying on to the dresser. 'Yes. Between you and me, Nancy is very taken with Bertie and I can quite understand why. He's such a lovely young man.'

'Yes, he is. The trouble is, my son is quite taken wi' *you*.' Mrs Watkins heaved a sigh. 'Why are things never straightforward, lass? What I mean is, you ain't taken wi' him, are yer?'

Ginny knew she must be straight with her. 'No, I'm not,' she said in a small voice, 'not in that way. But it's nothing to do with Bertie, Mrs

349

Watkins. At the minute, all I can think about is getting my family back together again.'

'Oh, now I wasn't tryin' to make yer feel guilty,' Esther assured her. 'You've been through the mill lately, lass, so it's no wonder yer feel that way. As it happens I reckon Nancy an' Bertie would make a fine pair, but I'm a great believer that what's meant to be'll be, so let's just leave 'em to it, eh, an see how things work out. In the meantime, you're always welcome here, as yer know, so you just concentrate on seein' that little brother o' yours.'

It was mid-afternoon when Ginny said tentatively, 'Would you mind very much if I set off back to the Hall now? I'd like to be early as I still have a few things to do before I leave for Hull tomorrow.' Her stomach was already churning at the thought of the journey ahead. She had never set foot outside of Nuneaton before, apart from to visit the Coventry pot fair with her parents once a year, and Hull sounded like the other side of the world to her.

Seeing Nancy's face fall, she instantly added, 'You don't have to come, Nancy. You stay and come back when you're ready. You'll walk her home, won't you, Bertie?'

'Of course,' he said chivalrously, and so after giving them all a hug, Ginny set off.

The next morning dawned bright and clear, and Ginny hurried around saying her goodbyes. Diana was almost in tears as she told her, 'I shall miss you.' They had devised their own little sign language between them and Ginny was touched to see how upset the girl was.

'I shan't be gone for too long,' she promised, then she carried her bag down to the hall and placed it by the front door before going in search of Mrs Bronson. The carriage was already outside waiting for them, so she knew the woman wouldn't be far away. It was as she headed for the kitchen to say goodbye to Cook that she noticed the housekeeper's door was ajar. Glancing in as she passed – she froze as she saw the master and Mrs Bronson locked in each other's arms.

'Hurry back to me safely,' she heard the master whisper into the woman's hair then he kissed her tenderly on the lips.

Ginny turned on her heel and raced silently back to the front door to wait there. What could it mean? Both the master and Mrs Bronson seemed totally devoted to the mistress, yet here they were, behaving like lovers! She was still reeling from what she had seen when she saw Mrs Bronson coming towards her with the master close behind her.

'Are you quite ready to go, Virginia?' the housekeeper asked.

'Yes, ma'am,' Ginny answered politely, managing to appear calm.

'Well, I hope the visit is a great success and that you both enjoy it,' the master told them with a smile, then turning about he headed for his study and Ginny began to wonder if she had just imagined the passionate embrace. Once again they were polite but formal with each other and appeared to be no more than employer and employee.

Outside on the drive, Mrs Bronson ushered Ginny into the carriage, pleased to see that the girl had made an effort with her appearance. If she was a little quiet on the way to the railway station, the woman put it down to the fact that she was probably nervous about the journey ahead and thought no more of it. For her part, Ginny was grateful for the peace as she tried to put her thoughts into some sort of order.

Ginny's nerves nearly overwhelmed her as they stood on the railway platform some time later and she saw the train steaming into the station. All thoughts of the master and Anna Bronson fled. The engine looked like a huge, fire-breathing dragon as it bore down on them and Ginny went quite pale as her hand rose to her mouth.

'It's all right, my dear. It's quite safe, I assure you,' Mrs Bronson told her kindly as she saw the girl's eyes widen with alarm. A porter lifted their luggage aboard for them and they took a seat in their carriage.

Ginny stared from the window in consternation. This was the part of the journey she had been dreading and it was every bit as nerve-racking as she had feared. Steam was pouring from the engine to float like fog on the platform and the noise was deafening.

'It will quieten down when the train gets underway,' Mrs Bronson assured her, taking Ginny's hand comfortingly in her own and she was pleased when the girl gripped it tightly. Then suddenly a whistle blew and doors began to slam, and very slowly the huge monster roared or rather chugged into life, picking up speed as it left the station.

Ginny gazed at the countryside flitting past through the window, and as fear was replaced by excitement, she released her grip on her companion's hand. The fields were full of cows and sheep, and she watched with interest as they passed through the small villages on the way.

'How long will it take to get there?' she asked.

Mrs Bronson smiled indulgently. 'Well, we shall have to change trains soon but we should be there for teatime.'

The little bubble of excitement in Ginny's stomach grew to epic proportions. Within a few hours she would be seeing her little brother for the first time in months, and she could hardly wait.

By mid-afternoon, Ginny was stiff from sitting for so long and the novelty of her first train journey had well and truly worn off, so it was a great relief when the train finally pulled into the station.

'My uncle said he'd send a conveyance for us. It should be outside,' Mrs Bronson told Ginny as they left the station and sure enough as soon as they emerged on to the street a man approached them, took their luggage and led them towards a carriage. Ginny's eyes were almost popping out of her head at all the unaccustomed sights, sounds and smells. Over the rooftops she could see the sails of the ships in the Humber Dock and the tangy salt air was completely different to anything she had ever experienced before.

She stared in awe as the horse clip-clopped over the cobblestones, noting that the houses they were passing looked dismal and uninviting. But then they were climbing to the better area of the town where the view opened up and she got her first proper glimpse of the sea. She had seen many pictures of it in books, but somehow it looked even more never-ending in real life. The dingy terraces gave way to smart detached residences here and Ginny couldn't help but be impressed. Very soon now she would be seeing Charlie, and her heart began to thump wildly at the thought. At last the carriage turned into a tree-lined drive and once they came to the end of it, a beautiful house appeared, surrounded by sweeping green lawns.

'Here we are,' Mrs Bronson said as the carriage drew to a halt at the bottom of some curved stone steps – but she had no time to say any more for suddenly the front door banged open and Charlie, closely followed by an elderly gentleman, appeared and raced down towards them.

'*GINNY!*' His face was alight as she almost fell out of the carriage in her haste to get to him and hugged him to her in a fierce embrace. They were both laughing and crying all at the same time but at last she held him at arm's length and looked him up and down.

'My goodness,' she gasped, 'I'm sure you've shot up at least twelve inches!'

He giggled. 'That's what Uncle Edward says. He says it's 'cos of the fresh air an' 'cos I never stop eating.'

He was dressed in a smart little navy suit under which he wore a waistcoat and a starched white linen shirt, and he looked every inch the young gentleman. He also looked remarkably well and Ginny could barely believe the change in him. He was clearly being very well looked after and he appeared to be happy.

Mrs Bronson and her uncle exchanged a smile as they looked on fondly but then the house-keeper appeared on the step to tell them, 'Tea is laid out in the drawing room, sir.'

'Ah, thank you, Mrs Page.' He beamed a welcome at Ginny before saying, 'Shall we go in? I'm sure you must be hungry after your journey.'

Holding Charlie's hand with one hand and her bag with the other, Ginny climbed the steps and gazed about. The house was nowhere near as big or as grand as Lamp Hill Hall but it was very impressive all the same.

'I'll take you up and show you my room after you've had something to eat,' Charlie chattered on, and again she was amazed at the change in him. He had always been such a nervy child but now he seemed confident.

After the guests had been relieved of their coats and had had time to wash away the traces of their journey, Charlie led them into a room where sandwiches, a large pot of tea and a sponge cake were laid out on a table. Politely allowing the visitors to help themselves first, he heaped his own plate with goodies, saying, 'This is just to keep us going till dinnertime, isn't it, Uncle? We've got roast pork an' apple sauce for dinner, an' Cook said she might do us an apple crumble and custard too. You will love that, Ginny.'

It was clear that the staff were all very fond of her dear little brother, and for the first time,

Ginny felt fearful. What if he'd become so settled that he wouldn't want to come home to her when she'd found them somewhere to live? There was so much she wanted to ask and tell him but she felt unable to speak freely in front of Mrs Bronson and her uncle, so for now she held her tongue. Surely they'd be able to snatch a little time alone together later on? And then she told herself to stop worrying. She was here, they were together again at last – and for now that was more than enough.

Chapter Thirty-Six

'So how are you *really*, Charlie?' Ginny asked him that night in his room when they were finally alone.

'I'm all right now. Uncle Edward is kind to me. But I didn't like it in the workhouse.' Charlie shuddered as he thought back to that terrible time and tears started to his eyes. 'It was cold in there and they didn't give us anything nice to eat, but if we didn't eat it they said we were ungrateful and we got the cane, then they'd sit us in front of the meal again and leave us there until it had all gone.' A solitary tear slid down his cheek and he dashed it away with the back of his hand. 'One night, one little girl cried so much that she was sick over her dinner but they still made her eat it. She used to wet the bed an' cry for her mam an' all, an' they caned her for that too. But then she got ill an' they took her to the hospital ward an' I never saw her again.'

Ginny paled at the visions he was conjuring up.

'Then one day, just when I thought I'd be there for ever, Uncle Edward came an' took me away,' he continued. 'At first I cried an' told him that I didn't want to go with him, 'cos I was waitin' for you to come an' fetch me, but he promised me that I'd be able to see you ... an' here you are,' he ended brightly.

'Yes, here I am,' Ginny said emotionally as she gave him a warm hug.

'But what about our dad, Ginny? Where is he, an' when will he be comin' home? Will we be goin' back to live in the cottage?'

Ginny sighed before answering cautiously. 'Dad has had to go away for a time, and no, we won't be going back to live in the cottage. But I will be finding somewhere new for us all to live.'

'Oh.' Charlie sniffed. 'But couldn't you an' Dad come here to live with me an' Uncle Edward?'

A pain pierced Ginny's heart. She was pleased to discover that Charlie was so happy where he was, but hurt that he preferred to stay here rather than come back to the Midlands.

'Well, whatever happens it won't be for some time,' she said eventually. 'I have to save up and find somewhere suitable for us all first, and Dad might be away for a while yet.'

Charlie nodded and then scampered away to fetch some of the books Uncle Edward had bought for him. Ginny was shocked to find that he had, as well as a nanny, a governess who came in daily to do his lessons with him.

'If it's nice tomorrow I'll take you to see the ships in the docks with Nanny,' Charlie gibbered on, and swallowing the huge lump in her throat Ginny nodded silently. They had dined with Mrs Bronson and her uncle, but she hadn't worn the dress that Diana had insisted she should bring. It felt too grand so instead she had simply tidied her hair and worn the dress she had travelled in. She felt decidedly uncomfortable. Back at the Hall she was merely a servant but here she was being treated as a guest and it felt strange. Charlie on the other hand might have been born to it and seemed completely at home, especially with Mrs Bronson.

Ginny had barely recognised her when the woman had come down to dinner. She wore a pretty blue shot-silk crinoline skirt and her hair had been teased into soft curls hanging down each side of her face rather than the severe bun she normally wore. Charlie had greeted her like a long-lost friend and it was obvious they were easy in each other's company. Even so, during the meal Ginny had managed to hold her own, and thanks to her love of reading had been able to contribute to the conversation which covered everything from the state of the British Empire to free education for all children.

Now she glanced around Charlie's room. Despite the fact that the spring days were warming, it tended to still go nippy at night and a fire was burning in the grate. His bed was piled with soft feather pillows and warm blankets, and toys and books were everywhere she looked. It was evident that he was receiving the very best of care and she couldn't help but feel a tiny bit peeved. She had expected him to be begging her to take him home, but whilst he was clearly very pleased to see her it was also obvious that he was very happy where he was. She felt guilty for feeling as she did. After all, she could have wished for no better home for him – but she couldn't help herself. He seemed so well too, with no sign of a cough or a weakness in his chest.

Brother and sister continued to look at the books he brought to her until eventually a young woman appeared. She was plump with rosy cheeks and soft brown curly hair that looked in danger of escaping from beneath a crisp white cap.

Charlie smiled at her, telling Ginny, 'This is my nanny. She lives here too. Her name is Flor an' we have great fun together.'

Nanny bobbed her knee and gave Ginny a friendly smile. 'It's nice to meet you, miss,' she said politely. 'Young Charlie has been so looking forward to your visit. But now, if you don't mind, it's time to get his lordship here ready for bed.'

'Of course.' Flummoxed, Ginny rose from her seat feeling totally out of her depth. Nanny could be no older than she herself was, and here she was bobbing her knee to Ginny as if she was gentry born and bred. It all felt very strange.

'I'll see you in the morning then, shall I, Charlie?'

Charlie threw his arms about her neck and planted a wet kiss on her cheek. 'All right, Ginny. Good night, sleep tight, hope the bed bugs don't bite.'

The familiar words brought tears stinging at the

back of her eyes again as Ginny nodded and hastily left the room, feeling somewhat in the way. How was she ever going to match the sort of care that Charlie was getting now? she asked herself. Here he was, being treated like a little lord, whereas all she would ever be able to offer him was a couple of rooms in a house somewhere or a small rented cottage at best. She knew she was being unreasonable and ungrateful but couldn't seem to pull herself out of it as she found her way to her own room to think. This, again, was like nothing she had ever known. There was expensive wallpaper on the walls and heavy drapes at the window to keep the cold out, and she could see her face in the highly polished rosewood furniture. Someone had turned the bedcovers back for her and laid her simple cotton nightgown across it, and the fire had been made up too. I could get used to this way of life, she found herself thinking, but then gave herself a mental shake. One day their father would come home and somehow she *must* have a home ready for Seth Thursday to return to.

As Ginny was preparing for bed in Hull, back at Lamp Hill Hall, Diana was sneaking out of the house to go and meet Joe. She missed Ginny already, but her absence did have its advantages. Ginny guarded her carefully whilst she was there but now there would be far more opportunities to see Joe. Once outside, she drew her cloak about her and tripped across the lawn in the direction of the summerhouse. He had promised he would be there waiting for her.

He was, and her heart skipped a beat at the

sight of him. However, she became concerned when he stared at her mournfully as she entered the small building and took her hands in his.

'Oh my darling...' he said brokenly. 'I'm afraid I've remembered some more and it isn't good.'

'What do you mean?' She stared at him fearfully from trusting eyes.

'I ... I remembered whose funeral I was attending,' he said in a theatrically choked voice. 'It was my parents'. They had been killed in an accident when their carriage overturned.'

'Oh, sweetheart, how dreadful for you,' she gasped, thinking of the macabre coincidence of the same tragic fate having killed her own beloved parents.

'Yes, but that's not the worst of it.' He hung his head as if he was too ashamed to look at her. 'You see, after I had arranged the funerals I had to listen to their will and it seems my father's business had collapsed. I shall have to sell their house to meet his debts and I shall be left with nothing. Do you understand what that means? I shall never be able to ask your uncle for your hand in marriage now because I have nothing to offer you – *nothing*.'

'But that doesn't matter,' she told him immediately, terrified of losing him. 'I have money, or at least I shall have when I marry.'

'No,' he said dramatically. 'I have too much pride to live off my wife. What would people think of me?'

'I don't care!' Diana said with a determined set to her jaw. 'We love each other, so what does it matter whose money we live off?'

'I doubt your guardians would look at it that way,' he pointed out. 'No doubt they had high hopes that you would make a good marriage.'

'But it's what I want that is important,' she said desperately then enfolded him in her arms. 'It is a terrible thing to happen, losing both your parents at a stroke. I know, because it happened to my brother Seb and me.'

Scrubbing at pretend tears with the back of his hand, he carried on, ignoring what she had just said, 'I've remembered my surname too. It's Peters. I am Joseph Peters.'

'And one day soon, I hope to be Mrs Diana Henrietta Peters,' Diana said with feeling.

He tugged her into his arms and kissed her passionately, gratified to feel her respond. She was his for the taking now, and it was all he could do to stop himself from laughing aloud.

'So what do we do now?' Celia asked her husband the following morning as he perched on the edge of her bed before leaving to visit one of his businesses. 'I am desperately sorry to hear what the young man has gone through, but he's hardly suitable husband material for Diana, is he? And I fear that is what she is thinking of him.'

'No, he certainly is not,' James agreed with a grim expression on his face. 'I spoke to him earlier on but he showed no inclination to leave. I thought he would, once his memory had returned.'

'In fairness it doesn't appear that he has anywhere to return *to*,' Celia pointed out as she sipped at her tea from a dainty china cup. Then as

362

an idea occurred to her she asked, 'Couldn't you perhaps offer him a job? At least he would have an income of sorts then and perhaps he'll go and find himself somewhere to live.'

'I suppose I could,' James agreed cautiously. 'But what sort of job do I offer him? He says he still can't remember what he did before he was attacked.'

'Mm, I see what you mean.' Celia sighed. 'I'm afraid we are in rather an awkward position now, aren't we? What I mean is, Diana won't thank us if we give him his marching orders, will she?'

'I don't suppose she would.' There was something about Joseph that James instinctively mistrusted. 'But anyway, don't you get worrying about it. I'll have a talk to him and we'll go from there. Now I really must be off. Have a good day, darling.'

He kissed her affectionately and as he left the room he almost collided with the very person they had just been speaking of. Joe was yawning and had clearly only just got up. He was dressed smartly as usual, however, in the clothes that he had borrowed from Giles, and didn't look as if he had a care in the world.

'Morning, sir,' he chirped brightly as he headed for the stairs.

'Morning,' James answered. 'Just off for breakfast, are you? You'll have Cook grumbling again. Everyone else finished theirs ages ago.' Only the night before, Cook had complained bitterly to him and with good reason. Joe seemed to expect a meal whenever the fancy took him. James had managed to placate her by saying that their guest probably wouldn't be with them for that much longer and suddenly he decided that now was as good a time as any for their chat. It wouldn't matter if he was a little late getting to work. The manager there had the factory running like well-oiled clockwork.

'Actually I'm glad I bumped into you. I'd like a quick word. Shall we go to my office?'

Not feeling like he had much choice, Joe reluctantly followed him down the stairs.

'So,' James said when they were in the privacy of his study. He had taken a seat at his desk and was staring at Joe across his steepled fingers. Joe felt a little like a naughty schoolboy who had been called in front of the headmaster for some misdemeanour. 'I spoke to Diana last night and she tells me that you've regained some more of your memory. I'm sorry to hear about your parents.'

'Thank you, sir.' Joe hung his head looking very sorry for himself as James observed him closely.

'Do I take it from the other things she told me that you now have no income?'

'I'm afraid not.'

'Ah, well there at least I can help you.'

Joe raised his head to stare at him curiously as James went on, 'The doctor informs me that you are now back to full health physically and of course I am well aware that you must now be longing to take control of your own life again.'

What he means is you've outstayed your welcome here, Joe thought as his expression turned sullen but he remained silent.

'And so what I thought was, I could perhaps offer you a job in one of my businesses,' James

364

went on. 'Then with an income you could choose where you would like to live and start over.'

Joe felt a flutter of panic in his stomach. In a very polite way, Walton-Hughes was giving him his marching orders.

'Well, I ... I suppose I could,' he blustered, not quite knowing how else to answer. No doubt he should at least appear to be willing to work, even if it was the last thing he wanted. 'But I shall miss Diana when I leave,' he ended pointedly.

James shook his head. 'Diana is a very young and impressionable girl,' he said calmly. 'And I apologise if she has made a nuisance of herself.'

'Oh, but she *hasn't* – quite the contrary. You see–'

'I think it might be best if you don't say any more, Mr Peters.' James' eyes were icy cold. 'As I said, Diana is very young. I'm sure she'll soon get back into her old routine once you have left. In the meantime, I shall start to see what jobs are available. You are, of course, welcome to stay on here until I find one that might be suitable for you. But now if you will excuse me, I really must get on.'

'Of course. Thank you, sir,' Joe forced himself to say as his hands clenched into fists of rage. Then he turned and strode from the room.

'It's too bloody soon,' he muttered to the empty hallway as he took the stairs two at a time back to his room. Suddenly his appetite had fled. Once inside his sanctuary he found Barbara making his bed.

She turned to smile at him but his voice lashed her when he bellowed, *'Get out!'*

365

She scuttled away like a frightened little rabbit, almost stumbling in her haste, as Joe stood by the window staring out across the grounds. He had no choice now, he had to bring his plan of action forward. Come hell or high water he would take Diana's virginity before Ginny returned – and then her uncle would be only too pleased to see him marry her. Feeling slightly better about things a cruel little smile lifted the corners of his lips.

Chapter Thirty-Seven

'Oh, please let me take him, Nanny,' Ginny implored the young nanny the following morning. She had promised Charlie that they would walk to the docks and had been hoping that they might have some time to themselves.

'But you might get lost – you don't know your way about,' Nanny objected.

'I have a tongue in my head. If I should get lost I know the address and I can ask someone the way,' Ginny answered.

'I'm sure they'll be fine on their own, Nanny,' Mrs Bronson interrupted. 'Charlie will be perfectly all right with his sister. Why don't you put your feet up for an hour and enjoy a break whilst they're gone?'

Nanny's face brightened at the offer. 'Well, if you're quite sure, miss.' She bobbed a curtsey and scurried away before Anna could change her mind as Uncle Edward looked on indulgently.

'Off you go then, you two,' he urged. 'But have him back for lunchtime, would you, Virginia?'

'Of course, sir. Thank you.' Ginny grabbed Charlie's hand and as they set off Mrs Bronson watched them go through the crisp white lace curtain that hung in the window.

'They're so happy to see each other,' she sighed and he nodded in agreement.

'And that's just as it should be.'

'So what do you think of Virginia?' she asked then.

'She's charming. Her parents did a good job with both of them, it's just so sad that...' His voice trailed away as he saw the sorrow cloud Anna's eyes. 'I'd be more than happy to have her here too,' he went on, changing the subject slightly.

His niece smiled at him ruefully. 'I thank you for that and I have suggested it to her – but she's set on getting somewhere for them to live for when ... or if, her father comes home.'

'But surely we could arrange that?'

'And what reason could I give for doing so? I think Ginny already senses that there's something more than I'm telling her. She's a very intelligent girl.'

'So why don't you just come out and tell her the truth and be done with it?'

Anna shook her head. 'I can never do that while Celia is still alive,' she said quietly. 'I would die rather than hurt her.'

Edward shrugged. 'In that case, my dear, it seems we have no choice but to go on with the deception.'

Down at the docks, Charlie and Ginny were having a great time as they watched the boats of various sizes bobbing about on the water. Many of them were fishing boats and men were zipping up and down the gangplanks with huge buckets of wriggling fish of every shape and size that would be sorted before being sold. The air was tangy with salt and the smell of fish was strong.

'I never imagined the sea would look like this,' Ginny remarked, looking out to the horizon where sea and sky merged into one.

'Oh, I'm used to it now,' Charlie replied airily and again she was shocked at the change in him. It was as if the timid little boy she remembered no longer existed. They moved on past girls who were gutting herrings with their hands tightly bound with rags, and as they left the docks behind them they came to a small stretch of beach.

'Shall we have a splodge?' Without waiting for an answer, Charlie bounded on to the sand and headed for the water as Ginny followed in a more leisurely fashion. By the time she reached him he had discarded his shoes and socks and his breeches were rolled up to the knee.

'Come on, Ginny,' he encouraged. 'The water'll be cold but you'll like it.'

Ginny wasn't so sure and eyed the waves nervously but then Charlie was splashing into the foam shrieking with laughter and she glanced across her shoulder to see if anyone was watching. It did look very tempting, she had to admit.

'Come on, scaredy cat!' he yelled and dropping on to the sand she removed her shoes and stockings. She then lifted her skirt above her ankles and ran to join him, gasping as the ice-cold water took her breath away. They raced up and down like the two children they still were, laughing without a care in the world until at last they waded out and dropped breathlessly on to the beach.

'Nanny lets me do this sometimes,' Charlie confided, 'but she says I'm not to tell Uncle Edward in case she gets into trouble. Sometimes on a Sunday she takes me to the pier an' we watch the Punch an' Judy Show. It used to scare me, the way the puppets batter each other but I like it now.'

Ginny eyed him before asking, 'So are you happy here, Charlie?'

He ran his hand through the sand and watched it sift through his fingers. 'Yes,' he said eventually. 'But I still miss Mam an' Dad an' the others ... an' you, of course. I wish we could go back to how it used to be.'

'I do too,' Ginny whispered as she cuddled him to her and they sat like that for some time watching the spring sunshine playing on the crests of the waves, each deep in thoughts of days gone by that could never come again.

'I was beginning to think you weren't going to come,' Joe said when Diana joined him at the stables later that afternoon. They had decided to go riding the day before, but because Ginny was away Diana had felt she ought to spend a little time with her aunt, who didn't appear to be too well again.

'I'm sorry I'm late. I was with Aunt Celia.'

Diana was looking very attractive in a dark green riding habit with a long plumed feather in her hat, and she allowed Joe to help her mount her side-saddle.

Minnie, her pony, pawed the ground impatiently while Joe mounted Giles' horse and then they trotted off down the drive side by side. Joe wasn't a confident horseman although he was improving day by day.

'Let's head for the Blue Lagoon,' Diana suggested when they came to the lane, and without waiting for an answer she dug her heels into Minnie's side and set off at a gallop, leaving Joe to cling on to his own mount for dear life as it cantered away to keep up with her.

When they at last arrived, Joe was breathless and as he dismounted his legs threatened to buckle beneath him. A large lake lay spread out before them. It was a local beauty spot and many young people came to swim there at weekends, but today it was deserted and there was nothing to be heard but the sounds of the birds and the bees buzzing contentedly amongst the wild flowers.

'It's so peaceful here,' Diana said dreamily. This had always been one of her favourite places although she had never been allowed to come here without Giles or Sebastian. Her smile disappeared, however, when she glanced at Joe and saw his glum expression. Taking his hand, she sat down on the grass, drawing him down with her before asking, 'Is anything wrong, my love? Did I ride too fast for you?'

He played with her fingers, avoiding her eyes. 'No, it isn't that.'

370

'Then what? I know there's something.'

'It's ... it's your uncle. We spoke this morning and he as good as told me that it's time I was moving on. I can't blame him. After all, he's already done far more for me than he need have done. He offered to find me a job so that I could look for lodgings somewhere.'

'*No!*' Her head wagged from side to side in distress. 'You can't leave. I won't let you. I'll tell him that I love you!'

'My darling, I fear it would do no good,' Joe sighed. 'I mentioned how much I would miss you and without actually saying it, he let me know in no uncertain terms that there is no future for us. I'm not good enough for you, you see?'

'But you are!' she said passionately. 'And I told you I have enough money coming to me for both of us to live more than comfortably. I'll be eighteen in a few weeks. Uncle can't tell me what to do!' Because of her distress her voice had risen to its old screech and it grated on Joe's nerves, although he didn't show it.

'Oh, my sweet love, how shall I live without you?' he groaned as he laid her down on the grass, and then he was kissing her hungrily and she responded to him. Until his hands began to wander across the material over her breasts that was, and then he felt her stiffen.

'It's all right, I won't hurt you, I promise.'

She looked up at him from frightened eyes. Her hat had come off and the pins had escaped from her hair and now it spilled on the grass like a golden sheet around her.

'I ... I think we should stop now,' she said.

Ignoring her protests, he began to undo the buttons on her riding habit.

'It's all right,' he rasped as his hand finally closed about her bare breast. A million strange emotions flitted through her – fear and ecstasy uppermost, all rolled into one. And then his lips fastened on her nipple and it immediately stood to attention as his hand roamed down to lift her skirt.

'Please, Joe, no,' she gasped, although half of her didn't want him to stop. The other half knew full well that what they were doing was wrong.

'I can't.' His hand was stroking the bare skin above the hem of her long cambric drawers, making her shiver with apprehension and pleasure as they approached the opening in the fabric. 'I've waited so long, my darling. I can't wait any longer.' Then suddenly the full weight of him was upon her, crushing her, and after yanking her drawers aside she felt a sharp pain that took her breath away as he thrust into her. Suddenly the pleasure was gone and she began to cry as he plunged in and out, in and out, as if he might never stop. The pain was indescribable but at last, after what seemed like an eternity, he gave a guttural grunt, and then slowly rolled off her to lie breathless on the grass beside her.

Diana was crying so hard that she could see nothing as the enormity of what they had just done came home to her. So this was what married couples did to make babies? It wasn't at all as she'd expected it to be. In fact, she hadn't liked that part of it at all but – perhaps it got better with time? Then suddenly Joe leaned up on his elbow and stared down at her saying, 'I'm *so* sorry. I don't know what came over me. I just love you so much. Please forgive me.'

He was instantly forgiven as she gathered him into her arms. 'Of course,' she said with a little catch in her voice. They lay like that for a time then slowly he began to caress her breasts again and this time she put up no resistance. It didn't hurt quite as much the second time although Diana couldn't have truthfully said that she enjoyed it. However, she loved Joe so much that she would have forgiven him anything. When they eventually mounted their horses and headed for home, Diana was somewhat subdued and wondered if anyone would guess what they had done by looking at her. Her insides ached and she was sore and feeling dirty, but worse than that was the fact that she had left the house as a girl and was returning as a woman. Her uncle would have to let her marry Joe now, for she knew all too well that no one else would ever want her now.

Chapter Thirty-Eight

'I think we should be looking at leaving within the next couple of days, Virginia dear,' Anna announced one evening that week as they all sat together at dinner.

Ginny felt sad at the thought of leaving Charlie but knew that Mrs Bronson was right. They were both needed back at the Hall and it wouldn't be fair to stay away for too long. She was surprised to find that she was looking forward to seeing Sebastian again too. She'd missed their little strolls in the garden and their chats.

'But will you be all right if we go back, Uncle?' Anna asked then.

Edward had developed a chill and Anna had insisted that the local doctor came in to check him over the day before.

'Of course.' He waved aside her concerns. 'Tough as old boots, I am. It's only a bit of a cold.'

'Even so, you know you have a tendency for it to go to your chest so you must look after yourself,' she scolded. He had eaten barely any of his favourite roast lamb cooked just as he liked it, and Anna felt torn. She needed to get back to Celia, yet felt reluctant to leave her uncle.

'Well, if you're sure,' she said uncertainly.

'Do stop *mithering*, woman. I've got a houseful of staff to see to my needs, haven't I? Now why don't you plan to go back the day after tomorrow? That way, Ginny and Charlie can spend a last day together.'

The two young people beamed at each other across the table and so it was agreed, although Anna still felt unhappy about leaving Edward.

The last day spent with Charlie was bittersweet. Ginny had loved being with him and was dreading leaving him when she went back to the Hall. Even Charlie, who was clearly very happy in his Hull home, was inclined to be tearful. He loved living with his new uncle but of course he loved his big sister too.

'When will you be back?' he asked. They had

gone to the little beach again and he was skimming pebbles across the surface of the sea.

'I don't know,' Ginny said truthfully. 'But we can write to each other now, I'm sure your governess will help you, and I shall be saving every penny I can until I can afford to find us somewhere to live.'

They began to look for shells and shortly before lunchtime they set off back to the house hand in hand. The rest of the day seemed to pass in a blur and before she knew it Ginny was tucking him into bed as Nancy bustled about tidying his toys away.

'I shall be gone in the morning when you get up,' Ginny said gently. 'So we'll say our goodbyes now.'

Charlie sat bolt upright and threw his arms about her neck as tears spurted from his eyes. 'You won't forget about me, will you?' he sobbed.

'As if I could!' Ginny cuddled him close. Her throat was tight but she didn't want him to see her cry. At last she gave him a final kiss and went to her room where she could indulge in the tears she had so valiantly held back. She was still crying half an hour later when someone tapped lightly on the door.

'Come in.' Ginny quickly dashed the tears away with the back of her hand as Mrs Bronson's head appeared around the door.

The woman instantly noted Ginny's flushed cheeks and watery eyes but tactfully didn't mention it. 'I was just wondering if you needed any help with your packing?'

Ginny managed a smile as she said, 'No, thank you. I didn't bring that much with me so it will only take a few minutes in the morning.'

'Very well.' Anna hovered uncertainly for a moment. She would dearly have loved to give Ginny a comforting word and a cuddle but sensed that this might just make her feel worse. 'I'll wish you good night then and see you downstairs at seven in the morning,' was all she was able to say.

'Ah, home at last,' Mrs Bronson said happily late the following afternoon as the carriage that had met them from the station drew up outside the front door at Lamp Hill Hall. Jim Grady and Johnny came around to help them both out and unload their luggage as Anna tripped lightly up the steps. She could hardly wait to see Celia and James again. However, her happy smile disappeared the instant they set foot through the door as the sound of angry voices reached them from the library. Ginny stayed where she was as Anna Bronson quickly hurried towards it.

Sebastian, James and Ventriss were inside and Sebastian was clearly very angry whilst James looked slightly nonplussed.

'Do you have any idea at all of what you've done?' Sebastian demanded as Ventriss hung his head.

'I were only tryin' to protect the stock, sir,' he mumbled, shamefaced.

They noticed Anna standing in the doorway then and James informed her of what was going on. 'Ventriss laid mantraps in the woods again and a local man was caught in one of them last night. He'd been lying there for some time and if Ventriss hadn't found him when he did, the fellow might have bled to death. His leg is in an awful state, by all accounts, and he's in the cottage hospital.'

'But what was he doing in the woods?' Anna asked.

'Poachin', ma'am,' Ventriss told her. 'He'd got a couple o' rabbits he'd snared at the side o' him.'

'The poor chap was probably just trying to feed his family,' Sebastian roared. 'You know there's a strike on at the local pit.'

'No disrespect, sir, but that ain't no excuse fer poachin' on private property,' Ventriss muttered.

'I wonder if you'd say that if your children were going to bed with empty bellies,' Sebastian retorted.

'All right, all right, you two, that's quite enough. This is getting us nowhere,' James interrupted. Then to Ventriss, 'I did tell you some time ago that I wasn't in favour of mantraps, Ted.'

'Aye, yer did, sir,' Ventriss nodded. 'But I didn't know how else to stop the poachin' unless I stayed up every night walkin' the woods.'

'Well, just give me your word that they'll not be used again and we'll say no more about it. I know you were only trying to do your job.'

The man shuffled away mumbling beneath his breath as James ran his hand through his hair.

'But what about the poor chap that's been injured?' Sebastian demanded.

'I shall make sure that he and his family are taken care of until he's recovered and back at work,' James promised, and slightly mollified, his nephew thanked him and left the room.

'Well, this is certainly some homecoming,'

Anna remarked with a wry smile as she undid the ribbons of her bonnet.

'I'm so sorry, my dear.' He crossed to close the door then taking her in his arms he kissed her gently on her lips. 'We've missed you.'

'I missed you too – but how is Celia?'

He shook his head and stepped away from her. 'Not good, I'm afraid, but I'm hoping that she'll perk up now that you are home. How was your trip and how is little Charlie?'

'He's as happy as Larry with Uncle Edward and growing like a weed,' she told him. 'But come along, I'm keen to see Celia now.' And so together they made their way upstairs to the mistress's room.

Meantime, Sebastian had spotted Ginny in the hall; he felt a pang at the sight of her. Her black hair was gleaming like coal and the sea air had put roses in her cheeks. The little break had clearly done her the power of good.

He told her about the incident in the wood and she looked concerned. 'But how will his family eat if he can't work for a while?' she asked.

'That was my point exactly but Uncle has promised to make sure they can manage financially until the man is back on his feet. Morally, he could turn him in to the police for poaching because the chap was in the wrong at the end of the day, but Uncle would never do that. I'll go round to their cottage myself later on and see his wife and put her mind at rest.'

He hefted Ginny's bag, saying, 'I'll carry this up to your room for you, shall I? Between you and me I'm relieved to see you back. I don't know what's wrong with Diana but she hasn't been herself at all for the last few days.'

'Oh? Is she ill?'

He shrugged as they climbed the stairs together. 'I don't think so, she's just awfully quiet. Perhaps she'll tell you if there's something on her mind.' When they reached Ginny's room he placed her bag down and left. The door closed behind him and Ginny smiled fondly. He was nice, was Master Sebastian – really nice – and she was so happy to see him again. But then she quickly removed her bonnet, washed her face and hands and tidied herself in the mirror. The holiday was over and it was time to get back to work.

She found Diana staring from her bedroom window. The girl obviously couldn't hear her come in but when Ginny went to stand beside her she looked up and threw her arms about Ginny saying, 'I missed you.'

'I missed you too,' Ginny told her in the strange little sign language that they had devised. 'But have you been unwell? You look awfully pale.'

Diana lowered her eyes. 'I'm fine. How was your trip?'

So Ginny went on to tell her all about the things she and Charlie had got up to until Diana interrupted and told her, 'I'm just slipping along to Joe's room for a moment.'

Ginny said nothing as the young woman left but set about tidying her messy room, and very soon it felt as if she had never been away.

Nancy was also pleased to see her and later that evening she told her shyly, 'Bertie called in to see me yesterday. He was all dressed in his uniform an' he looked ever so smart.'

Ginny raised a surprised eyebrow. 'Why was that then?'

Nancy glanced about before lowering her voice. 'I went into town fer Cook. She needed a couple o' bits off the market an' while I were there I popped in to see Mrs Watkins fer a cuppa. She told me I were welcome to call by any time. Anyway, I forgot me shawl what wi' it bein' so warm, so Bertie returned it fer me. I thought Cook would gi' me a roastin' but she didn't. But weren't that kind of him?'

'It was indeed.' Ginny smiled. Perhaps Bertie was finally beginning to see what a lovely young lass Nancy was? From where she was standing they were perfect for each other and she for one would be delighted to see them become a couple.

Nancy then went on to tell her in a hushed voice about what the master was proposing for Joe. 'I overheard Cook tellin' Barbara that the master's gonna find him a job so as he can afford to get lodgin's somewhere. I can't see Joe bein' none too happy wi' that after the comfy billet he's had here, can you? I don't reckon Miss Diana is very pleased about it either.'

'No, I don't suppose she will be,' Ginny agreed. 'Although it had to end somewhere. Joe couldn't just expect to stay here for ever as if he's one of the family.'

'Huh! I reckon that cheeky young sod would be happy to do just that,' Nancy retorted.

'Oh well, I ought to be getting on. I've still got to help Miss Diana undress,' Ginny said, and

380

bustled away only to find that Diana's room was empty. It didn't take much to figure out where she might still be, so with a sigh Ginny settled on a chair to wait for her to return.

It was two weeks later on a bright sunny morning when Ginny helped Diana into her riding habit. She and Joe went for a ride most mornings now, weather permitting, and Joe's skills as a horseman were improving vastly. Ginny was secretly happy for her to go as she and Sebastian had taken to having a stroll about the gardens in his sister's absence. They were completely at ease in each other's company now and Ginny enjoyed their chats. This morning, however, when Diana met Joe at the stables she found him in a rare bad humour. He was looking very handsome in Giles' riding habit and as always, Diana's heart fluttered at the sight of him, although she had no idea what might have put him in such a bad mood.

'Is anything wrong?' she asked as they trotted down the drive.

'Your uncle called me into his study last night to inform me that he's found a job for me,' Joe told her with a face like thunder. 'Working in the *quarry!*'

'Oh!' Diana couldn't quite picture Joe working there and getting his hands dirty somehow, but she said tentatively, 'Perhaps it won't be as bad as you think?'

He snorted with disgust before urging the horse into a gallop and she had no choice but to follow him. As Joe whipped the horse, an idea occurred to him. If Diana were to have a fall – just a *little* one – and injure herself, she would want him close to her, and that might postpone the job starting. With an ugly smile he led his horse into the woods with Diana trotting trustingly behind him. After a while he urged her to go ahead of him. The horses were nervy as branches brushed across their flanks and their eyes, but that was just what Joe had hoped for. Unseen by Diana he snapped an overhanging branch from a tree as he passed underneath it, then raising it above his head he brought it down hard on the hindquarters of Diana's pony, Minnie. The poor animal snorted with shock and tossed her head as she reared on to her back legs. Just as Joe had planned, Diana gave a shriek before flying through the air and landing heavily on the earth floor, where she lay quite still, like a broken little rag doll.

Joe frowned as he dismounted. That had gone a little *too* well. He'd only meant her to sprain her ankle or perhaps break her arm at most. Why was she lying so still? Then he saw the blood flowing from beneath her head and seeping into the patchy grass and his heart jolted. Her head had landed on a large stone and who knew what damage it might have done. Suddenly he saw everything he had planned for slipping away from him and he panicked. *What if he'd killed her?* Then common sense took over. Diana would have no idea what had caused the horse to rear and neither would anyone else, so the best thing he could do was go for help as quickly as possible – and that was exactly what he did.

By the time Joe dragged the horse to a halt in

the stableyard the poor creature was foaming at the bit, but flinging himself from the saddle, he paid him no heed as he raced across to Johnny Grady who was in the process of cleaning out one of the stables.

'I need help,' Joe babbled breathlessly. 'Where's Jim?'

Hearing the commotion, Johnny's father appeared from another stable to ask, 'What's goin' on then, lad?'

'It ... it's Diana, she's fallen from her horse. I think she's badly injured.'

Jim took control of the situation immediately. It was clear that Joe was in no state to do so. Turning to his son he told him, 'Run an' fetch Ted Ventriss fer me, lad. Then ride to the quarry an' let the master an' Master Sebastian know there's been an accident. After that, call in at the doctor's an' tell him to get here as fast as he can on yer way back. Is Master Giles in?'

Johnny shook his head. 'No, Dad. He went out on his horse an hour since.'

'Right, well, me an' Ted'll have to try an' get her back then. Go on, lad. There's no time to lose.'

Whilst Johnny ran to do as he was told, Jim dragged an old door from the back of the barn, telling Joe, 'We'll have to carry the lass back on this.'

Minutes later, Joe was leading them back to where Diana lay injured as Johnny rode like the wind on one of the horses to fetch the master and the doctor. Diana was lying exactly where he had left her and her face was so white that he feared she was already dead.

'I can't understand it. Miss Diana is a fine horsewoman. What could have caused this to happen?' Ted fretted as they laid the door down at the side of her.

'It was a snake ... an adder, I think. It slithered out in front of the horse and startled it,' Joe lied.

Very gently Ted and Jim lifted Diana on to the door. Her pony, calm again now, was cropping at the grass, and as the other two men carried the injured girl carefully back to the house, Joe led Minnie back to the stables behind them.

Mrs Bronson and Ginny were waiting at the door for them when they arrived. Johnny had told them what had happened and Mrs Bronson ordered, 'Bring her into the day room and lay her on the couch.'

The men did as they were told then quietly departed leaving Diana in the women's care. They had done all they could now.

Ginny had a lump in her throat as she stared down at Diana's still face. Blood was trickling from a gash above her left ear and she was deathly pale.

'Is she dead?' she asked fearfully.

Mrs Bronson shook her head. 'No, but her pulse is very thready. I hope the doctor comes soon. Meantime all we can do is clean her up a bit.'

They had towels and hot water all ready and gently the housekeeper began to bathe the wound as Ginny held Diana's hand tight and looked helplessly on.

Soon after, the master and the doctor arrived together.

'Stand clear and let me have a good look at her,'

Dr Gifford ordered. After a moment he told them, 'This gash is going to need stitches. I shall do it now while she's still unconscious. Luckily the wound is in her hair so the scar won't be visible when it heals.'

Ginny couldn't bear to look but kept her eyes on the window as he trimmed away the hair and sewed Diana up as neatly as he could. He then sent James from the room and got the women to undress her so that he could examine her properly, but thankfully he could find no evidence of any broken bones. Mrs Bronson helped to put Diana in a nightgown, but she had shown no sign of regaining consciousness whatsoever as yet.

'So how bad is she?' James asked worriedly as he was allowed back in and stared down at his niece's bloodless lips. Sebastian had arrived by then too and he was also sick with worry as he stood next to Ginny feeling utterly helpless. They had lost their parents – he couldn't bear to lose his sister too.

The doctor proceeded to wash the blood from his hands in the bowl of hot water Barbara had brought in for him. 'It's hard to tell what's going on at this stage,' he told them honestly. 'She's obviously deeply concussed, but all we can do for now is wait until she regains consciousness.' He refrained from telling them that there was a possibility that she might never wake up. That she might just slip away. 'Would you like me to have her transferred to the cottage hospital?'

'Oh no, we can look after her here,' Anna said straight away, and Ginny nodded in agreement. It would be awful for Diana to wake up amongst strangers. And so James carried his niece upstairs to her room, tenderly tucked her into her bed – and the terrible wait began.

Chapter Thirty-Nine

'Come on now, you're going to be ill yourself at this rate,' Mrs Bronson scolded early the next morning. Ginny had sat beside Diana all night, refusing to leave her side. 'Why don't you go and try to get some sleep? I can sit with her now.'

Ginny yawned but shook her head. 'Not yet, I'm all right for a while. Sebastian has kept me company for most of the night. I'll tell you when I need a rest, I promise.' She again rinsed the calico cloth in the bowl of cool water at the side of Diana's bed and bathed her forehead.

'Well, if you're quite sure,' Mrs Bronson responded. 'But I don't want you getting ill too. I'll go and see to the mistress and then I'll come back to check if there's been any change. Millie will bring you up a tray of food. You must eat to keep your strength up.'

Ginny merely nodded. She was too weary to get into any conversation. Sebastian had gone to his room to get washed and changed but she had no doubt he'd be back soon. He'd been wonderful company throughout the night, taking it in turns with Ginny to bathe his sister's forehead and fetching them warm drinks from time to time. They hadn't spoken much, yet Ginny had felt comforted by his presence. Just as she'd thought, he was back in no time. Millie had brought a tray up with enough food for both of them on it and he bullied and cajoled Ginny into eating something. The food stuck in her throat but she did manage to drink two cups of hot strong tea and felt much better for it.

'Right, now you go and get changed,' Sebastian ordered. 'She'll be quite all right with me and I'll call you straight away if I need you.'

While she was gone Joe stuck his head round the door asking, 'How is she?'

'No change,' Sebastian answered shortly. He knew that he was being unreasonable. It wasn't Joe's fault that Diana had come off her horse while she was out riding with him, after all – but what the hell had they been doing in the woods in the first place? Diana knew that it spooked the horses.

'Oh right. Well, I'll be off to get some breakfast then.' With that Joe disappeared.

Sebastian's lips curled with contempt. Joe had made damn sure he had a good night's sleep, which showed how concerned about Diana he was despite the fact that he was always fawning over her. *He doesn't love Diana. He's just after her money.* Once the thought had occurred to him, Sebastian couldn't seem to shake it off. The sooner the scoundrel was away from the Hall the better as far as he was concerned. However for now there were more pressing things to worry about so the young man returned his attentions to his sister.

The doctor returned mid-morning but found no

change in the patient whatsoever. It wasn't a good sign. The longer the girl remained unconscious, the less chance there was of her ever waking up, but he had no wish to distress the family any more than they already were, so he wisely kept his concerns to himself. 'Just keep doing what you're doing,' he told Ginny kindly. 'And I'll call in again this evening after surgery. Should you need me before, don't hesitate to send for me.'

'Thank you, sir.' By now, Ginny was so tired that she could hardly stay awake. Her eyes felt sore and gritty. I'll just lay my head on the side of the bed while I hold tight to her hand and rest, she thought and within seconds she was fast asleep.

Mrs Bronson found her that way shortly afterwards and gently smoothed the black hair back from her cheeks before tiptoeing from the room.

Two whole days passed and they were all beginning to despair. Celia was unwell too, so Anna had to divide her time between the two sickrooms, although Ginny did more than the lion's share of caring for Diana.

Joe was kicking himself by then as he saw his big dreams slipping away from him. Why did she have to fall so heavily, or land on a stone? Sebastian was barely civil to him, leaving him in no doubt of what he thought of him, and the master's attitude towards him had changed subtly too. Luckily the family were all so concerned about Diana that the suggestion of him working seemed to have been put to one side for now – but he had no idea how long that might last and he wasn't relishing the prospect of toiling in the dirty quarry at all. Every, time he saw the master he expected James to give him his marching orders, and he felt as if were walking on a knife-edge. Damn and blast Diana – why didn't the silly bitch bloody wake up!

Striding out into the fresh air, he thrust his hands deep into his pockets and almost collided with Giles, who had been just about to come in.

'So what's going to happen now if Diana dies?' Giles spat. He had no love for his cousin, but he would miss the money Joe had promised him.

'Then I'll be out on my arse, won't I?' the other man snapped.

Grabbing his elbow, Giles moved him away from the doorway. 'So was it really an accident?'

'Of course it was,' Joe spluttered. 'I'm hardly gonna kill the goose that was about to lay the golden egg, am I?'

Giles glared at him suspiciously. He knew how unscrupulous Peters was and wouldn't have put anything past him. 'Then we have to hope she comes round – for both our sakes, don't we?' he hissed, then turned and strode inside without another word, leaving Joe to kick at the stones on the drive with a sullen expression on his face.

'How are you feeling today?' Anna asked as she put down the tray and as she drew back the curtains in Celia's bedroom to admit the early-morning sunshine.

'Oh, not too bad.'

Anna knew that she was lying. The poor woman's face was the colour of bleached linen and the fact that she was worrying herself sick about Diana wasn't helping matters.

'How is she today?' Celia asked then.

Anna kept her voice light as she answered, 'About the same but no worse, which is something to be grateful for. Ginny is doing a grand job of looking after her.'

Since returning from Hull, Anna had taken to using the shortened version of Ginny's name and the girl had noticed. It marked another little shift in their relationship.

Celia sighed as she fiddled with the bedsheet, pleating it and unpleating it in her agitation. 'I feel so useless, not being able to take my turn at nursing her,' she fretted.

'She'll be fine,' Anna comforted her, with far more conviction than she was feeling. 'She's young and strong so she'll be able to fight this, and while she's asleep her body will be healing.' She crossed to the woman she had come to love, and helped her to sit up, noting the way Celia winced as she moved her. The growth on her stomach was so big it made her look as if she was six months pregnant now and Anna knew that it must be causing her enormous pain although the dear soul rarely complained. She started to butter some toast for her, but Celia said weakly, 'Just a cup of tea for now, dear.'

Sighing, Anna poured her a cup, just the way she liked it, and watched as the woman sipped at it. Her heart ached. There was nothing she could really do to help either Diana or Celia, apart from ensure they had the best care they could get at present, and it grieved her.

When Celia had finished, Anna then gently

washed and changed her; it was an effort for Celia to even get out of bed now. Then, when she had made sure that her mistress was as comfortable as she could possibly make her, Anna went along to Diana's room to check on her. She found Sebastian there keeping Ginny company, which was no surprise. The pair seemed remarkably easy with each other but they both looked drained. Hardly a surprise as neither of them had had much sleep since the accident.

'Any progress?' she asked, crossing to the bed to gaze down at the girl who lay as still as a statue.

Ginny answered with tears in her eyes. 'I ... I just wish there was something I could do,' she said huskily, and Anna noted the way Sebastian took her hand and squeezed it gently.

'You're doing all you can – you both are,' Anna said then crept from the room leaving the young people to their vigil.

That night, Ginny insisted that Sebastian should go to bed. 'There's no sense in us both sitting here,' she told him. 'If you go and snatch a few hours' sleep I'll do the same when you come back to take over the watch,' she coaxed.

'All right – if you put it like that, I will.' Giving an enormous yawn, he rose and stretched painfully. He seemed on the verge of saying more but then thought better of it and quietly left the room.

Once he was gone, Ginny struggled to keep her eyes open. The house was silent; there was nothing to be heard but the sound of Diana's soft breathing and the ticking of the clock...

In the early hours of the morning, something made her stir from a light doze. She opened her eyes groggily, trying to figure out what it was, and then suddenly it came to her. Someone was applying a gentle pressure to her fingers. She was instantly awake. Diana was staring at her and Ginny gave a whoop of joy.

'Oh, darling, you're awake.' She could barely speak for the tears that were clogging her throat and raining down her cheeks. 'Just lie still – I must go and tell Mrs Bronson. This is marvellous!' Then she was racing along the landing, not caring a jot how noisy she was, calling the housekeeper's name at the top of her voice. Doors began to open and sleepy heads appeared. 'Diana is awake,' she trilled happily as she headed for Anna's room.

Minutes later, they were hurrying back up the stairs together. Anna's fair hair was tied in a thick plait that hung like a rope down her back and she was in her dressing robe, making her look years younger.

'Oh my dear, what a scare you have given us,' Anna told Diana as she hung over the girl. 'How are you feeling now? Would you like a drink?'

Diana blinked her eyes, looking confused as the room slowly filled with people. Sebastian was there and her Uncle James. Millie and Barbara too, and of course Ginny – but there was no sign of Joe. Of course, it was dark so he was probably sleeping.

She opened her mouth as if she were trying to say something then raised her hands to either side of her head and pressed on her ears.

'Are you in pain?' Anna asked, her face full of concern.

A tear trickled from Diana's eye and made its solitary way down her cheek. 'N ... no. But everything is so loud. You see, I can hear you!'

Chapter Forty

'It's nothing short of a miracle,' Celia declared the next morning as Anna was washing her. 'But how could it have happened after all this time?'

Anna smiled. 'The doctor has no idea. He says perhaps the bang on the head could have done it. Whatever the reason, we're not complaining, are we?'

'Certainly not.' Celia was perky this morning following the good news. It seemed to have given her a new lease of life. 'We should do something to celebrate,' she said thoughtfully, then her face lit up. 'How about a party? It's years since there's been one in this house and it will be Diana's birthday soon.'

'Hmm, I'm not sure about that,' Anna wavered as she lifted the brush and started to brush Celia's hair. 'Diana is still very weak. She's not going to recover overnight.'

'But it isn't her birthday for another six weeks yet,' Celia pointed out. 'It might give her something to look forward to. Just think about it, Anna. Think how wonderful it would be. We could have dancing, perhaps hire a band – and Diana will be able to hear the music.'

Celia was so animated that Anna didn't have the heart to raise any more objections. In truth, Celia could be right. It might be just what Diana needed.

'Why don't you talk to James about it and see what he thinks of the idea,' she said tactfully, but sensed that she was wasting her breath. Celia's eyes already had a faraway look in them as she planned the event in her head.

Shortly afterwards, Anna went along to check on Diana. Dr Gifford had warned that she must stay in bed and rest for a few days, after telling her what a lucky young woman she was.

'We thought we were going to lose you for a while back there,' he'd admitted with a glimmer in his eye. 'And now here you are, not only back in the land of the living but with your hearing restored. Perhaps the fall was a blessing in disguise.'

The instant Anna walked in, Diana smiled at her. She had heard the door opening.

'And how are you feeling this bright morning?' Anna asked cheerfully.

Diana winced. 'Still trying to get used to all the noises,' she said. 'After living in a silent world for so long, everything sounds magnified now and I keep jumping.'

'You'll soon get used to it,' Anna reassured her. 'But is there anything you need before I go about my duties? I've insisted that Ginny goes to lie down for a while. She's quite exhausted as she's hardly left your side since the accident happened. Can you remember anything about it?'

'Nothing at all. One moment I was trotting

along on Minnie and the next thing I knew, I was lying here and able to hear everything.'

Anna noticed that Diana's speech had already improved vastly. She was no longer shouting or spacing her words out. The conversation was interrupted then when Joe appeared.

He nodded casually at Anna before bending to kiss Diana's cheek and Anna had to stifle a sigh of annoyance. The young man was very forward. He hadn't even bothered to tap at the door before entering but had breezed in as if he owned the place – and Diana too, for that matter.

'That'll be all, thank you, Mrs Bronson,' he said, dismissing her, and Anna bristled with rage as she swung about and marched from the room. That'll be all indeed! Just who did he think he was? But then she took a deep breath to calm herself. This was a special, day, after all, and she didn't want anything to spoil it.

James was striding along the landing towards her on his way to see Celia and he beamed at her.

'Who would have thought such a terrible accident could have such a wonderful outcome, eh?' he asked.

She nodded in agreement. It was nice to see him smiling again after all the worry of the last few days.

'Quite – and I think you'll find Celia is perky this morning as well. She has an idea to put to you, as it happens, and I don't think it's a bad one.'

'Really? What's that then?' He looked intrigued but Anna tutted.

'That's for her to tell you – and now I really have to get on.' James laughed as she hurried on her way before proceeding to his wife's room. He was delighted to find her sitting up in bed with a writing pad and a pen spread across her lap.

'Hello – and what's all this then?' he asked teasingly as he gave her a big kiss.

'I'm making plans for the party.'

'Party? What party?'

'I was saying to Anna that we should celebrate Diana getting her hearing back – and as it's almost her eighteenth birthday, what better time? What do you think, darling?'

'Well, in principle it's a splendid idea and I'm sure that Diana would love it,' he said cautiously. 'But are you sure that you're up to it, sweetheart?'

'Oh yes, truly I am,' she told him. 'I shall enjoy planning everything. I get quite fed up stuck up here all day on my own and it will give me something to do. I even plan to attend it myself.'

When he saw how expectantly she was staring at him, he knew that he was lost. It was hard to deny Celia anything; she asked for so little.

'Very well,' he agreed. 'But don't tire yourself out. Get Anna to help you.'

'I will,' she promised, and then to his amusement she seemed to forget that he was there as she turned her attention back to the fast-growing list in front of her.

'Oh,' Diana said nervously when her uncle told her of the plans later that day. She had never been to a proper grown-up party before. 'Will there be many people coming?'

'Half the county, I should think, if your aunt has her way,' he told her wryly. He had expected his niece to be a little more excited about it. 'So now you just have to concentrate on getting well.'

As Diana lay in bed, alternating between dozing and being wide awake, she had plenty of time to think about everything.

'Is there anyone that *you'd* like to invite?' she asked Ginny later that day.

'Well, as it happens, there is. I'd like to invite Bertie Watkins. He's a policeman friend of mine and I have a feeling that he and Nancy have something lovely growing between them.'

'Then of course he must come. And we shall both need a new dress, of course.'

It was there that Ginny put her foot down. 'I don't need a new dress; I still haven't worn that beautiful cream one that you so kindly gave me. But you must have one, naturally. We could perhaps go shopping together for the material and the pattern for it when you're back on yer feet.'

'Yes, I suppose we could,' Diana answered half-heartedly. She still felt very unwell. 'But I think I'll have a nap now, if you don't mind. I'm feeling rather sick and giddy. My head is throbbing.'

'I dare say that's only to be expected,' Ginny told her kindly. 'The doctor said you had a severe concussion and so it will probably take a few more days before you start to feel right.'

Diana nodded before burrowing beneath the covers.

'A party? Here in this house?' Cook was astounded when Ginny told her of it later that morning.

'Yes, but don't worry, I think the mistress is

talking of getting caterers in to see to the food.'

'There will be no need for that,' Cook declared indignantly. 'I'm not having strangers rampaging around *my* kitchen. I'm more than capable of seeing to everything meself. It's not as if it's going to happen tomorrow or next week, after all, is it? I have plenty of time to organise a menu with the mistress and plenty of time to prepare it – so that's an end to it.'

Word spread through the staff like wildfire and soon everyone was getting excited at the prospect of a party and vastly relieved that the young mistress was on the mend.

'Miss Diana must be really looking forward to it,' Nancy said to Ginny as they were having a tea break in the kitchen.

'Actually she didn't seem overly keen on the idea when her uncle first told her about it, but then she has been very poorly. I dare say she will be more excited when she's feeling better.'

Over the next few days Diana showed a gradual improvement although she still seemed very subdued. On the third day the doctor allowed her to get out of bed and sit in the chair by the window for an hour, but as Ginny helped her she suddenly clapped her hand across her mouth and gasped, 'I think I'm going to be sick!'

Ginny raced away to fetch a bowl – and only just in time as Diana emptied the entire contents of her stomach into it.

'It's probably the after-effects of the crack on the head,' Ginny consoled her and Diana nodded miserably.

Throughout the following week the same thing happened every single morning and a little niggle of unease began to grow in Ginny's mind. The last time she had seen anyone with morning sickness as severe as this had been when her mother was expecting her last baby. Waiting until Diana was having a nap one afternoon, Ginny went to the drawer where Diana kept the cloths that she used for her monthly courses, only to find them all there. It was Ginny's job to take them down to the laundry to be soaked and boiled each day, and now that she came to think of it, Diana should have begun to menstruate on the week of her accident. She mentioned it casually as they shared dinner together in Diana's room that evening and the girl shrugged.

'It's probably the accident that's thrown my body out,' she replied and Ginny fervently prayed that she was right.

The first of June dawned sunny and warm, and the house was a hive of activity as preparations for the party the following week got under way. Cook was barking orders at everyone like a sergeant major and baking from dawn until dusk and the maids were furiously spring-cleaning every nook and cranny of the house. Diana was now up and about again but she seemed to have lost all of her sparkle. She was still being violently sick each morning and Ginny was very concerned about her. The only time she seemed to smile was when she was with Joe, who still hung around her like a dog near a bitch on heat.

'Come on,' Ginny said brightly that morning as

399

she threw the bedroom curtains open. 'We have to be in town early today so that you can have the final fitting for your dress.'

Diana groaned as light flooded into the room. 'But I don't feel well enough to go into town.' She then threw the bedclothes back and hurtled past Ginny into the bathroom. Diana had now missed her second flow and Ginny knew that the time had come to voice her suspicions.

When Diana returned from the bathroom looking like a limp rag and with her face the colour of putty, Ginny said quietly, 'As well as feeling sick all the time, does anywhere else feel any different, Diana?'

'As a matter of fact my breasts are slightly swollen and they're very tender.' Diana felt embarrassed talking of such things. She had led such a sheltered life and was very naïve in some respects. 'Why do you ask?'

'Well...' Ginny cleared her throat as she laid the dress Diana would be wearing that day over the end of the bed. 'I couldn't help but notice that you've missed your second course.'

'So?'

'Usually, missing your bleeding and having tender breasts are the first signs that a woman is with child.'

Diana stared at her for a moment, then as comprehension dawned her face collapsed. 'What? You mean I might be having a baby?'

'Only you could know that. I mean, have you and Joe...'

The colour that flooded into Diana's cheeks was her answer.

'Perhaps we should get the doctor to examine you,' Ginny suggested tactfully as Diana sat heavily on the nearest chair.

'I ... I need to speak to Joe.' Diana's face was as white as a sheet as she rose and without another word, hurried along the landing to his room. She was desperate to catch him before he left for his morning ride.

He was just making an adjustment to his cravat when she tapped and entered his room, and he looked surprised to see her still in her dressing robe.

'Good morning,' he said pleasantly, and then seeing her stricken face he asked, 'Is anything wrong, darling?'

'I ... I don't quite know how to tell you this,' she gulped. 'But the thing is ... I think I might be going to have a baby.'

She watched his face closely and was relieved when he strode across to her, exclaiming, 'But that's wonderful!'

'I don't think my aunt and uncle will think so,' she answered wretchedly.

'Oh, I'll handle them, and we shall have to be married as soon as possible,' he told her with genuine delight. Things had worked out even better than planned. Only the day before, James had informed him coolly that he was to start work the day after the party. James saw no reason to postpone it any longer now that Diana was recovered from her accident and if truth be told he'd had more than enough of Joe and would be thoroughly glad to see the back of him.

'I shall speak to your uncle at his earliest convenience,' Joe promised her. 'There's no way on earth that he'll refuse to let us be wed now.'

Diana wept with relief as she melted into his arms.

Chapter Forty-One

The night of the party arrived. Lanterns had been strung amongst the trees in the garden and a large marquee had been erected on the lawn. Inside, tables groaned beneath the weight of the food placed upon them on top of crisp white cloths. There were all manner of treats. Whole cooked legs of pork, baked hams, sides of beef, pickles and pies of every shape and size along with baskets of freshly baked bread. Another table held the desserts – cakes, fruit flans, trifles and tarts. Cook was fair worn out but more than pleased with her efforts and she hoped that everyone else would be too. Another table held a selection of fine wines and champagne. As James had pointed out, it was a very special occasion; after all, it wasn't every day you cheated death and regained your hearing at the same time! For those that preferred it there were barrels of ale and a selection of spirits. A wooden floor had been laid in the centre of the marquee for anyone who cared to dance, and the band that James had booked were already tuning up their instruments on a raised dais to one side of the enormous tent.

In Diana's room, Ginny was dressing the girl's

hair. There was a new fragility about her since her accident, and with her huge blue eyes and softly curling golden hair she looked like a tiny doll. Her dress, a frothy concoction of pale lilac satin and lace, was a work of art, and Ginny sighed with satisfaction as she stood back to admire her. Since the accident the girls had grown even closer and Ginny looked upon her almost as a sister now.

'You look stunning,' she breathed and she meant it.

'You look very beautiful yourself,' Diana told her as she secured the diamond stud earrings that her aunt and uncle had given her for her birthday. They winked in the light as she turned her head this way and that.

Ginny self-consciously fussed with the skirt of her own gown. She had never worn anything so fine in her life before and she had to admit that she felt nice and wondered what Sebastian would think of her.

'So when is Joe going to speak to your uncle?' she asked then – and the smile instantly slid from Diana's face.

'Any time now. He wants to do it before the party so that we can announce our engagement this evening.'

'I suppose it's as well to get it out of the way,' Ginny said practically, although inside she was quaking. Surely there would be a big row! She could only begin to imagine how angry the master was going to be when he found out that Diana was expecting a baby.

Downstairs, Joe took a moment to gather his

courage before tapping at the library door. Millie had just informed him that James was in there waiting for the first of the guests to arrive.

'Enter.'

Joe came into the room, making sure to close the door behind him.

'Peters.' The master, who was seated at his desk, looked mildly surprised to see him. 'Well, what can I do for you?'

'I was wanting a word, sir.' The young man folded his hands behind his back and went to stand confidently in front of the desk.

'Then fire away – but I hope this isn't going to take long. I will be needed to greet our guests at any minute.'

'Very well, I'll get straight to it, sir. The thing is ... I've come to ask for your permission to marry Diana. I've already asked her to be my wife and she has agreed.'

James was rendered temporarily speechless. He merely stared back at Joe, stunned, as if he could hardly believe his ears.

Joe raised his chin. 'I am asking permission to marry your niece, sir,' he repeated. 'I thought we might announce our engagement at the party tonight.'

'*What!* You will do no such thing, young man!' James roared, suddenly finding his voice again. 'Diana is only eighteen years old today and you can't be much older. What are you – nineteen, twenty?

'Age is irrelevant,' Joe answered cockily. 'It's what we both want so I see no need to wait.'

There was a tap at the door then and Barbara

poked her head round it to tell the master, 'Sorry, sir, but the first of the guests are just arriving. The mistress an' Miss Diana are already in the hall waitin' to receive them an' the mistress told me to fetch you.'

'Thank you, Barbara. Tell my wife I shall be there in a second.' He waited for her to leave the room before turning back to Joe and saying coldly, 'I think we'll have this conversation in the morning when we have more time. Something so momentous shouldn't be agreed on a whim. Meanwhile I forbid you to make an announcement this evening.'

Slightly disappointed, Joe shrugged. 'As you wish sir, but I warn you we shan't change our minds.' With that he rudely turned on his heel and left without another word.

James stood there seething with rage. The insolent young pup! He had a strong urge to knock his block off! But then with a huge effort he pulled himself together. A lot of time and hard work had gone into preparing for this evening and he wanted nothing to spoil it, so he would do his best to forget that he and Joe had ever had this conversation. Until the morning, that was, when he would make his feelings abundantly clear.

He found Celia, Diana, Giles and Sebastian in the hallway waiting for him. The young people were standing to greet their guests but Celia, who looked remarkably pretty this evening and more like her old self, was sitting on a chair that the staff had fetched for her, with Anna standing behind her watching over her solicitously.

They greeted their first guests – a local solicitor and his wife and daughter – then there was a constant stream of invitees and James slowly began to relax and get into the party spirit. In no time at all the house and grounds were teeming with people. The women in their elaborate crinolines flitted about like butterflies, their jewels sparkling in the light of the lanterns as the sun went down, and the men formed into small groups discussing politics and cricket and the state of the country. The young people were dancing to the band in no time and the waitresses that James had hired for the night moved efficiently around with their silver trays laden with drinks in fine crystal goblets.

James took a seat next to Celia in the marquee and leaning towards him she whispered happily, 'Doesn't Diana look beautiful tonight, darling?'

'Yes, she certainly does.' As he looked across at her James saw that Joe was standing close by her in a possessive stance, and as their eyes met, James glared at him.

He won't be so keen to stop me marrying his precious niece tomorrow when he finds out she's got my kid growing in her belly, Joe thought smugly and knocked back the rest of the whisky in his glass. He'd already had more than a few and was feeling quite amorous. His eyes roamed around the young ladies present and came to rest on Nancy, who'd treated herself to a new dress especially for the occasion. All the maids were there to join in the celebrations, including the cook, and they were all clearly enjoying themselves enormously. It wasn't often they were given a whole night off, especially to attend a party. His eyes moved back to Nancy. She was standing with a tall young man and laughing at something he'd said. This must be Bertie, he supposed, the young man Diana had told him about. He was a friend of Ginny's. Joe had never seen Nancy without her maid's outfit before and was surprised to note how pretty she looked. She had a nice figure an' all from what he could see of it and the thought made him harden. He wouldn't mind betting she'd be more fun in bed than Diana, who always lay there like a plank when he was making love to her.

After a time, he led Diana on to the dance floor and they started to waltz. Anna had been giving her dancing lessons and she seemed to be enjoying it. But his gaze kept straying back to Nancy. Unbeknown to anyone, he'd already bedded Barbara. He'd also tried it on with Millie but like Ginny she was having none of it. Glancing around the dance floor he saw Ginny dancing with Sebastian and his lip curled. She was smiling up at Sebastian as if the sun shone out of his arse yet she couldn't find a civil word for him, the bitch! Now he came to think of it, he realised that Ginny and Sebastian were seeing quite a bit of each other lately. At the end of the dance he snatched another drink from a passing waitress, a glass of wine this time, and swallowed it in two quick gulps. The evening moved on and the moon and stars appeared in a black velvet sky, washing the grounds of the Hall with a soft light. The wine was flowing like water and everyone was happy, eating, drinking and dancing. It was quite clear that the evening was proving to be a great success. He noted that the mistress was beginning to look deathly tired though. Sure enough, before long the housekeeper and the master were leading Celia towards the house, with her saying her goodbyes to the guests on the way.

Diana was speaking to some young people who were complimenting her on her dress so Joe took the opportunity to slip closer to where Nancy and Bertie were standing observing the proceedings with smiles on their faces and glasses in their hands. After a time, Bertie leaned over to her and whispered something in her ear before striding off towards the house – heading for the privy, no doubt. Joe saw Nancy step out of the marquee, to get a breath of fresh air. She began to wander across the lawn in the direction of the copse, and after furtively glancing across his shoulder to make sure that no one was watching, Joe began to follow her, keeping to the shadows. She had almost reached the trees when he made himself known.

'May I say how nice you're looking this evening?' he called out.

Startled, Nancy twirled about to face him then laughed with relief. 'Oh, you made me jump.'

'Sorry, I didn't intend to.' He flashed her his most charming smile. Then spread his hands, saying, 'Isn't it a wonderful evening?'

'Yes, it is,' she replied innocently. Just like Diana, Nancy had led a very sheltered life and saw no harm in anyone.

'Actually, I've been watching you all night hoping to get you alone for a minute.' He sidled up to her and she felt the first flickers of fear spring to life in her stomach.

Reaching out, he began to wrap a curl that had escaped from one of her clips around his finger and instinctively she moved away, saying, 'I err ... ought to be gettin' back now. Bertie'll wonder where I've gone.'

'He's your young man, is he?' Joe asked, his eyes glowing eerily in the light of the moon. Nancy realised then just how far she had strayed from the party. It could barely be heard from here and suddenly she was keen to get back to the marquee.

'He's not my young man, just a friend,' she faltered.

'Is he now? Have you never kissed him or let him make love to you?'

'No, I have not!' Nancy retorted indignantly, feeling more uncomfortable by the second.

So she's a virgin, Joe thought. Just the way I like 'em!

Nancy made to pass him then but he put out his hand to stop her. 'Don't be in such a hurry,' he urged. 'Let me show you what a real man can make you feel like.' And then without warning he snatched her up as if she weighed no more than a feather and strode into the trees with her struggling with all her might in his arms.

'*Please ... let me go!*' she begged as tears spurted from her eyes but he only laughed as he threw her roughly down on to the grass, knocking the wind from her body and temporarily silencing her.

By the time she had managed to get up on to her elbow, Joe had undone his flies and was dropping to his knees beside her. He reached out and grabbed at the buttons on her bodice and they popped off in all directions and rolled into the grass.

'*NO!*' Nancy was kicking and lashing out with all her might now but she was no match for Joe. He was so much heavier and bigger than her and she knew that she was lost.

Opening her mouth, she let out an ear-splitting scream but then a blow to the side of her face stunned her. She felt him crush her with his weight and start to lift her skirt. She could feel the cool air on her thighs and gasped as he ripped her drawers aside ... then suddenly he grunted and she felt him being lifted from her.

Sobbing with relief, she rolled herself into a ball as she tried to cover her breasts, praying for this nightmare to be over. Yards away, two men were fighting and she realised that it was Bertie and Joe. Bertie must have come looking for her, bless him! As her eyes slowly became accustomed to the gloom she saw Bertie drag Joe to his feet and push him brutally.

'If you know what's good for you, you'll scarper now, you filthy swine! Think yourself lucky I ain't killed you. And don't think you've heard the last o' this, not by a long shot!'

She saw Joe stagger towards the break in the trees and then Bertie was on his knees and gathering her to him, rocking her gently to and fro while she sobbed with shock and relief. If Bertie hadn't come when he did ... she shuddered as she thought of what might have happened.

'It's all right, lass. You're safe now,' he crooned, then, 'Nancy, did he...'

When she shook her head he thanked God while he continued to hold her tenderly until she had calmed down a little.

'Do you feel up to making your way back yet?' he asked eventually.

'I ... I can't go back to the party now. Not looking like this.'

'Hmm, well, let's sneak you into the house the back way, eh? All the rest of the staff are at the party so you shouldn't be seen.' He helped her to her feet then ground out angrily, 'If it weren't for spoilin' Miss Diana's party, I'd go to Mr Walton-Hughes right now an' tell him what that bastard tried to do, but as, it is I think we'd best wait till tomorrow, do you agree?'

'Y ... yes,' she managed with a hitch in her voice as he led her towards the opening.

'Soon as I've got you safely inside I'll go an' find Ginny an' get her to come in to you,' he promised as she leaned heavily against him. They skirted the trees until they came to the stable block, then after crossing the yard Bertie gently pushed her through the kitchen door, telling her, 'Don't worry, lass. I'll see as he gets what's comin' to him.' He then lowered his head and kissed her tenderly on the lips and suddenly a million butterflies came to life in her stomach.

It's a strange life, the girl thought as her hand rose to stroke her lips. How could the touch of one man repulse her so much, yet another's could set her senses spinning?

Chapter Forty-Two

'How are you feeling today?' Ginny asked as she entered Nancy's attic room the next morning. She had been appalled when Bertie had taken her to one side last night and told her that Joe had tried to rape Nancy. Up until then, Ginny had been enjoying herself enormously, dancing the night away in Sebastian's arms... Today however, she was in a quandary. Should she tell Diana about Joe's attack? She knew that it would break her heart.

'I'm all right,' Nancy groaned as she dragged herself up the bed, but she didn't look it. In fact, she felt as if she had been run over by a carriage and there was a painful bruise on her cheek where Joe had clouted her.

'You poor thing!' Ginny hurried over to her and gave her a quick cuddle. 'Why don't you stay in bed today? I'll tell Cook you're not feeling very well.'

'I might just do that, if you're sure she wouldn't mind.' Nancy flicked her tongue out to lick a tear from the end of her nose. 'Oh Ginny, just think what would have happened if Bertie hadn't come along when he did. Joe was going to—'

'Don't think about it any more,' Ginny advised. 'Bertie will be coming along to report to the master about what went on last night and then all hell will break out! I can't see Joe being able to

412

wriggle his way out of this one.' Her loathing of Joseph Peters had increased a hundredfold.

'But what if everyone thinks it was my fault?' Nancy asked timidly.

'Don't be so silly. We all know you better than that. Joe has gone a step too far this time. He's tried it on with most of the maids and now he's going to get his comeuppance. But snuggle down and rest now, and I'll go and get you some breakfast and a nice hot cup of tea. Diana is having a lie-in so I have time.'

In the kitchen Ginny took Cook to one side from her supervision of the big operation to clean up after the party and told her in a hushed voice what had happened. The plump little woman was horrified. Ginny knew she was bound to find out sooner or later, so it was best to tell her now.

'Good Lord,' Cook gasped. 'That lowlife scoundrel! After all we've done for 'im, the ingrate. I thought there was somethin' amiss when Nancy disappeared so early. She seemed to be havin' such a good time. The poor little lamb. Ooh, I'd like to get my 'ands on 'im! But what'll happen now?'

'Bertie is coming to see the master this morning,' Ginny said. 'But goodness knows what this will do to Diana. She worships the ground that Joe walks on.'

Cook shrugged. 'Happen it's for the best that she finds out what he's like now rather than after he's put a ring on her finger,' she said pragmatically.

Ginny wondered what Cook would say if she knew that Diana was carrying Joe's baby but wisely said nothing. Things were quite bad enough

413

as they were. She then made up a breakfast tray and carried it up to Nancy before returning to the kitchen for another one for Diana.

She found the girl sitting on the side of her bed with a sunny smile on her face. 'Morning! The party went well, didn't it?' she burbled. 'Everyone seemed to enjoy it, although I don't know where Joe disappeared off to. He was there one minute and gone the next, and when I went to see him before I went to bed, he'd locked his bedroom door.'

Ginny silently placed the tray down and started to pour Diana a cup of tea. What could she say?

'It was disappointing that Uncle James wouldn't allow us to announce our engagement,' Diana went on. 'But at least he didn't say we couldn't get married. He's going to talk to Joe about it this morning.'

Diana nodded as she shook out the dress Diana had worn the night before and put it on a hanger to take down to the laundry for attention. She felt torn in two. Half of her wanted to tell the girl what had gone on, but the other half of her instinctively held back. She didn't want to be the one to break her heart.

At that moment, downstairs, Barbara was answering the front door to Bertie. The young man's lips were set in a grim line. He'd spent a sleepless night thinking of what might have happened to Nancy, and now he wanted to make sure that Joe got his just deserts.

'Is there any chance of speaking to Mr Walton-Hughes, please?' he asked politely, and noting his police uniform, Barbara invited him in while she

414

went off to the library to see if the master was there.

Very shortly she was back to tell him, 'The master will see you now, Constable. Would you please come this way?'

'Good morning,' James greeted him when he was shown in. 'I hope it's nothing serious. How can I help you?'

'I'm not actually here on police business, sir,' Bertie explained as he removed his helmet. 'But I think you should be aware of an incident that occurred here last night.'

He then went on to tell James of what Joe had done, and as he heard the details of the assault on Nancy, James' face turned an ugly red colour and he clenched his fists.

'I *knew* that young scoundrel was no good,' he fumed. 'I should have followed my gut instinct and sent him packing weeks ago.' Then, remembering his manners, he said, 'Thank you for informing me of this, Constable Watkins. No doubt Nancy will refuse to take the matter further for fear of besmirching her good name, poor lass. And to think it happened under *my* roof where she should be safe! Constable, you may rest assured I shall deal with it immediately.'

'Very good, sir. Good day to you.' Bertie rose and left the room, hoping for a glimpse of Nancy but there was no sign of her. It wasn't until he'd seen Joe attacking her that he'd realised how much she'd come to mean to him – and now he just wanted to tell her so and hope that she felt the same. But there would be time for that when this whole sorry mess had been sorted out. If he had his way, of course, it would be a police matter.

'Barbara, tell Joe I wish to see him *immediately*,' James boomed sticking his head into the hall.

'Yes, sir, right you are.' Barbara scuttled away. She couldn't ever remember the master raising his voice like that before and wondered what was wrong.

Joe was sitting on his bed fully dressed when she reached his room, as if he had been expecting to be summoned, and he never even flinched when she told him that the master wished to see him right now ... this minute. Unfortunately, drink had got the better of him the night before and he'd made a grave mistake, but he still held the trump card as far as he was concerned. Once the master knew that Diana was with child he'd be begging him to marry her and save her from disgrace.

Joe strolled down the stairs as if he didn't have a care in the world and unhurriedly made his way into James's library.

'So what have you got to say for yourself?' James spat.

Joe shrugged insolently. 'If you're talking about the incident that occurred with your maid last night, I'm afraid Constable Watkins got the wrong end of the stick. She followed me when I went for a breath of fresh air to cool down and tried to seduce me.'

'Really?' James said impassively. 'Then let's fetch Nancy herself in and see what *she* has to say about it, shall we?'

Once again Barbara was despatched to run and fetch Nancy. The two men had to wait while she threw some clothes on and a tense silence stretched between them.

'Y … yes, sir?' Poor Nancy's knees threatened to give way when she entered the room and found herself standing right next to the man who had tried to rape her the night before.

'You're not in any trouble, my dear,' James told her gently, noting the livid bruise on her cheek. 'But I'd like you to tell me in your own words what happened last night. And while she does so, you can wait outside, Peters!'

Joe angrily left the room, casting a withering glance in Nancy's direction as he went.

'Right, now tell me: did he try to hurt you?' James asked when they were alone and falteringly she began to speak. Although she found it painful and humiliating, under the master's kindly encouragement she managed to get the story told, and even offered to show him her ruined gown, ripped apart in the violent assault.

'Thank you, my dear. You may go now. Send Joe back in on your way out. Oh, and do take the day off and rest.'

Nancy dropped a curtsey and hurried away, flinching as she passed Joe, who sauntered back in.

'So, if what you say is true, how do you explain the bruise on Nancy's face?' James asked, his voice deceptively calm.

Joe shrugged. 'She must have done it when she fell when I tried to push her off me.'

'And how did the buttons on her dress get torn off? Did she do that too?' James was being openly sarcastic now. He knew which of the two he believed and it certainly wasn't the creature standing in front of him.

'I've no idea. But do you seriously think that I would even look at a maid when I'm going to marry your niece?'

'Oh, I wouldn't be too sure about that,' James said grimly. 'Putting last night aside, how do you propose to keep her? By your own admission you don't have a penny to your name.'

'We'll get by,' Joe said. He paused for a second, then with a sneer he told him, 'The thing is, we *have* to get married. Do you understand what I'm saying?'

James stared at him for a moment ... then as he realised what Joe was saying he leaned heavily on the edge of his desk.

'Are you trying to tell me that my niece is carrying your child?'

Joe nodded. 'I'm afraid so – so you see, you'll have to let me marry her. You won't want the child to be born a bastard, and we can live quite comfortably on Diana's inheritance.'

Suddenly everything became crystal clear. Joe wanted Diana for her money. He didn't love her and she'd probably have a terrible life with him, but if James were to send him away she would never forgive him. He was well and truly trapped between the devil and the deep blue sea. Poor Diana. There could be no happy outcome here. And then suddenly he knew what he must do. He'd put Joe to the test.

'In that case, you are quite right. I can't stand in your way but it won't be easy for you. I suppose I should be grateful to you for being prepared to take the girl on with no money.'

Joe frowned, 'What do you mean – no money? There's her inheritance.'

'Quite, but she can't touch that for another three years. Sebastian could have his, should he marry before his twenty-first birthday, but that does not apply to Diana. Her parents left a codicil in their will to that effect – to deter fortune-hunters, you understand?'

Joe had gone pale and sweat stood out on his brow. 'So how would we manage until then?'

Now it was James' turn to shrug. 'I've no idea. I suppose you will have to start work and find somewhere for you both to live. That is, if Diana still wishes to marry you when she discovers what you tried to do to Nancy.'

James would have liked nothing more than to go and tell his niece right now what Joe had done the night before, but she was not only pregnant but still fragile from her accident. Things were already bad enough as they were. The best he could hope for now was that Joe would clear off and never come back, then he could try to sort out this whole sorry mess.

A vision of himself living in some hovel with a clinging wife and a screaming brat suddenly flashed in front of Joe's eyes and he panicked. Walking out without a backward glance, he took the stairs to his room two at a time then began to throw some clothes into a bag. Once he was packed, he kicked the bag under the bed where it wouldn't be seen. He then scribbled a note to the master and placed it on the shelf above the fire. The sooner he was away from this place the better as far as he was concerned now, but he intended to choose his time and go with a little more than a few of the clothes Giles had lent to him. The rooms in Lamp Hill Hall were full of miniatures and trinkets that must be worth a small fortune, and he fully intended to help himself to a few before he went on his way.

Chapter Forty-Three

'The master's got a face on him like a slapped arse,' Cook whispered to Ginny when she went into the kitchen later that morning.

'Yes, I know,' Ginny whispered back. 'Bertie has been to see him about what Joe tried to do to Nancy, so that's probably why the master is in such a bad mood.'

Cook nodded and tutted. 'Well, let's just hope that young rogue gets what's comin' to 'im!'

Everyone was rushing about trying to get the house and grounds back to rights and tidy again, and Ginny had promised to help too whilst Diana sat with her aunt for a time. Diana was already fretting because Joe hadn't been to see her as yet that morning and she was anxious to know if he had spoken to her uncle again.

At that moment Joe was on his way to the stables when he bumped into Giles. 'So what's going on then?' Giles asked irritably. 'I thought you were going to announce your engagement to my cousin last night. Didn't you get time to speak to my grandfather?'

'Oh, I spoke to him all right,' Joe ground out.

'And?'

'*And* he told me that we can wed ... provided I'm prepared to keep her for the next three years ... which I'm not!'

'What are you talking about? Diana will come into her money if you get married. That's the agreement we had – and then you'll see I get a cut too.'

'You're wrong. As it happens she won't get a penny afore she's twenty-one because of some codicil or another her parents left in their will,' Joe spat angrily. 'And as for our agreement ... huh! I owe you nothing, and before I leave I shall make damn sure your grandather knows that it was *you* who stabbed me and why. You ain't exactly gone out of your way to make me feel welcome here, have you? It was what you did to my sister that got us in this mess in the first place. Thank God I shall be out of this dump for good tonight.'

'But ... you can't walk out on me like this!' Giles was appalled. He was even more heavily in debt now and had been relying on that money. In his wallet was all the cash he had left in the world: two sovereigns, three florins, a shilling piece and a few farthings. The people he owed a small fortune to were not the type to be crossed.

'Oh, get out of my way,' Joe stormed, pushing him roughly aside and heading for the stable block. 'I'm goin' for a ride.'

As Giles watched him go, the colour drained out of his cheeks. If Joe did tell James that it was he who had stabbed Joe – after getting his sister pregnant to boot – then Giles would be in even deeper shit than he was now! He stood there as if in a trance until Joe galloped past him, dangerously close, and screaming abuse at the poor horse he was riding. Somehow he had to stop him. If Joe did carry out his threat, Giles knew that his grandfather might well disown him – and then where would he go? He would be ruined and living on the streets.

Giles raced off to the stables, saddled his horse himself in record time and minutes later was pounding down the drive. At the end of it he looked to left and right, and seeing a cloud of dust to the left he turned his horse in that direction. He soon spotted Joe in the distance heading for the disused quarry in Hartshill. The quarry was fast filling with water now and was a favourite spot for young people who liked to go swimming there in the summer. Digging his heels into the horse's sides Giles spurred the beast on, and sure enough there was Joe trotting the horse around the quarry edge. There was a perilous drop to the water below and suddenly Giles knew what he must do. Joe could ruin his whole future if he opened his mouth, and Giles was prepared to do whatever it took to stop him.

As he approached Joe, the chap's head swung round and he snarled. 'What the hell are *you* followin' me for? Leave me in peace, for Christ's sake. I've said all I'm goin' to say to you.'

'It's more what you're planning to say to my father that worries me,' Giles retorted. A far better and more experienced rider than Joe, he started moving his horse closer to Joe's.

Joe's horse snorted with fear as it found itself being edged towards the drop.

'Stay back, you bloody fool, else you'll have us all over the side!' Joe roared, then leaping from his horse, he turned to face Giles as the horse ambled away and began to crop the grass.

Giles grinned as he urged his horse on again and Joe nervously backed away from him. His brash manner was gone now as he saw the evil glint in Giles' eyes and realised what he was trying to do.

'Look, man, be sensible. You don't wanna find yourself danglin' at the end of a rope, do you?' Joe tried to inch away from the edge of the deep chasm behind him, but each time he did so, Giles blocked him with his horse. Glancing from side to side, Joe prayed to see someone who might help, but there was not a soul in sight. Terror engulfed him. Then suddenly when the horse was almost upon him, Giles slashed the poor beast with his whip and the animal reared in distress.

Joe let out a bloodcurdling scream as one of the horse's hooves caught the side of his face and then he felt himself falling backward into the void. Just for a second he seemed to be hanging suspended in the air ... then he was hurtling down the face of the quarry towards the deep water below, bouncing off the jagged rocks as he fell. There was a loud splash and Giles watched, his chest heaving with effort, as Joe hit the water spread-eagled and began to float across the mirrored surface. Even from such a great height Giles could see the water around him changing colour and knew that it was

Joe's lifeblood seeping out of him. The next scream took him by surprise. It couldn't be Joe, surely? He could never have survived such a fall. Then a young boy appeared at the water's edge gazing up at him with a horrified expression on his face. He had been fishing but now he threw his rod down and fled in the direction of the town, screaming blue murder.

Panic set in then as Giles cursed. He'd been seen – and just as Joe had said, if he was caught he'd breathe his last at the end of a rope. *What can I do, what can I do?* he chanted to himself, and eventually the answer came. He would have to get away from here – and quickly!

Go somewhere no one would ever find him.

Turning his horse about, he began to gallop away as if the hounds of hell were snapping at his horse's heels, and as he went he devised a plan. He would head for the nearest coast and once there he would adopt a new name and a new identity and go aboard a ship. Sail to pastures new. He knew that he would never be able to go home again now, but that was the least of his concerns. He'd never wanted to be a part of his father's businesses anyway. Surely a life on the ocean waves would be preferable? It was a known fact that sailors had women in every port, so it could turn out to be quite an adventure and a chance to see the world. He urged his horse on with not a scrap of remorse for what he had just done. Guttersnipe Peters had finally got what was coming to him, and if Giles had his time over, he would have done exactly the same again.

As Giles was making his escape, little Tommy Gunn who had witnessed the whole tragic affair was entering Tuttle Hill where he flagged down a passing horse and cart loaded with farm produce for the market.

'Help!' he gasped, pressing his hand to his side where he had a stitch. 'Th ... there's just bin a murder – back yonder at the quarry. A man were knocked over the top an' he's floatin' in the water!'

'Slow down, son. I can't understand a word yer sayin',' the kindly farmer told him. So Tommy tried to catch his breath and repeated what he'd said more slowly.

'Bloody 'ell! 'Ere, give us your hand, me young feller. We'd best get you to the police station so's yer can tell 'em what you've seen soon as yer like.'

Bertie Watkins just happened to be on duty and manning the front desk in the police station. He listened to the little lad's story with the attention it deserved.

'So do you know the man that was pushed?' he asked as he reached for his helmet.

Tommy shook his head. 'No ... but I know who pushed him. It were the young master from up at the Hall. Me dad works fer Mr Walton-Hughes, see, so I recognised Master Giles straight off.'

Heart in his mouth, Bertie hurried away to tell the sergeant what had been reported and before long, four policemen set off to check out what Tommy had told them.

By the time they reached the quarry there was no sign of a body floating there and Bertie asked sternly, 'Are you sure you're not havin' us on, son? It's a very serious matter, to waste police time, you know.'

'I swear I'm not,' Tommy insisted. 'The body landed just over there an' it were floatin' about when I did a runner. Happen it's sunk.'

'Then those of us as can swim had better strip off an' go in an' take a look,' one of the policemen said, then on a brighter note, 'As it happens it's quite a nice day to take a dip. You stay here with the nipper, Bertie.'

Bertie and Tommy stood side by side, their eyes fixed on Bertie's three colleagues who were dipping and diving beneath the surface of the water in nothing but their long johns. Then suddenly one of them broke the surface and spat out water before shouting, 'Here, chaps. There's something down below caught in the weeds.'

It was mid-afternoon before Joe Peters' lifeless body was hauled on to the side of the quarry, and as Bertie looked down at him he felt nothing but relief that never again would this man be able to abuse another woman. As far as he was concerned, the lousy bastard had got his just deserts and the world would be a better place without him.

It fell on Bertie to be the bearer of the bad news. At just after six o'clock that evening he stood with another two officers and his sergeant on the steps of Lamp Hill Hall.

'Could I see the master of the house, please?' he asked Barbara when she opened the door to them.

'Yes, do come in.' She left the men sitting in the

hallway while she hurried to the study to let the master know that they were there.

'Police officers to see me, you say?' James sighed and rubbed his forehead where a raging headache was throbbing. It had not been a good day, what with one thing and another. Diana was fractious because Joe had avoided her all day, Celia was worn out from the excitement of the party, Nancy was still in bed following the horrific attack the night before, and he'd not seen hide nor hair of Giles since the morning, when he'd noticed him galloping off down the drive like a madman.

What now? he wondered wearily. 'Show them in, please,' he told Barbara.

'So how can I help you?' he enquired when Constable Watkins and Sergeant Berry had entered his room. The other two constables had been instructed to wait in the hallway. 'If this is about what we spoke of this morning, Constable Watkins, I can assure you—'

'Could I stop you there, please sir,' the sergeant said, tucking his helmet beneath his arm and looking very solemn. He then cleared his throat and went on, 'I have a warrant here for your grandson Giles' arrest, Mr Walton-Hughes.'

'You have a *what?*' James looked astounded and horrified.

'I believe you have had a Mr Joseph Peters staying here with you for some time?'

James nodded numbly, thinking this must be something to do with the attack on Nancy – but if it was, why did they have a warrant for Giles' arrest?

'I'm afraid Mr Peters was killed late this morning when he was pushed over the edge of the disused quarry in Hartshill. His body was recovered from the water this afternoon. There was a witness, who can verify that they saw your grandson force him over the edge, so we are here to arrest your grandson, Giles Walton-Hughes, on a charge of murder.'

James thumped down on to the nearest chair. He felt as if he had had all the air knocked out of him, but he managed to croak, 'Th ... there must be some mistake.'

'I'm afraid not, sir.' The sergeant shook his head gravely. 'The witness was quite clear on what he saw, so if you could just tell us where your grandson is we'll get this over with as soon as possible.'

'I don't know where he is,' James told them truthfully. 'I haven't seen him since he went out on his horse this morning. In fact I was just beginning to get concerned.'

'I see. Then would you have any objection if we checked his room and searched the house?'

'Is that really necessary?' James asked. 'My wife is not well and I dread to think what this news is going to do to her.'

'I'm sorry, sir, but it's our job. A murder has been committed.'

'Then I suppose you will have to go ahead; I'll get the maids to show you around,' James answered, in deep shock and wondering how the hell he was going to break this to Celia.

'That won't be necessary, sir. We'll find our own way around and I promise we shall be as discreet as possible.' The sergeant nodded before leading Bertie from the room as James dragged himself out of the chair.

Anna entered at that moment and seeing his ashen face, she asked, 'Whatever is wrong? You look as if you've seen a ghost. And what are all these police officers doing here?'

'Oh, Anna, thank goodness you're here.' He ran a hand distractedly through his hair making it stand on end. 'Will you please go up to Celia and warn her that the police will be wanting to look around her room shortly. I'll explain everything later to both of you, I promise, but will you please just stay with her for now?'

Sensing that something awful had happened, she left without a word to do his bidding.

An hour later the police were back in the hall, having searched the house from top to bottom. The staff, still weary after the party, were all agog wondering what on earth was going on, and Anna was still upstairs trying to calm Celia.

'Thank you, sir.' Sergeant Berry put his helmet back on as he prepared to leave. 'We're satisfied that your grandson isn't here, as you said, but I must ask you to inform us the moment that he returns.'

His lips set in a grim line, James nodded his agreement, and after seeing the police out he made his way upstairs. Celia would have to be informed of what was going on sooner or later, so he might as well get it over with now. Deeply shocked himself, he feared for her life, once she had heard this terrible news: that her grandson was being hunted down for murder. And then he would have to speak to Diana too, and he quaked at the thought. The father of her unborn child was dead. Dear Lord, this was every parent's worst nightmare come true.

Chapter Forty-Four

Celia took the news every bit as badly as James had feared she would, but now that he had left her in Anna's safe pair of hands, he braced himself to speak to his niece. Anna had informed him that Diana was downstairs in the drawing room with Ginny so he slowly made his way there, with his wife's sobs following him down the stairs.

Outside the drawing-room door, he rubbed a hand over his eyes then straightened his shoulders before striding into the room. Ginny and Diana were sitting on either side of the fireplace. They rose and looked at him expectantly when he entered and he gave a nervous cough to clear his throat, wishing that he were anywhere but here.

'Why were the police here, Uncle James?' Diana asked immediately. 'They insisted on coming into my room and snooping around,' she ended indignantly.

'My dear, I'm afraid I have some very bad news for you,' James said quietly. 'Perhaps you would like to sit down?' He went on to tell her that the reason the police had come to the Hall was to look for Giles who was wanted for murder. And then, very gently, he told her that Joe was dead.

She immediately shook her head.

'No, he can't be,' she gasped. 'It must be some-one else. We're going to get married and I'm carrying his child. Joe will be coming in to see me any time now.'

'I'm afraid it is true.' James could almost feel her pain.

'*No!*' Diana screamed. 'And what's this about Giles? Why would Giles want to hurt him?'

'I can't answer that, I simply do not know.' James was a broken man.

Diana sprang up and began to pace the room like a caged animal as her head wagged from side to side, setting her golden curls dancing. 'They've made a mistake,' she said after a while. 'It's someone else they've pulled out of the quarry. It can't be Joe. Can it, Ginny?'

She twirled about to confront Ginny and when the girl merely lowered her head with tears in her eyes, Diana became still and her face crumpled. She stood motionless for some seconds then suddenly from somewhere deep inside her there came a groan that was so heartrending it turned her uncle's blood to ice.

'*No –NOO–NOOO!*'

Ginny was at her side in a second, gathering her into her arms as James crept from the room. He had his own grief to deal with and felt as if he had been stretched to breaking-point. As he stumbled into the hall he found Barbara waiting for him.

'Sir, when I went to light the fire and turn the bed back in Mr Peters' room earlier on, I dis-covered a bag full of clothes shoved under the bed along with some of the items from the cabinets in the drawing room, and this letter was on the shelf. It's addressed to you but I didn't want to give it to you until the police had gone.' Joe had used and abused her and she felt no allegiance towards him whatsoever now.

'Thank you, Barbara.'

She looked at James and hovered for a moment as if there was something she wanted to say, but then thinking better of it she went on her way, feeling heart-sorry for him. He was a good man was the master, a kind man, and he didn't deserve all this grief.

James meanwhile stared down at the letter in his hand before walking on leaden legs to his study. He'd have a stiff drink before he opened it, he decided, in case it contained any more shocks. He wasn't sure he could take too many more. It was actually three whiskies drunk in quick succession later before he finally slit open the envelope and began to read what Joe had written. As he did so, his face creased with agony. So it was Giles himself who had stabbed Joe after the latter came looking for him to tell him that after raping his sister, Giles had left her pregnant. Worse still was the fact that Giles and Joe had plotted to get Diana wed to Joe so that they could both get their hands on his niece's money.

What did I breed? he thought wretchedly – and yet all he could see in his mind's eye was Giles as a little boy. His first tooth, taking his first step, learning to ride his pony on a leading rein in the manège. Giles was his grandson, his own flesh and blood, and despite the fact that he had been selfish for some long time and spoiled beyond belief, James had continued to love him. Now when he was found, he would probably end his short life with his neck in a noose and James could hardly bear to think of it. Laying his head on his arm, the sorrowing man wept as if his heart would break.

James stayed up until late that night watching for a sign of Giles returning but eventually he made his way to bed, peeping in at Celia on the way. She was asleep but her closed eyes were puffy and Anna, who was sitting in a chair at the side of her, placed her finger on her lips and quietly ushered him back out on to the landing.

'She's only just dropped off,' she whispered. 'I gave her the sleeping draught the doctor left for her.' Then looking into his tired face she said, 'I'm so very sorry, my darling.'

'I know, my dear.' He swiped the back of his hand across his bloodshot eyes. 'I think I've spent most of the day trying to convince myself that the police had made a terrible mistake, but the fact that Giles hasn't dared to come home speaks volumes, doesn't it?'

She nodded sadly. 'I'm afraid it does. Where do you think he might have gone?'

'I have no idea, although I rather suspect he'll try to board a ship somewhere and get out of the country. He always said he wanted to be a sailor when he was a little boy.'

'Then there's nothing you can do for now, so why don't you try to get some rest?'

'Very well, but I'd like you to read this first.' He handed her the letter that Joe had left for him, and as Anna quickly scanned the page she looked horrified.

'So Joe's sister is having Giles's baby? But that means it will be your great-grandchild!'

'Quite. It just gets worse, doesn't it? Of course I shall have to go and visit the family and make financial arrangements for the child, but would you mind keeping this to yourself, Anna? I think this might just tip Celia over the edge.'

'Of course. But now I insist you go and lie down. I shall nap in the chair at the side of the bed this evening in case Celia needs anything.'

'I really don't know what I would do without you,' he said, seizing her hand and raising it to his lips. 'If only things could have been different. You deserve so much more than life has dealt you.'

'I'm not complaining.' She gave him a little shove in the direction of his bedchamber before disappearing into the shadows of Celia's room again and he, heavy with care, wearily did as he was told.

The police were back early the next morning to see if Giles had returned, although they must have known that he hadn't, for they'd posted a policeman to stand at the end of the drive all night. Everyone was up and about. Few in the household had slept well that night, especially Diana, who was beside herself with grief. Ginny had stayed with her all night, offering what comfort she could but the girl was inconsolable.

'There's no point in going on without Joe,' she wept over and over again.

'Don't be so silly. You have the child to think

about now, and while you have that you'll always have a little part of Joe,' Ginny tried to tell her but Diana just ignored her, pacing up and down, up and down, until Ginny was sure she would wear a hole in the carpet.

Diana refused to go down for breakfast, saying she wasn't hungry, and Ginny felt anxious. Surely the way Diana was going on couldn't be good for her unborn baby?

She sought the master out and said as much to him, and James agreed to ask Dr Gifford to look in on Diana when he paid a visit to Celia later that morning. Up until now, Diana had not had the pregnancy confirmed. She had hoped that she and Joe could be wed before they made it common knowledge, but there seemed no point in concealing it now. Soon everyone would know – and now there was no chance of her having a ring on her finger. This would present the family with yet another problem – that of an illegitimate child. It seemed there was no end to their troubles.

Then suddenly, about mid-morning, Diana's tears stopped abruptly and she sank on to a chair by the window staring sightlessly out across the lawns. Ginny wasn't sure which was worse, the girl's tears or the terrible silence. Diana didn't even answer when spoken to, so Ginny slipped away to the kitchen to get a well-earned cup of tea. She bumped into Sebastian in the hall on her way and seeing how fagged-out she looked he gently took her hand and asked, 'Are you all right, Ginny?'

She felt a little shock travel up her arm at his touch. 'Yes, *I'm* fine. It's Diana you should be worrying about,' she told him sadly.

He shook his head, still holding her hand, and her weary heart wished that they could just stay there like that for ever.

'I … I should be getting on,' she said eventually. 'I don't want to leave Diana alone for too long at the moment. I'm just going to have a quick cup of tea while she's resting.'

'Of course.' He released her hand. 'We'll talk later.' She nodded and hurried on her way.

'Aw lass, yer look all in,' Cook sympathised when she entered the kitchen. 'Come an' sit down an' take the weight off yer feet fer a few minutes. I bet you ain't had a wink o' sleep, have yer?' The plump woman bustled about, spooning sugar into a cup and adding the strong tea and a drop of milk.

'Get that down you,' she advised, then in a sombre voice: 'Whoever would have thought it, eh? I allus knew Master Giles were a handful but I never dreamed he'd be capable o' murder. Don't get me wrong, I had no time fer Joe, but he didn't deserve to die like that, did he?'

'Maybe he did,' Ginny said as she sipped at the hot drink. 'I don't know what to think.' Then she asked, 'Is Mrs Bronson still in with the mistress?'

'No, she's had to go into town again. Said she'd got an appointment wi' someone, though she didn't say who, so Millie's in wi' the mistress at present. She's disappeared off a few times recently, come to think of it.'

Ginny sat silently for a while then when she'd drained her cup she rose and carried it to the sink where Nancy was washing pots. The young girl looked much better than she had the day before, although she was still terribly pale.

'Sorry to make you more work,' Ginny said and hugged her as she handed Nancy the cup before going back upstairs.

Diana was sitting exactly where she had left her and it was a relief when the doctor came in a short time later. He had been informed of what had happened, but then Ginny supposed everyone in town would know by now. It would no doubt be headlines in the local newspaper.

'Mr Walton-Hughes asked me to look in on Diana,' he told Ginny, glancing towards the motionless figure sitting by the window.

'Has he told you that we think she may be...'

'Expecting a child? Yes, he has, my dear, but now if you would get her on to the bed for me, we'll have a good look at the young lady, eh?'

Ginny led Diana towards the bed and helped her off with her dress as Diana stood unprotestingly as if she was carved from stone. Once she was lying down the doctor gently pressed around her stomach and nodded.

'Yes, it's still very early on, but she's certainly with child. As for the state she's in now... Well, it's probably delayed shock. There's not too much I can do for that, I'm afraid, but I'll give her something to help her sleep. Rest is always the best tonic after a trauma. Get someone to call at the surgery and I'll leave a draught there for her.'

'Thank you, Doctor.' Ginny pulled the covers up over Diana who lay staring up at the ceiling, and left the room with him. She wanted to see how the mistress was faring.

Mrs Bronson was back by then and she gave Ginny a tired smile as the girl entered the room. 'Hello, dear, how is Diana?' she said quietly.

'Not too good to be honest,' Ginny replied sadly, noting that the mistress looked even worse.

'The police have just been to tell the master that they've managed to discover Joe's address,' Mrs Bronson confided in a quiet voice. 'He lived with his family in Rugby, not far from where Sebastian and Giles went to school, apparently.'

'Do they know what's happened yet?' Ginny asked and Mrs Bronson shook her head.

'I think the police are going to tell them today. And there's still no trace of Giles. I hope in a way that he does manage to escape. Not because I think he shouldn't be punished for what he's done, but because it will kill the mistress if they catch him and he's hanged.'

Ginny nodded in agreement. Celia lay in a drugged sleep; she looked ghastly. It was hard to believe that just a couple of days ago she had been laughing and playing the hostess at Diana's party. Anna herself looked little better. The situation at Lamp Hill Hall remained all very confusing, Ginny thought. She had once seen Anna wrapped in the master's arms – yet the housekeeper clearly adored her mistress. With a little sigh, the girl left the room and went back to sit with Diana. Ginny herself was no stranger to tragedy, and adversity had strengthened her powers of endurance. However, she felt heartsore for the family here, almost as traumatised as they were. It looked set to be another very long day.

Chapter Forty-Five

Ginny was so exhausted that night that she was asleep in the room adjoining Diana's almost before her head hit the pillow. Sebastian had come to spend time with her and Diana during the afternoon and it only went to reinforce what she thought of him, that he was a truly kind and honourable person, so different from his cousin Giles.

It was in the early hours that something made her stir – and she was instantly awake. For a moment there was nothing but silence and she was just about to turn over and go back to sleep when she heard what sounded like a groan. With a sigh she slid out of bed and pulled her dressing robe on. Diana was probably crying again, poor lass.

She padded along the landing in bare feet, and when she tapped on the door and entered the room the groan came again, much louder this time. Ginny fumbled her way forward in the dark until she reached the small table where the oil lamp stood and after a while she managed to light it and the shadows in the room were chased away.

Diana was curled in a ball beneath the blankets but her forehead was visible and Ginny saw at a glance that she was drenched in sweat.

'What's wrong?' she asked, and Diana's

agonised eyes looked up at her.

'My ... stomach,' she gasped.

Realising that something was very wrong, Ginny's head spun. And then it came to her – Mrs Bronson: she would know what to do.

'I won't be a moment,' she promised then fled from the room and along the landing, nearly tumbling down the dark staircase in her haste.

Mrs Bronson answered the pounding on her door almost immediately, knuckling the sleep from her eyes as she asked, 'What is it?'

'It's Diana. She's in terrible pain and I don't know what to do.'

'I see. Wait there a moment while I get my robe.' Minutes later they were rushing up the stairs together and Ginny looked on from frightened eyes as Mrs Bronson leaned over Diana and asked, 'Where is the pain, my dear?'

'It's in my back ... my stomach ... *everywhere,*' the girl moaned.

'Right, then let's get you up in the bed and see what's going on.' The woman was instantly in control of the situation and she beckoned to Ginny to get hold of one of Diana's arms while she grasped the other. Once they had her in a more upright sitting position Mrs Bronson drew back the blankets and gasped. The bed was like a bloodbath: Diana was having a miscarriage.

'Run down to the stables, Ginny, and get Jim Grady to ride into town for the doctor. Say it's urgent.' Then Anna whispered: 'Say it's a matter of life and death.' If Diana carried on bleeding like this, it was certain she would haemorrhage to death.

Ginny needed no second telling but was off like the wind. When she returned, she nearly bumped into the master who was just leaving his room.

'I thought I heard someone crying. Is it my wife?' he asked blearily.

'No, sir. It's Miss Diana.' Ginny quickly told him what was happening.

He accompanied her to Diana's room, only to be told brusquely by Mrs Bronson, 'Go back to your room and get some rest. This is no place for a man at the moment and there's nothing you can do. We've already sent Jim off to get the doctor.'

'In that case I'll go downstairs and wait so that I can let him in, the moment he arrives.' James melted away as Mrs Bronson told Ginny, 'We're going to need hot water, lots of it, and towels. Can you see to that?'

Ginny was relieved to escape from the room with a job to do. Diana was clearly in agony and she hated to see her that way.

Downstairs in the kitchen she raked the glowing embers of the fire back into life and threw some more coal on to them and once it was blazing again she swung the kettle over it to boil while she raced away to collect some clean towels.

It was almost an hour and a half later when the doctor arrived, but by then it was all over. Diana lay in a spent heap on the bed, her breathing laboured.

'I'm sorry,' he told Mrs Bronson. 'All we can do now is clean her up.' He removed the small bloody mess from between Diana's legs and after placing it in a bowl he covered it whilst Mrs Bronson gently began to wash her.

'What's happened?' Diana whimpered. She was so relieved that the searing pains had stopped.

'I'm afraid you've lost the baby, my dear. It was probably all the shock of the last few days that caused it to happen,' Mrs Bronson explained with great tenderness.

'So I've lost Joe *and* his child now,' Diana said dully as a solitary tear slid down her cheek. And then she turned her face to the wall.

Ginny's spirits lifted slightly the next day when Millie brought up a letter for her that had arrived in the post. She knew it was from Charlie instantly by the handwriting, and as Diana was fast asleep she settled down in the chair by the window to read it straight away.

For the first time in what felt like days, she found herself smiling. Charlie still sounded happy and contented, which was something to be grateful for at least. At the end of the letter, her brother added a postscript to say that Uncle Edward would still be very happy for her to join them permanently in Hull, and Ginny felt more than a little tempted. But then she glanced at Diana's sleeping figure and knew that she couldn't leave her. The poor girl had gone through so much recently; she couldn't abandon her now. Ginny had just folded the letter and popped it in her pocket to read again later when the door inched open and Sebastian appeared with a cup of tea for her.

'I thought you might be ready for this,' he said glancing at his sister. 'Anna just told me what happened during the night.'

Ginny took the cup and saucer with a word of

thanks. 'It hasn't been the best couple of days, has it?' she said ruefully. 'And to think that not so long ago, everyone was happy and preparing for Diana's party.'

Sebastian took a seat, his eyes still on his sister. 'How has she taken it? Losing the baby, I mean.'

'Badly, I'm afraid.' Ginny sighed.

'Why don't you go and snatch a couple of hours' sleep when you've had your tea,' he suggested thoughtfully. 'I can stay here and keep an eye on Diana. I shall read the newspapers.'

'Are you sure you don't mind?' Ginny was sorely tempted for her eyes were gritty from lack of sleep.

She finished her drink then rose and gave him a grateful smile. It was as she was passing him that he caught her hand and told her, 'You're a very remarkable girl, Ginny, and I can't thank you enough for what you've done for Diana. My sister never really had a proper friend until you came along.'

The touch of his fingers sent a tingle up her arm and she snatched her hand away, telling him brusquely, 'But I'm paid to look after her. You mustn't forget that.'

He frowned, wondering what he might have said to offend her as she rushed from the room. Once out on the landing, Ginny silently cursed herself. What did you have to go and say that for? He was only trying to be nice! But that was the problem, she suddenly realised. He was *too* nice and she was beginning to get silly notions about him, which would never do. They were from different classes, as Joe and Diana had been –

and look what had happened there! All the same she found that it was hard to put him from her mind.

In her room she lay on the bed. Yawning, she decided that she would just have forty winks, but exhaustion caught up with her and the next time she opened her eyes she found herself in a darkened room. With a sense of panic, she hurriedly tidied her hair in the mirror and shook out the creases from her dress as best she could before hurrying along to Diana's room.

Sebastian was still there and he smiled at her, saying, 'That was a good sleep. You look a little more rested now.'

'I'm so sorry, I only meant to have a short nap,' she said guiltily as her eyes moved to the bed. Diana was lying with her back to her and Ginny couldn't tell if she was asleep.

Sebastian beckoned her out on to the landing where he told her in a low voice, 'The doctor dropped by this afternoon again and said everything seemed all right with my sister – or as all right as it could be under these circumstances. But she hasn't eaten a thing. I had to almost bully her even to take a little drink. She's going to make herself really ill if she goes on like this.'

'Oh the poor, dear girl.' Ginny chewed on her lip before asking, 'Has there been any news of Giles?'

'No, they're still looking for him but the police came by to say that a young man answering his description left his horse at an inn in Warwick late last night. Jim Grady is planning to go there on the train tomorrow and identify it – and if it is

Storm, he'll bring him home. Giles could be anywhere by now. Oh, and that young constable called in this evening to enquire after Nancy and left her a bunch of flowers. I don't know if it's my imagination but they seem to be quite smitten with each other, don't they? Nancy didn't have time to exchange more than a few words with him because she was helping Cook to prepare dinner when he arrived, but she went as red as a beetroot.'

Ginny smiled. 'I think you may be right – I hope so, at any rate. They'd make a lovely couple. But now I'm going down to the kitchen to prepare a few treats for Diana to see if I can persuade her to eat anything. As soon as I come back I'll take over and you can go and get some rest then.'

'We'll see,' he answered. 'I'm not particularly tired. I've only spent the afternoon relaxing and reading so I'll sit with you for a while if you wish before I turn in. Diana isn't much company at the minute – in fact I don't think she's uttered so much as a single word all day.' Ginny thanked him, relieved that he hadn't taken umbrage, and there was a spring in her step as she headed for the kitchen.

Despite all their best combined efforts, Diana firmly refused to eat so much as a mouthful of the food Ginny brought to her, so she and Sebastian shared it as he told her about his plans for schooling the children of his uncle's workers.

'Uncle James has told me there's an old cottage in the grounds that isn't being used and it would be an ideal place for a little school.'

Ginny saw the excitement in his eyes as he

spoke of it.

'Of course it would need some work doing on it first. Quite a considerable amount of work as it happens. A new roof for a start-off. The place has stood empty for some long time. And then even when it is ready I'd have to get a teacher in to help me run it. I can't be there all the time if I'm going to work with Uncle James as well.'

'It will be wonderful,' Ginny said. His enthusiasm was infectious. 'And how gratifying that your uncle is agreeable to your plans. So many employers prefer to keep their workers and their families ignorant, but times are changing. Everyone should have the opportunity to read and write now.'

Before they knew it, they were swapping ideas about how the new school should be run and time passed in the blink of an eye as Diana lay in an uneasy sleep full of troubled dreams.

Chapter Forty-Six

As Giles staggered out of the inn at Portsmouth it occurred to him that he had nowhere to sleep and he cursed as he scratched his head and looked up and down the road. He was very close to the docks but he doubted he would get taken on by any of the ships now with it being so late. He'd have to wait for the morning tide. He supposed he shouldn't have had so much to drink as well. There wouldn't be many captains willing to take him on in the state he was currently in. It might be better if he found a cheap lodging house some-where then try for a ship in the morning – but which way should he go? He had no idea where he was although he knew the area was seedy to say the least.

The inn had been full of sailors of every shape, size and colour, and some of them had looked like they'd cut their own mother's throat for sixpence. There had also been a gaggle of women who looked to be of dubious repute, which was why he'd kept his hand on his pocket where his money lay. He frowned as he thought of the dodgy pawnbroker he had sold his watch to when he'd first arrived in the town late that afternoon. The watch was a solid gold hunter – a grand affair bought for him by his mother, and the chap hadn't given him a fraction of its worth, the bastard. Still, things would improve tomorrow if he could just get taken on board one of the vessels leaving the docks.

As he stood there, the door of the inn opened behind him and he shrank into the shadows. He was still looking over his shoulder expecting the long arm of the law to tap him on the shoulder at any minute but it was a woman who emerged, staggering drunkenly. He recognised her im-mediately. She had been making cow eyes at him all night.

'Are you looking for a good time, boyo?' she asked as she spotted him.

He was on the verge of telling her to piss off but then thought better of it. She'd no doubt have a room to take him to and anything was better than having to spend the night in a shop doorway.

'I might be,' he answered, stepping into the dim glow of the streetlight, and her eyes lit up greedily. She'd been keeping tabs on him all evening. He was very well dressed, not short of a bob or two no doubt, and he was young and handsome too.

He, on the other hand, was less than impressed with her. The ragged dress she was wearing was so low-cut that her flabby breasts looked in danger of spilling out of it at any second, and she smelled rank. Her face was heavily made up with rouge and her lips were cherry red – but it didn't disguise her heavily pockmarked cheeks nor the fact that she was fast approaching middle age.

'Come along then,' she said as she sashayed jauntily towards him and placed her arm through his. 'Let Pearl show you what a Portsmouth girl can do for you.'

She giggled and hiccupped, and as he caught a waft of her foul-smelling breath it was all he could do to stop himself retching. She began to lead him through a labyrinth of cobblestone alleys, over which he could see the masts of the ships bobbing in the docks. Now and again he glanced behind him, convinced he could hear footsteps following them – but each time there was no one to be seen. And then they emerged next to what looked like a deserted warehouse right on the water's edge.

Suddenly nervous, he looked around before asking, 'Is your room near here somewhere?' But he had no time to say any more, for suddenly someone thumped him squarely in the middle of his back from behind, knocking him to his knees and driving the wind from him.

Pearl sniggered as she stepped aside. 'That's it, lads. You give 'im what for, the stuck-up young sot. I saw his lip curl when I took his arm back there. Check his pockets, quick.'

Still dazed, Giles felt himself being roughly turned over so that he was flat on his back as someone began to rummage in his pockets. He realised then that there were at least two men, but at the thought of being robbed he began to fight back, kicking and swearing as loudly as he could. It was too dark to see his attackers' faces but as his foot connected with one of their shins they squealed in outrage and began to kick him in the ribs.

Giles curled himself into a ball then tried to crawl away but in seconds they were on him again and he knew he was no match for two of them. He could hear the filthy water slapping on the side of the docks and he began to panic as a hand found its way into his pocket and fastened about the money there.

'I've got it!' A triumphant shout went up and Giles saw the shape of Pearl dart forward and snatch it from the man's hands.

Then: 'Is that all there is?' she grumbled as she dropped the coins into her pocket. 'There ain't no more than a few measly sovs there. Try his other pocket.'

Giles was manhandled once more then as the men searched the rest of his clothes, and as he heard his jacket tear he began to lash out again. He could already feel one of his eyes closing and taste blood in his mouth, but he wasn't prepared to give up without a fight.

'I'll have the law on you, you just see if I don't,' he gurgled as he blindly hit out with his clenched fist. It connected firmly on someone's chin and they yelped with pain.

'Right, that's it,' the man said threateningly. 'You'll get what's coming to you now, shipmate.'

As he spoke he was hauling Giles to his feet as if he weighed no more than a feather and Giles felt his feet leave the ground as the bloke held him up by the neck of his jacket. He was a positive giant. And then a cold blade sliced through his fancy waistcoat and he felt it sink in near his heart.

Instantly his mouth began to fill with blood and he realised with horror that he had been stabbed. Something warm was spilling out of him and his hand was suddenly sticky. He felt a great darkness racing towards him then he had the sensation of flying before he hit the water in the dock. The shock of plunging into the cold sea snatched the breath from his lungs and he flailed about helplessly for a moment before sinking slowly below the debris and the flotsam. His brain told him that he must try and reach the surface as he stared up, but everything seemed to be happening so very slowly now. He could vaguely see the distorted shape of the moon high above him but the effort of moving his arms was causing a pain in his breast so he stopped struggling. And then a strange lethargy swept through him and he felt weightless and calm. It was pleasant to float down beneath the waves, and as he closed his eyes for the very last time, Giles Walton-Hughes was smiling like the innocent child he had once been.

At the beginning of July, James set off to visit Joe's family with no idea if his great-grandchild had been born or not yet. Celia was now gravely ill and Diana wasn't much better, so both Ginny and Anna were being kept very busy caring for their charges.

Celia still had no idea why Joe had come to the house in the first place, so James told her a white lie and said that he would be away on business for just one night, leaving her in Anna's capable hands. When he eventually reached the small village on the outskirts of Rugby where Joe had lived, he was appalled at the abject poverty he found there. Almost all the men worked at the local pit and everywhere seemed to be coated in a thin layer of soot and grime. There were rows and rows of terraced two-up two-down cottages with a narrow cobbled street dividing them, where raggy-arsed, snotty-nosed children were playing. Most of them were barefoot, and as James strode purposefully along, searching for the address Constable Watkins had given him, they eyed him curiously.

'Here – you, lad.' James addressed a thin child who looked to be about six or seven years old and as the child approached him James saw that his hair was crawling with headlice. 'Can you tell me where Primrose Lane is? There's a penny here for you if you show me the way.'

The child's eyes lit up hungrily as he picked at a scab on his arm. A penny would get him two currant buns. 'It's this way, mister. Foller me.' He shot off ahead so fast that it was all James could do to keep up with him. The boy led him through lanes that all looked exactly the same, then stopping at the beginning of one he told him, 'This 'ere is where yer want, mister.'

'Thank you. Would you happen to know which one the Peters family live in?'

'Third one down on that side.' The boy pointed, then with incredulous eyes snatched the shilling James tossed to him instead of the promised penny before scampering gleefully away.

James moved on. There were women standing on their doorsteps gossiping and he was aware of their eyes on him. He looked very out of place in his smart clothes and they wondered what a toff might be doing in these parts.

He stopped outside the door the child had pointed to and as he did so, the sound of a baby crying reached him from inside. There was no door knocker so he rapped on the wood and soon heard footsteps slapping towards it. A woman of indistinguishable age opened the door and peered at him. Her hair was greying and she was as thin as a rake.

James cleared his throat as he removed his hat respectfully and asked, 'Mrs Peters?'

She looked at his grand clothes and scowled. 'Yes, what do yer want?'

'A word, if I may. I'm Giles Walton-Hughes' grandfather.'

She gawped at him for a moment then said tightly, 'Yer'd best come in.'

He stepped into the room and tried not to gasp at the smell and the unbelievable poverty he was confronted with. A table stood in the middle of the room, leaning at a precarious angle on a hard-packed earth floor. Four young children were huddled around a small fire; he saw that they were all painfully thin and dressed in little more than rags.

'I believe that my grandson and your daughter–'

He had no time to say any more as she gestured towards a drawer which contained a wailing infant. 'The result o' them pair is over there,' she told him bitterly.

'I'm so sorry for everything that has happened,' he said sincerely. Words seemed so inadequate in a situation like this. 'I was hoping that you would let me reimburse you for your son's funeral and give your daughter some financial help towards the upkeep of the child.'

'Huh! You'll 'ave a job,' she sneered. 'Fer a start-off we 'ad to 'ave our Joe buried in a pauper's grave. We ain't got the money fer fancy funerals. An' our Meg died havin' the young 'un, so now it's down to me to bring it up. As if I ain't already got enough on me plate.'

James was so horrified that his mouth gaped as he looked towards the drawer again. A tiny baby lay squalling there and his heart went out to it.

'Is it a boy or a girl?' he asked eventually as he inched towards the drawer. The baby was wrapped in a ragged piece of sheeting that was a dirty grey, and its tiny hands and feet were blue with cold.

'It's a girl. There's a woman down the row comes in to feed it twice a day. The rest o' the time it 'as to make do wi' a bit o' milk from a pap bag.' Her eyes were angry now. 'Thanks to your son I've lost me son *an'* me daughter an' I'm left

453

wi' *that*,' she said scathingly.

James felt as if he was being torn in two. He couldn't even argue with her, she was speaking the truth. Half of him wanted to scoop the baby up and take it home. She was his great-grand-child, after all, but the other half knew that the shock of it could well kill Celia. She still wasn't aware of the baby and he was too afraid to follow his gut instinct.

'I 'ope when they catch 'im they 'ang the bastard by the neck till 'e's *dead*,' the woman spat and again James didn't know how to answer. He would probably feel exactly the same in her position. But at least he could make things easier for her financially.

Taking a large money bag he'd got from his bank, filled with coins to the value of £10 from his pocket, he placed it on the table.

'Please use some of this to ensure that the child has all it needs,' he told her. 'And of course you may use the rest to do with as you wish. Be assured I shall call every few months from now on to give you some more.' He guessed that it would have been a waste of time leaving a huge sum all in one go. The woman would probably have gone through it in no time, or at least her husband would have, from what he'd heard of him. Most of it would no doubt have gone across the bar of the local inn whilst the baby and the children went hungry.

Snatching the money up, Mrs Peters hid the bag in the pocket of her dress.

'Well I dare say that'll be a big 'elp at least – an' I don't suppose I can blame you fer your gran'son's wrong-doin's,' she said grudgingly.

'I shall never be able to apologise enough for his behaviour and for what has happened,' James told her again, and the woman had no doubt of his sincerity. 'But now, before I go, may I hold the baby for a moment?'

'Don't see why not. She's your flesh an' blood as much as mine at the end o' the day, ain't she?'

James tentatively lifted the tiny bundle from the drawer and she instantly stopped crying and stared up at him hopefully from eyes as blue as bluebells. Her hair was a soft golden colour but it was matted and tangled and he tried to imagine what it would be like if it were washed and forming a curly halo about her head. She really was a pretty child, or at least he thought she would have been, had she been clean. The ripe smell of urine that rose from her almost made him gag and there were tears in his eyes as she curled her tiny hand around one of his fingers.

'Have you named her yet?' he asked and when the woman shook her head he asked, 'Would you consider calling her Emily?'

'I suppose it's as good a name as any other,' she agreed with a sniff, slightly mollified at the small fortune he had given her.

'Thank you, and believe me, as I said I will return. Meantime my apologies for my grandson's appalling behaviour once again. Good day, Mrs Peters.'

She nodded and he quickly laid the child back in the drawer and stepped outside where he could at last let his tears fall unchecked. Although this was the first time he had met his great-granddaughter, he felt as if he was leaving a little part of himself behind and he knew that he would never know another moment's peace, and that her tiny pinched face would haunt him for the rest of his days.

Chapter Forty-Seven

'Come along, Diana. A walk in the fresh air will do you good,' Ginny encouraged one afternoon late in July. It was always a relief to escape the stifling atmosphere in the house these days. The mistress was now in the end stages of her illness and the whole of the staff were creeping about like mice so as not to disturb her. Sometimes Ginny felt that it was only the short spells she spent with Sebastian that kept her sane.

Diana was still seemingly locked away in a world of her own and was painfully thin. No doubt she would have been thinner still had not Ginny frequently bullied and encouraged her to eat just a little bit. But Ginny still suffered all manner of guilt feelings because she couldn't do more for her.

Now Diana rose lethargically from her seat as Ginny took her hand and led her towards the stairs.

'We'll get Cook to make up a basket for Sebastian and the men who are helping him work on the cottage.' Ginny said, keeping her voice light. 'I bet they'll all be glad of a bite to eat by now, and you like watching them work, don't you?'

She didn't expect a reply and she didn't receive one. Diana barely said a word nowadays but at least Ginny was managing to get her out of the house for short intervals now, which was something. As they set off through the orchard and across the lawns with a loaded basket, Ginny kept up a cheerful chatter.

'Isn't it a beautiful day? Just look at those clouds floating across the sky. We should go on a balloon flight one day and see if we could touch them.'

Diana merely plodded woodenly along at the side of her, a shadow of her former self.

Ginny often went to watch the progress on the cottage. Sebastian spent most of his free time working on it nowadays. Some of the master's employees had almost finished replacing the roof and Sebastian was now busily working inside. He hoped to have it all finished for the winter so that he could start his free school before Christmas, although Ginny wondered if he wasn't being slightly optimistic. He and the men had done marvels but there was still an awful lot of work left to do. The two girls passed the lake and soon afterwards the cottage came into sight and the sound of banging and hammering disturbed the silence.

The men had cleared all of the old woodworm-filled furniture from the cottage some time before and it stood in a massive pile that would be burned along with all the rest of the rubbish when they were finished. It was certainly going to be some bonfire, Ginny thought as they passed the towering heap.

They found Sebastian inside lime-washing the walls and Ginny giggled when she saw him. He seemed to have more in his hair and on his face and clothes than he did on the walls, but the place was looking better, fresher already.

'Having fun?' she asked as she stood in the doorway blocking out the light with Diana trailing behind her.

He grinned as he wiped the sweat from his forehead and threw the brush down. 'Hello, Ginny. Hello, Sis. I'm not sure you'd call it fun, exactly. I'm just discovering I'm not very good at this, but I'll get there in the end.' He looked at the basket then and said, 'I hope there are some drinks in there. It's enough to roast you in here even with the doors and windows open. Not that there's any glass in the windows yet but we'll make that the next job when the men have finished getting the roof watertight.'

He gratefully accepted a glass of the lemonade that Cook had sent and gulped it down thirstily as Ginny looked on with a smile. For the last few weeks she had forsaken her Sundays off because she didn't like to leave Diana alone for too long. It was also a chance for Nancy and Bertie to get to know each other better, and judging by the way Nancy was swooning around the place with a love-struck look on her face, Ginny's plan was working and they were now a couple. Instead of going to the Watkins family, Ginny had been spending part of her Sundays visiting Mrs Bevins and the rest with Diana here at the cottage, helping Sebastian out in whichever way she could. The pair of them were now so at ease with each other that no one would have known, had they seen them together, that she was a maid and he was the nephew of her employer. They chattered away together about anything and everything from politics to farming, and the more Ginny saw of him, the fonder she grew of him although she knew deep down that they could never be more than friends.

Now she and Sebastian stood close together and watched Diana, who remained outside in the small garden that surrounded the cottage, kicking listlessly at the profusion of weeds that grew there, a faraway look in her eyes.

'How has she been?' Sebastian asked.

Ginny shrugged. 'Much the same. She doesn't eat enough to keep a bird alive and she's taken to wanting to go for walks around the top of the quarry where Joe fell.' She shuddered. 'I don't think it's healthy for her to keep going there, but I always accompany her because I'm afraid of what she might do if she went alone. It's as if she's lost the will to live, poor soul.'

'My poor sister. What a nightmare she's been through. I dare she'll snap out of it eventually,' he said philosophically. 'It's just a matter of time, isn't it? They do say it's a great healer. Meantime Giles is still out there somewhere. He's certainly doing a great job of lying low. I know he doesn't deserve to get away with what he's done but it's a blessing in a way. It would finish my aunt Celia off if they *did* catch him. I reckon he's hopped on a boat and left the country.'

Ginny nodded before taking drinks out to the men.

459

That evening as Diana sat at her bedroom window staring out at the balmy night, she suddenly began to speak. 'Do you know, Ginny,' she said quietly, 'I don't know what I would have done without you over the last few weeks. You've become the sister I never had.'

'Oh, what a lovely thing to say!' Ginny was in the process of hanging up the clothes that Diana had worn that day and was deeply touched. These were the first words Diana had uttered for days, and she prayed that the girl was returning from the dark place in which she'd been imprisoned. Then she laughed.

'As it happens I've become very fond of you too. Who would have thought it after the way you treated me when we first met?'

'I'm truly sorry about that now,' Diana said regretfully. 'I was a spoiled brat back then but I've had to grow up quickly since...' Her voice trailed away but Ginny knew that she was thinking of Joe and the baby she had lost.

Quickly crossing the room, Ginny gave her a hug and was shocked when Diana kissed her tenderly on the cheek. She had never been so openly affectionate before.

'What was that for?' she asked.

Diana shrugged. 'I just wanted you to know how much you mean to me.'

Ginny went back to what she was doing, and when she'd finished and had got the bed ready for her, she asked Diana, 'Is there anything else I can get for you before I turn in?'

Diana shook her head. 'No... Nobody can get

me what I really want, but thank you, Ginny – for everything.'

A finger of unease climbed up Ginny's spine. 'You're talking as if you're never going to see me again,' she said.

Diana smiled. 'Go on, get yourself off to bed. You look tired.'

Ginny did just that but she couldn't quite shake off a feeling of foreboding and she had a restless night. The next morning, she got up before her usual time and went down to collect Diana's breakfast tray from Cook.

'My, my, you're an early bird,' Mrs Martin commented, glancing at the clock.

'I didn't have a very good night,' Ginny told her, 'so I thought I might as well get up early and see how Diana is today. She was in a very strange mood last night.'

'Oh, in what way?'

'I'm not quite sure,' Ginny said thoughtfully. 'She was just more ... well, talkative, I suppose.'

Cook chuckled as she placed a full teapot on the tray. 'Well, dearie, I would have thought that was a good sign. You young 'uns look for trouble, I swear. Now get this up to her while everythin' is nice an' hot, though I doubt she'll barely touch it.'

When Ginny tapped at Diana's door, there was no reply so she tapped again, louder this time. The girl must still be asleep. Again nothing so she inched the door open and peered inside. The bed was empty; the covers thrown back – but there was no sign of Diana. The bad feeling was back now, stronger than ever as Ginny checked the bathroom to find that that was empty too. Diana's dressing gown was flung across the end of the bed and her house shoes were still tucked neatly beneath it, but there was no sign of the girl having got dressed, so wherever she was, she must still be in her nightgown.

Ginny felt a bubble of panic in her stomach as she raced out on to the landing, almost colliding with Mrs Bronson, who had just left the mistress's room.

'Why, my dear, whatever is the matter?' the woman asked as she lightly gripped Ginny's arm.

'It's Miss Diana, she isn't in her room,' Ginny gabbled. 'And she's gone out dressed only in her nightgown.'

'I see.' Mrs Bronson frowned. 'Now stop panicking, that isn't going to help anything. I want you to go and get Barbara and Millie to check and see if she's in any of the downstairs rooms. It might be that she just couldn't sleep and went downstairs. Meantime I'll check the upstairs – but I don't want the mistress disturbed. She's had a very bad night.'

Ginny nodded and flew off as if there were wings on her feet to do as she was told. Half an hour later, there was still no news. No one had seen hide nor hair of the missing girl. Mrs Bronson had informed James of what was going on by then and they all went into the library to discuss what they should do next.

'Get Ventriss and the Gradys to search the grounds,' James told Barbara, and bobbing her knee she rushed away.

Another hour passed before the men reported

back to say there'd been no sighting of her. During this time Ginny had paced anxiously up and down the drawing room and with every minute that passed she became more afraid.

'But where could she have gone, dressed in her night-gown?' James asked for the fiftieth time – and it was then that it came to Ginny in a blinding flash.

'I think she might have headed for the quarry where Joe died,' she said fearfully, as an icy hand gripped and squeezed her insides. 'She's been going there more and more often of late, even though I told her she shouldn't torture herself so. She said she feels close to him there.'

'Right, come along, men. There's no time to lose,' the master said, stony-faced, and they all piled out into the early-morning mist.

The small group marched purposefully through the dewy grass and in no time at all the hem of Ginny's dress and her shoes were soaked through, but she didn't even notice as she almost ran to keep up with the men. Her hair was loose and flowing down her back, as black and shiny as midnight, and Sebastian hung back to keep pace with her and catch her arm when occasionally she stumbled.

At last they came to the edge of the quarry. Here they all stopped, panting, to stare down fearfully at the deep water below but it was shrouded in mist. It looked set to be another fine day when the sun shone through, but for now it was hard to see anything. Ginny's anxiety increased as she clung to Sebastian's arm and tried to get her breath back.

'We're going to have to climb down there and walk around the water's edge if we're to see anything.' James' sombre voice broke the silence and as one they all trooped towards the steep path that curved down the face of the quarry. It was treacherously slippery underfoot and the going was slow. More than once Ginny was convinced that she was going to topple into the water but Sebastian guided her, keeping a close grip on her arm and eventually they arrived on the shores of the old quarry. The mist was still swirling and eddying above the surface but suddenly Sebastian stopped and pointed.

'I thought I saw something over there.' He could barely get the words out. 'Something white floating in the water.'

Ginny's hand flew to her mouth as she thought back to the voluminous white nightgown trimmed with guipure lace that Diana had worn the night before, but she refused to let herself believe the worst. Sebastian must be mistaken! He had to be.

They all stood for seconds that felt like hours peering in the direction of his pointing finger and then suddenly the mist cleared for a second and they could all see it. There *was* something floating there.

'I'm going in,' Sebastian declared, kicking off his shoes and shrugging off his jacket.

'No, the water will be cold and it's dangerous.' Ginny tried to hold him back but he gently put her away from him.

'It's all right. I'm a very strong swimmer. I used to come here for a swim sometimes when I was a child, although I didn't let on to my aunt or uncle, of course.' He smiled at James apologetically then waded into the water as Ginny watched with her heart in her mouth. The mist swallowed him up for a while but they could hear his powerful arms slicing through the still surface and then there was a shout.

'I've got her. I'm bringing her back to shore.'

The wait seemed endless but at last he appeared again. He had the edge of the white material in his hand and was towing it behind him with one hand as he swam to the shore with the other.

Then willing hands were helping him back on to dry land and they were hauling his tragic cargo up on to the grass. It was Diana, and as they gently turned her over, her sightless eyes stared up at them.

'Is ... is she dead?' James asked hoarsely as he gazed at the girl who had become like a daughter to him.

'Yes, Uncle, my poor beloved sister is dead, and her suffering is over. Strangely enough, she was floating in almost the exact same place as Joe was when we found him.' And Sebastian wept while those around him bowed their heads in respect.

Chapter Forty-Eight

Diana was buried with the minimum of fuss as Sebastian and James requested. The family had endured so much grief lately that they both felt it was better that way. They told Celia that the girl had slipped from the top of the quarry whilst out walking. James knew that should she learn the truth of her suicide, it would increase her grief a hundredfold.

It was on the evening of the day of the funeral when James found Ginny waiting for him in the hall.

'Might I have a word, sir?'

It was the last thing he felt like doing but he nodded politely and led her into his study.

'I was thinking...' She swallowed nervously. 'That as I was employed as Miss Diana's companion ... I now no longer have a post so I thought it only right that I give you notice.'

James looked horrified. 'But you can't leave!' he exclaimed. 'As it happens I was going to ask you if you would stay on to help Ann ... Mrs Bronson to care for my wife. As you may be aware, Celia requires twenty-four-hour attention now and it is proving rather too much for Mrs Bronson on her own. If there were two of you, you could take it in turns and then at least you would both get to have some rest.'

Ginny looked uncertain. She was still fiercely proud and didn't want him to feel that he had to invent a position for her.

'You would be doing me a very great favour,' he sighed. 'I could quite easily employ a nurse but my wife wouldn't like strangers caring for her whereas she feels comfortable with you and Mrs Bronson. But first you must go and have a little holiday with your brother in Hull for a few days. I know how fond of each other you and Diana had become and how difficult this must have been for you.'

466

It was then that Ginny started to cry and James felt his own heart breaking. He would have liked to take the poor girl in his arms and comfort her, but of course that wouldn't have been right. Thankfully Mrs Bronson entered the room then, and without saying a word, she gathered Ginny to her and let her weep.

'I ... I feel so guilty,' Ginny said between sobs as she dabbed at her eyes ineffectually with one of her lace handkerchiefs. They had been a present from Diana and were the finest she had ever owned. 'I felt that something was different about Diana the night before it happened... If I hadn't left her, she might still be here.'

'But that's quite ridiculous,' Mrs Bronson told her. 'I'm afraid that even if you had stayed with her that night, Diana would have done it at the first opportunity she got. Losing Joe and the baby completely devastated her, and I think this was her way of feeling that she was going to be close to them again. Who knows – perhaps she is?' The housekeeper wiped her own eyes. 'We can only pray that she is finally at peace, so you must stop thinking such silly thoughts. You couldn't have done more for her.' She glanced at James then and said, 'Have you asked Ginny yet if she is prepared to help me with the mistress?'

The couple had clearly already discussed it.

'Yes, I have as it happens, but I haven't had an answer yet.'

'Then let me tell you that you would be doing me an enormous favour if you did stay on.' Mrs Bronson smiled ruefully at the girl. 'I can't re-member when I last got a proper night's sleep and

I'm not sure how much longer I can keep it up.'

'In that case I'd be happy to, for now at least,' Ginny sniffed. 'But first the master says I may have a few days off to visit Charlie, if that's all right with you?'

'I think that's an excellent idea,' Mrs Bronson said warmly. 'I shall make the necessary travel arrangements for you today. A little break will do you the world of good.'

Ginny nodded and quietly left the room, but as she climbed the stairs her mind was in a muddle. Why, once again, were the master and Mrs Bronson being so kind to her? Had they invented the new post just to help her? Mrs Bronson had always seemed to manage caring for the mistress quite well on her own.

Once inside the privacy of her own room, Ginny stared thoughtfully into space. An idea had been growing in her mind for some time now but she had been trying not to acknowledge it; now she felt she had to. Could it be that it was *Mrs Bronson herself* who had left her father at the door of the workhouse all those years ago? It made sense. After all, why else would she have gone to so much trouble for herself and Charlie if she didn't have an immediate link to them?

Ginny sighed. Everything seemed so sad – and also to be getting more complicated by the day – and yet she was reluctant to leave Lamp Hill Hall because that would mean she would never see Sebastian again. Worn out with grief, she pulled her bag from the wardrobe and began to pack it. At least seeing Charlie would cheer her up a little. Choking back more burning tears as she thought of Diana, she tried to concentrate on what she was doing and shut everything else from her mind. She just couldn't deal with any more heartache at the moment.

Later that evening, as Ginny sat at the kitchen table enjoying a leisurely cup of tea with Cook, Mrs Bronson came in to ask her, 'My dear, it just occurred to me, you've never travelled as far as Hull on your own before, so I suggested to Sebastian that he might feel in need of a little break too and he's offered to come with you. How would you feel about that?'

'Fine,' Ginny answered as her heart began to race. She had rather been dreading the thought of facing the journey on her own but she wondered if Sebastian had only agreed to accompany her out of kindness.

'Good, then I shall arrange the train tickets for the end of the week and I'll get a letter in the post this evening informing my uncle that you'll both be coming. He will be expecting you then and no doubt be thrilled to see you.'

She then swept away through the green baize door, and when Ginny glanced at Cook she saw a funny look on her face.

'Takes a great interest in you, don't she?' the woman said observantly. 'I ain't never known her be like it with any of the other staff in all the years I've worked here.'

'I know – I had noticed,' Ginny admitted. 'It's a mystery. But why do you think it is?'

Cook glanced around the kitchen to make sure that Nancy was out of earshot before whispering,

'I've got me own thoughts on things but it wouldn't be my place to say owt, so we'd best stop right here, eh?'

Ginny nodded slowly. So Cook had her suspicions too but didn't dare to voice them. She wondered if she should confront Mrs Bronson outright – but then shied away from the thought. Her heart was wrung out, and with everything that had gone on lately she didn't feel up to a confrontation. Best to get her visit to Charlie over with first, no doubt.

When she and Sebastian set off for the station in the master's carriage a few days later it was an immediate relief to get away from the house of mourning and sickness. Sebastian was subdued and grieving for his sister, but Ginny was glad of his company and very much looking forward to seeing Charlie.

'Thanks, Jim,' Sebastian said to Mr Grady when they arrived. 'I can handle the baggage from here. We only have a small case each.'

'Right y'are, sir. Have a pleasant trip.' Jim Grady tipped his cap then climbed back into the driving seat and urged the horse on as Sebastian carried their luggage on to the platform.

Like most of the other staff, Jim had worked for the Walton-Hughes family for years. The master was a fair man and Jim had always felt that he'd dropped on his feet when he got a position at Lamp Hill Hall. He was heartsore for the family when he thought of the tragic events they'd had to endure over the last few months, and his sympathy went out to Master Sebastian, whom he had known since the day the orphaned boy and his sister had come to live with their aunt and uncle. It was Jim who had taught the lad to ride, spending countless hours leading him around the manège on his first pony when he'd been just a tiny boy. He'd done the same for Miss Diana. The thought of the girl brought a lump to his throat. Well, she'd be doing no more riding now, that was for sure, God bless her soul. With a shake of his grizzled head he went on his way.

Both Ginny and Sebastian were quiet during the first part of the journey, each lost in their own sombre thoughts, but as the journey progressed they began to relax. They'd seen little of each other since the morning Sebastian had dragged Diana from the deep water of the quarry, but now at last he felt ready to talk about it and he poured his heart out to Ginny, and by doing so felt as if a lead weight had been shifted from his shoulders.

'I always felt very protective of her,' he confessed. 'And I can't help but feel I should have done something to prevent her from doing what she did.'

'I feel exactly the same,' Ginny told him and he stared at her in surprise.

'But why should *you* feel that way?'

She went on to tell him about Diana's strange behaviour the night before she had thrown herself from the quarry top. 'I should have stayed with her,' she said regretfully, much as she had to the master.

'But you couldn't have stopped her if that's

what she had in mind.' Sebastian looked shocked then at what he had said, and as they stared at each other, it occurred to him that he couldn't have stopped her either. From that moment on, the guilt they both felt began to loosen its grip.

Charlie raced outside to meet them the moment the cab they had hired to bring them from the station pulled up outside – and once again Ginny was amazed at the change in her little brother. He seemed to have shot up at least another three or four inches in just a few months.

'This is Sebastian,' she told him as he stared warily at the tall fellow at her side.

'Is he your young man?' Charlie asked innocently and Ginny blushed to the roots of her hair. She opened her mouth to answer him, but before she had a chance, Sebastian bent to Charlie's level and replied for her.

'No, I'm not,' he confided, 'but I wish I was.'

Ginny gaped in amazement and just for a moment their eyes locked and she saw all she needed to see. Sebastian felt the same way she did – but it gave her no joy. For some time she had been trying to deny her true feelings for him but now she couldn't hide from them any longer. She loved him! But all she could see were further complications ahead. Even so, she was determined to enjoy her time with Charlie so leaving Sebastian to collect the bags from the carriage she took her brother's hand in hers and as they climbed the steps she asked him brightly, 'So what would you like to do in the morning then?'

'I thought we could take our nets on to the

beach again and go crabbing like we did last time you came,' Charlie told her eagerly.

'Well, I hope I can come along too,' Sebastian piped up from close behind them. 'I love crabbing.' And so it was decided.

The next few days passed in a pleasant blur. They wandered around the docks looking at the boats and played on the sand. They went paddling in the sea, and during the evenings Sebastian and Charlie played board games whilst Ginny sat and chatted easily to Uncle Edward. Sebastian and Charlie were clearly getting along famously and it did Ginny's heart good to see it – not that she would allow herself to dream.

At last it was time for them to leave and Sebastian seemed almost as reluctant to go as she did.

'Will you come again ... soon?' Charlie pleaded and it amused Ginny to see that he was addressing Sebastian. They were obviously the best of friends now.

'You can bet on it,' Sebastian assured him as he tousled his hair.

It was Ginny's turn to say goodbye then, and her little brother clung to her for a moment although he didn't ask her not to go this time. He was very happy where he was, which was surely a blessing.

He watched as they clambered into the cab then waved until the carriage turned the corner and they were out of sight.

'He's a lovely little chap and he seems very happy and contented,' Sebastian observed as he settled back in his seat.

'Yes, he does, doesn't he?' Ginny sighed, her

mind in turmoil, then she turned her attention to the sights beyond the window. Saying goodbye was always difficult and it was always hard to leave him. Sometimes now she wondered if her father would ever come home or if they would ever be a family again. Only time would tell.

Chapter Forty-Nine

'Are you sure you feel up to this?' Anna asked as James prepared to leave.

Ginny and Sebastian were due to return that day but James had decided that it was time to pay his great-grandchild another visit.

'I'm sure, but are you going to be all right with Celia?'

'Of course, aren't I always?' she said indignantly and he grinned.

They said their goodbyes and as James set off Anna hurried upstairs to be with his wife.

It was later that day before he finally tapped on the cottage door in Primrose Lane and once again he was greeted by the sound of a baby crying.

This time when Mrs Peters admitted him, she looked better nourished, as did her children, and her tattered gown had been replaced by one of a slightly better quality. On seeing James, her eyes sparkled at the thought of the money he would give her.

'The baby's over there,' she said carelessly and

sure enough, there was Emily lying in exactly the same place she had been the first time he called. But now he noted that her wails were weaker and she looked pale and unwell.

'Has she been ill?' he asked in alarm as he gazed down at the child's pasty face. She didn't appear to have put on an ounce of weight since his last visit. In fact, if anything she looked even frailer than before.

The woman sniffed, clearly not much bothered one way or the other. 'Lots o' little 'uns round 'ere never make it to their first birthday,' she said matter-of-factly. 'I lost five o' mine an' she ain't the strongest o' babies.'

James lifted the child tenderly and she nestled into his chest and tried to suckle his finger as she looked for food and affection. He had battled with his conscience ever since the first time he had clapped eyes on her, but now he knew what he must do, whatever the consequences. Her father had been a great disappointment to him, but Giles was his flesh and blood just as this little one was ... and James found that he could turn his back on her no longer.

'Mrs Peters,' he began, choosing his words carefully, 'I realise how difficult it must be for you to be left with another child to care for so I am prepared to take responsibility for her from now on.'

'What? Yer mean yer want to take 'er away?' The woman was alarmed. What about the money she would lose if she allowed this? She had no feelings for the child whatsoever but now she saw her as a source of income.

'I would settle a sum of money on you, of course, for all the inconvenience and heartbreak you've been put through,' James assured her quickly, seeing the way her mind was working, and an interested glint appeared in her eyes.

'Just 'ow much money are we talkin' of?' she asked warily. 'Yer see, she's all I 'ave left o' my Joe now an' it'd break me 'eart to lose the sweet little soul.'

James was almost gagging at the rank smell that was rising from the child and he was determined that she shouldn't stay in this hell-hole for a moment longer than necessary.

'I was thinking ... two hundred pounds,' he stated.

'Two 'undred pounds!' Mrs Peters was dumbstruck. It was an absolute fortune but she was canny and knew that it wouldn't do to appear too eager.

'Hmm ... well, I'd 'ave to think about it,' she said musingly, tapping her chin with one grimy finger.

'In that case I shall leave you.' James made to lay the child in the drawer again but just as he had prayed she would, the woman said hastily, 'Very well then, if yer promise me yer'll take good care of 'er.'

'I assure you she will want for nothing.' His face was calm as he straightened with the child still in his arms. 'But I would want you to sign a document that my solicitor will draw up agreeing that you will never try to take her from me again. If I take her now, it must be for ever – for her sake. If you agree to that, I shall have the money and the document to you within a week and then, Mrs Peters, you will be able to get on with your life.'

She barely hesitated before saying, 'Agreed.'

James had to stop himself from crying aloud with relief. 'Then I shall leave you with some money today and my groom will bring the document for you to sign and the rest of the money within days. Now, have you something warm I might wrap her in for the journey back?'

She snatched an old shawl from the back of a chair and passed it to him as he fumbled in his pocket and removed, as before, a bag containing coins amounting to the value of £10. Heaven knows, she and her children could do with it. He only hoped she had the wisdom to keep her good fortune to herself. Just as she had before, she snatched it up barely before it hit the table and hid it in her pocket.

'That's it then,' she said, showing not an ounce of regret. 'I'll let yer be on yer way, but make sure yer send the rest o' the money, mind.'

'I am a man of my word, Mrs Peters,' he said coldly and with that he strode away with the baby wailing loud enough to waken the dead as the woman stood on the doorstep, watching him go.

Emily had cried herself to sleep by the time he reached the Hall and when he strode in with her tucked against his chest, Anna stared at him curiously. She had just come downstairs to fetch her mistress a cup of hot chocolate and to see if Ginny and Sebastian were home yet.

'Whatever have you got there?' she asked, but before he could answer the baby suddenly woke up and let out a thin wail.

'My God!' Her hand flew to her mouth. 'You've brought the child *here?*'

'I didn't have much choice,' James confessed, clearly all of a fluster. 'I'll explain everything later, but meantime, can you get one of the staff to feed her? The poor little mite is starving. I think she's in dire need of a bath as well.'

'Of course.' Anna gently took the child from him, wrinkling her nose at the smell that was issuing from her. 'I'll take her through to the kitchen and get Millie or Barbara to go and light a fire in the nursery. No one has slept up there for years so it will need a good airing.' Her face softened then as she looked down at the whimpering infant and she hurried her away as James sank on to the nearest chair, exhausted. It had been a difficult journey and now he had a lot of explaining to do.

'So you are telling me that we have a *great-granddaughter?*' Celia asked incredulously some time later as he sat holding her hand at the side of the bed. He'd had no option but to be brutally honest with his wife about Giles fathering a child, but instead of it upsetting her, as he had feared it would, she seemed to be delighted.

He nodded. 'Yes, we have. Barbara is bathing her now. Luckily we still have some baby clothes from when Giles was tiny and the staff are getting the nursery ready. I shall have to hire a nanny, I suppose.' He looked shamefaced then. 'I'm so sorry I didn't tell you before, darling, but I feared it might make you ill.'

'I'm already ill,' she told him, solemn now. 'And

you must face up to that, James. This illness is not going to go away and I fear I don't have much longer. But now at least I can spend the time I do have left getting to know our great-grandchild. Does she have a name?'

'Yes. It's Emily.'

His wife smiled approvingly. 'And when may I see her?'

'As soon as she's clean and fed, my love. Shall I ask Anna to bring her up to you?'

'Oh *yes,* please.' Her face was animated for the first time since Diana had died. 'I can hardly wait.'

Bemused, James shook his head. Women could be strange creatures. Here he had been thinking that Celia would be horrified to learn that they had an illegitimate great-grandchild and yet she was acting as if she had been given some great gift, which he secretly felt she had – they both had.

'Now we shall have to think about what we are going to tell the staff,' he said. 'They're bound to wonder where this little scrap has come from, and who she is.'

'We shall tell them the truth and start as we mean to go on,' Celia declared firmly, surprising him still further. 'I won't have her feeling that we are ashamed of her. She must grow up knowing that she is wanted and loved. Every child deserves that.'

'Have I told you lately that you are a very special woman? You never fail to surprise me,' he told her lovingly as he rose and planted a kiss on her hair. 'And now I shall go and tell Anna to bring a certain Miss Emily to meet her grand-mamma.'

Emily, who was now content and fast asleep after a bath and a feed, was duly carried into the mistress looking like a completely different infant to the one who had arrived at the Hall a short while before. Just as James had imagined, her soft blonde hair now formed a halo around her head and her long fair eyelashes were curled on her cheeks. She was dressed in one of the tiny lawn nightgowns, warmed by the fire, that had once belonged to her father and which Celia had never been able to part with, and she was wrapped in a fine woollen shawl.

'Here she is,' Anna said, as she tenderly placed the infant into her great-grandmother's frail arms, and Celia fell in love with her instantly. Tears sprang to her eyes.

'If only things could have been different and her father could have seen her,' she said in a choked voice.

Anna personally doubted that Giles would have wanted to even acknowledge his baby daughter, but she kept that thought to herself. The mistress was looking radiant and Anna wanted nothing to spoil it.

At that moment Ginny and Sebastian were rattling down the drive in a cab. The break had done them both the power of good and now although they were both still devastated at the loss of Diana they had at least come to terms with the knowledge that there was nothing either of them could have done to change her state of mind.

When they entered the house they looked around in confusion. The staff were rushing about like busy little ants with broad smiles on their faces, and the air of gloom that had hung over the place was gone.

'What's going on?' Sebastian enquired as Barbara hurried forward to take their coats.

'The master has brought a baby home,' she babbled excitedly. 'She's in with the mistress at the minute but she's a bonny little thing. Eeh, it'll be grand to have a child in the house again.'

'A baby?' Sebastian was more confused than ever now but when he looked towards Ginny she could only shrug, as baffled as he was. 'But who is it?'

'We've no idea yet, sir, but the master said he'd talk to us all this evening.'

Glancing at Ginny, Sebastian told her, 'I'd best go and see what's happening. This place is like a madhouse!'

She grinned as he took the stairs two at a time then followed him at a more leisurely pace to take her bag to her room.

'Can yer believe it!' Cook exclaimed later that evening when the staff were gathered together in the kitchen enjoying a cup of cocoa before retiring. 'To think that Master Giles had a daughter.'

'*And* that he wasn't married to the mother,' Barbara added.

Cook frowned at her. 'That's neither here nor there, young lady. The child didn't ask to be born an' I think it took courage fer the master to bring her home as he did. So she'll be given the respect that's due to her whether she were born in or out o' wedlock! Do yer hear me? The master an'

481

mistress will have enough gossip goin' on outside
o' the house without the staff addin' to it.'

'Yes, Cook,' Barbara said meekly, feeling as if
she had been firmly put in her place.

Nancy caught Ginny's eye and they smiled at
each other but it was another half an hour before
Nancy was able to have a private word with her.
Ginny had helped her to clear the cups from the
table and now Nancy whispered, 'While you were
gone, Bertie asked me to be his girl, so it's official
now. We're walking out together.' She eyed Ginny
cautiously. 'Is that all right with you?'

'All right?' Ginny laughed. 'Why, it's wonderful
news and I think you're just perfect for each
other.'

Nancy sighed with relief as her eyes sparkled.
'And Ginny, guess what? He proposed to me!
He's going to take me shopping for an engagement ring soon,' she confided. 'Cook said I could
swap my Sunday off for a Saturday one week so
that we can go into town an' choose one. Would
you like to come?'

Ginny chuckled. 'Thank you very much for the
offer but I think it's a case of two's company and
three's a crowd on an occasion like this. I shall
look forward to seeing it though and I hope you'll
both be very, very happy.'

Ginny was in a strange mood when she finally
retired that night. Only days before, the whole
house had been mourning the death of a loved
one, and now they were all celebrating a new life.
It just went to show that the cycle of life went on.

As she snuggled down in bed her thoughts
returned to the lovely time she had spent with

Sebastian and Charlie, and when she finally fell asleep only happy dreams took her through the night.

Chapter Fifty

Baby Emily seemed to have breathed new life into the house and within no time at all the whole of the staff were besotted with her, including the new nanny the master had employed to look after her. Mrs Weatherspoon was a plump, matronly figure with a ready smile who believed that children thrived on love. However, as Emily flourished the mistress's health declined further, and as it neared the end of November, everyone sensed the lurking presence of Death.

'I fear it could be any day now,' Anna whispered to Ginny one morning as they tiptoed about Celia's room. The doctor had prescribed a high dose of laudanum to be administered to her every few hours, for she was in a great deal of pain now and slept for most of the time. The master had left the running of most of his businesses to Sebastian as he wished to spend as much time as he could with his wife.

Ginny nodded tearfully. There was nothing any of them could do for Celia now except to make her as comfortable as possible. She picked up the bowl of water they had just used for washing her and crept from the room, leaving Anna to keep her vigil. However, she had been gone for no more than a few minutes when Celia's eyes flickered open and she grasped Anna's hand.

'Ah. You're awake, dear.' Anna tenderly stroked her hair from her feverish forehead. 'Is there anything I can get for you? Would you like a drink?'

'No ... but I need ... to speak to you.'

Anna leaned closer as Celia stared at her from pain-filled eyes. 'I want you to ... promise me something.' Each breath was an effort now and Anna's heart broke afresh. 'Of course. Anything.'

Celia smiled. 'You have been ... so good to me. I have come ... to love you as a sister ... over the years.'

'And I love you too,' Anna whispered, her throat tight with tears.

'So when I am gone ... I want you to promise me that you will look after James ... and little Emily.'

'But of course I will.'

Celia moved her head restlessly. 'No, I mean ... you and James must finally ... come together. You have my blessing. I know that you ... love each other. I have known ... for years.'

Anna gasped in distress but Celia raised a frail hand and placed it gently across her lips. 'I'm not upset about it. Just ... sorry that I couldn't be ... the sort of wife that he deserved. But ... you can be. You ... both deserve some happiness now.'

'Please, don't talk like that. You're not going to die yet,' Anna said, openly sobbing now.

The effort of talking had worn Celia out and now her hand dropped on to the counterpane. 'Remember what I said. It's what ... I want for you both.' And then her eyelids fluttered shut and she was asleep again as Anna looked on, feeling bereft and guilty. To learn that the dear soul had known about her and James all these years was almost more than she could bear.

The doctor was sent for at eight o'clock that night. James had spent the last few hours ensconced with his wife, holding her hand and telling her how much he loved her, but she was already in a place where she could no longer hear him and by the time Dr Gifford arrived she had slipped away peacefully in her sleep.

'I'm so sorry, James,' the doctor said gravely as he finished examining her, 'but I'm afraid she's gone. If there's a heaven she'll surely be an angel, for Mrs Walton-Hughes was one of the kindest women I ever knew.'

He left then and James spent the rest of the night beside her, refusing to leave her even when the undertakers arrived.

'We'll come back in the morning,' they told Anna, and, grey-faced, she nodded. The master's sobs could be heard all over the house and everyone was in mourning for their kindly mistress.

Anna sat outside the room on a hard-backed chair and finally as dawn lit the sky and he became quiet she joined him and he fell into her arms. But his eyes were dry now as he told her, 'She knew about us, and yet all this time she never said a thing. She told me that we must find happiness together now and that is exactly what I intend to do after a suitable period of mourning. This house has seen enough heartache but soon I want it to ring with the sound of laughter again, for Emily's sake. When the funeral is over I mean to fetch all the skeletons out of our closet and be truthful about our past.'

'Are you quite sure about this?' Anna asked and when he nodded her heart felt lighter. Soon the secret they had been forced to live with all these years would be out in the open.

It was late in November when Ginny was summoned to James' study, along with Anna. The mistress's funeral had taken place only days before and once again, Ginny now had no official role at Lamp Hill Hall so she supposed she was about to be dismissed.

'Yes, sir.' She bobbed her knee as she went to stand in front of James' desk and clasped her hands together to try to stop them shaking.

'Ah, Ginny.'

Anna had gone to stand beside him in the high-necked black bombazine gown that she had adopted for her mourning period. It set off her fair colouring and Ginny thought she looked quite regal in it. It reminded her a little of the one she had seen Queen Victoria wearing in the newspapers, for it was known that her beloved Prince Albert was very ill.

James and Anna glanced at each other and then after clearing his throat, James said, 'Please sit down, my dear. I'm afraid that what you are about to hear may come as something of a shock to you.'

Ginny gingerly did as she was told, wondering what was about to follow.

'The thing is...' James cleared his throat again before going on. 'The thing is, Anna and I have been forced to keep a secret from you and now it is time for you to hear it. You see, Anna came to work for my wife and myself shortly after our son, Timothy, was born. It was after his birth that Celia became an invalid, as you may be aware. We were told in no uncertain terms that to have another child could well kill her, and I couldn't risk that happening, so our marriage became ... shall I say, like two friends living together, rather than man and wife.' He gave a little cough, looking embarrassed.

Ginny blushed. This was very personal information and she couldn't think why he might be sharing it with her.

'Anna had no need to work, for as you know, she came from a well-off family, but like most young people she felt she wanted to spread her wings. Within no time at all, she and my wife became very close. And then I too started to feel an attachment to her.' He glanced down then as Anna gently squeezed his shoulder. This clearly wasn't easy for him. 'Eventually Anna and I ... behaved inappropriately and we suffered all manner of guilty feelings to think that we had betrayed the woman we both loved. Even more so when we discovered that a child would be the result of our liaison.'

Ginny gasped. So her suspicions had been right all along then: Anna *was* her father's mother!

'We couldn't bear to hurt Celia so Anna returned to her home in Hull, but when her father learned of her condition he disowned her. She then went to live with her Uncle Edward and when the child was born she returned to the

Midlands and was forced to give the baby up.'

'That baby was my father, wasn't it?'

James looked at her levelly before shaking his head and Ginny frowned.

'But I suspected... I mean, he was brought up in the workhouse and he always told me that Mrs Bronson was very kind to him.'

'I *was* very fond of your father,' Mrs Bronson replied, taking up the story. 'But in actual fact the child I gave birth to was your mother.'

Shock coursed through Ginny as she stared back at her. 'B ... but my grandparents died when I was very small. They lived in the town,' she stuttered, totally confused.

'Yes, I know; it was to them that I entrusted Emily. That was the name I gave her. They were middle-aged and had never been able to have children of their own so my Emily was a blessing, and James settled a sum of money on them to ensure that our daughter would never want for anything. At least with her being in the same town we could watch her grow from afar. It almost destroyed us, not being able to acknowledge her, but we were fearful of the effect it would have on Celia should she ever find out. Despite what we had done, we both loved her, you see?'

Anna gave Ginny a few moments to digest what she had said before going on, 'It was by pure chance that your mother then met your father when he left the workhouse and we heard that they were to be married. Your father Seth was always such a lovely child that I knew he would be good to her and I rejoiced for them. I even sent them a wedding present. You may remember it – it was a pink china tea set?'

Ginny nodded. 'Yes, it was Mother's pride and joy and we were only ever allowed to use it on high days and holidays.' There was a silence then as she tried to take everything in.

'So this means ... that you are my grand-parents?' Ginny said eventually, and when they both nodded, everything began to fall into place. The way they had always been so kind to her. The way Anna had fetched Charlie from the work-house and placed him safely with her uncle. She could even see the likeness between Anna and her mother now, and wondered why she had never seen it before. She felt dizzy with it all. It seemed as if her whole life had been turned upside down in a matter of minutes.

'So what will happen now?' she managed to ask.

'Now at last we will be able to acknowledge you as our granddaughter and ensure that you have what is rightfully yours,' James told her softly as he took Anna's hand and smiled up at her. 'On her deathbed my wife confessed that she had always known that Anna and I had feelings for each other. She said that she wanted us to finally come together and she gave us her blessing. In fact, it was what she wished for. She was quite a remarkable woman.'

'Is ... is that why you have called Giles' baby Emily?' Ginny asked then, and when James nodded, the tears at last began to roll down her cheeks.

'Yes, and we intend to lavish all the love we could never give to your mother on her and bring her up as our own. In six months' time, Anna and I shall be quietly married, and we shall also make it common knowledge that you and Charlie are our grandchildren. There is one more thing we need to tell you, my dear; it's about your father. You see, we always felt that Seth had been wrongfully imprisoned, and so Anna and I have been working closely with a lawyer who has been fighting his case. That was where Anna kept disappearing to from time to time. A couple of months ago the man your father injured agreed to admit that it was he himself who had started the fight – in return for a rather large sum of money, of course! Anyway, the long and the short of it is that after his confession, the barrister was able to start an appeal and I'm pleased to tell you that we won it.'

'What does that mean?' Ginny asked nervously. Her mind was spinning now.

'It means, my dear girl, that your father will be coming home. Possibly as soon as this very week, as it happens.'

Ginny's face lit up like a ray of sunshine. 'What? Father is coming home? But we don't have the cottage any more!'

'He is fully aware of what I'm telling you. My lawyer went to see him last week to explain everything and he'll be coming here.'

'Here?'

'Yes, here – and we have already put a few ideas to him. You see, Anna now owns the house in Hull where Charlie is living with her uncle, but she has bequeathed it to you as her oldest living relative. She also owns half of a very lucrative shipbuilding business, as you are aware, so we thought your father might like to go and live there with Charlie and her uncle and manage the business. Seth seems quite keen on the idea as it happens and Uncle Edward will be only too happy to hand the reins over to someone else now that he's getting older.'

'But what about me?'

'Ah! Now *you* have a number of choices,' James smiled at her kindly. 'You can, of course, go to live in Hull if you wish – it will soon be your house, after all; or, you might prefer to stay here and help Sebastian with the school. I know he is very keen for you to stay. In fact, I know he has feelings for you – he has confessed as much to me and I fear he would be heartbroken to see you leave.'

'B ... but if you and I are related..?'

James shook his head. 'If you and Sebastian are in love with each other there is no reason on earth why you shouldn't come together. Sebastian was my wife's sister's child – which means he is absolutely no blood relation to me. But don't feel that we are pushing you in that direction, my dear. You are now a young woman of means in your own right and if you don't return his feelings then you now have a choice.'

'Oh, but I *do!*' Ginny gasped, blushing furiously. She had loved him secretly, hopelessly, for such a long time.

'I'm very pleased to hear it!'

Ginny leaped out of her chair – and as she twirled towards the door she saw Sebastian standing there with a wide grin on his face.

'Sorry,' he told her. 'But I knew you were in here and I couldn't wait any longer to find out what your decision would be. Will you *please* stay, Miss Virginia Thursday? I don't know how I'd cope if I were to lose you now.'

Suddenly they were all laughing and crying at the same time and in an instant Sebastian had crossed the room to take her in his arms.

'I've wanted to tell you for ages how I felt,' he whispered, almost forgetting that his uncle and Anna were in the room. 'But you're such an independent soul I was worried that you'd send me away with a flea in my ear.'

'Never,' she breathed happily, feeling as if she had been caught up in a dream.

James and Anna looked on with joyful smiles on their faces. At last, all the years of lies and secrets were over and now they could all look forward to the future.

Ginny's birthday was celebrated quietly, which suited the girl just fine. Cook baked a cake and the family all dined together. Ginny had been like a cat on hot bricks with her eyes constantly on the drive waiting for a glimpse of her father ever since they had told her that he would be coming home. She still hadn't quite taken everything in and wondered how she would ever manage to call Anna and James 'Grandmother' and 'Grandfather', but they didn't seem overly concerned about it.

'You can call us whatever you like, so long as you stay close to us from now on,' James had told her fondly. They had spoiled Ginny shamelessly on her birthday and she had come down in the morning to a pile of presents. At last they could make up for lost time. Amongst the gifts were two beautiful dresses and a bracelet set with blue stones that made her gasp. From Sebastian there was a filigree gold locket, carved in the shape of a heart. She fastened the slender chain around her neck immediately, vowing that she would never take it off again.

The birthday meal was held that evening and the atmosphere was light as they all sat around the table. Even Nanny was there with baby Emily so that she could join in – although to their amusement she slept through most of it. Anna and James absolutely adored the dear little girl, who was thriving. Ginny wore one of her new crinolines – a lovely frothy concoction of pale blue satin and lace – and Sebastian could hardly keep his eyes off her.

They had just sliced the cake when the door suddenly opened and they all turned as one to see who it was.

The room seemed to spin for a moment as Ginny's hand flew to her mouth.

'Happy Birthday, sweetheart. Is a piece of that there cake for me?' The man who spoke looked gaunt and fragile. His wonderful thick black hair was peppered with grey now and he had lost an enormous amount of weight, but even so to Ginny he looked miraculous.

'*Daddy!*' With a squeal of delight, she launched herself out of her chair and into his arms as everyone looked on with happy tears in their eyes.

Over his shoulder, beyond the window, the

moon suddenly sailed from behind a cloud and Ginny remembered all the stories Seth had told her when she was a little girl. So many heartaches and tragedies had been acted out within the small community of Lamp Hill Hall over past seasons, but tonight the man in the moon appeared to be smiling. At long last, all was at peace and their futures looked bright.

Acknowledgements

I would like to say a massive thank you to Maddie, my editor, Florence, Olivia and all the team at Little, Brown for your support and encouragement. Not forgetting Joan Deitch, my copy editor, and my wonderful agent Sheila Crowley.

The publishers hope that this book has given you enjoyable reading. Large Print Books are especially designed to be as easy to see and hold as possible. If you wish a complete list of our books please ask at your local library or write directly to:

Magna Large Print Books
Magna House, Long Preston,
Skipton, North Yorkshire.
BD23 4ND

This Large Print Book for the partially sighted, who cannot read normal print, is published under the auspices of

THE ULVERSCROFT FOUNDATION